P9-CFL-080

Falling
to Pieces

Falling to Pieces

~ a Shipshewana Amish Mystery ~

Vannetta Chapman

ZONDERVAN

ZONDERVAN.com/
AUTHORTRACKER
follow your favorite authors

ZONDERVAN

Falling to Pieces
Copyright © 2011 by Vannetta Chapman

This title is also available as a Zondervan ebook.
Visit www.zondervan.com/ebooks.

This title is also available in a Zondervan audio edition.
Visit www.zondervan.fm.

Requests for information should be addressed to:

Zondervan, *Grand Rapids, Michigan 49530*

Library of Congress Cataloging-in-Publication Data

Chapman, Vannetta.
    Falling to pieces : a Shipshewana Amish mystery / Vannetta Chapman.
        p. cm.
    ISBN 978-0-310-33043-1
    1. Amish women — Fiction. 2. Female friendship — Fiction. 3. Murder —
Investigation — Fiction. 4. Shipshewana (Ind.) — Fiction. I. Title.
PS3603.H3744F36 2011
813'.6 — dc22   2011020586

Any Internet addresses (websites, blogs, etc.) and telephone numbers in this book
are offered as a resource. They are not intended in any way to be or imply an
endorsement by Zondervan, nor does Zondervan vouch for the content of these
sites and numbers for the life of this book.

All rights reserved. No part of this publication may be reproduced, stored in a
retrieval system, or transmitted in any form or by any means — electronic, mechani-
cal, photocopy, recording, or any other — except for brief quotations in printed
reviews, without the prior permission of the publisher.

Cover illustration: MaryAnn Lasher ©
Interior design: Matthew Van Zomeren

Printed in the United States of America

11 12 13 14 15 16 17 18 /DCI/ 19 18 17 16 15 14 13 12 11 10 9 8 7 6 5 4 3 2

To my mom, Wanda Van Riper

Glossary

ack—oh

aenti—aunt

bedauerlich—sad

boppli—baby

bopplin—babies

bruder—brother

daed—dad

dat—father

danki—thank you

Dietsch—Pennsylvania Dutch

dochdern—daughters

eiferich—excited

Englisher—non-Amish person

fraa—wife

freind—friend

freinden—friends

gegisch—silly

gelassenheit—calmness, composure, placidity

gern gschehne—you're welcome

Gotte's wille—God's will

grossdaddi—grandfather

grossdochdern—granddaughters

grandkinner—grandchildren

grossmammi—grandmother

gschtarewe—dead

gudemariye—good morning

gut—good

in lieb—in love

kaffi—coffee

kapp—prayer covering

kind—child

kinner—children

mamm—mom

naerfich—nervous

narrisch—crazy

onkel—uncle

rumspringa—running around; time before an Amish young person has officially joined the church, provides a bridge between childhood and adulthood.

schweschder—sister

was iss letz—what's wrong

wunderbaar—wonderful

ya—yes

Prologue

DAISY STOOD in the center of her garden, admiring the chaos of flowers. May rains and warmer days had brought a burst of color. Brilliant orange flowers dotted with butterflies spread across the ground, white false indigo had grown waist-high, and the purplish-pink blossoms of Joe-pye-weed fought for their place in the sun. Unfortunately grass and common weeds had also shot up with extra zeal. Her garden looked almost like a thing abandoned.

She glanced back toward the quilt shop. Paperwork waited for her there. The garden beckoned her here. And where was Max? As if he could read her thoughts, the sixty-pound yellow Labrador bounded past her, practically knocking her on her keister.

"Catch a ground squirrel and I won't be bandaging your wounds," she called after him. Of course she would. She loved the dog more than she would have thought possible—she supposed turning seventy-six last March had softened her a bit. Also, she had no family in the area. The Amish community had accepted her, and the Englishers—like herself—were as close as neighbors could be. But Max, well, Max was her constant companion; he protected her, he played with her, he listened to all her problems without judgment, and he loved her unconditionally.

"Wonder where I left that hand rake. I had it last time I fought these weeds." Daisy circled left, then right, finally spying the red handles of her tool set by the fence which bordered the alley running behind her shop and little side yard. With a sigh, she hustled back along the brick walk, aware that she was already losing the day's light. She'd just reached down to pick up the bucket of tools when she saw movement in the alley—a flash of color in the gap between two of the six-foot bayberry shrubs that lined the fence.

Most folks stuck to the main street, and Daisy was curious. Peeking through the evergreens, she glimpsed a man rounding the corner of the deserted alley. She didn't recognize the editor of their small town newspaper at first. It wasn't until he'd crept closer and stopped next to the dumpster behind Pots and Pans, a shop that sold old-fashioned kitchenware to tourists, that she was sure it was Stakehorn.

Just as Daisy was about to call out, he opened a Shipshewana shopping bag and peered down into it, as if he wasn't sure what he'd find. He pulled an item out, studied it in less than the amount of time it would have taken her to sew a whip-stitch, and dropped it back into the bag. Then he examined his hand, as if it had bit him.

"Now that has to be the oddest— "

Before she could complete her thought, Stakehorn turned and darted between Pots and Pans and the new floral shop which had been taken over by Georgia Stearn's sister. The place didn't even have a name yet, which Daisy thought was a shame. Every store needed a name, or how would you look it up in the yellow pages?

She reached down and picked up her bucket of garden tools. When she did she felt a tightening in her chest, that uncomfortable pressure she'd been meaning to talk to Doctor Pat about. Could be indigestion. She'd had one of those new microwave sandwiches for lunch and sometimes they didn't sit well. With one hand she rubbed her chest and with the other she turned toward the flowers, but the sleeve of her blouse caught on the evergreen. She reached to loosen it, which was when she saw the second person enter the alley.

This person she didn't know. Must be from the market. He wasn't from Shipshewana. She'd lived here long enough to know everyone, and a man like that? She would remember if she'd seen him before. He scanned the backs of the buildings as if he couldn't decide where he was going. As he walked, his attention moved to the ground. Twice he squatted down and touched the dirt. When he stopped outside Pots and Pans, at the same place Stakehorn had stopped, Daisy saw him pull something out of the inside of his jacket.

It took her a moment longer to realize it was a gun.

Chapter 1

Shipshewana, Indiana
June 1

DEAD BODIES had never bothered Deborah Yoder.

Discovering old Mrs. Daisy Powell facedown in her garden had been a surprise. Her friend had died there between the butterfly weed and white indigo, had died with the dog she loved so keeping her company. Deborah had found her when she stopped by to deliver a casserole, rushed to her side and knelt there, not even thinking to go for the police, but she hadn't been upset.

Amish considered death a natural part of the cycle of life, and Daisy Powell had lived life to its fullest.

Deborah focused on the neat row of stitches in front of her, on the slight tug of the needle as she worked it through the layers of the quilt, on the satisfaction of watching the blue, gray, white, and black pieces fit perfectly together.

She focused on the quilt, but her mind went back to the evening she discovered Daisy's body in the midst of her flower garden.

Three weeks had passed, Daisy's body had been properly placed in the ground according to English customs, but still Deborah and her *freinden* had no answers to their problem.

Of course she noticed when the voices around her grew silent.

She snipped the thread, pocketed her small scissors, worked

the needle through her apron for safekeeping, and looked across the quilt frame at her two best friends.

Melinda and Esther waited expectantly.

They didn't state the obvious.

They didn't spoil the moment—this moment she loved when the three of them completed something they'd worked on for weeks.

They didn't even voice the questions crowding her sitting room and stifling the summer morning.

Suddenly Joshua's cries pierced the morning, quickly followed by baby Hannah's wails, and Leah's holler of "*Mamm.*"

"Perfect timing," Deborah declared brightly, standing and surveying their work.

Melinda and Esther didn't actually argue with her; instead they shook their heads and spoke as if she were deaf, or worse invisible.

"Perfect timing, indeed," Melinda muttered, standing and pushing up her glasses with one hand; with the other she touched the strings of the *kapp* covering her honey-brown hair.

Esther stood as well—posture straight, shoulders back, never attempting to minimize her five-foot-ten height. Her hair was darker, though you'd never guess it looking at her—she kept it perfectly covered by her *kapp*. Smoothing her dark apron, she looked pointedly from the finished quilt in front of them to the stack in the corner of the room. "Good thing she has four other *kinner* in addition to the crying *boppli* in the other room, or our pile of finished quilts would reach the ceiling."

Deborah merely smiled and strolled into the nearest bedroom where their three youngest children had taken up quite the chorus.

Melinda scooped up baby Hannah, planted a kiss on the six-month-old's neck, and inhaled deeply. "I adore the way she smells."

Esther crinkled her nose. "If I'm not mistaken, that odor is

14

a wet diaper." As she sat on the bed, her two-year-old daughter crawled into her lap, then promptly snuggled into a ball and closed her eyes.

"We're lucky they're young and still take such a good morning nap—gives us more time to sew," Deborah reasoned as she changed Joshua's diaper. The fourteen-month-old giggled and reached for the strings of her prayer *kapp*.

"Definitely what we need—more time to sew." The teasing had left Melinda's voice, and what crept into its place sounded like a note of despair.

Deborah lifted Joshua out of the crib, and turned to Melinda and Esther. "Why don't we have some tea and talk about this? Surely we can find a solution."

Esther smiled as she led Leah to the bathroom across the hall. "You're good with solutions, Deborah. But even you can't sell quilts in a shop that's closed."

"I had so hoped this would solve our problems." Melinda stared out the window. She didn't speak again for a few moments. When she did, her voice took on a wistfulness like the sound of the June breeze in the trees coming through the open windows. "It seemed like such a good idea when we began, but now everything that can go wrong has gone wrong. And we haven't earned a dime."

Deborah's gaze locked with Esther's as she walked back into the room.

When they'd first started their venture, she'd assumed it would be Esther who would need the income the most. After all, it was Esther who had lost Seth in the accident. Esther who was trying to raise her *boppli* alone.

Oh, she had the church to help her, and her family pitched in as well. Even as they sewed, Esther's *bruders* were at her place tending to the fields. Still Deborah had assumed Esther would need the added income more than any of them.

Yes, when she'd first had the idea to sell their quilts in the store on Main Street, it was with Esther's needs as her primary concern. By the time they'd approached Daisy though, Melinda had finally confided with her about her middle *kind's* condition.

Aaron's situation was more serious than Deborah had imagined.

She should have known, but then she'd never seen the disease before.

Deborah had known the boy was sick, known how important it was for them all to pray for him, and even known about Doctor Richard's visits. The boy had seemed so improved though.

In reality, the situation was precarious health wise. Financially it was quite dire.

Of course they helped one another whenever anyone had health costs, since it went against their teachings to participate in health insurance programs. Instead they pooled their resources and helped pay for one another's expenses. But the toll on Melinda's family would go far beyond merely what the medical costs totaled, and the extent of what Melinda had shared had been shocking.

Although Deborah believed things would work out for the best, although her faith remained strong, it took only one look at her friend's face today to see that she remained worried.

She'd been right to go to Bishop Elam about offering the quilts in the English store.

"We'll find a way to sell the quilts," Deborah assured her.

"It's been nearly a month since Ms. Powell passed, Deborah." Esther sat on the side of the bed, allowed Leah to crawl back into her lap. "Daisy's Quilt Shop has been closed all this time, and it doesn't look as if it's going to reopen."

"We can't very well sell our quilts in a store that is closed." Melinda attempted a smile and pushed up on her glasses.

Even from across the room, Deborah could see the tears shining in her eyes. Though she turned away and pretended to focus on changing Hannah's diaper, Deborah could feel the depth of her anguish.

Which is why she told them what she knew.

"I didn't want to mention what Jonas said to me last night, until I had been to town." She laughed uneasily as Joshua reached for her nose, then satisfied himself with chewing on the toy she snatched out of the cubby near his crib and handed to him.

"Tell us what?" Esther asked.

"What did Jonas say?" Melinda turned toward her as she bundled up the wet cloth diaper and placed it in her diaper bag.

Both women faced her now, holding their *kinner*, and Deborah was struck with the thought that families and friendships were like quilts—each person intricately connected to the other.

"Jonas said someone has moved into the apartment above Daisy's Quilt Shop—a woman, and I'm going to see her this afternoon."

"And you didn't tell us this earlier?" Esther's voice rose in irritation.

"Maybe she didn't want to get our hopes up."

"But we're in this equally."

"Esther's right. I should have mentioned it when you first arrived."

"Is this woman opening the store up again?" Melinda asked.

Esther scooted closer on the bed. "Is she here to stay?"

"He didn't have any other information. We need to find out though. We deserve to know."

Esther nodded. Pulling in her bottom lip she glanced down quickly, suddenly completely engrossed in running her fingers over the hem of Leah's dress.

Deborah realized with a jolt that while her own life had moved forward since Seth's passing, perhaps Esther's hadn't. She had lost a good friend, but Esther had lost the man she loved.

Esther always seemed like the strong one, seemed to take

everything in stride; but then at moments like this one, melancholy practically poured from her.

The accident causing his death had happened just over one year ago, and it wasn't the Amish way to linger over such things. Still Deborah knew her *freind* was struggling, could see the sadness written on her face, hear it in her voice.

Together she and Melinda moved toward Esther, each sitting beside her on the small bed.

Deborah gazed out the window and could just make out Jonas in the far field, working with the plow and the large horses. He was such a good man, a good husband to her and a kind *daed* to their children. The three of them stayed that way—Deborah, Esther, and Melinda, each holding their *boppli*.

For a few minutes, they remained there, in the morning sunshine, the breeze occasionally stirring through the window. It was enough that they were together and there for each other. They'd find a way to sell the quilts.

⁓

Callie Harper pulled the quilt over her head and focused with all her mental powers.

Surely she could go back to sleep. How hard was it? She wanted to go back to sleep. She needed to go back to sleep. She had no reason not to go back to sleep.

The whining lump taking up the entire bottom half of the bed inched forward.

Callie ignored it, focusing instead on sheep in a pasture, jumping lazily over a fence.

The lump whimpered.

Callie peeked out from under the pillow she was using to block the bright sun.

"No, Max."

She must not have put enough energy into the scolding.

At the sound of his name, the yellow Labrador launched himself at her, licking what portions of her face he could find.

"Bad dog. Stop! Bad, bad dog."

Callie burrowed deeper under the covers, and Max retreated to the end of the bed, tail thumping hard and a whine sounding in his throat. Unable to ignore her guilt or forget that the glimpse at her bedside clock had revealed it was well past noon, Callie threw back her covers and stared at the sixty-pound, golden dog.

"I'm not a good pet owner," she explained.

Instead of answering, Max crept closer — though much more slowly and infinitely more carefully this time. He didn't stop until he was mere inches away, giant brown eyes staring into hers.

"What am I going to do, boy?"

A single bark was his only answer.

"Right. Well, I suppose that makes sense."

Rolling out of bed, Callie grabbed her robe, made a quick stop by the bathroom, then clipped the nearly new leash she'd found in the hall closet to Max's collar. Though she wasn't sure if there were leash laws in Shipshewana, she'd been trained well in the better suburbs of Houston.

Max practically pulled her down the stairs, out into the bright sunlight, and across the small parking area that served her aunt's quilting store. Callie walked past the empty spaces — distressingly vacant, reminding her again that she had no car. She continued through the gate and into the side yard that resembled an overgrown forest.

She supposed she'd have to find a way to mow it.

Who was she kidding? A mower wouldn't cut through this grass. She'd have to find a machete.

After she'd securely fastened the gate behind her, she unclipped Max, then trudged through the tall grass to what must have once been a sitting area. Sighing in relief, she sank into the Adirondack chair under the tall shade tree.

Maybe if she sat there long enough she'd think of some answers. It had been nearly a week, and still she had no idea what she needed to do next. Truth was, she couldn't make a real guess as to what day it was without booting up her computer or turning on her phone.

Which was when she remembered she'd lost her phone. Maybe she should have ordered a new one when she'd realized it was missing, but it had seemed so pointless. No one would be calling her anyway. What friends she'd had in Houston had slowly distanced themselves since Rick's death three years ago. That wasn't really fair. Perhaps she'd been the one to choose distance. Immersing herself in her work had been easier than pretending to be comfortable among her friends, people she suddenly found she had nothing in common with. Now she didn't even have her work. The final argument with her boss had been her last one. No, she wouldn't be needing a phone anytime soon — which was good, because her aunt's service had apparently been disconnected some time ago. She was lucky the electricity had been automatically paid each month from her checking account.

From the looks of things, Max was nearly done with his business though.

They could go back upstairs.

Take a nap.

No doubt life would make more sense to her later in the afternoon, after a few more hours sleep.

The Labrador made a final lap around the yard, then skidded to a stop at her feet, head tipped to the side, ears alert, eyes expecting answers — or at least breakfast.

"Let's find you some food." Callie leaned forward, clipped the leash back on his collar, and was headed out of the gate when she remembered that she had no dog food. She'd used the last of it the evening before.

20

A sinking feeling came over her as she realized the full measure of her predicament.

She couldn't actually let Max starve. She'd have to shower, dress, and then venture out on foot to the grocery store. She had seen a grocery store when the cab had dropped her off last week. Hadn't she? Was it close enough to walk to?

Then Callie remembered seeing a chicken dinner in the freezer. Dogs could eat chicken. Maybe she'd warm up the dinner and go to the store later.

Relieved to have found a way out of going out into public, she started toward the opened door, then paused to push the pile of newspapers out of the way.

She heard the clip-clop of horse hooves and the unmistakable clatter of buggy wheels, which was not an unusual sound in a town that was largely Amish.

What was unusual though was that the buggy was turning into her parking area, and the woman driving—unless she was greatly mistaken—was waving as if they knew one another.

Callie was sure of so little these days, but she was absolutely sure she did not know anyone in this town.

Chapter 2

CALLIE WATCHED as a young Amish woman stepped out of the buggy. She tethered her horse to one of the antique hitching posts installed in front of each parking space, then turned back toward her buggy and stuck her head inside, pulling out a stack of quilts—piled nearly to her chin.

"Gudemariye," the young woman called, closing the space between them.

Callie's heart sank.

Despite the quilts, despite the fact that she was staying above her aunt's store which was in fact named Daisy's Quilt Shop, she'd held on to an irrational hope that the woman might be visiting the furniture shop next door.

No such luck.

Cinching the belt of her robe more tightly, Callie moved closer to the Labrador. "Stay, boy."

"Oh, you don't need to worry about Max. He and I are old friends."

Max thumped his tail, but didn't move. He did gaze up at Callie as if he were waiting for something.

"He wants your permission. Max never greeted a customer unless he had Daisy's consent."

Callie had been looking down at the dog, but at the sound of her aunt's name, her head snapped up and blood rushed to her cheeks.

Who was this person? She knew Max. She knew Aunt Daisy, and she was apparently well acquainted with the store.

Callie shaded her eyes against the sun and stared at the woman in front of her.

Slightly older than she first thought—mid- to late-twenties. Amish, of course, given the long, gray dress, white apron, and matching hat with strings. What did they call it? Callie searched her memory for the word … a cap, no a prayer *kapp*. Blondish-brown hair was pulled neatly back into a bun, though a few strands had escaped.

Amber-colored eyes studied Callie calmly. The young woman wore no makeup, but she didn't need any either—her complexion was beautiful. The general impression looking at her was one of health and quiet energy.

Callie couldn't stop her hand from patting down her own hair. She'd not bothered to run a comb through it, which was a tad embarrassing. Now she found herself wishing she'd at least brushed her teeth and splashed some water on her face.

"I've caught you at a bad time," the woman said. "I'm sorry. I heard you were here, living upstairs, and I thought I'd bring these by."

"They look heavy; let me help you." Callie took the top half of the stack, smelled the clean cotton cloth, and wanted to lie down on top of them right there in the parking lot. "They're beautiful."

"*Danki.*"

Callie had been studying the quilts, but she pulled her gaze away and toward the woman at the sound of the unfamiliar word. "I don't understand."

"I'm sorry. You haven't been here long enough to understand German Dutch. *Danki* means thank you."

"I guessed as much. What I don't understand is why you're here, with these quilts."

"I'm bringing them to you."

Callie took a step backward, bumped into Max and nearly tripped.

The woman moved forward as if to help, but Callie shook her head. "I'm fine."

"I haven't even introduced myself. I'm Deborah Yoder—"

It was habit for Callie to shake hands. "Callie Harper. Listen, Miss—"

"Yoder."

"Miss Yoder." Callie pulled in a deep breath, tried to think clearly, but she hadn't had coffee in, well in days and a headache throbbed in her temples.

"Call me Deborah, please. We're not very formal in Shipshewana. The thing is I had an agreement with Daisy to sell quilts I made. I don't make them alone of course—two friends and I make them."

Callie shifted from one slipper-clad foot to the other. "Deborah, I don't know what arrangement you had with my aunt, but Daisy's Quilt Shop is closed."

They both turned to stare at the little shop. Unread newspapers lined the walk. Weeds fought with flowers for space in the beds, and the weeds were definitely winning. Mud from recent rains splattered the front windows, and yellowed MAY SALE flyers remained in the display case outside the door.

Daisy's Quilt Shop was definitely not open for business.

"This all must be very difficult for you," Deborah said softly.

Tears stung Callie's eyes. She blinked rapidly, shifted the quilts so she could maintain a better grip on Max's leash, though he had decided to lie down at her feet, in the shade of the raspberry-colored awnings and study the two women.

Callie glanced again at the stack of quilts in her arms and

noticed a diamond-in-a-square pattern, solid dark blue surrounded by purple and bordered in black. It reminded her so much of a quilt which once covered her mother's bed. A deep ache started from somewhere in the middle of her chest, and she thought she might drop to the pavement right beside Max.

"Are you all right?" Deborah moved forward, juggled the quilts, reached out, and touched her arm.

"I'm, I'm fine. I was wondering, what do you call this, this pattern?"

Deborah smiled, readjusting the quilts in her arms. "It's called a medallion quilt. I'll tell you about it, but let's go inside first. I think you could maybe use a cup of tea or some *kaffi*. You looked a bit pale there for a minute."

Callie hesitated, then realized she was standing outside in her robe, and Main Street traffic was beginning to pick up.

"All right. I suppose we could go inside long enough to straighten this out."

Walking in through the back door, she looked longingly at the stairs that led up to the apartment, but instead she continued down the hallway and led Deborah through the side door that opened into the shop.

Fifteen minutes and one cup of tea. Let the woman have her say, then she'd send her back outside to her buggy, and she'd send all the quilts with her.

∽

Deborah walked to an empty counter where they could set the quilts. Her heart sank as she gazed around at Daisy's shop.

A fine layer of dust covered every shelf, countertop, and even the quilts she had left to be sold two months ago. The plants which Daisy had so lovingly tended now lay brown and wilted in the front window. Even from across the room, she could see that a few cobwebs had settled on the displays of cloth.

Less than a month had passed since Daisy Powell had died; yet her shop showed the neglect of each and every day. It occurred to Deborah then that a shop was like a living thing. It required constant care and maintenance.

From the way Callie was looking about in confusion, it seemed as if she hadn't even stepped into the shop before this moment. She had been here for a week and done nothing? And why had it taken so long for anyone to show up in the first place?

Who was Callie Harper? She claimed to be Daisy's niece, but she was nothing like the woman. Perhaps there was a slight physical resemblance — the pert nose and the dark chocolate-colored eyes.

But any comparison ended there.

Daisy's dark eyes had been warm, calm, and of a normal size.

Callie's were large like a doe's, and looked somewhat frightened. In fact, her eyes were her most striking feature, seeming to take up most of her face. Dark hair barely reached the collar of her robe, spiking in several different directions around her head. Shorter than Deborah — barely five foot, three inches if she were to guess — and thinner. Like many of the English women Deborah knew, Callie was probably afraid to eat.

Deborah could say with certainty that Callie Harper was unlike any Englisher she had ever met.

Was she still grieving the sudden death of her *aenti*?

Deborah realized Englishers regarded death differently than the Amish.

But there was something more wrong here.

Past noon and the woman was still in her pajamas.

Jonas had told her the woman moved in nearly a week ago. The only reason news of her arrival hadn't traveled around their small community was because she hadn't stirred from the little apartment above the shop.

What was she doing up there?

What was amiss?

And when did she plan to reopen Daisy's Quilt Shop?

"I don't know if there's tea down here," Callie confessed. "And I'm fairly sure there's none in the apartment."

"There'll be some in the store's kitchen."

"Kitchen?" Callie set the quilts on the dusty counter, squinted at her in confusion.

"Daisy kept the kitchen well stocked." Deborah moved around the counter, past the little office, to the pocket kitchen tucked across from the customer bathroom. "She liked to be able to pop in here for a quick cup of tea. Often she would set hot beverages and cookies out for customers as well."

"I didn't realize any of this was here."

Opening the cabinet to the left of the sink, Deborah pulled out a plastic container, opened it, and turned to show Callie a variety of tea bags. "What do you prefer?"

"Anything is fine."

"There's chamomile, lemongrass and spearmint, ginger, or Earl Grey."

"Lemongrass and spearmint sounds all right."

Deborah pulled two of the bags out, smiled again, and filled the little coffee pot with water. "She only ran water through this percolator. So it stayed clean. If customers wanted *kaffi*, she had different flavors of instant."

"I thought Amish weren't allowed to use electricity."

"At work we may. I helped out in the shop from time to time."

"You seem to know a lot about my aunt," Callie murmured.

"I counted her among my closest *freinden*." Deborah had begun to wipe the counter, but she stopped, turned and studied Callie before continuing. "I found Daisy in the garden, the evening she passed. She looked as if she'd laid down among the flowers to rest."

Callie's eyes widened. When tears began to pool there, Deborah reached into her pocket and pulled out a freshly laundered handkerchief, and pushed it into Callie's hands.

"You found her?"

"*Ya*. Max was there, waiting by her side. I had brought her a casserole for her evening meal. Actually I came by several times a week since she started carrying my quilts. But truthfully Daisy, and this store, had been a central meeting place for women in our community as long as I can remember. We all felt very close to her."

Callie nodded, busied herself with removing the tea bag from the package and setting it in the cup Deborah had placed on the counter.

At that moment, Callie's stomach growled loudly.

"I believe there are some cookies here as well," Deborah said. She wondered when Callie had last eaten.

"Oh, I'm not—"

Max wedged his way between their legs and uttered a pitiful whine.

~

Callie smiled sheepishly. "We, uhh, ran out of food for Max this morning. I was on my way to buy some more when you drove up."

Deborah's eyes widened and she purposely did not look at Callie's night clothes.

"After I dressed, that is." Callie sank onto the single stool in the small kitchen. "I'm a terrible pet owner. Max knows it. I know it. Soon all of Shipshewana will know it."

Callie looked up at Deborah with big brown eyes. Max, beside her, had the same expression. Deborah tried to hold in the smile, but a giggle escaped. In a moment, she was laughing out loud, and trying desperately to stop.

"It's not funny." Callie stood, cinched the belt on her robe, and pushed the cup and saucer away.

"Of course it's not. I'm sorry, Callie." Deborah managed to get herself under control. She hoped she hadn't offended Daisy's niece. Too much depended on their relationship. "I just—I don't know—I just enjoy your honesty." Deborah poured hot water over the tea bag and handed it back to her.

Callie accepted the tea, focused on dunking the bag in and out of the hot water. She shrugged, as if ready to move on. "I do feel bad about Max," she said. "He ate the last of the dog chow last night. Do you think we could give him the cookies?"

"I think Daisy kept some extra dog food here in the kitchen."

Deborah began going through the counters on the right, and Callie opened the ones on the left. They met in the middle where they found a rather large bin of dog chow. Max let out a full-blown woof, then sat, his tail beating a happy rhythm on the linoleum floor.

"Found a dog bowl in this one," Callie declared.

It took no time for them to put water and food out for Max, and he was soon eating with gusto.

"One problem solved," Deborah said with a smile, as she found an unopened package of cookies and set them on the counter as well. "How's your tea?"

"Good, thank you." Callie nibbled around the edge of a short-bread cookie, then set it back down on her plate. "Miss Yoder—"

"Mrs. But please call me Deborah."

"Mrs.?" Callie looked at Deborah's left hand.

Deborah nodded. "I'm married, though we don't wear rings. It often confuses Englishers. My husband Jonas comes into town with me when he can, but today he is working in the fields and the barn. He was able to keep my youngest *boppli*—"

"Your what?"

"Oh." Deborah had forgotten that some of her words were different than Callie's. *"Boppli*. We say *boppli*, it means—"

"Baby."

"How did you know?"

"If it's your youngest, it would have to be baby, or farm animal, and why would he keep your youngest farm animal?"

"Right." Deborah nodded and realized Callie would learn their ways quickly. "Jonas had finished his field work by the time I needed to leave, so he offered to keep the *boppli*. Joshua behaves quite well in the barn, though he's barely fourteen months old."

"Look— " Callie said, and Deborah knew her welcome had worn out.

"I know," Deborah said, standing up. "It's time for me to go."

Callie looked guilty and started to apologize.

"It's okay," Deborah said. "I'm glad we were able to visit for a little while. Already I feel like we're old friends."

"But we barely know each other." Callie stared at her in amazement, and again Deborah wondered if she had gone too far. But something told her this was exactly what Callie needed to hear.

"Sometimes it isn't merely how long two people know each other," Deborah said. "It's also the times they've shared. We've shared a cup of tea, and the searching of food for Max." They both turned to look at the dog, who had finished licking his bowl clean. "And now we're going to share a business relationship." She smiled a little, hoping Callie would hear the friendliness in her voice.

Callie began shaking her head, moved to the small sink and rinsed out her cup. "No, no I never said that."

"But my agreement with your *aenti*— "

"Was just that, an agreement with my aunt. It wasn't with me."

Deborah had a sinking feeling in her belly. She rinsed out her cup, placed it on the dishcloth beside Callie's. "Are you saying you won't sell my quilts in your shop?"

"I'm not selling anything in the shop." The Englisher turned now, looked her directly in the eye as if her flat, no-nonsense voice wasn't convincing enough. "The shop is closed, and I have no intention of reopening it."

Chapter 3

CALLIE FELT A TWINGE of guilt at the look of distress in Deborah Yoder's eyes, but she knew it was best to be straightforward with her.

She'd disappointed enough people in the last few years—no surprise that she'd just let down one more.

"I don't understand."

"I'm not staying in Shipshewana. I'm here to see to my aunt's things—that's all."

Deborah fidgeted with the strings of her *kapp*. "So you mean to sell the shop?"

"I suppose. I mean yes, of course. I have no use for it. I certainly know nothing about running a craft store."

"You could learn."

The moment seemed to freeze—even Max stopped nudging the bowl around the floor. Amber eyes met brown ones, and Callie almost thought Deborah was daring her. She closed her eyes, took a deep breath, and pushed the ridiculous idea away.

"I can't possibly stay in Shipshewana." Callie left the small kitchen and walked toward the quilts Deborah had brought with her.

"I see." Deborah followed slowly behind.

At the counter they both stood looking at the quilts.

"When I received word that my aunt had died," Callie said quietly, "I meant to come right away." Her hands came out, as if she could explain better with motions than with words. "But everything became complicated. My job didn't understand why I needed more than three days off. When I insisted, they made me choose work over family. I had a big argument with my boss, and then I walked out."

Callie laughed, but even she heard the nervousness and pain behind her words. The memory was too raw. "We have family leave laws, but suddenly I was too tired to fight. Suddenly I knew I needed out of that job. I don't know why I'm telling you all of this."

"At times it helps to talk things out." Deborah shrugged, and Callie thought of what Deborah had said about seeming like old friends. It did feel good to have someone to talk to.

"Anyway. I didn't know what to do," Callie continued. "I had financial obligations I suddenly couldn't meet. The lawyers were saying I had to get to Chicago and sign probate papers. I finally put my things in storage, since I knew I'd have to find a new place to live — not to mention a new job when I returned. I let the lease go on my car, and got here as soon as I could."

"It sounds as if things have been very difficult for you."

"I certainly wasn't expecting — this. And what happened with my job, well, it wasn't the first disagreement I'd had with my boss. We hadn't seen eye to eye in quite some time. It's complicated, but ultimately I figured I'd be better off doing something different. If I only had some idea what." Callie glanced around the room, shook her head, and pushed on. "Now what am I left with? A dusty old shop in a state I know nothing about — and all my things are still in Texas, where I should be looking for employment."

Callie fingered the medallion quilt, the one that reminded her of her mother. She may not be keeping the shop, but she was still interested in hearing about this beautiful item.

"You were going to tell me about this one."

"Yes, it's a traditional Amish pattern, typically done in deep, rich tones. As you can see it's a diamond-in-a-square design with wide borders. It's quite popular among our families, and we had hoped it would sell well."

"The work is exquisite."

"Danki."

Callie hesitated, then plunged on—since Deborah was leaving, there was no harm in speaking with her. It wasn't as if she'd ever see her again.

Running her hand over the medallion quilt, she said, "My mother had a quilt like this. Seeing it, I feel as if I were a girl again."

Deborah retrieved a stool from behind the counter and offered it to her.

Perching on it, Callie shook her head, shook herself free from the memories which held such heartache. "I knew my aunt owned a craft shop—"

"Quilt shop," Deborah corrected her gently.

"Right." They were quiet for a moment. "I didn't even make it for her funeral," Callie whispered.

"I took care of the arrangements."

Callie looked up in surprise.

"It was a pleasure for me to do so. We had heard there were problems with her family making it from such a long distance. Your *aenti's* final ceremony was well attended. The community thought a lot of her. She was liked by everyone."

Pulling in a deep breath, Callie again ran her hand over the medallion quilt sitting between them. "Where I come from, quilt shops—craft stores—are pretty much one and the same. They're quite large and owned by chain stores."

Deborah tilted her head, rather like Max did when she spoke to him. Instead of jumping in with a comment, she waited.

Callie pushed on. "I haven't seen many chain stores in Shipshewana. Anyway, I didn't realize my aunt had left her store to me. The last time I was here, I was four or five years old."

"Just a *kind.*"

Callie shook her head. If she had ever thought of staying in Shipshewana, she would need to buy an Amish-English dictionary.

"Child," Deborah explained.

"Yes, I was only a child. I can remember the flowers in her garden, the smells of cooking, even the sound of the buggies out on the road. I think she had a dog then too, but seems like it was smaller." Callie ran her fingers through her hair, thought again of how she needed to shower, needed to find a rental car, needed to buy some food, find a realtor, do so many things—oh yes, and purchase another phone.

"I don't know how to do ..." with her hand she gestured to include the entire shop, the apartment above, even Max, "this."

"We would help you."

"No. I don't belong in a town like Shipshewana."

"So you have family back at home?"

Callie stood, placed both palms flat on the dusty counter, but didn't look at Deborah, couldn't look at her. She seemed, after all, to be a nice person. "I'm sorry I can't help you. I really am."

"You're leaving soon?"

"As soon as I can clean this place up and find a buyer."

Deborah ran her fingers from the top of her *kapp* strings to the bottom. "Jonas, my husband, knows a man here in Shipshewana who is a good realtor. I don't have a phone, but I'm running some other errands while I'm here in town. I can see if he's in. If he's not, Jonas will know how to reach him. We'll ask him to come and see you."

A small amount of hope surged through Callie for the first time in the last week, actually in a lot longer. If she could sell the shop, maybe she could use the money to go in some new direction. Callie brushed her hair down with her fingers. "I would appreciate it very much."

"It's no problem at all. What else do you need?"

Looking down at Max, Callie pulled in her bottom lip. "Any idea where I could buy a cell phone? I lost mine."

Deborah laughed again, the sound reminding Callie of springtime and hummingbirds and Texas. "We rarely use phones. When we do, we have phone shanties that are set up for the purpose of placing calls, or sometimes we have phone cards and go to the General Store here in town where there is a phone the owner lets us use."

"It's really different here," Callie said, scrunching her face up as Max turned in a circle and flopped on the floor between them.

"*Ya*, which is why we like it." Deborah's smile broadened. "If you walk down the street to the corner light and make a right, you'll find a small grocer. An Englisher, Mr. Cooper, owns it. He may sell the disposable phones. If he doesn't, he can tell you who does."

"You've been a wonderful help. Thank you so much."

"It's no problem. We're a small town, and we help each other. Now I have a favor to ask you."

Callie felt her insides tighten in a knot, but she forced a smile. "I'll try."

"Allow me to leave the quilts here. I'll pick them up in a few days."

Callie let out the breath she didn't realize she'd been holding. It was a small favor, and one that wouldn't complicate things in any way. It was the least she could do considering how much help Deborah had offered. "I suppose there would be no harm in leaving them here, but why?"

"It's just that I hadn't planned on taking them back with me, and I need to pick up supplies while I'm here in town. My buggy will be full, and I don't want to soil them."

Walking Deborah outside, she waved good-bye.

She didn't have many answers, but at least Max was fed and she knew where the grocery store was.

It wasn't much, but it seemed from the perspective of where she'd been while huddling under the covers that it would be a start.

~

Jonas had begun to snore when Deborah slipped off her house shoes and crawled into bed. Pressing her cold hands against the small of his back, she wasn't surprised when he startled awake.

"What's wrong? Who needs me?" Jonas sprang up, reminding Deborah of the way the *kinner* bounced on the seats in the buggy.

"Nothing's wrong, and I need you." She laughed softly and pulled him back down under the summer quilt. "Now lie still and let me warm my hands."

"How can you be so cold? It's summer." His voice was gruff, but he took her small hands between his own, brought them up to his lips, and kissed them gently.

"I was rocking Joshua until he fell asleep, and then I sat out on the porch a little while, thinking about the English woman." She burrowed into his arms, into his warmth. "There's a breeze tonight."

"Which is why you should be in bed."

"I was trying to puzzle it out though."

"Not another of your puzzles." Jonas began to breathe deeply, and Deborah realized he was on the verge of falling asleep again. She placed her toes against his ankles, and he jerked his legs away.

"Your feet are like ice, woman."

"Talk to me until I warm."

"You talk. I'll listen." He touched her face, ran his fingers down her neck, sent shivers zipping all the way down her spine.

"I believe she'd like to stay — the look in her eyes when I asked her if she had family back home ... Jonas, it cut to my soul."

"And how can you help her?"

"We have a good community here. People would support the store if she were to reopen it."

"She told you no."

"But she didn't mean no."

"What makes you think that?"

"Intuition."

He didn't argue with her. They rarely argued, though when they did it was short and fierce—like the storms that raged in the spring.

Deborah allowed him to fall into a deep slumber, nestled in his arms.

She wondered if Callie Harper had found her groceries and her cellular phone.

Who did she plan to call with it?

Were there people who would come and help her to restore Daisy's Quilt Shop to its former condition?

And then would she put it up for sale with Mr. King? Jonas had promised to speak with him tomorrow.

Deborah didn't know how this new twist would end for her and Melinda and Esther.

She was, however, glad she had managed to leave the quilts on Callie's dusty counter. It didn't guarantee that the woman would change her mind, decide to reopen the shop, and agree to honor the deal to sell the quilts; but Deborah had seen the wistful way she'd stared at the medallion quilt. It was the only time she'd shown real interest in her surroundings. Surely that had been a sign.

She'd stop back by soon.

Until then, she'd pray that the quilts worked their way into Callie's heart.

∽

He stood under the canopy of one of the older shops, one of the shops he knew didn't have security cameras. Pulling out his cell phone, he punched in the boss's number.

"The package isn't in his house."

He listened a few more minutes, then disconnected the call.

As far as locations went, Shipshewana wasn't the worst, but it could be the most bizarre. Just as he was about to cross the street, a horse and buggy appeared out of the darkness, causing his heart rate to accelerate, causing him to reach for his gun.

That was the last thing he needed to do—shoot some farm animal in the middle of Main Street. One more reason he hated being here.

Find the package and he could head home.

Which was exactly what he intended to do, no matter what measures were required.

Chapter 4

CALLIE WAS SITTING in front of the windows of her upstairs apartment. It was mid-afternoon of the next day, and she was astounded at the number of people on the street below. When had Shipshewana become so busy?

Her fingers traced the letters on the cover of the book in her lap—JOURNAL. She'd found it while cleaning this morning. It seemed almost like trespassing to look inside, but her desire to know more about her aunt had won over the slight twinge of guilt.

She slowly traced the J with one finger, traced it and thought about the single page she'd randomly opened to. February 4th, four years ago—

My heart aches for Callie, Father. I know her newborn daughter is in your arms, safe with you, but I also know her pain is great. Comfort her today. Comfort Rick. Show them your love, even in their time of sorrow.

Earlier she had slapped the journal shut and pushed it back into the drawer on the night stand. Reading about those days, even from her aunt's perspective, caused the wounds to bleed anew. She found it easier to concentrate on the basket of laundry that needed folding. It had stacked up over the last week. But as she'd folded her mind kept going back to the journal. Now she sat holding it, wondering what else was there, wondering whether she had the courage to read more. She had begun reading again when not one but two buggies pulled up in front of the shop.

Two men with long beards, straw hats, dark pants, light-colored dress shirts, and suspenders stepped out of the buggies. They stood looking at the shop and talking. One of the men carried a cane, though he didn't seem to be leaning on it.

"I'll never get used to people not calling first," she confessed to Max.

For his part, the dog looked thrilled to have company. He ran to the door and waited expectantly for her to clip on his leash.

Checking the mirror over the hall table, she decided at least her appearance had improved since yesterday's fiasco.

She was dressed.

She was clean.

And she'd eaten.

These days it didn't get much better.

Clipping Max's leash to his collar, she hurried down the stairs, and exited the door at the same time the two men started up the walk.

The younger of the two men nodded, but didn't offer his hand. "Hello. I'm Jonas Yoder. I believe you met my *fraa* yesterday."

"Deborah?"

"*Ya.* She asked me to bring Eli by." Jonas nodded at the older gentleman, who put his hand on his hat and nodded at her. Light streaks of gray peppered his beard, and gentle lines feathered out from his blue eyes.

"My name is Eli King. I help people buy and sell their property."

"You're a realtor?" Callie's heart tripped a beat, as she realized one of her problems might be solved.

"*Ya*, I suppose that's what you English would call me." He shared a smile with Jonas, leaned on the cane. The old guy seemed spry enough. Callie had the oddest feeling the cane was more of a prop than a necessary aid. "You might have noticed we do things a bit differently here in Shipshewana."

"I noticed." Callie tucked her hair behind her ear. "Can you help me sell the shop, Mr. King?"

"I believe I can."

No one spoke as Max settled between the three of them.

"Can't say as I've been in the shop before, though of course I knew Ms. Powell." Eli studied the building, then turned and looked her directly in the eye. "I'm sorry for your loss."

"Thank you."

Tapping the side of the stucco wall with his cane, he smiled mischievously. "I remember when this building was first put up. Construction's good."

"Nice to know."

"Can't sell it like it is though. Folks don't like to buy a place that looks abandoned."

Callie's head snapped around, and she glanced at Jonas to see if she'd heard the old guy right.

Jonas grinned and stooped to scratch Max behind the ears.

"I suppose you know the shop's been empty since my aunt died. I only arrived last week."

He nodded. "Landscaping will have to be tended, windows washed, displays redone."

Callie hurried to catch up with Eli King, who was indeed surprisingly spry.

"I don't want to reopen it. I want to sell it."

He turned to study her. "Reopening it is a fine idea. I'm glad you suggested it."

"I didn't suggest it. I said—"

"Of course it's your decision, but you'd have the best chance of getting top dollar for a business that's open and thriving versus one that's …" His voice trailed off as his cane took in the state of the parking lot where weeds had run rampant.

"Abandoned?" she asked sarcastically.

"Excellent choice of words."

Callie closed her eyes and pulled in a deep breath. When she opened them, Eli had disappeared around the corner of the building. Suddenly remembering Max, she turned and nearly bumped into Jonas.

"He can be a bit opinionated," Jonas said, handing her the dog's leash.

"A bit?" she accepted the leash and hurried to catch up with Eli King.

Jonas kept pace with her. "*Ya*, but on the other hand, he's usually right."

After Eli had surveyed the exterior of the building, he walked through the inside, then asked to see the apartment. Callie was relieved she'd at least picked up the dirty laundry upstairs. Jonas wrote down Eli's suggestions as they walked through each room. By the time they'd returned to the buggies, the list covered two sheets of paper.

"You want me to do all of this?" Callie's voice rose like the birds chattering in the trees.

"Where are you from, Miss Harper?" Eli studied her from beneath bushy eyebrows.

"Texas."

"In Texas, do you not clean up a piece of property before you attempt to sell it? Put on the best possible face, as if you are preparing it for a grand celebration?"

"Yes, of course we do, but I don't want a celebration. I simply need to sell this place, and go …" the word *home* almost slipped from her lips, but she blocked it. Instead she allowed the afternoon sounds of Shipshewana to fill the silence.

"Selling property is never easy," Eli said, not unkindly. "But in a small town, like Shipshe, it's even more difficult. Most of the Amish people live on farms. While they are appreciative of the stores, they haven't the resources or the desire to own one."

"What about Englishers?" The word fell clumsily off her tongue. "Like myself?"

"It's rather far for them to commute from Elkhart or Angola, and though of course we have some Englishers who live among us, most—like yourself—prefer not to live in such a small rural place."

Something in Callie's stomach sank like a stone, and she found herself wishing she hadn't eaten the cheese bagel and egg earlier. "So you're saying it's useless for me to try and sell Daisy's Quilt Shop?"

"Not at all," Eli said.

"Of course not," Jonas added.

She studied them both. "Then what am I missing?"

"Hope, perhaps." Eli reached out, patted her arm.

Callie stiffened at the touch, in spite of herself. When had she grown so unaccustomed to something as simple as a hand on her arm?

"This list though ..." Callie studied the two sheets in her hands. "I don't even know where to begin. And opening the store—I'm not sure I can do that. I'm not sure I want to do that."

"A decision you'll have to think on and pray about," Eli agreed. "But an open and thriving business will sell much more quickly than—" he turned and looked once more at her aunt's shop, at her shop. "More quickly than one which has been deserted."

Callie sighed and stared back down at the sheets of paper.

"As far as the list," Jonas said. "I believe Deborah might have some ideas."

They all looked up as another buggy entered the parking lot. As soon as it stopped, the doors opened and four children tumbled out, followed by Deborah holding a toddler.

~

By the expression on Callie Harper's face, Deborah worried things were not going well.

However, Eli greeted her children exuberantly, and Jonas grinned as if he hadn't seen her in months.

"Danki for sending me over to meet Miss Harper, Deborah." Eli tapped his cane on the ground. "This is a beautiful shop, and I think we can find a good buyer in a few short months."

"Months?" Callie's voice squeaked, reminding Deborah of the mice Joseph sometimes snuck in from the fields to hide in a shoebox under his bed.

"I wish I could stay, but I have a meeting with the bishop this afternoon." Eli nodded to everyone, patted the last of the children, and climbed into his buggy.

"Did he say months?" Callie's gaze jumped from the departing buggy to the children standing stair-step beside Jonas.

Deborah and Jonas both nodded yes, waving after Eli as he drove away.

"Are these all your children?" Callie covered her mouth with her hand, as if she could draw the words back. "I'm so sorry. That sounded rude."

"It's no problem," Deborah said.

"Englishers are often surprised by our large families," Jonas agreed, accepting baby Joshua from Deborah's arms.

Deborah reached out and pulled down on Joseph's wool cap, which was about to fall off his head. "Callie Harper, meet Martha, Mary, Joseph, Jacob, and this is baby Joshua. Ages ten, six, the twins are five, and the baby is fourteen months."

Callie smiled weakly. "Hello."

The children all nodded, and a few murmured their hellos. Deborah motioned toward the paper. "Eli's famous for his lists. I thought we might be able to help."

"We?" Callie asked, her eyebrows arching in disbelief.

Jonas shifted the baby in his arms. "Everyone except myself and baby Joshua. We'll be headed back to the barn. I will stop by tomorrow to take care of those trees that need trimming and the mowing in the side yard."

"You don't need to do my yard work. I can find someone —"

"Be happy to do it. Daisy's place has helped our town for years. It's the least we can do in return." Jonas ran his hand down Deborah's arm, then headed toward his buggy, carrying the baby as if he were a sack of potatoes. Joshua grinned at them over his dad's shoulder.

"If there's anything else on that list I need to do, just mark it down," Jonas called out as he climbed into his buggy. "I'll be here after lunch."

"All right children. Unload the supplies." When Deborah turned back toward Callie, she found she still hadn't moved.

"I don't feel right accepting your help."

"It's the way we do things here, Callie. We support each other. Is it not this way where you come from?"

"In Texas? Sometimes, perhaps, in the smaller towns." She clasped her hands around her waist.

"But not where you lived?" Deborah asked.

"I lived in Houston, and well, I traveled a lot actually and didn't know my neighbors very well." Callie shifted her weight from one foot to the other, still staring down at the list. "Even if you could help, this will take days. I'm not even sure where to start."

Deborah peered at the lists, at her husband's handwriting. "Many hands make the work light. I'll send Martha inside the store with you to begin. She's *gut* at housework. The other children and I will start out here."

Callie looked from the paper to the crowded road and sidewalks. "Deborah, why are so many people here today?"

"Market days," Martha said, as she handed a bucket with

paper towels and cleanser to her younger sister and led her toward the shop's front windows.

"What are market days?"

"They are what Shipshe is famous for," Deborah explained as she corralled the boys toward the front flower beds. "Our little town of six hundred swells to nearly thirty thousand on market days. Tuesdays and Wednesdays from May through October."

Callie froze where she was, halfway between the littered walk and the front door of the shop. "Did you say thirty thousand?"

"*Ya*. It's one of the reasons the shops do so well." As Deborah and Callie spoke, they were interrupted by two ladies asking if the shop was reopening. When Callie said she hadn't decided, Deborah nearly squealed in victory. They'd moved from a no to a maybe.

"Lots of tourists visiting and buying things." With a smile on her face, she directed the boys to pulling weeds. Perhaps the idea of all those tourists buying her stock would convince Callie Harper to stay and reopen the shop for at least a few weeks.

Chapter 5

Three hours later, Deborah handed Martha her change purse and sent her with the younger children around the corner to the grocer. "One small piece of candy each. Not enough to ruin your dinner."

"Yes, *Mamm*." Martha blinked once, accepted the purse, and tucked it in the pocket of her apron.

"I'll be sure the boys stay out of the syrup this time." Her tone indicated she understood the seriousness of her role as oldest sister. She and Mary took their positions on the end, with the twins in the middle. Arms linked up like cars on the train that passed through town, they made their way down the sidewalk.

It did Deborah's heart good to see them that way — taking care of one another. She had *gut* children, who had worked hard the last few hours, and the results brightened everything in front of her.

Sparkling, clean windows.

Weeds pulled from flower beds and dumped in the mulch pile behind the store.

Well-swept walk.

Passing the window display, she noted with approval that the dead plants had been removed and the dust bunnies banished.

The inside of the store shone like the outside.

Callie stood behind the counter, an expression of confusion on her face. Max lay on the floor near her feet, sleeping blissfully.

"Something wrong?" Deborah asked.

"I don't know how we did it. I keep checking the list, and nearly everything's done. Not all of it, of course. I still need to set up new window displays—"

"You'll want to check Daisy's catalogues for summer suggestions."

"And I should create new flyers to place outside."

"When you decide what you want to advertise."

Callie sank on to the stool, finally raised her eyes from the paper she'd been staring at since Deborah had walked into the shop. "Am I actually going to do this? Am I going to reopen Daisy's Quilt Shop?"

"Do you want to reopen it?" Deborah moved closer to the sales counter, close enough to reach across and give her hands a comforting squeeze. Though she'd only just met Daisy's niece, she found herself thinking of her like a younger sister.

"I don't know. Maybe. I didn't think that I wanted to, but I must say things look much better now. Before, everything seemed so overwhelming."

"And are you overwhelmed now?"

Callie laughed, pulled her hands back, and tucked her hair behind her ears. "No. I'm exhausted, but I'm not overwhelmed. I can see this is a business, just like—" She bit on her bottom lip, stopped the words she'd been about to say. "Well, it's no different than any other."

"Of course it isn't, and we'd be glad to lend a hand." Deborah felt hope surge. Maybe she'd be able to carry good news to Esther and Melinda after all.

"We? You and the children?"

Deborah's laugh joined with Callie's. A light breeze ruffled the curtains, and it seemed to Deborah that the beginning of trust breezed through the room, washing out some of the tension.

"My children are wonderful workers, but only Martha knows anything about quilting, and she just began sewing a few years ago."

Callie smiled but didn't interrupt her.

"No, when I said we'd be glad to help you I was referring to my friends — Melinda and Esther. Most of Shipshewana would also be happy to help. We'd all like to see the shop opened again."

Callie nodded and traced a finger down the sheet of paper, tapped something written on the bottom, then checked it off with the pen she kept tucked behind her ear. "I hadn't realized how important Daisy's shop was to this town."

"So you'll do it?" Deborah aimed for a casual tone, but in her heart she was remembering sitting in the baby's room — positioned between Esther and Melinda, and their hopes and needs.

~

Callie stood and walked toward the front of the store, to where she could look out the front windows and see the little sign that proclaimed "Daisy's Quilt Shop." It was the only remaining legacy to her aunt, to her family. If she left now, if she sold the store, what would the name be changed to? She couldn't stay indefinitely, but maybe she could stay long enough to regain a sense of who she was, of who Daisy was. Maybe, here in Shipshewana, she could find a way to put her feet on solid ground again.

"To be honest, I don't have any reason to hurry back to Texas."

"That's *gut*."

"And Eli said the property would bring a better price if it's open."

"Eli always speaks the truth, even when it causes more work."

Callie returned to the counter and replaced the pen behind her ear. "I suppose I don't have to know about quilting per se to sell quilting supplies."

"Of course you don't. Any questions, just ask." Deborah beamed at her.

Callie had the distinct impression that if the counter wasn't between them she might find herself enfolded in a hug. Were the Amish always so demonstrative with their emotions? She realized then that she had grown used to being rather reserved and the touching left her a little unsettled.

Callie again pulled in her bottom lip, then placed both her hands flat on the counter as if to brace herself against a big wind. "I'll do it then. I'll reopen Daisy's Quilt Shop."

"Wunderbaar!" Deborah exclaimed.

Max rolled over in his sleep, let out a sigh, as if he understood what Callie had decided.

Callie smiled and found that she actually felt good about the decision. "When I arrived, someone met me here at the door with a key and Max, but I don't even recall the man's name. I don't believe he was Amish, but I was so tired that evening, I remember very little. Any idea who looked after Max for the last month?"

"That would have been Mr. Simms. He always had a soft spot in his heart for your *aenti*."

Cocking her head to the side, Callie looked at her quizzically. "Soft spot? As in romantic feelings?"

"Oh, I don't know. Do you mean was he *in lieb*? I really couldn't say."

Callie began to giggle, picturing Daisy on a date. "My aunt was in her seventies, Deborah."

"Do you think such things stop with age?"

"Last week I would have said so, but then last week I wouldn't have imagined myself owning a quilt shop either." Callie made a mental note to look through the journal and see if Daisy had mentioned Mr. Simms.

"I think it's a *gut* decision. I'm very happy for you." Deborah paused, then pushed on with what was troubling her. "There is one more thing." She nodded at the stack of quilts she'd left the day before.

Callie stepped out from behind the counter. "Martha and I moved them here while we were dusting." She picked up the top two, brought them back, and stood beside Deborah. "It's expert craftsmanship," Callie said softly, almost reverently, her mind flashing back again to the quilt her mother had owned. "I assume you know that."

"Danki."

"Explain to me what your agreement was with my aunt."

"Daisy agreed to sell them here in the shop, for an 80/20 split."

"You had a contract?" Callie's fingers traced the pattern of the medallion quilt.

"No, we had a verbal agreement. You'll find that often Plain folk do business this way."

Callie wondered if she should be tactful, then decided as a business owner — even a temporary one — it was more important to be clear. "I'd prefer to have something on paper."

"All right." Deborah didn't even hesitate. "If it makes you more comfortable."

"I think it would be best." Callie glanced up at her. "It helps to keep good business records."

"Of course."

"I could draw them up on my laptop and have them ready for you next time you come into town. Did you have a set price that you wanted to ask for each quilt?"

"Actually that was something I wanted to talk to you about. I'd like to change the way we were offering the quilts. In fact, I'd like to try something completely different. Something I don't think Daisy knew how to do, but I have a feeling you will."

Nearly all the tension had drained out of Callie's shoulders as the mountain of work had been completed in the last few hours. At Deborah's words, it all came crashing back in an instant. "I don't know what you have in mind, but I doubt seriously there's anything different I can do."

"That is your laptop, your computer?" Deborah nodded at the slim black box resting on the other side of the counter.

"Yes ..." Callie drew the word out, wondering what an Amish person, someone who didn't even use electricity, could possibly know about a laptop.

"I would like you to sell our quilts on ibby."

"Ibby?" Callie realized again there was going to be a learning curve to this Amish language thing.

"Yes, ibby." Deborah frowned, pulled one of the strings of her prayer *kapp* forward and began fiddling with it. "Ibby is on your computer. It is a big store."

"I'm not sure what you're talking about, but I've never heard of Ibby."

"Ibby. It's like our auction houses, except much larger."

"eBay?"

"Yes. Maybe. I'm not sure. Is it an auction house?"

"Oh, my. Yes, it is an auction house. Deborah, where did you hear about eBay?"

Deborah smiled, standing taller. "We are not ignorant of English things, merely because we choose a different way."

"But you don't have electricity; isn't that correct?"

"*Ya*, but our teenagers go through a time of *rumspringa*—a period where they're allowed to sample English ways."

"And they have computers?"

Deborah shrugged. "What they have changes with the times. I don't know exactly what things they sample now. It's been a few years since my *rumspringa*. I can remember one of the boys from our church kept an old motorcycle in the back of the shop where he worked." She looked at Callie and smiled mischievously. "Several of us would sneak out at night and ride all over the county."

Callie didn't even try to stop the smile that spread across her face, in part because she was thinking of her own teenage years. "I had no idea."

"Most people don't. It's not a problem in our community. All is done before we join the church — a time to, how do you say it, try our wings."

"And now teens have laptops?" Callie reached down to pat Max as he stood, shook himself, and trotted toward the front window.

"Possibly. I heard my nieces talking about this eBay. Apparently someone had a way to participate in the auction."

"Could have been a laptop computer or even a cell phone with internet capabilities, like a BlackBerry."

"How can one get on the internet with berries?"

"I'll explain it later. Tell me what you know about eBay."

Deborah shrugged. "However they did it, these teens were able to purchase some items — one bought a new horse, and another bought some farming tools. I've even heard of a young man in the next district buying a racing buggy on auction. Could that be possible?"

"Oh, I'm sure it's possible. I've seen almost everything offered on eBay. But why would you want your quilts auctioned that way? It's summertime. From what you've told me about market days, and the amount of shoppers on the streets, it seems Shipshewana has plenty of tourists and buyers."

Max whined softly as Deborah's children came into view. No longer linking arms, this time they were walking in a straight line, each focused on the candy they were eating. Martha stopped them outside the window. She and Mary set the twins down on the bench, then wiped their hands and faces with a handkerchief. Both boys squirmed as if they were being tortured, but they didn't move from the bench. Callie watched the scene play out and wondered what a childhood here would be like then she turned back to Deborah.

"You have good kids."

"Danki," Deborah said softly.

Something passed between the two then, something Callie wasn't sure she was ready to share yet, something she might have once called friendship.

"Do you worry about them walking in the crowds?"

"No. They didn't go far, and the other shop owners will watch out for them."

Callie nodded and smiled as Jacob tugged on his cap.

"Why the wool caps in the summertime?"

"It's what their *dat* wore, and their *grossdaddi*. It's our way."

Callie thought of all that must include, then glanced down at the quilts.

"It's true we have a good amount of tourists during the summer, especially on market days, but more look than buy. Daisy had the quilts up for three weeks and no one had bought any."

"That's not a lot of time."

"Yet many people came and went."

Callie ran her hand over the medallion quilt again. "Are any quilts sold at the auction house here in town, the one you spoke of?"

"Ya, and we could sell ours there."

Callie waited.

"We need to make more money than that. Ours need to stand out, need to be different. You have a good eye, and you were correct when you said — how did you say it? That you noticed expert craftsmanship. Melinda, Esther, and I were always considered the best quilters in our age group. We have sold the occasional quilt at the auction house or to raise money for a benefit, but now we need to —"

Deborah stopped, turned, and walked toward the window. She waved at her children. Again Callie waited instead of pressing her. When she turned around, Callie was surprised to see tears in her eyes.

"It's not my place to tell you the needs of my friends, but I believe there's a reason God gave them this talent, a reason he put the three of us together, and a reason that you are here now to help us with this."

Callie shook her head. "Deborah, I'm probably not staying here for long. I'm certainly not ready to say that God has anything to do with my being here."

"Just tell me you'll try. It's very important or I wouldn't ask."

Callie pulled in a deep breath, glanced around at the shop that looked as if a miracle had occurred there in the last three hours, then turned back to the woman responsible for it all—the same woman who had seen to her aunt's funeral arrangements when she hadn't made it back in time to do so. "All right. If that's what you want, I'll do it. We'll need to set a minimum bid."

Deborah named a number.

"That sounds like a good starting price to me. I think the quilts will bring more, but I'll search the listings of completed auctions to be sure—not that I expect to find many Amish quilts there. Also, I want to start by placing only three for sale."

"How long do you think it will take?"

"We'll start the bidding the day I open. Today's Tuesday. I don't see how I could open before—"

"Saturday?"

"Saturday would be good. And we'll close the bidding on the first quilt in ten days—long enough to attract notice, but not so long that people will lose interest."

Callie barely had the words out of her mouth, when she found herself enfolded in a hug. She held very still and waited for Deborah to back away. When she did, Callie couldn't help returning the woman's smile. Her enthusiasm was a bit contagious.

"Are you sure you want to do this, Deborah? It seems like a big step, seems very different for you and your friends to conduct business this way."

Deborah stood straighter, a look of confidence replacing whatever had caused the tears earlier. "It's what we need to do. The bishop will understand."

"The bishop ..."

"Don't worry about it. I'll speak to him. You take care of the auction."

Callie agreed, called Max to her side, then followed Deborah outside.

As she watched Deborah and her children climb into the buggy, watched the horse and buggy trot gracefully down the road into a nearly picture-perfect sunset, it occurred to her that the day had certainly taken some bizarre turns.

She was still on her own, still lonely if she was honest about it, but at least her life had a bit of purpose. More than in her last job. She didn't miss the endless traveling or the traffic jams one bit.

Selling Amish quilts on eBay. She didn't tumble out of bed ten hours earlier imagining she'd be doing that, which went to show that you never knew where a day would lead you.

Chapter 6

SATURDAY MORNING new plants graced the front window display. Deborah's friend Melinda had brought them by, insisting they were welcome-to-the-community gifts. Quiet and friendly, wearing glasses, and carrying a baby, Melinda reminded Callie of a cousin she had played with at summer reunions. Played with might have been the wrong word. They sat side by side near the creek behind her grandmother's place, reading their books together and staying away from the boys who insisted on catching grasshoppers and throwing the insects at them for some unfathomable reason.

With the plants placed among the yards and yards of white lace Callie had found on a top shelf in the store room, the green and white made for a bright, inviting window treatment.

The grounds outside the window were also in pristine shape, thanks to Jonas who had stopped by and done much more than was on Callie's list.

But of course what people had been stopping to point at for the past twenty-four hours was the centerpiece displayed in the front window—the medallion quilt. A placard at the bottom read, *Available ONLY on eBay*. Beneath that was the item number.

Callie had also purchased a wireless router for her laptop and a secondhand computer from the local tech expert who had helped her set everything up. Where the old button bin had once taken up a nice corner, she now had an eBay station. Customers could place their bids immediately or browse and wait until they were home to shop. A laminated instruction card was tacked next to the computer terminal and flyers were stacked beside it that customers could take home. Reconnecting Daisy's phone service and internet had been easy enough, and she had been able to purchase a replacement cell phone from Mr. Cooper, the grocer. It had all come together seamlessly.

Esther's cookies filled two plates that rested on a table near the electric coffee pot, which Callie had filled with hot water. Next to the drinks was the basket full of a variety of instant coffees and teas.

Callie surveyed her shop and decided she was prepared—even excited—for Shipshewana's Saturday morning tourist crowd. She had made an effort to keep things much like her aunt had them while still adding her own flair. Instead of using the Styrofoam cups Daisy had kept stocked in the pantry, Callie had set out a peg board, placed hooks on it, and filled it with a variety of mugs she'd found in the cabinets above the sink. Beside the table she'd placed a bucket, with another sign directing customers to place used cups there. She'd never liked the taste of Styrofoam herself and liked the homey feel the old-fashioned cups lent to the refreshment corner.

Max padded over to her and placed his head against her leg.

"You ready, boy?"

He didn't answer. Why would he? But he did allow her to fix the blue bandana around his neck. It nicely matched the blue summer dress with spaghetti straps she'd chosen to wear over a white short sleeved T-shirt. She'd always liked wearing layered clothes, but it had been too casual in her last job. She planned to indulge herself as far as wardrobe if she was going to be a shop owner.

Checking her reflection in the mirror one last time, she marched to the front door, turned the CLOSED sign to OPEN, and unbolted the door.

No one waited on the benches.

No one walked inside.

Sticking her head outside, she peeked down the road a bit. A few people walked up and down the sidewalk, but the roads were surprisingly quiet. She'd grown used to Shipshewana's busy foot traffic.

"Hmm. I wonder where everyone is."

Closing the door she walked back inside and moved behind the counter, which was when she spotted the clock sitting next to the register—it read seven a.m.

"Might explain why there are no shoppers out yet. Come on, Max. Looks like we have some time for you to take a run."

Clipping his leash to his collar, she walked him out to the freshly mowed side yard. While he ran about, acting as if he hadn't just been there less than an hour before, she sat on the bench in the early morning light, and tried to envision what her first day as a shop owner might be like.

Three hours later, she looked up from the register into Deborah's laughing amber eyes, baby Joshua on her hip.

"Busy morning."

"Yes, it has been." Callie peered around her to see if any customers waited in line. Sighing in relief, she dropped on to the stool. "Good thing I worked a few summers in a General Store back in Houston. That was years ago, but they used this same type of register. Pricing hasn't been a problem. Daisy had everything tagged, but I have no idea how to note what inventory I'm selling. I'll have to work out a system of some sort."

"I take it you haven't had a rest?"

"Not at all. It's been a steady stream of customers since eight this morning." Callie raised her hand in a high five, but when

Deborah merely looked at her quizzically she dropped it back to the counter.

"I was supposed to do something?"

"It's nothing."

"Show me, Callie. I want to celebrate with you."

"It's silly. My friends and I used to high-five when we received a high grade on a paper or returned a good volley." She realized that she hadn't high-fived anyone in a long time—and that it felt good to have something to celebrate.

"Volley? So you play volleyball?"

"I did, but that was years ago—in high school and then a little in college for fun. I don't know why I thought of it just now."

"Then high-five, to the grand reopening of Daisy's Quilt Shop." Deborah held her hand up beside her, as if she were about to take a pledge.

Shaking her head, Callie leaned across the counter and slapped it. Baby Joshua giggled and bounced in Deborah's arms, attempting to slap at her hand like his mother.

"Your English ways are a bit strange, but I'm glad things are going so well."

"I'm glad you talked me into opening."

"I didn't talk you into it. I believe you convinced yourself."

"Maybe so. Maybe I did. Certainly it's better than sitting around feeling sorry for myself." Callie suddenly busied herself straightening things on the counter. The truth was, though she did feel better, she still had moments when she wanted to turn the sign to CLOSED, make her way back up the stairs, and climb under the old quilts covering Daisy's bed.

Deborah cocked her head and waited, but she didn't question her—it was one of the things Callie liked about her. Deborah rarely asked questions, waiting instead to see if Callie wanted to share more.

"Good news about your quilt. I saw several tourists stop and write down the item number. A few also logged onto the eBay site. Tonight I'm going to print out some cards that look like bookmarks—I want to put pictures of all three quilts on them along with the corresponding item numbers."

"You're a natural businesswoman," Deborah said. "I never would have thought of doing such a thing."

Callie felt a blush creep up her cheeks at the compliment. She reached for the pen stuck behind her ear and studied the notebook where she'd begun keeping all her work notes.

"A good businesswoman would have already ordered a new phone over the internet. I suppose I wasn't in a hurry to replace it because there wasn't anyone I wanted to talk to."

"Replace the one you lost in the airport?"

"I told you about that?" Callie ran her fingers through her hair, trying to remember.

"You did, the first day I was here. Along with the fact that you had no automobile."

"I'm still working on the transportation problem, though to tell you the truth I've become used to walking. I think I've found a car rental firm that I can lease from weekly and will deliver straight to Shipshewana, but it costs more."

"Where are they located?"

"The closest seems to be Elkhart."

"It's less than twenty miles away. I know a driver who can take you. Her name is Elaine."

"A driver? You have a driver?" Callie leaned forward, her face resting in her hands as the bell rang over the door. Two ladies entered, followed by an older gentleman carrying a small notepad and wearing a scowl. Deborah nodded to all three as if she knew them, but suddenly Joshua grew restless in her arms, claiming her attention.

"Welcome to Daisy's Quilt Shop," Callie called out. "Let me know if I can help you."

"All Amish people have a driver," Deborah explained in a hushed voice, as Callie stepped out from behind the counter. "We can't very well drive our buggies long distances, so we hire someone who owns an automobile. I'll tell Elaine to stop by and talk to you. She's a sweet, older English woman. You'll get along fabulously." Joshua continued to fuss. "I better run. Time for his nap."

Callie waved as she made her way toward the two ladies. Though she'd had several men in shopping, this elderly gentleman did not seem to be browsing. Something about him raised her defenses. At the moment he was standing in front of one of Deborah's quilts, jotting down the eBay number. If anything, the frown on his face had deepened.

"Is there anything in particular I can help you find?" she asked the oldest woman.

"Oh, no. We were visiting Shipshe for the day, and saw your lovely shop. How long have you been here?"

"I reopened the store today, but my aunt ran Daisy's Quilt Shop for over thirty years."

"We saw the For Sale sign in the yard. So you don't plan to stay?"

"No. I'm afraid I can't. I have obligations in Texas." Callie's consciousness twinged slightly at the lie, but fortunately she didn't have to dwell on it. The shorter of the two women had problems retrieving a pattern book from a rotating display.

Callie helped her with the book, invited them to enjoy the refreshments, then turned back in time to see the older man scowling at the second quilt.

Gathering her courage, she stepped toward him.

"Can I help you, sir?"

Max moved with her, pressing himself against her leg.

The man remained focused on the quilt, which was actually the third that Callie had placed on auction. The first was the medallion quilt which was in the front display window. The second was a nine-patch block design. Callie had confirmed the names with Melinda when she brought by the plants.

The final quilt, the one the gentleman scowled at now, was the signature quilt.

"Melinda, Esther, and Deborah know that you are auctioning their quilts?" His voice sounded as if it had sand in it. "Auctioning them on the *internet*?"

He practically spat the last word as he glared at the computer center she'd set up.

When he turned to look at her, Callie had the urge to step back. She didn't, but the desire was strong. She thought for the second time that day of her old volleyball games.

"Never give up court space," the memory of her coach murmured.

"Excuse me?" Callie kept her voice even.

"I asked you, Do the girls know that you are auctioning their quilts on the internet? You're not deaf are you?" The man glanced at her again, as if she were a pesky fly he'd rather not have to bother with.

"Who are you?" Callie asked, matching his rudeness with a firmer voice of her own.

"I'll take that answer as a no."

"No?"

"No, they do not know what you're doing. How could they? After all they're only three *Plain* women." The man continued to scribble on his small pad. What little hair he had was gray and cut uniformly, one-half inch in length. It grew in a circle around the top of his head, rather like a crown.

Callie had a perfect view of his shiny bald spot because she could look down directly on it — he couldn't have been over five feet tall.

He might have been old, but he wasn't frail.

The man was built like a tiny Sherman tank — bulky and solid. When he finally looked directly at Callie, blue eyes pierced her as if she'd committed some crime.

"I don't suppose you asked their bishop about this?"

"About what?" Callie's voice now settled into what she'd learned years ago to use with her most difficult clients. She took a deep breath, held it a moment, then let it out slowly. "I didn't speak to their bishop about what?"

Obviously he was referring to the quilts, or the eBay auction, or both, but she refused to give him the satisfaction of admitting she understood the problem. Deborah had assured her there was no problem, and besides, it was none of his business.

"Never mind. I heard you say you don't plan on staying, apparently you didn't take the time to learn anything about Amish ways either."

"Mr. — " she waited for the rude little man to fill in his name. When he didn't she pushed on. "I'm not sure what you're in a tizzy about, but if you'd tell me perhaps we could work this out."

"Tizzy? Is that how you speak to your elders in Texas?"

"What?"

"I would have thought Daisy's niece would have been more respectful." And with that, he snapped his notepad shut, tucked it into his shirt pocket, and marched out of the shop.

~

Deborah sat rocking and quilting. She didn't hear Jonas walk into the living room, didn't realize he was there until he rested his hand on her shoulder.

"You plan on quilting until dawn?"

Deborah reached up, patted his hand, then continued with her sewing. "I'd keep you awake if I came to bed now. Best that I sew here for a while."

Instead of trying to convince her otherwise, Jonas walked over to the kitchen, retrieved the milk from the gas-powered refrigerator, and poured two cups. Then he pulled the cookies that Esther had brought by out of the cabinet. Bringing it all to the living room, he sat down near her.

"Kind of late for a snack."

"Never too late for Esther's cookies. Wonder what she puts in these things."

A little of the tension eased from between Deborah's shoulder blades as she shook her head at her husband, then took a bite of the cookie he held out to her. "You'll make me fat yet."

"You look perfect to me, and you know it."

"What if the bishop says no, Jonas? What if he says Callie can't auction the quilts on the internet? Then what will we do?"

"You explained to him she's already placed the quilts for sale?"

"*Ya*. He only will say there is no hurrying God's wisdom. How will I explain to everyone if his answer is no?"

Jonas popped one of the oatmeal chocolate cookies into his mouth and considered her question. After he'd chased it with half the glass of milk, he finally answered. "We have to trust Bishop Elam to do what is best for Melinda and Esther."

"But do you think he understands?" Deborah rocked the chair a bit harder.

"Do you doubt that he understands?"

Deborah paused mid-stitch. Suddenly it occurred to her that she was doing it again—she was taking on the role of provider for her two closest friends.

Jonas reached over, rested his hand on top of hers. "The bishop is a fair man. He promised to think on it, and he will. Perhaps he'll give you an answer when we meet for church tomorrow."

"*Ya*. You're right."

"If he decides against this eBay idea, then you'll go back to selling them in Callie's shop."

Deborah felt the tears she'd been holding back all night spring to her eyes. "And what if Callie closes the shop, or sells it? What if Melinda doesn't get the money soon enough? What if Esther—"

Jonas's thumb gently strumming up and down the back of her hand stopped the questions, stilled the avalanche of fear.

"Small steps," he reminded her.

She nodded, blinked the tears back, and stored the pin in her apron.

Small steps, but as Jonas set the dishes in the sink and they readied for bed, she couldn't help praying that the quilts would sell through the online auction, and that they would sell for a very high price.

Chapter 7

ON SUNDAY, Shipshewana was closed.

Callie rested—a little. She was uncomfortable about the idea of having too much free time, sure she'd end up huddled back under the covers. The feelings of depression she'd been submerged in just a week ago were never far away. So she'd allowed herself only a few hours of downtime before asking Deborah's driver, Elaine, to take her to Elkhart for the rental car. Elaine was in her fifties with short-cropped gray hair and was definitely an Englisher.

She entertained Callie with stories of her aunt for the twenty-five minute drive—stories that had Callie wishing the drive were a bit longer.

Why hadn't she come to visit Daisy sooner?

Why hadn't she made time?

Why had she waited until it was too late?

Pushing the regrets away, she paid Elaine for the ride, then picked up her rental car. She'd arranged with the customer service rep to rent the small Ford on a weekly basis, since she still had no clear indication as to how long it would take to sell the store.

Though it had been only thirteen days since she'd flown into Indiana, not even two weeks since she'd had her own car at her disposal, she realized as she adjusted the driver's seat and checked the rear view mirror just how much of her sense of independence was tied to a vehicle. It felt odd to be driving out of the parking lot—odd but invigorating.

How did the Amish do it?

Depending on others to transport them around, being locked into a ten-mile radius, it was so confining.

Of course she had managed to meet quite a few of the local people that she probably wouldn't have otherwise.

Callie set the radio on low as she began the drive back to Shipshe, her mood drastically improved.

A stop at the warehouse discount store located on the edge of Elkhart cheered her even more. She didn't buy much, but delighted in noting what they carried and that it was only twenty minutes away. She did pick up a giant bag of dog food and more bandanas for Max. No use having a dog if you couldn't dress him up. She also purchased office supplies for printing her flyers, sales sheets, and bookmarks.

The expenses were adding up, but she'd sat down and made out a budget the night before. If she was going to run a successful business, then she needed to put a percentage of the assets Daisy had left back into the quilt shop. Even though she didn't plan on staying in Shipshe long, she knew she'd be able to sell the business for a higher price if she could show it was profitable. She actually felt good about investing some of the money she had received from her aunt's estate.

Once home, she spent the remainder of the afternoon photographing the quilts, then made the bookmarks containing the eBay information. They turned out even better than she'd imagined, thanks to the new color printer her aunt had recently purchased.

As she readied for bed that evening, she reached for Daisy's journal. It was fast becoming a habit, reading Daisy's words before sleeping. Usually she opened the journal up randomly. Her aunt didn't write long entries and often they were about people around Shipshe that Callie didn't know. Reflecting on small cares, praying for the needs of others, admitting when she'd occasionally lost her temper. It was surprising to read that her aunt could be moody. Maybe she'd inherited more than she realized from her mom's sister.

Callie was surprised to find herself mentioned in the pages so often. As her aunt's only niece, she didn't realize how much time Daisy had spent thinking about her, praying for her. She opened the book to June, five years earlier —

> My niece is married now, Lord. And I'm sitting here with Max and this sprained ankle. Can you blame me for fuming? But I'm not writing to complain. It's my own fault that I was carrying too big a load down the stairs and tripped. No, I'm writing to thank you that Callie has found such a fine young man. She sent me pictures of her and Rick. He sounds very special. I'm so glad you blessed her with a good man, someone who will care for her. You're a good Father. They look very happy. Since I can't be there, I'll use my time to crochet a blanket for them.

The other entries which mentioned Rick or her baby had left Callie feeling as if the deep ache might burst open, but tonight's entry only brought a smile. "Come on, Max. You can sleep up here." Max bounded on the bed, settled his head across her stomach.

She still had the blanket Daisy had crocheted them — it was a lovely blue and yellow. When she drifted off to sleep, it was with memories of her first year with Rick sifting through her mind.

∽

Downtown shops were traditionally closed on Monday, so Callie spent the next morning perusing the internet and in the afternoon decided to visit a local herb farm.

What would it hurt to start a small container garden?

She'd always wanted to have one in the city, but she'd never been home enough to take care of plants, let alone a dog. Max nosed his way into her lap as she sat cross-legged on the ground in her yard and potted the nursery plants.

Thyme, sage, oregano, and dill.

She could envision cooking with every one of them.

Monday evening she even had time for a little reading — something she hadn't done in years. Perusing her aunt's shelves in the tiny apartment above the shop, she was surprised to find a very good collection of old Agatha Christie novels.

So her aunt loved a mystery did she?

Pulling one off the shelf, Callie curled up in the recliner with a light blanket across her lap and Max at her side.

"*Dumb Witness* was published in 1937, Max. Now why do you think Aunt Daisy would have ordered a new copy of it?"

She pulled out her aunt's bookmark, turned back to the beginning, and began to read.

Tuesday dawned clear and sunny. Callie was actually looking forward to going back to work. She dressed to match Max again. Might be silly, but it was fun. What was wrong with a little fun? This time she chose a blue-jean skirt with a short-sleeved red sailor sweater. She'd found a bandana that was red with white ship anchors at the warehouse, and she tied it around Max's neck. He looked at her rather sadly, but he didn't argue.

"I know. I'm pitiful, but you'll learn to like me." Adding a white headband to her hair was a nice touch. "We look like we're ready to go sailing, not to work." Still, it gave her a bit of a lift for the day. That — and some very strong coffee — was all she needed.

This time people did start arriving as soon as she unlocked the door, and surprisingly the crowds were as large as Saturday's. She'd expected things to be a bit slower, but as Deborah had promised sales were brisk. Then she remembered that Tuesdays were market days. The streets were bustling.

She was pleased to see that every time she glanced up, a customer was logged in at the eBay terminal, and her bookmarks went quickly. In fact, she had to sneak into the small office at lunch and print off additional copies.

Callie didn't want to get her hopes up, but she thought word might be circulating about the quilts, even among the Amish community. As she was checking customers out at the register, she overheard snippets of side conversations — nothing specific, but it had to be about the auctioned quilts.

"Do you think these are the ones?"

"Must be ..."

"And the auction is on the In-ter-net?"

Callie finished ringing out the customer and approached the two Amish women standing in front of the nine-patch quilt.

"Did you have a question about the quilt?"

"Oh, no. *Danki.*" Both women glanced down at the ground, and it seemed as if the heavier one began to fidget.

"All right. Well, I'll be at the register if you have any questions."

They murmured their thanks, then hustled off to look at the spools of thread.

It went that way all morning.

Even a few Amish men stopped in, claiming they needed to pick up supplies for their wives. Though she saw many English couples on Saturday, Deborah had explained that in general, Amish men took care of their shopping at the feed store or hardware store while women shopped for sewing supplies. Today seemed to be the exception.

Most customers were open and friendly, but not all. Callie looked up a little before lunch to see one middle-aged English woman practically hiding behind a newspaper. (Even she was beginning to split the customers into two categories — English and Amish.)

She had noticed the Amish customers tended to buy only supplies — fabric, thread, and notions. No doubt they sewed their own quilts, though several did stop to admire the finished quilts. Probably they knew Deborah, Melinda, and Esther.

When Callie approached to see if she could help, the rather hefty woman stuffed the paper in her bag, murmured something that sounded like, "Well I never would have thought — " then hurried out of the store.

Staring after her in disbelief, Callie wondered if perhaps she'd heard her wrong. With a shrug, she picked up the bucket of dirty coffee mugs and carried them to the kitchen, but she'd barely made it into the little room when the bell over the shop door rang again.

"Maybe she remembered what she never would have thought," Callie muttered, wiping her hands on a dish towel. Hurrying around the corner, she nearly plowed over Deborah.

Deborah was wearing a pale blue dress with a white apron and her customary flip-flops. All the Amish women seemed to wear flip-flops, except the very old ones who wore the black laced up shoes.

"I didn't expect to see you back in town today."

"We need to talk."

"I know. I thought about driving out to see you tonight, but I didn't know where you live. Of course I could have asked someone, but — "

"We need to talk now." Deborah reached out and grabbed her hand, pulling her toward the counter. "Are there any customers in the store at the moment?"

"Not unless they're hiding behind the bolts of cotton. Is something wrong?"

"Yes. I'm afraid so. I take it you haven't seen today's paper."

Deborah opened the *Shipshewana Gazette* and placed it on the counter, smoothing it with her hand.

They both stood there, gazing down at the front page. The top half was covered by a picture of colorful plants, set up in a pattern to resemble a quilt, and now in full bloom.

"Am I supposed to be upset about The Living Quilt picture? Because I think the gardens are quite beautiful." Callie didn't touch the paper, didn't open it, but she did look Deborah in the eye and wait for her response.

"Page three, right column. You better sit down."

~

Deborah went into the small kitchen while Callie read. She pulled down two coffee cups, placed a lemongrass and spearmint tea bag in each one, and poured hot water over the top.

"You must be kidding!"

Deborah didn't walk into the main room immediately, opting instead to snag a few of the cookies off the refreshment table, hoping to give Callie time to finish the article, and perhaps calm down a bit.

"He can't write this! He can't say these things. There are slander laws against this. We're in Shipshewana, not a third world country. Do you realize how much damage this can do to my business?"

Deborah carried the mugs of tea, each topped with a saucer filled with several cookies, over to the counter.

"Perhaps you should have some tea." She hoped her voice sounded calm; after all, Callie had never dealt with the editor of the *Gazette* before — calmness worked best.

"Tea? You want me to drink tea?"

"*Ya*, it's nice and hot." Deborah removed the saucer from the top of the mug and pushed it toward her. She knew the lull in activity wouldn't last, and she wanted to calm Callie down before any customers arrived. Perhaps she should have waited until the store closed, but she didn't want to risk her hearing about the article from someone else.

"He can't say these things, Deborah." Callie folded the paper in half, then in half again, until only the offending editorial showed, then she whacked the counter with it — as if she meant to kill a fly. "He can't, and he won't. I'm going to make him take it back."

"But Mr. Stakehorn is the editor of the paper."

"I don't care if he owns the paper. He still can't print lies."

"Callie." Deborah again nudged the tea toward her as she glanced out the window at two English women who had paused outside the store to gaze up at the medallion quilt. One woman was holding a copy of the *Gazette* in her hand, and the other was pointing at the eBay sign. "I'm sure if we give it a few days, the story will —"

"Disappear? Do you think it was typed with invisible ink that will fade away after twenty-four hours?"

Deborah bit into the cookie and smiled at her. "You're kidding, right? I've never heard of this invisible ink."

"Of course I'm kidding. It's not as if we're living in a Harry Potter book."

"Harry who?"

"Oh, never mind."

Deborah stood and picked up her saucer as the two women outside the shop proceeded around the corner and up the walk. "You have customers. I should go."

"Do you need to get back to your family?"

"Not right away. The children went to their *grossmammi's* today. Why?"

"The store closes in another thirty minutes. I want you to show me where the newspaper office is located. We're going to have a talk with Mr. Stakehorn. We're going to set him straight about the quilts and the auction. You can explain to him that it was your idea to auction them on the internet, and that I did not corrupt you!"

74

"Perhaps it is best if we go to see him together," she agreed.

Deborah turned to greet two regular customers. It was good to see that Daisy's faithful customers were supporting the shop.

Glancing back at Callie, she added, "I brought my quilting bag. I'll sit by the window and stay out of the way until you close. As long as I'm home by six, Jonas won't worry."

"You'll be home by six. We'll have this cleared up in five minutes. Mr. Stakehorn can print a nice retraction on page one of the next edition."

As Callie walked off to assist the customers, Deborah wondered if it would be so easy. Shipshewana was a small town, and she'd had dealings with Mr. Stakehorn before. The man wasn't the most agreeable Englisher she'd been around.

Could be she'd always caught him on a bad day. Or maybe he only had bad days.

She'd find out in a half hour.

For Callie's sake, she hoped today Stakehorn's temperament would be different.

Chapter 8

DEBORAH PUT BOTH HANDS on her hips and nodded toward the front seat. "It's only a horse and buggy. What's there to be *naerfich* about?"

"I realize it's a horse and buggy. And I don't know what nar-fitch is." Callie tucked her dark hair behind her ears and crossed her arms. She looked for all the world like Martha, Deborah's oldest, when she didn't want to do something.

"*Naerfich*, you know, a little green in the face. Maybe you haven't ridden a horse before? I promise, buggies are perfectly safe."

"We have horses in Texas." Callie's voice hardened and her eyes darted from the horse to the little blue car and back again. "I don't see why we can't take my car. It would be faster."

"Sometimes slower is better."

Callie shook her head, as if Deborah's reasoning made no sense at all.

"I'm a *gut* driver," Deborah added.

"I'm a good driver too."

"*Ya*, I'm sure you are, but Cinnamon is tired of standing here, and I know where the newspaper office is."

Callie's look softened a bit. "Her name is Cinnamon?"

"The children named her, because of her light brown color. We've had her three years now, and she's a very good mare."

Callie looked doubtfully at the mare. "All right, but next time we take my Ford, which I haven't named yet."

"Sure. Next time you drive. Where are we going next time?"

"I don't know. Maybe to pick up the retraction Mr. Stakehorn is going to write. Or to dinner to celebrate the awesome price you ladies will receive from your quilts."

"That's a *wunderbaar* idea."

Deborah clucked to the mare and they started off, out of Daisy's Quilt Shop's parking area. Callie clutched the seat, obviously still agitated about Stakehorn's editorial.

"Buggy riding is generally soothing. Might help settle you down a bit."

"What makes you think I'm unsettled?" Callie let go of her grip on the seat and turned around to look at the two cars slowing down behind them on the road.

"Possibly the way you slammed things as you were closing up the shop."

"I slammed things?"

"Or maybe the fact that you've been muttering under your breath since the minute you read the first line of his editorial."

"He called me a robber."

Deborah flicked Cinnamon's reins, pulling her to the right when the road broadened to four lanes. The cars behind her sped up and passed, but she maintained a steady, even pace.

"*Ya*, Stakehorn had quite a few inaccuracies in his editorial."

"The title alone was enough to make my blood boil." Callie sat back against the buggy seat, slapping the folded paper against her leg. "New Shop Owner Robs Amish — what was he thinking?"

"He was thinking about selling papers, and no doubt he sold quite a few." Deborah's voice was an extension of her thoughts, calm and quiet like the summer afternoon's breeze. Its effect on Callie was mild but evident nonetheless.

She stopped slapping the paper and closed her eyes for a moment as they completed the drive down Main Street.

Deborah breathed a quiet prayer of relief. She'd been a bit concerned with the way Callie had first slammed the paper on the counter, practically thrown the mugs into the sink, even banged the door shut when she locked up the shop. Deborah didn't doubt Callie was a good driver, but she had no desire to ride in the little blue car with her driving in her current state.

Even Max had scampered to the far end of the yard and sat gazing at his new mistress, head cocked, ears perked—as if he could somehow hear what was wrong by listening more closely.

"You're awfully quiet over there. I suppose it takes a lot of concentration to drive one of these?" Callie's voice went up at the end as Deborah pulled Cinnamon to a stop in front of the red light on Main Street.

"Oh, it doesn't take as much focus as you'd think. Cinnamon is very used to the traffic. Now if we'd brought our other mare— Lightning, I would need to pay very close attention."

"You have a horse named Lightning?" Callie's eyes widened, and she cornered herself in the buggy so she could study Deborah more closely.

"*Ya*, she's midnight black with a white streak between her eyes. Jonas brought her home a few months ago. I didn't think we needed another, but he made a good trade, and he likes to ride in the buggy races."

"You have buggy races?"

"We're not all work and no play, Callie. We even have volleyball games. I was going to ask you to join us sometime."

Callie's eyes lit up instantly for what seemed to Deborah like an unguarded moment, but then she turned and stared back out over the front of the mare. "Sounds like fun, but I don't know how long I'll be here. Depends on when the shop sells."

"Of course. If you're still here on Sunday though, perhaps you could come by."

A smile played on Callie's lips. "Don't you have church on Sunday? I thought Amish were very religious."

"We do take our commitment to the church and our faith very seriously, but we only gather together for services twice a month. This Sunday there is no service, so several families are meeting at our home for lunch and some games."

Callie cut her gaze sideways, but didn't turn. "Maybe we should try that in Texas."

"Try what?"

"Alternating Sunday church with a week off now and then for food and games."

Deborah laughed as she pulled the buggy to a stop in front of the *Shipshewana Gazette*. "It's been our way for a long time."

Callie was out of the buggy before Deborah had come to a complete stop. By the time she had Cinnamon tied to the post, Callie had already disappeared inside the small newspaper office.

"Mr. Stakehorn has already left." Mrs. Caldwell sat at the front desk, plainly closing up for the day.

"We need to talk to him though."

Mrs. Caldwell had been the receptionist at the *Gazette* for as long as Deborah could remember. She was in her early sixties, with short gray hair cut in a bob, and glasses perched on her nose. She was also close to two hundred pounds — not in a soft grandmotherly way, but in a tough no-nonsense way. Deborah had often wondered what the woman had been like in her younger years, but it was difficult to imagine her as anything but what she was now — the guardian of the *Gazette*. No one seemed to remember a Mr. Caldwell.

She looked at Deborah and nodded. "Afternoon, Deborah."

"Afternoon, Gail."

She turned her attention back toward Callie, looked over the top of her glasses, and pursed her lips together. "You're welcome to come back tomorrow. Mr. Stakehorn's always in the office by nine."

"I have to be at my store at nine. I'm Callie Harper, the new owner of Daisy's Quilt Shop." Callie offered her hand. Mrs. Caldwell looked again at Deborah, then back at Callie with a look of impatience, but she finally shook her hand halfheartedly.

"Nice to meet you," Callie said.

Mrs. Caldwell glanced pointedly at her wristwatch.

Deborah stepped forward, her instincts telling her it would be best to intervene before there was a problem, and placed a hand on Callie's arm. "We're sorry to bother you. Perhaps Callie could have Mr. Stakehorn call her tomorrow."

"Actually I want to talk to him tonight."

Mrs. Caldwell released an exasperated sigh, blowing up her bangs which were cut straight across her perfectly arched gray-blue penciled eyebrows.

The bell on the door behind them rang again, and Mr. Hearn walked into the room. Nearly Deborah's age, he was the only welder in town. Over six feet and lanky, he had dark black hair cut short and dark eyes to match.

"Afternoon, Baron." Mrs. Caldwell looked put out with the three of them, but stated the obvious anyway. "We're closing in case you haven't noticed."

"No problem. I'm here to drop off my ad for Saturday's paper." Baron Hearn handed her a large envelope, then turned to smile at Deborah, lifting off his ball cap as he did. "Mrs. Yoder."

"Mr. Hearn."

"I need to know where he is," Callie insisted. "There's a matter I need to clear up in today's paper—he grossly misstated what we're doing at Daisy's Quilt Shop, and I'd like him to print a retraction."

Baron Hearn stepped back, stuck his hands in the back pockets of his jeans as if to enjoy the show, or the view of Callie, Deborah wasn't sure which.

Mrs. Caldwell all but rolled her eyes. "Sweetheart, you obviously haven't been in Shipshewana very long."

Callie uncrossed her arms, and lowered her hands to her side, but her voice lost some of its forced politeness. "What does how long I've been here have to do with anything?"

"See this sign behind my desk?" Caldwell pointed to a cheaply painted corrugated tin that read — *I can only please one person a day, and today's not your day. Tomorrow's not looking too good either.* "Came to work for Mr. Stakehorn twenty-seven years ago. First six months I was here, so many people came in here asking for retractions — I had to purchase this."

"She the new owner of the quilt store?" Hearn asked Deborah, jerking a thumb toward Callie.

Deborah nodded, but didn't take her eyes off Callie and Mrs. Caldwell. She could sense a buggy wreck when it was about to happen, but she had no idea how to stop it.

"She talking about the editorial in today's paper?"

Deborah nodded again.

"That was a bad one, even for Stakehorn." Hearn sat down, legs stretched out in front of him and crossed at the ankles, apparently caught up in seeing how this was going to play out.

"So this is the way ya'll operate a paper here?" Callie took a step closer to the desk.

"Don't include me in the group, little miss. I don't own stock in the company."

"You work here, don't you?" Callie put her hands on the desk, actually leaned over it.

"I do, and I'd appreciate it if you'd step away from my desk before I call the sheriff."

"Call the sheriff?" Callie's voice rose, like a baby bird calling to its mother.

"You heard me."

"But I'm the one with a complaint. What Stakehorn wrote was pure lies. He had no right to say those things."

Caldwell pointed to another plaque, this one under the *Shipshewana Gazette* banner. It read *"The First Amendment—don't like it, move to a different country."*

She stood, pulled a large black purse out of the bottom drawer of her desk. "Unless we voted it out, the First Amendment still stands. Doesn't it, Baron?"

"For better or worse, I believe it does." Baron tugged again on his Indianapolis Colts ball cap.

Deborah stepped forward. "Why don't we go, Callie? We'll talk to someone about this tomorrow."

"You bet we will. You haven't heard the last from me. Stakehorn is going to regret he ever started this."

Deborah linked her hand through Callie's arm, attempted to pull her toward the front door of the newspaper office.

Caldwell was staring at her now, as if she was seeing some odd sort of farm animal, perhaps a newborn calf with two different-color eyes. Baron Hearn was still grinning from ear to ear—no doubt ready to run out and tell what he'd witnessed to everyone at the Main Street Café. Deborah knew how gossip spread in their town—this scene would feed the rumor mill for a good twenty-four hours.

"Maybe Shipshewana is used to this type of poor reporting, but in Texas we get retractions—" Callie nearly stumbled over the lip of the doorway. "Or we get even!"

~

Callie stood in front of the buggy, in front of the horse, who shook her head a bit, then resumed reaching for the green grass growing beside the sidewalk.

She turned and looked back into the front window of the *Shipshewana Gazette*.

Mrs. Caldwell had picked up the phone and was talking into it.

The man she had referred to as Baron walked out after them, smiled, and murmured, "Afternoon, ladies." He then sauntered down the walk.

"I think he enjoyed that." Callie narrowed her eyes after him.

"I have little doubt. Baron Hearn enjoys a scene as much as he enjoys a good wager on a competition, and trust me he's been known to take pleasure from both."

Callie shook her head, hoping to clear it. "You know him?"

"I do," Deborah said with a nod.

"Will he report what he just heard?"

"He will."

"You're not doing much to cheer me up here."

Deborah untied the mare, patted her gently, and smiled at Callie.

"How do you remain so calm, Deborah? I feel as if I've finished running a marathon."

"Put your hand on Cinnamon."

"Why?"

"Try it."

Callie stepped closer, placed her hand on the side of the mare. Her body warmed by the afternoon sun, she felt snug, satiny, and solid. She allowed her hand to travel the length of her neck, then repeated the process two, three times.

"Better?"

"A little."

"*Gut.*"

"I still want to find Stakehorn, and I will."

"I don't doubt it, but perhaps you should think about how you're going to handle the situation when you do."

They both climbed into the buggy, and Deborah turned the buggy back toward Daisy's Quilt Shop.

"That didn't go so well, did it?" Callie leaned forward, placed her forehead in her hands, massaged at her temples.

"At least she didn't actually call the sheriff."

"Does Shipshewana even have a sheriff?"

"Yes, we do, and let's hope you never have cause to meet him."

~

Two hours later, Callie rose from a nap she had not intended to take. Max stretched, yawned, and pushed his nose into her hand.

"Message received." After making a pit stop herself, she clipped his leash and walked him to the side yard. Once there, she realized there was enough light left for the short walk to the deli down the street.

Of course she could take the blue car, but perhaps Deborah was right — perhaps slower was sometimes better. Leaving Max in the yard to enjoy his romp with the birds, she started down Main Street.

Her nap had helped her to realize another thing: She needed to approach this situation more calmly.

Reacting like the high-pressured salesperson she had been would not work with the people of Shipshewana. She would only make enemies — and though she didn't plan to stay here long, she needed all the friends she could possibly accumulate.

Or as her mother had been fond of reminding her, "You can accomplish more with a big glass of sweet tea . . ." A bit of a twist on the traditional saying, but for Stella Harper it made perfect sense. She knew her daughter, knew her tendency was to storm in, and often reminded her that in the South, patience and manners was the better way to win someone's favor.

So she should try sweet tea.

Sweetness, Mr. Stakehorn, and the *Shipshewana Gazette* seemed incompatible, but perhaps not.

Chapter 9

CALLIE SAT DOWN at a table to wait on her order. Probably owing to the fact that it was a Tuesday, a market day, the deli was quite busy. Plus, Shipshewana didn't offer many places to eat in the evening.

The thought brought a smile to Callie's face. In Houston, many places stayed open until well past midnight. But in Shipshewana, most places closed up when the sun went down. She was grateful the deli stayed open an hour later than the others.

She seemed to be the one person waiting on a to-go order.

More than a dozen people sat at various tables or at the old time soda-fountain bar.

Some sat with their families, talking about the day's events as they enjoyed their meal.

Some sat alone, like her. She'd been eating alone since Rick died.

Her gaze traveled to the window, to the twinkly lights in the trees lining the walk outside. Summer had been Rick's favorite time. He loved everything about it—water-skiing, hiking, bike riding. He was a bit of an outdoors enthusiast. A lump filled her throat until she was sure she wouldn't be able to swallow past it.

Two years, nearly two years now. Shouldn't something as simple as eating her evening meal be easier?

On the other hand, if it became easier what would that say about her? That she didn't really love him? She did though. She loved him, and she missed him more than she'd miss her arm if someone were to walk in and cut if off at this very moment.

"Can I get you some iced tea while you wait, Miss Callie?" Beth, a young Amish girl, smiled as she stopped at her table. Blonde hair peeked out from the prayer *kapp* Callie was growing accustomed to seeing. A dark blue dress was covered by a white apron which matched the *kapp*.

"That would be wonderful. Yes, thank you, Beth."

"Mango-peach, like before?"

"I would love that. You have a good memory."

"Danki." The girl blushed slightly, then skittered away from the table.

Callie pretended to read the menu, though she'd already ordered. In truth, she studied the other customers. Many were people she'd met in her shop over the last few days.

The thought brought her up short—*her shop*.

Was that what it had become?

Her shop?

When had she started to feel a personal sense of ownership for the place?

She'd been numb for so long—since Rick's death, since her friends had deserted her, since she'd lost her job. Maybe longer. Maybe since she'd lost the baby.

The words on the menu blurred, but she blinked, forced back the tears.

Now was not the time to grow sentimental, and certainly not over an old shop that she had no ties to—no ties except Aunt Daisy.

Daisy had always been such a gentle soul, her monthly letters a balm over the last few years. True, they were short and usually filled with ramblings about her day-to-day life. What old person's letters weren't?

Who even sent letters anymore?

In a day of emailing, texting, instant messaging, and tweeting, Callie had always thought her aunt eccentric.

But she'd kept every one of those letters, tied them with a bit of lace, and placed them in her mother's hope chest back in her apartment in Houston.

She'd always meant to come back and visit her aunt. The occasional postcard she'd sent to her from wherever she had happened to have been located for that week's sales emergency now seemed like such a hollow gesture.

What kind of person was she?

She hadn't even taken the time to connect with her only remaining family.

The deli owner, Mr. Simms, was an old gentleman with a full head of white hair. He walked to the counter and hollered, "Stakehorn, your order is ready."

Callie clutched the menu in her hand. She watched in disbelief as a short older man walked up to the counter. It was the cranky old bald guy who had given her such a hard time in her shop on her first day. She moved toward the door as Mr. Stakehorn accepted the to-go order in a white paper bag, pulled out his wallet, and paid his bill.

He turned around, and she saw the same piercing blue eyes she'd stared into before.

"You." Callie could barely choke out the word.

Stakehorn looked, if anything, bored. "Step out of my way, girl."

Callie didn't budge. "You came into my shop, snooped around, and wrote things down in your little notebook. You didn't even bother to check your facts with me first." Callie shook her finger in his face. "Then you wrote lies about me in your paper."

Around them the deli grew as quiet as snow falling across the plains of the Texas Panhandle.

"If you have a problem with my paper, Miss Harper, I suggest you write a letter to the editor."

"A letter to the editor?" Callie thought the top of her head might literally come uncorked. "You are the editor, and I will not write a letter. I don't need to write a letter, because you are going to print a retraction."

Callie slapped the menu she still held down on top of the nearest table. "You wrote lies about me — lies that could very easily hurt my business. That, Mr. Stakehorn, is cause for a libel suit, which I have no reservations about pursuing."

"Be my guest, Miss Harper." Stakehorn rattled his paper bag. "Now if you don't mind, I'd like to take my dinner home and eat it before it becomes soggy."

"That's it? Just like that? You won't even consider being reasonable?"

"Harper, do you even have any proof what I wrote was untrue, or are you harassing me for the fun of it?"

"Harassing you?" Callie heard her voice rise an octave and she fought to regain control. "You're the one who filled your paper with drivel."

"So you have no proof, as I thought. Now if you'll excuse me."

Stakehorn inched right to move around her, but Callie had seen far quicker moves from elderly receptionists trying to avoid sales reps — trying to avoid her! She moved right as well, determined he wouldn't leave with the smug look on his face.

"Oh, I'll excuse you, all right."

Unfortunately at that moment Beth walked up with her tea. Not knowing what to do with it, she set it on the table nearest Callie and once again dashed away.

"I'll excuse you the minute you admit that you're a liar and you're only interested in making a profit."

"Who is only interested in profits here? At least the people who buy my paper realize what I'm about, what I'm doing." Stakehorn took two steps forward, what Callie later realized was his biggest mistake.

Stakehorn lowered his voice. "But you have to admit that those poor women have no idea how much you're taking them for. They don't even use electricity, and you're hustling their wares on the internet highway. Robbery, Miss Harper. Plain and simple."

"Plain and simple? What's plain and simple is that you will regret making an enemy of me."

When he laughed his self-righteous little laugh, Callie lost the last remnant of her flimsy control.

The tea was too close.

The temptation too great.

Callie picked it up and with one flick of her wrist she dumped the entire thing on the top of Mr. Stakehorn's head.

Then she turned and stormed out of the deli.

~

Sitting in a far back booth, the man continued eating his pastrami on rye and watching Stakehorn.

The scene with the little shop owner had been interesting.

But did it change anything?

He'd need to factor it in to what he already knew, to what he had planned.

The waitress rushed over, handed the editor a dishtowel. Stakehorn used it to pat himself dry, though it did nothing to remove the stain the tea had left on his shirt.

Scowling, Stakehorn picked up his to-go order and pushed his way out the door of the deli.

The man counted to five. Then he tossed a ten-dollar bill down on the table, and he followed the editor out into the gathering dusk.

~

Deborah stood at the sink with her mother-in-law, cleaning up the dinner dishes, looking out the window, which gave a good view of the approaching evening.

"So you trust this English woman?" Ruth's voice was smooth and calm as the surface of the pond behind the old farmhouse.

As she rested her hands in the warm rinse water, Deborah stared out at the fading image of the pond in the subdued sunset—a mingled display of blues and grays and blacks.

Ruth slipped another dish into the soapy water, sponged it off, then handed it to Deborah to rinse and dry.

"*Ya*, I do trust Callie. I can tell she's an honest person, in the same way Daisy always dealt fairly with us. It wasn't even Callie's idea to put the quilts on the computer auction. It was my idea. I heard some boys in town speak of it."

"And the bishop hasn't made a decision yet?"

"No. I believe he might stop by this weekend." Deborah dried the dish and placed it in the cabinet. Like nearly everything else in Ruth's home, the dishes weren't fancy. Plain off-white, no pattern bordered the edge. The dishware was old and dependable and had been used at Ruth's table for many years—long before Deborah was a girl of sixteen and had started coming to the Yoder home, courted by a young boy who made her heart beat like the wings of a hummingbird.

"I'm worried he'll say no," Deborah confessed. "Melinda and Esther sorely need the income. They need as much as we can earn."

"It wouldn't hurt you and Jonas either," Ruth pointed out.

"*Ya*, but I know that we have you and Saul to help us."

"It's true." Ruth handed her a bowl. "But it's not the two of us that you put your trust in, Deborah. It's the Lord."

"You're right. Jonas said as much to me last night. Didn't the Lord give us the gift of quilting though? And he brought Callie here. Callie who knows how to sell things this way. So how is it wrong?"

"Don't be giving me your arguments, child. I'm sure you already presented them to the bishop." Ruth washed the last dish and pulled the plug from the sink, watched the water swirl away. "Sometimes our dreams are like this water. They drain away and we don't understand why."

Ruth sat down at the table, reached for the knitting she always kept close.

Deborah pulled out a chair and joined her. "Tell me there's more to that example, or I'm going to be a bit depressed."

Ruth peered at her over her glasses, gray hair peeping out from under her *kapp*. When she smiled, wrinkles folded around her eyes, across her forehead, down her cheeks. In her mid-sixties, she seemed ageless to Deborah—energetic and healthy, though signs of her age were beginning to show, like the gray and the wrinkles. Deborah realized anew how lucky she was to have this woman in her life, this mother who had replaced the one she'd lost all those years ago.

Focusing on her knitting, Ruth clucked her tongue. "Ah, but life is a bit sad at times. A bit like that dishwater swirling down the drain—slipping away. We don't understand it, why it has to be so, but it is."

A screech came from the other side of the room, where the children played on the rug and Jonas and his father read *The Budget*, though they'd no doubt poured over it from cover to cover the day before.

Ruth followed her gaze. "Other times life is like what you see there—full of joy."

"I don't understand what you're telling me."

"Merely that we're not meant to comprehend everything. We'll have moments of simple joy, like watching our loved ones enjoy an evening together. And we'll have moments of pain, like the illness of Melinda's child, where you want to help but aren't sure how."

"Or the death of Esther's husband." Deborah felt her throat tighten with the pain of her best friend's loss.

"Yes, that too." Ruth's hands knitted the blue yarn so quickly, Deborah wondered if her tears were clouding her vision. "Much like the water swirling down the drain, you want to reach out and stop the pain for her. But you can't always bring an end to pain—anymore than you could have stopped the water once I pulled the plug."

Deborah shook her head, needing to argue with her.

Ruth pushed on. "It isn't always our job to stop the pain. Even if we don't like it, pain has a place in this life."

Sighing, Deborah pulled the bowl of walnuts toward her, picked up the nutcracker, and set to work. Ruth would bake in the morning, and she'd heard the boys ask for oatmeal walnut cookies. Ruth might talk about pain and the inability to ease it, but she spoiled her grandchildren considerably.

"I don't know what the bishop will decide," Deborah admitted, "but what Stakehorn did was wrong."

"*Ya.* It's not the first time he's stretched the truth."

"Pulled it clear out of shape." Deborah cracked a walnut with extra gusto, separating the meat from the shell. "Callie needs some proof to take to him tomorrow—something more than our word."

"What would convince Stakehorn?"

"You know how stubborn he is. It would take something solid. Something like ..." Deborah dropped the nutcracker on the table. "Like a recording."

Pushing her chair back, she stood up, looked around as if seeing her mother-in-law's house for the first time. "That's it—we need a recording."

"And you have such a thing?" Ruth smiled, but didn't slow in her knitting.

"We do!" Deborah reached down and hugged Ruth. "We certainly do."

Pausing just long enough to clean off the shells and toss them into the trash, she gathered her things. "Jonas, we need to go. Hurry *kinner*, find all your things."

"We're leaving?" Martha looked up from where she was lying

stretched out on her belly, sprawled on the rug, paging through a book. "Now?"

"I've only started reading the paper," Jonas said, a frown forming between his eyes.

"You already read that paper, Jonas. I need to stop by the phone shack on the way home."

She heard some rumblings about women and phone cards, but within minutes everyone had climbed into the large buggy and they were off. She'd dropped the smaller buggy at the house earlier, after seeing Callie, then ridden over with Jonas in the larger buggy so they could all ride back together after dinner.

"Have any more children and we won't fit in a single buggy — even this large one." Jonas smiled over at her, his eyes twinkling in the dim light given off by the small battery-operated lamp they kept in the front.

"Are we having more children, *Daed*?" Martha's head popped up from the back seat.

"Not that I know of, but you'd need to ask your *mamm*." Jonas murmured a soothing word to Lightning as the mare trotted down the lane.

"Let's not talk of more *bopplin* tonight, Martha. I have my hands quite full." Deborah turned around to settle the twins and found they'd given Joshua a frog to pet.

She took the frog and tossed it out the side of the buggy.

"I was planning to take him home," Jacob fussed.

"We weren't hurting him," Joseph added.

"Weren't hurting your baby *bruder* or weren't hurting the frog?" Deborah did her best to sound stern, but baby Joshua was having none of it. He giggled and bounced in Martha's arms. Mary smiled at her.

The twins stuck their heads together and sank back into the corner of the back seat — no doubt to keep any other varmints they might have a secret.

"Don't forget to stop at the phone shack," Deborah murmured to Jonas.

"I gather this is important."

"You gather correctly."

"Must have to do with the quilting." The teasing sound again entered his voice.

"It does—quilting and the terrible news story that came out in the *Gazette*. I think I found a way to change Mr. Stakehorn's mind, thanks to your mother."

"My mother?" It was Jonas's turn to sound surprised.

"Slow down or Lightning will gallop right past it."

"*Ya, ya.* I know where it is." Jonas had barely stopped the buggy before Deborah jumped out.

"Go with your *mamm*, Joseph. You can hold the flashlight."

Joseph followed behind her, shining the beam of light on the path that led to the wooden shack.

Walking around to the back, Deborah opened the door and they stepped inside. Approximately two-feet-by-two-feet, the only thing inside the structure was a pay phone and a small countertop.

Deborah placed her coin purse on the countertop. "Shine your light up here, Joseph."

Deborah found the card easily enough, though entering the numbers was a bit more difficult, since Joseph—and his light—kept jogging left to right and back again.

"Can you hold it a bit more steady?"

Joseph nodded solemnly, holding the light with both hands. The boy's eyes were dark chocolate brown and wide as an owl's. He reminded her very much of Jonas at that moment. She bent down and kissed him on the cheek as she waited for the phone at Daisy's Quilt Shop to ring.

She'd memorized the number at the shop years ago, and Callie had mentioned having the service reconnected earlier in the week. Though she'd also jotted down Callie's new cell phone number, she was hoping she could catch her at the shop.

Chapter 10

CALLIE PICKED UP Max's leash off the hook near the gate, clipped it to his collar, then walked slowly to the shop's door.

What had she done?

What had she been thinking?

Of course the jerk deserved it, but still—she had better self-control than to throw an entire glass of tea on the man.

Shaking her head, she started up the stairs to her apartment when she heard the phone ringing in the shop below.

Who would be calling the shop at this hour?

Could it be Stakehorn?

Could he have realized how wrong he was? Maybe her iced tea had worked as a wake-up call.

Rushing back down the stairs, she grabbed the phone before the caller disconnected.

"Daisy's Quilt Shop. This is Callie Harper."

"Callie, this is Deborah."

"Deborah?" Callie reached down and unclipped Max, who shook himself and padded off toward the window. "I don't understand. Is something wrong?"

"Everything's fine. I thought of the answer to our problem. I thought of a way you can settle things with Stakehorn."

"How are you calling me?" Callie hadn't learned everything about the Amish in the two weeks since she'd arrived, but she had learned that they didn't have electricity or phones.

Deborah quickly reminded her about the phone shack, then hurried on. "Callie, I think there's a video recording of our conversation. Our first conversation. When I came into your shop and asked you to auction the quilts on the internet."

"You want to say that again?" Callie sat down on the cashier's stool with a hard thump.

"Are you at the counter now? Near the register?"

"Yes."

"Look under the counter, behind the curtain, back behind the extra rolls of register tape."

Callie turned on the lamp next to the register, squatted down on her knees, and poked her head into the space between the two shelves.

"Do you see it?"

"Oh my goodness." Callie's pulse raced as she stared at the machine.

"You see it."

"When did Daisy purchase this? Why did Daisy purchase it?"

"I'll explain later. I don't understand how it works—"

"I do. If it was still recording, we might have what we need."

Deborah's long sigh carried over the phone. "No reason it wouldn't be. Daisy only signed up with the service last Christmas. She'd had a minor break-in at the shop, and the insurance company wanted to go up on her premiums. Daisy talked them out of it—"

"By installing a security system."

"*Ya.*"

"You're a genius, Deborah. I might not have ever seen this here."

"I believe the bill is deducted from her account once a month. You would have noticed it on her next statement."

"By then Stakehorn's editorial will have already done its damage."

"I'm not sure readers will even believe what was in that article."

"If anyone believes then he should print a retraction. It's wrong, and I won't tolerate it."

"Everyone in Shipshe knows that it is an effort at times for him to fill his paper with news." Deborah paused, said something to one of the children. "Everyone knows that sometimes what he prints is not truthful."

"But this time what he printed was about me — about us, Deborah. I can't just let that go. I'm going to hang up and try to find the correct day on the recording."

"It would have been last Tuesday. The day you decided to reopen the shop."

"The day you came over to help me. You and your children."

A silence filled the line as Callie tried to think of how to thank her, tried to find words to express what it meant to have someone on her side for once.

"Esther, Melinda, and I are quilting tomorrow morning. We'll come into town when we're done to visit you at the shop."

"Thank you." Callie hung up the phone, reached out to pet Max who had nosed his way over to investigate.

"We can do this, Max. Looks like the same model some of my clients used, back in Houston. Back in the old days — you know, two months ago."

The surveillance system allowed for instant playback, which apparently Daisy had never done, since it wasn't currently connected to any type of monitor.

There was a small television upstairs, which Callie had turned on less than a half dozen times. With no cable, she hadn't been able to get reception to more than three local channels. She dashed upstairs, retrieved the small set, and placed it on the counter in the shop.

Within fifteen minutes she'd found the recording of the day she and Deborah had decided to auction the quilts on eBay—an auction which was now going well above minimum bid. But their success wouldn't impress Stakehorn.

He was out for blood—English blood.

What might convince him was the somewhat grainy image replaying on the screen.

The camera lens was apparently mounted on the wall's southeast corner, so much of the recording looked down on Callie's and Deborah's head—but even Stakehorn wouldn't be able to argue about who said what. The audio recording was crisp and clear.

Daisy had bought a newer model, so the system had the ability to record, much like a combination VCR/DVD. Callie found a stack of blank DVDs in a cupboard, placed one in the slot, and after finding the correct spot, hit the RECORD button on the security box.

"Are you sure you want to do this, Deborah? It seems like a big step, seems very different for you and your friends to conduct business this way."

"It's what we need to do. The bishop will understand."

She hit STOP, then ejected the DVD from the player. "This should convince him."

This could all work out, she thought. With a retraction, Stakehorn's little stunt might even benefit her in the long run, with all the free advertising. Callie booted up her laptop and searched online for the phone number of the *Gazette*, then called it from her cell. On the eleventh ring, Stakehorn picked up.

"I have your proof," she said, not bothering to introduce herself.

"What you have is a cleaning bill coming your way. I'll expect it to be paid first thing tomorrow."

"I have proof that it was Deborah's idea to auction the quilts on eBay."

"If you plan to drag the little Amish woman over here, forget it. No doubt you've coached her plenty since you had your little fit at the deli. Now if you'll excuse me, I have a paper to—"

"I have a recording."

Stakehorn stopped talking. Callie could hear the sound of a printing press running in the background. She sat down on the cashier's stool, put her left hand on top of Max's head for comfort, and waited.

"What do you mean you have a recording?"

Instead of answering his question, she fired back with one of her own. "Do you want to see it or not? If not, I'd be happy to take it to the owner of your paper and show him—or her—what shoddy drivel you print in your *editorial* section. They might be interested in knowing."

"If you have a recording, which I strongly doubt, and if you bring it to me, and if I agree that it proves what you think it proves, then I'll print your retraction, young lady. But those are three mighty big ifs."

"I can be there in ten minutes."

"Give me an hour. I have a paper to print, and I'm behind schedule since someone baptized me in mango-peach tea."

The line went dead.

The man was infuriatingly rude. She didn't care though. All that mattered was she'd won, and in an hour he'd know it.

This time, Callie drove to the *Gazette*. She had no problem finding it since she'd so recently been there with Deborah. It sat on the east side of Main Street, sandwiched between the post office to the north and an antique store to the south. Both were closed. Across the street was the local feed store, which was also dark.

This town closed up at six, rolled the carpet up and tucked it inside in case there was rain. Not that she missed the big city lights of Houston. She'd once counted eighteen lanes on the highway—from frontage road, across the southbound lanes of the freeway, central HOV lanes, then across the northbound lanes and frontage roads. Eighteen lanes of concrete.

No, Houston-ites could keep their big city ways.

She might not end up staying in a place as small as Shipshewana, but she wasn't ready to go back to a metropolitan area—that much she knew.

She parked in front of the building, walked up to the door and tapped on the glass.

No answer.

Mrs. Caldwell's desk sat empty, though Callie wouldn't have been surprised if the battle axe had jumped out of the shrubs and shooed her away.

Pressing her nose against the glass-paned door, she could see past Caldwell's desk to the small hall leading beyond the reception area she'd been in earlier. At the end of the hall was a door which must open into the main part of the building.

From the street lights on Main, Callie could see well enough to make out a small square window in the door separating the two areas, but she couldn't see through the window. It seemed to be covered with some sort of film.

She moved to the right, to the large plate glass window for a better look and saw a light beyond the door. A yellowish glow emanated weakly through the tiny window. Pressing her ear to the cool glass, she could hear the thump-thump-thump of the printing press.

She walked back to the door and tried the knob, even rattled it a bit, but of course it was locked.

Pulling her cell phone out of her pocket, she redialed the last number. After fifteen rings, it turned over to a recording. "You have reached the *Shipshewana Gazette*. We're closed for the evening. Please leave a message and we'll—"

Callie snapped the phone shut and looked around in frustration.

Stakehorn was in there. Either he couldn't hear her, or else he'd never intended to meet with her in the first place.

Stepping back toward her car, she spotted the sign. *Deliveries drive down alley to back.*

Bingo.

Drive or walk?

You're not in Houston anymore. No need to be afraid of a dark alley. Might as well walk. But she couldn't help wishing she'd brought Max along for company.

Callie breathed a sigh of relief when she reached the end of the alley.

Which was ridiculous.

It ran the length of the building—no more than fifty feet, and she was never in complete darkness. There was a single street light at the end she'd started from, and light from the window of the printing room of the *Gazette* at the other.

Plus she was a grown woman and not afraid of a little darkness.

Still she was sure she'd heard a rat or some sort of varmint by the large trash dumpster. And the way her sandals had crunched against the asphalt and pieces of broken glasses had sent small shivers down her spine.

"I'm getting what I deserve for reading Agatha Christie novels. I'm more nervous than a catfish on a hook."

She tried the back door of the *Gazette* and nearly fell down when it opened easily on her first tug.

"Mr. Stakehorn? Hello?"

The printing press continued to roll with an ear-splitting thump-thump-thump. From inside it sounded like a train rolling through the room.

Stepping past the small area for deliveries, Callie pushed through the double doors and into the main press room.

She was instantly overwhelmed by light. Overhead fluorescents shone down from the twelve foot ceilings, revealing yellowed tile, old presses, and stacks of paper everywhere. The unmistakable odor of ink filled her nasal passages.

Her mind flashed back to sitting at her father's feet, playing with something. What had it been? Colors. She'd sat there with colors and a pad while her father read the paper. She could hear the rustle as he turned the pages, see the black letters on gray print when she'd glance up at him. And the smell, the smell was the very same — the smell of newsprint.

"Mr. Stakehorn?" This time, Callie raised her voice, trying to be heard above the din of the press.

She walked the length of the room and peered out front, into the reception area she'd been in earlier in the day. She could see through to the front, see her car parked by the curb and the deserted street beyond.

A dark, sepia flap covered the window over the door — which would explain why the light looked dim to her from out front. No doubt it helped to keep the office area cooler.

"Bet these presses heat up the place later in the summer." Her words echoed in the room.

But where was Stakehorn?

Had he stepped out for a minute?

Callie pivoted back toward the alley door. When she did, she saw that something was wrong with the press. The newspapers rolled off the belt and dropped into a giant crate on the floor, but the crate was full and overflowing.

Papers continued to spew in every direction.

The scene was almost comical. It looked as if a child had been set loose inside the newspaper office, allowed to play with the machines. Except it wasn't funny.

It was somehow wrong.

She turned slowly in a circle and that was when she spied the small corner office — no bigger than a closet. She could just make out two aluminum folding chairs and the edge of an old oak desk, papers stacked six inches high on both it and the chairs. Some of the papers had even fallen and scattered across the floor.

But that wasn't what caused her mouth to fall open, and her hand to clasp her throat.

On top of the stack of papers, rested Stakehorn's outstretched hand.

Chapter 11

MAYBE HE'D FALLEN ASLEEP.

Or maybe it wasn't him at all.

She couldn't tell from where she stood. She'd have to walk into the office.

Callie attempted to swallow, but found her throat was too dry. Her hand was also still wrapped around her neck. She pressed her palm against her heart, took three deep breaths to slow her heart rate, then reached into her purse.

With one hand she still held her cell phone. Flipping it open, she keyed in the numbers nine, one, one, then positioned her thumb over the call button. With her other hand, she hunted through her purse, found and clutched her tactical flashlight. The thirty thousand candle power might not succeed in blinding someone in a fully lighted room, but then again it might.

On top of that, it was solid polymer construction — she'd bought it after taking a self-defense class. If anyone waited in there for her, she stood a good chance of being able to clobber him or her with it.

Heart thrumming in rhythm to the noise of the press, she moved toward Stakehorn's office. Her sandals echoed against the linoleum floor, seeming to out-shout even the noise of the machine behind her.

As she inched closer, she noticed brown liquid on the floor — splattered from the corner of the desk and across the nearest stack of papers. Puddled on the floor.

Could he have fallen asleep and knocked over his coffee?

Callie reached up to brace herself against the doorframe before entering the room. When she saw the hand in front of her, shaking and garish in the fluorescent lights, she almost didn't recognize it as her own — then she saw her grandmother's wedding band that she wore on her index finger.

Why was she so shaken? For all she knew, he was merely passed out. Except her old training kicked in when she forced her gaze back toward the man at the desk.

Her heart rate thundered in her ears now.

Above it she heard her own breath gasp, even as her eyes took in the awkward tilt of Stakehorn's head across his arm, the lifelessness of his open eyes, the stillness of his body.

Her phone clattered to the floor.

Her flashlight slipped from her fingers.

Callie clasped both hands across her mouth in an effort to stifle her scream.

Then she realized no one would hear her.

Would they?

Twirling around she nearly slipped in the coffee on the floor. It had been coffee hadn't it?

Suddenly she needed out of the room, needed out of the office and back in her car.

Walking as quickly as she could, but not running, she hurried back through the press room.

It wouldn't do any good to run and fall. Every teenage horror movie she'd ever seen replayed through her mind — the woman alone at night, a dead body found, the murderer lurking in the shadows.

Except there weren't any shadows, and it hadn't been a murder. Had it?

Perhaps he'd had a heart attack.

Under the harshness of the fluorescent lights, Stakehorn's cold, lifeless form had looked so old — older than she'd remembered.

As she rushed back through the press room, the same lights glared down on her, revealing cracks in the linoleum, a piece of trash thrown in the corner, her hand reaching to push the door open.

Then she was flying back down the alley, back through the darkness, back toward the street.

A cat hissed, but Callie never slowed.

She turned the corner of the building and practically threw herself at the door of the little blue car.

Fumbling in her purse for her car keys, she hit the alarm instead of the unlock button. Its blare split the quietness of the night.

After the third try she managed to quiet the alarm and unlock the rental. Collapsing into the driver's seat, she slammed the door shut, hit the lock key, buckled her seat belt, and sat staring at the front door of the *Shipshewana Gazette*.

How long had she been in there? Ten minutes?

Ten minutes since she'd parked here, determined to prove to Stakehorn that she was right.

Now he was dead.

Her hands began to shake at the thought. She grasped the wheel to still them.

She needed to think clearly.

A dead man she barely knew was sprawled across his desk.

She'd spoken with him barely an hour ago. How was it possible that he was dead?

She needed to call someone, call the police.

Grabbing her purse, she began pawing through it, looking for her cell phone.

"Where is it? Where did I put it? I tried to call him from the front door. Then I had my thumb on the button as I walked toward—"

She dropped her purse onto the seat, suddenly realizing where her phone was.

It was in Stakehorn's office, on the floor, near his body.

She was not going back in there after her phone.

Okay. So she needed to drive to the police station.

Where was the police station?

Shipshewana was a small town. The police station couldn't be that hard to find. She'd drive around and look for it.

She retrieved her keys from the floorboard where they'd fallen, tried three times to put them in the ignition, but found her hand was shaking too badly to make the connection.

Finally she settled for clutching the wheel and resting her forehead against it.

The coolness settled her, helped her to even out her breathing, slowed her heart rate—until she heard the tap at her window.

This time she made no attempt to stifle the scream as she tried to leap across the car away from the window. Of course the seat belt held her in place, which only increased her panic as she fought it.

Her system had absorbed too much shock in the last half hour. The scream she released expressed the horror she'd felt since spying Stakehorn's hand stretched out across the stack of papers.

The man standing beside her car backed up two steps, flipped the flashlight to on, and spoke in an authoritative, no-nonsense voice. "Ma'am. Shipshewana Police Department. I'm going to need you to step out of the car."

Her terror momentarily fled, and she nearly collapsed with relief. She couldn't see his face because the flashlight blinded her, but she could make out the dark blue of a uniform and what looked like an officer's belt. She held one hand up to shield her eyes, and with the other, fumbled with the door handle.

"You'll need to unlock the door before exiting the vehicle."

If he was amused by her bumbling, his voice didn't show it.

Using the remote control, she unlocked the car, released her seat belt, opened the door, and stepped out. "Thank goodness you're here!" she began. Then she saw the expression on the officer's face.

He might have been called ruggedly handsome by some, except for the complete lack of expression. Blue eyes the color of ice took in everything, assessed her, pinned her where she was beside the car. Six feet tall and muscular, he wasn't your cartoon donut-cop. Hair the color of wheat was cut military length.

"A disturbance was reported a few minutes ago." He spoke in a clipped tone, waiting for her to explain.

"A disturbance?" Callie looked around in disbelief. Could something else have happened while she was in the newspaper office?

"Some sort of loud noise. Apparently it was related to a new model Ford, license number—"

"It was my car—my rental car. I couldn't get it unlocked, and I hit the alarm by mistake. Listen to me, Sir—

"Officer. My name is Officer Gavin."

"Officer Gavin. Forget about the noise." Callie pulled in a deep breath of night air, hugged her arms tightly around her body. "Stakehorn's in there, at his desk, and he's dead."

Gavin's hand went immediately to his firearm. "Say again."

"He's dead." Callie's voice rose and she hugged her ribs tighter. "He's at his desk, his coffee spilled everywhere, the press still spewing papers all over the floor."

Her legs started shaking and she wondered if she'd fall apart there by the car, crumble onto the asphalt.

"Ma'am, I need you to turn around and put your hands up on your car." Gavin's expression hadn't changed, but if anything the look in his eyes had hardened.

"Excuse me?"

"Do what I said, please."

"You must be kidding. I just told you there's a dead man inside and you're going to frisk me?"

"Ma'am, I'm going to *ask* you one more time."

Callie tried to laugh, but it came out as more of a groan. She followed his directions, turning and placing her hands against the top of her car. At least the coolness of the car's metal provided something solid for her to lean against. It didn't stop her legs from shaking, but it brought back some sense of reality.

Would he check her for weapons? The thought was so ludicrous it made her want to laugh.

Instead he stayed where he was and spoke into his radio. "This is Gavin. I need backup at Main and Fourth. We have a possible deceased person."

Someone cackled back with numbers that Callie couldn't comprehend. The night had taken on a surreal quality.

They stood for what seemed like ten minutes as the silence of the evening once again surrounded them.

She thought he might ask her more questions, but he didn't.

She hoped he might at least tell her she could sit down, but no.

Gavin was not a knight in shining armor. He wasn't even a compassionate officer.

Well if there was one thing she'd learned in the last two years, it was to not expect compassion.

Her thoughts were spiraling toward despair when they were interrupted by the sound of a siren and a patrol car driving down Main. Instead of pulling in beside them, it created a sort of blockade behind her rental. Once parked, the officer turned off his siren, but kept his emergency lights on—sending a warning into the night.

Good thing she couldn't get away—since she was so dangerous. She wanted to shout at them now. She wanted to throw a tantrum and holler, "Go check out the dead guy in the office!"

Then she heard footsteps, and a softer, older voice. "What do we have here, Gavin?"

"Followed up on a noise complaint. Found Miss Harper."

Callie jumped at her name. She hadn't given it to him, but then how many rental cars would there be in Shipshewana?

"She claims Stakehorn is dead inside the shop."

The newer officer sighed heavily, his breathing blending with the sounds of the night. His voice was still calm, measured, but it took on something of an edge. "Is there a reason you're treating Miss Harper like a suspect instead of a witness?"

"I was following procedures, sir."

"You're not in the military any longer, Gavin. We are a small town, and we adapt to the situation we're presented with. In this case we seem to have one frightened young shop owner." The voice drew closer, then the officer put a tentative hand on her shoulder.

Callie turned slowly around and looked into gentle brown eyes, framed with white eyebrows, and a face lined with wrinkles.

"Miss Harper, I'm Officer Taylor, senior officer of the Shipshewana Police Department. Why don't you come over and have a seat in my cruiser. No doubt you've had quite a shock this evening."

Unable to speak, nearly melting with relief, Callie nodded and followed him to the second police vehicle. Taylor opened the door to the back passenger seat, and she sat down, collapsed actually—her feet still dangling outside the car. No need growing too comfortable. Gavin might decide to shut the door and lock her inside.

Speaking of Gavin, she glanced up and saw that she was once again facing him. The man's expression hadn't changed. He remained completely unreadable.

Perhaps it was the shock or the old fatigue rising in her, but Callie had to fight an urge to stick her tongue out at him. Following procedures, indeed.

"Now, tell us exactly what you saw, Miss Harper." Taylor stood gazing down at her, a sympathetic look on his face.

"I had called Stakehorn earlier. He told me to stop by. I was supposed to show him ... something." Callie realized suddenly that the DVD was still in her purse. She thought of mentioning it, but Gavin interrupted her.

"How did you even get inside?" He crossed his arms and raised his right eyebrow. So his face did have the ability to move. Interesting. "The front door is always locked after Caldwell leaves."

～

"The front door was locked." She'd been directing her comments to Taylor, but now she spoke to Gavin. He didn't even blink. "I saw the light on in the back, and I tried to call, but there was no answer."

She looked down at her hands, noticed they were still shaking and tucked them under her armpits, hugging her arms around herself. It felt like a childish pose, but comforting somehow. "I saw the delivery sign, directing people around the back."

"You went down the side alley?" Gavin asked. "In the dark?"

"I'm from Houston, Officer Gavin. A dark alley in Shipshewana isn't exactly frightening." Callie remembered the rat she'd encountered on her trip down, and the screeching cat on her flight back, and nearly smiled at her own bluff.

"So what did you find at the back of the building?" Taylor pulled her back to the matter at hand.

"The back door was unlocked. I thought perhaps Stakehorn had forgotten about our meeting, so I walked inside. That's when I found him."

"And you're sure he's dead?" Taylor reached out, touched her shoulder.

Callie nodded. "Yes, I'm sure. He's at his desk."

Taylor stood straighter, hitched his service belt up over his protruding stomach. "I'll stay with Miss Harper. You go check it out. If he is dead, we'll need to call it in to county."

"He's dead all right, Officer Taylor." Callie's voice took on more strength. She didn't like being treated like a dim wit. She knew a dead body when she saw one.

"I'm not doubting what you think you saw." His tone wasn't patronizing. "We don't want to wake up Black if we don't have to."

Gavin strode off around the corner of the building, and Taylor stepped a few feet away from the patrol car, speaking into his radio.

Within five minutes, Gavin returned.

He reported to Taylor, glancing back over at Callie several times as he spoke.

The rest of the evening was a blur. Callie told her story again, this time in more detail.

The clock on her dash read twelve thirty by the time she climbed into the rental and drove back to Daisy's Quilt Shop.

She didn't remember she was once again without a cell phone until she'd looked up and saw the *Gazette* fading in her rearview mirror. Her morning would have to begin with another trip to see Mr. Cooper, since Gavin would insist that her cell phone was evidence. Not that anyone had determined there had been a crime. Apparently they were being "thorough" — their word. In Callie's opinion, they needed more crime to amuse the Shipshewana police.

~

He watched the entire thing from the building across the street.

It hadn't played out exactly like he'd hoped, but close enough. Close enough.

The important thing was that Stakehorn was dead, or at least that was the first step toward the most important thing. The next part would be easy now.

Probably Shipshewana's finest would determine the old man died of natural causes. If not, if they were smart enough to figure it out—which he doubted—then they could pin it on the woman. She was the perfect suspect since she'd been seen arguing with him earlier in the evening.

Chapter 12

By six the next morning, Deborah was in the kitchen preparing breakfast. She'd already been up over an hour — fixing lunches, laying out clothes, taking care of the baby who woke up crying with a wet diaper — then fell quickly back asleep.

She looked out the kitchen window and saw Jonas walking from the barn, carrying fresh eggs. Twice a week their neighbor Reuben brought some by, traded them for apples from their orchard in the fall.

"I'll use them tomorrow," she said, smiling at him as he banged through the back door. "Set them in the fridge for me, please. I hope you thanked Reuben for bringing them by."

Deborah set out a bowl of raisins and a jar of cinnamon sugar, then turned back to the gas-powered stove to stir the oatmeal.

"Eggs isn't all he brought, Deb. He brought some big news too."

Deborah gave him her full attention.

"Reuben and his cousin Tobias are both staying together at his *grossdaddi's* old place."

"*Ya*, I remember."

"Well, Tobias works at the feed store across from the *Gazette*, and he came in talking about Stakehorn last night. Seems he died."

"He what?" Deborah dropped the spoon she'd been stirring with into the pot of oatmeal.

Jonas handed her another to fish it out with.

"Dead? And he was sure?"

"Saw him carted off on a gurney with a sheet pulled up over his face."

"But how? I don't remember hearing he was ill." Deborah removed the pan from the stove, divided the breakfast into portions, then scrubbed the pan vigorously as she checked over her shoulder to see if the twins had made it down the stairs yet. "Did Tobias know what he died of?"

"No. He only said Gavin and Taylor stayed out in front of the shop until three a.m. Then the county people showed up and removed the body." Jonas poured himself a mug of *kaffi* and sat down at the table.

"The county people? Do you mean Shane Black?"

Jonas ran his thumb under his suspender, took a moment before answering her. "*Ya*. I think Tobias did say it was Black."

"Of course Black had to be called. That's standard procedure. He even checked on Daisy when I found her in the garden. I wonder if Callie knows Stakehorn is dead. She was supposed to meet with him."

"According to Tobias, Callie was there. She sat out front quite a long time answering questions—first from Gavin and Taylor, then from Black."

Deborah stopped drying the pan, set it carefully on the back of the stove, glanced at the twins as they clomped down the stairs. "I don't understand."

"That's all Reuben knew. Tobias was working late to put up a new delivery of feed. He didn't see her go in, but saw her rental car later when Gavin arrived."

Deborah let go of the pan she'd been grasping. Wiping her hands on the dish towel, she helped the boys settle at the table.

"I wanted cinnamon toast, *Mamm*." Joseph rubbed at the sleep in his eyes.

Jacob picked up his spoon and dug into his oatmeal.

Deborah kissed them both on top of the head, and smiled at Martha and Mary as they slid into their seats across the table. "I'd like to go and see her today."

Jonas nodded, and then reached for the sugar in the middle of the table and sprinkled it on top of his own bowl of oatmeal. He added some of the raisins, winked at the boys, and added a handful to theirs.

Deborah sank into her chair. "Jonas, I called Callie from the phone shack last night. She was going over to show him the recording of our conversation."

"I wouldn't worry. A recording can't kill someone."

Martha's eyes widened as she swallowed a spoonful of breakfast. "Who was killed?"

"No one was killed, darling. Mr. Stakehorn, the newspaper editor, died last night."

"I don't think I knew him," Martha said, squirming in her chair.

"Will we be going by his house?" Jacob asked, always looking for an excuse to go to town.

"It's doubtful. He was an Englisher, and they do things differently than the Amish."

"We went to Miss Daisy's funeral," Martha reminded her.

"I remember. I liked the cookies," Joseph piped up, finally looking awake. "Is it wrong to say you liked the cookies at someone's funeral?"

"No, son. It's never wrong to have a fond memory of someone." Jonas took another drink of his *kaffi*. The family fell into silence as each person focused on their breakfast—and Deborah focused on her memories, of Daisy, Stakehorn, and finally all of her previous dealings with Shane Black. She was startled back to the present by the boys' giggles as they played with extra raisins.

Jonas cleared his throat and said, "Speaking of remembering, I seem to remember two boys who have chores to do."

Joseph and Jacob glanced at each other, stuffed in two more bites, then scooted out of their chairs in a hurry.

"I get Lightning's stall," Jacob declared.

"You had her last time." Joseph hurried across the room to catch up with his brother.

"Both of you come back here." Jonas's voice plainly brokered no argument.

The boys froze in place, then turned and walked back to the table.

"Dishes." Jonas nodded to the bowls and spoons they'd left at their seats.

"Yes, *Daed*." Their voices sounded in unison. They picked up their breakfast dishes and set them in the sink, then looked toward the door. They didn't move though, only glanced at each other trying to remember what else they might have forgotten.

"Thank your mother for a good breakfast. She works hard for you."

"Danki, Mamm." Again their voices came out in unison.

"Gern gschehne." Deborah suddenly wished she could freeze the moment. Only yesterday they were Joshua's age. Where had the years gone?

With a nod from Jonas, they grabbed their straw hats from the hooks by the door and headed off toward the barn.

"They're *gut* boys," Deborah said as she moved toward the sink and added hot water and soap.

Jonas kissed her on the cheek. "That they are."

Martha went off to dress baby Joshua, and Mary joined her at the sink, though she had to stand on a stool to help dry the dishes as Deborah washed.

Deborah's mind flashed back on the previous evening, how

she'd stood in Mary's place as Ruth had washed dishes. It brought her some peace to know that certain things stayed the same from one generation to the next.

But when she pulled the plug on the drain and watched the water swirl down, she couldn't help wondering if more pain was in store for her friends—knowing, as Ruth had pointed out, she may not be able to stop it.

What would happen to the auctioning of their quilts now?

And what did the Lord have in store for Callie Harper?

Three hours later the boys were in the field with Jonas; Martha and Mary were at their *Aenti's* helping with some early summer canning. Baby Joshua had been up, fed, played for two hours, and was down for his morning nap.

Melinda and Esther were once again seated across from her.

"We can't just sit here and quilt," Melinda reasoned.

"We can, but we shouldn't." Esther looked down at the half-finished friendship quilt in front of them. "We should do something."

"*Ya*, I agree." Deborah stood, walked over to the window. "I think maybe we should go into town. See if there's something she needs. Should we wait until the children are up though?"

"They've slept in the buggy before." Melinda stood and began folding the quilt. "I needed to go by the General Store anyway. We can accomplish two errands at once."

In fifteen minutes they'd loaded up all three carriages.

Jonas had already pulled Cinnamon out, harnessed her up to the rig. "Thought you might want to leave early."

She smiled down at him as he handed up baby Joshua.

"Boy is growing," he added.

"Probably will look like his *daed* one day." The bantering helped to ease some of her worry. Surely Callie was fine. She'd seemed so much better since reopening the shop, and though Mr. Stakehorn's death was a shock—death was a part of life.

So why did she have this niggling feeling that their troubles were just beginning?

~

Callie stood at the counter, exhausted but awake thanks to three strong cups of coffee. Max lay near her feet, a green bandana tied around his neck, tail thumping—ever her faithful companion.

"I should have taken you with me last night," she murmured. "I suppose I've learned my lesson."

He stood, pressed his cold nose into her hand, then turned in a circle twice and flopped flat on the floor.

Looking out the window, she was surprised to see three buggies pull up at once. She'd had two customers so far since opening, but it had been a somewhat slow morning for a market day.

Peering out the window, she hurried around the counter when she saw Deborah, then Melinda, and finally Esther exit their buggies. She'd only met Esther once, when she'd stopped by to bring cookies for the opening. Melinda had been by twice. And of course, it seemed as if she'd known Deborah for years. All the women had their babies with them.

"Looks like a hens' meeting, Max. Hang on to your collar!" Her spirits lifted immediately though. She could use some feminine company, even if they weren't aware of what had happened last night. The only question was whether she should tell them of her evening's events.

Callie opened the front door and started down the walk, but she didn't make it halfway before being engulfed in Melinda's skinny arms. The smell of line-dried cotton overwhelmed her senses, even as she returned the hug. Melinda's show of affections surprised her. Callie was southern born and bred, where hugs were commonplace, but she'd always heard Amish folk were a bit more standoffish. So far the people she'd met in Shipshewana were shattering stereotypes.

"You poor thing. To think that you were at the newspaper so late, and you still opened this shop. I just don't see how you do it." Baby Hannah squirmed and cooed as she was pressed between the two women.

Callie stepped back. Melinda adjusted her glasses, and Hannah waved a fist into the air before she let out a shout.

"Did we squish her?" Callie asked.

"Of course not. It's time for her mid-morning feeding is all."

"There are some comfortable chairs at the back of the shop."

"*Ya*, Daisy used to hold a quilting circle back there."

Melinda moved past her, into the shop, but she was quickly followed by Esther, holding Leah's hand. Leah clutched a doll who was dressed in Amish clothing identical to her own — right down to the peach-colored dress and white prayer *kapp*.

"You must be exhausted," Esther said. Her voice was calm and even, but her eyes betrayed her concern, that and her offering. "We brought food."

Holding out a plate of breads and cheeses, her gaze met Callie's. She didn't smile exactly, but Callie saw something in her expression — was it understanding?

Before she could figure it out, Esther had bent down to speak with her daughter, and Deborah had squeezed between them.

"Are you upset?" She reached to touch Callie's arm, juggling baby Joshua onto her opposite hip.

"No. Maybe a little. It was a long night." Callie rubbed at her forehead where a headache had been threatening all morning.

"Should we leave? If it's a bad time—"

"Huh-uh. I'm glad you came. I've been chasing things around in my mind all morning."

"*Wunderbaar*. We'll chase them together."

Deborah corralled everyone to the back of the store, to the quilting area Melinda spoke of. Cushy arm chairs were arranged in a semi-circle facing the front of the store, and an Amish-made coffee table sat in the middle.

It was the one part of the store Callie had somewhat ignored. Though it was now clean, she hadn't decided how she wanted to use it—since she didn't exactly plan on staying.

It wasn't as if she could schedule classes.

Or start a quilting group.

Or invite friends over.

Everyone except Esther sank into a chair, leaving the one in the center—the one directly facing the front door—for Callie. Esther arrived with the hot water from the kitchen and four mugs, plus an array of teas.

"Best thing for a death is a cup of strong tea."

"How did ya'll know?" Callie accepted the mug as well as her usual lemongrass and spearmint tea. Though she hadn't had the stomach to eat any breakfast, suddenly the homemade bread array Esther had brought looked rather appealing. She selected a slice of banana nut from the tray on the table, then sat back, looking at the three women and waiting for an explanation.

Esther and Deborah shared a smile. Melinda simply gazed down at her baby.

"It's the Amish grapevine," Deborah explained. "We might not have telephones, but word travels fast from house to house when something of importance happens within our community."

"A gossip grapevine?" Callie asked, one eyebrow raised.

"It can be that," Esther acknowledged, "but most of us realize that if you spread gossip you'll one day be on the hurting end of it."

Callie thought of the logic in what she was saying, thought of Houston, and the hurt she'd suffered because of loose tongues.

"What Deborah's speaking of is a little different." Melinda traced her baby's face as she continued to nurse. "We communicate in the old way—from household to household. News spreads fairly quickly."

Deborah sat Joshua on the floor with his favorite toy, beside Leah who was playing with her doll. "Now tell us what happened.

We were very *naerfich* when we heard your car was in front of the building. Are you okay? And why did they keep you so long?"

Callie gave them the shortened version, stopping twice to help customers who came in for quilting supplies. She described Gavin's initial abruptness and how helpful Taylor had been.

No one seemed surprised.

"Gavin is a bit new on the force," Esther explained.

"I believe it was only six years ago last fall that he was hired." Deborah's voice was serious enough, but there was no mistaking the twinkle in her eye. "He's still trying to prove himself."

"So he isn't from here?"

"*Ya*, actually he is. He grew up and went to school in the area, but then he went away to college and after that joined the English military."

"That would explain how formal and stiff he is. You would think he expected his C.O. to show up at any moment." Callie reached down and stroked Max as she spoke.

"What is a C.O., Callie?" Esther looked troubled.

"Commanding Officer. No doubt Gavin was a favorite in his unit. I'm telling you, I don't think the man has a kind bone in his body."

"Perhaps you're being a bit rough." Deborah set her mug on the table. "We were hesitant to accept him at first, because of his military service. But he's always been fair with Amish people. He's more respectful than most. Your problem last night might have stemmed from the fact that he follows the rules so closely, and you didn't fit into the rules very well."

Callie realized then that some things were the same whether you were in a small community like Shipshewana or a huge metropolitan area like Houston.

Gavin was a newbie after having grown up there, moved away, and settled back in town for six years. Callie had felt like she didn't fit in while living in Houston once Rick died. She'd felt like she was someone from an alien planet, even though they had shared a life there for years. Would she ever feel at home here in Shipshewana?

She was twenty-seven now. So if she decided to stay in Shipshewana, how old would she be before she was accepted?

Callie nearly dropped the empty mug she was holding. Stay in Shipshewana? Where had that thought come from? She'd never even considered staying.

Setting down her empty cup, she straightened her green cotton blouse and looked around at her newfound friends. They were her friends. They'd proven as much this morning. "Anyway, on to the important thing: You don't have to worry about your quilts. The online auction is going well. We're well above the minimum bid." Callie used her napkin to brush her mouth, checking to see if she had stray cookie crumbs dangling anywhere. "And I don't think there will be any more rude editorials, though I feel very bad about the death of Mr. Stakehorn."

"*Ya,* we all do." Deborah murmured.

"I suppose it's up to the police to figure out what happened. As I explained more than once to the detective they brought in—I think his name was Black—"

"Shane Black?" Esther cut in. The three women exchanged glances.

"Yes, from the LaGrange County office," Callie said, wondering what the big deal was. "Have you met him? I thought Officer Gavin was rude, but Gavin's a puppy dog compared to Black."

Deborah leaned forward, picked up baby Joshua, and placed him across her legs, tummy down as he began to suck his thumb. "*Ya,* we've met him." Deborah rubbed Joshua's back in small circles.

Esther sat up a bit straighter, and Melinda pulled off her glasses, cleaned them with the hem of her apron.

Callie waited for them to add something else, but no one did.

Taking a page from their book, she sat back and waited.

Melinda was the first to break the silence. "What exactly did Black do, Callie?"

Her solemn eyes widened behind her glasses, or maybe it just appeared that way to Callie. It seemed suddenly as if the entire room had stilled, waiting for her answer.

She stood, began straightening the already clean area. Max padded over and pushed against her side, as if he too could sense her agitation.

"What did he do?" Her hands came out, encompassing the room. "He did what detectives are supposed to do I would imagine. It wasn't what he did. It was more the way he did it."

She paused, stared over their heads, trying to pinpoint exactly what it was about Black that had irked her to a point of near misery. Finally she waved it off and continued. "I told him exactly what I told Gavin and Taylor, but he kept asking the same questions. I swear, if Gavin is a bear protecting his community, Black is a lone wolf. The man would not let it go."

She clattered the dishes together on the tray, set the tray down on the table, and slumped back into her chair. "He acted as if I should know something, as if it was more than a coincidence that I happened to be the one who found Stakehorn's body. I was unnerved enough by then—"

"Of course you were." Melinda shook her head.

Esther smoothed out her skirt, an unreadable look on her face. "It's Black's way, though that doesn't make it right."

"So ya'll know him?"

"We've had ... dealings with Officer Black before. He isn't Amish, of course, and he no longer lives in Shipshewana, but he's assigned to our community for certain cases." Deborah looked as if she might say more, but a sharp look from Esther stopped her.

Callie started to ask whether she should be worried when the bell over the front door rang.

Grateful for the distraction, she practically sprang out of her seat. "Business goes on as usual," she chirped, gliding toward the front of the store.

Then she saw Shane Black and stopped dead in her tracks.

"Miss Harper."

"Officer Black. How can I help you?"

The man was maybe two inches taller than her, lean and muscular, and probably five years older. Dark black hair curled and touched the collar of his shirt. Piercing eyes the color of night seemed to take in everything at once.

Callie thought again of a wolf.

Despite her determination to remain calm, a shiver started at the base of her neck—traveled both directions simultaneously so that her scalp tingled and spiders danced down her spine.

Why did he intimidate her so?

It wasn't as if she'd done anything wrong.

"I need you to come with me."

"Come with you?"

"Correct." He didn't move, didn't glance away.

"Why would I come with you?"

Black stepped closer, stepped into her comfort zone—close enough that Max uttered a low growl.

Close enough that she caught the smell of summer on him, heard the creak of leather that had to be his holster under the light summer jacket he wore. "Come with me now and we can say it's only for questioning. Make me come back and you'll be under arrest."

Chapter 13

Deborah walked into the front room as Callie reached for the counter behind her, looking as if she needed to steady herself.

"Is there a problem here, Officer Black?" Deborah kept her voice soft and even. She knew from experience that Black responded best to reason, not emotion.

"No problem, miss." Though he didn't address her by name, his nod and gaze said he remembered her, as well as Melinda and Esther.

In fact, Deborah was willing to bet Black rarely forgot a name or a face—and that he never forgot a case.

Callie spun around, stepped close enough that only Deborah could hear. "He says I need to go with him. What will I do about the shop?"

"We'll take care of it. Do as he says, and we'll be along to see you in a few minutes."

"Max—"

"Taken care of," Melinda said, stepping closer. "Don't worry about a thing, Callie." Raising her voice so Black would hear, Melinda added, "I'm sure Officer Black won't need you for long."

Esther walked past the group of women, still holding her

daughter's hand. She opened the door to the shop, then turned, all business. "What's begun is sooner done, Callie. Two of us will stay with the shop, and one will follow along behind you. So you'll have a ride home."

Though her words were directed to Callie, her gaze settled on Black, dared him to contradict what she said.

Instead of arguing with any of them, he placed his hand lightly on Callie's arm, motioning her toward the door. "After you, then."

Though he wore no hat, he nodded at them, tipping his head.

Customers stopped on the sidewalk to gawk—everyone in town recognized Shane Black's car. Jonas had tried to explain to her that English viewed cars like Amish viewed their horses. It was hard to understand how anyone could love a yellow car with black stripes. Jonas had said it was a classic Buick. Deborah noticed Amish and English, a few sympathetic looks (like Mr. Simms), and a few unkind ones. Everyone stared as Callie and Black made their way from the store.

As Deborah watched them move down the walk, past the front of the shop with the bright little FOR SALE sign standing proudly near the street side windows, she wondered if what Shane was doing would help or cause the situation to spin further out of control.

∼

The door shut, and Deborah rushed to the front window, quickly shadowed by Melinda and Esther. They watched Callie duck into the back of the Buick. Black didn't handcuff her, and they considered that a good sign.

He also didn't put his light on top of the car.

When he'd disappeared down the road, headed toward the Shipshewana Police Station, they all started talking at once.

"What could he possibly want with her?" Melinda demanded.

"How dare he? It's the same as before. He's causing problems when he should be solving them." Esther nearly trembled with anger.

Deborah watched as she led Leah to the back room where Joshua and Hannah were sleeping.

"*Mamm*, what did that Englisher want with Miss Callie?"

"Don't worry, *boppli*. She'll be back soon."

"Can Max stay with me until then?" Leah reached out, ran her hand over and through the dog's coat. He seemed to endure her attentions well enough, lying down beside her.

Esther reached into her shoulder bag, pulled out a sheet of paper and some crayons she'd brought. "Yes, Max seems happy here for now. Do me a favor and color for a few minutes, Leah. I'll be at the counter with *Aentie* Deborah."

Deborah reached out, rubbed Esther's shoulder when she joined them back at the counter. "I know it's hard for you to see Black, but we need to stay focused on Callie. Black must think she knows something she hasn't told them."

"Or he found additional evidence since last night." Melinda greeted a customer who came in looking for blue fabric.

"I'll take care of this," Esther said. "You two figure out how we can help Callie. I do not want Black bullying her like he did me, but it's probably best that I stay here at the store. I don't need to be around that man."

Deborah watched her walk away.

"Esther's right," Melinda said. "She'll be more help here at the store."

"*Ya*. I suppose so. It's probably better if Esther isn't around Black at all. It seems her wounds have barely healed."

"We could be looking at this wrong. Perhaps facing Officer Black will bring some resolution to what still haunts Esther." Melinda's voice was soft, thoughtful, reminding Deborah of her mother-in-law the night before.

Deborah shook her head, tried to focus on the problems at hand. She had always been a good judge of character, and she was certain Callie wasn't involved with Stakehorn's death. "Whatever's going on, it bothers me. Callie's new here. She doesn't have much in the way of support—"

"She has us." Melinda smiled, straightened the eBay bookmarks on the counter.

"True. But some would say we are the reason she's in this mess to begin with. If it weren't for us badgering her to open the store—"

"And auction the quilts—"

"She never would have met Stakehorn."

Melinda sighed, sat carefully on the stool. "So what should we do? I have several more hours before I need to pick up Matthew and Aaron from their *grossmammi's*."

Deborah fidgeted with the hem of her apron, looked at the clock on the wall, then peeked over at Esther.

"What are you thinking of doing?" Melinda asked. "Since we were little, when you get that look in your eye it's meant you were considering doing something that might land us in trouble."

"Callie's already in trouble," Deborah pointed out. "I think I should go find Adalyn Landt."

"Adalyn Landt, the lawyer?"

"There's just the one Adalyn in town. She would know what to do. I only suggest it because I think Callie needs good counsel right now, and I'm not sure she's getting it from Black."

"Certainly we don't know all the ins and outs of the English system." Melinda stood and glanced back at the children. "I'll stay here and help Esther with the store and the *bopplin*. You go and find Adalyn."

Deborah hugged her, then hurried to the back to retrieve her purse.

"Deb, do you think Adalyn will do it?"

"She's always helped us before, and it's rare we use their legal system. If she'll help us, I have to believe she'll help Callie."

Melinda nodded. "Good luck then."

∽

Twenty minutes later Deborah and Adalyn approached the front door of the Shipshewana Police Department, located inside Shipshewana Town Hall. A small department of fewer than ten officers, it had nonetheless grown significantly since Deborah was a child.

She dared a glance at Adalyn.

Adalyn, who had barely waited to hear the entire story, before she'd grabbed her brown leather briefcase and hurried out the door.

"I love our officers, Deborah. They swore an oath to defend the town of Shipshe and defend is what they will do."

"What does defending Shipshewana have to do with Callie?"

"Exactly what I intend to find out."

As they pushed through the doors of the single-story building, Adalyn stiffened her spine, as if preparing for battle.

Adalyn was nearing fifty, with gray hair pulled back in a bun at the nape of her neck. Taller than Deborah, probably five-seven, and a bit overweight from the pie and coffee she loved, she was without a doubt the best lawyer in Shipshewana—not that there were many.

Deborah often wondered how the woman had enough customers to maintain a business, but then she understood little about the workings of a lawyer.

She did know that the few times she'd dealt with her, Adalyn had been honest and straightforward. More importantly, in the situation with Esther and the death of her husband, Adalyn had proven to be a true Godsend—both compassionate and savvy enough to guide them through the English legal system.

"I'm here to see my client, Miss Callie Harper." Adalyn offered the receptionist at the front desk a small smile — enough to be pleasant, but not enough to indicate she could be pushed around.

"Sure thing, Miss Landt." The receptionist looked as if she'd recently graduated from the English high school. In other words, maybe all of eighteen years old. Despite the short blonde hair, dangly ear rings, and makeup, she reminded Deborah of her own niece — very young. "If you'll have a seat in the waiting room, I'll tell — "

"I will not have a seat. My client is being questioned without benefit of counsel. I need to see her this minute."

The young girl's eyes widened, and she began punching buttons on her switchboard.

Deborah couldn't make out exactly what she said, but within less than a minute the girl motioned across the room. "If you'll go through the door on the far end of the room, Officer Gavin will meet you and take you to Miss Harper."

"Thank you."

Deborah hurried to stay up with Adalyn as she sailed toward the door.

"I'm sorry, miss, but Officer Gavin said only Miss Landt could go back."

Adalyn spun on her heel and drew her shoulders back, reminding Deborah of a cow protecting a newborn calf. "This young lady is with me. She's the closest thing Miss Harper has to family in this state. She will go through that door with me."

"Can't do it, Landt."

They both pivoted again.

Officer Gavin stood in the doorway, taking up most of it. Deborah had forgotten exactly how big the man was — it wasn't his height; he couldn't have been over six feet. He was built so solid though that he reminded Deborah of the door he stood next to.

This morning he looked exhausted, though no less intimidating. "Family isn't allowed, unless Harper's incarcerated."

He didn't smile, didn't relax his posture at all, but in Deborah's mind he must have searched through the English rule book and found something that might offer him a bit of comfort. "Of course if Harper is detained on a more permanent basis, Mrs. Yoder would be able to return during regular visiting hours and see her."

"That's not the outcome we're working toward, Officer." Adalyn moved past him, and Deborah could tell by the way she marched through the doorway without giving him so much as a second look that she wasn't the least bit intimidated by Gavin, the police station, or the prospect of defending a woman she'd never met.

Which all brought a measure of peace to Deborah.

She turned, sat in one of the plastic chairs, and pulled her knitting out of her bag. Idle hands being the mischief makers her *mamm* always claimed they could be, she best stay busy.

~

Callie refused to let Black frazzle her, but the truth was—and she could feel this deep inside her bones all the way to her toes—he was beginning to wear her down.

No, that wasn't quite right.

She'd passed exhaustion several minutes ago.

Passed puzzlement last night.

And she was sailing straight into the land of "you have rocked my boat and I'm about to jump back in your face."

She heard her mama's voice in her ear: *Remember your manners.* It was more than being polite though. Callie knew that if she released the last of her restraint, she would most likely land in a jail cell. If they had a jail cell here. Was she really being interrogated in City Hall? Or was this some sort of bizarre hallucination?

Black stood across the small room, leaning against the wall and scratching at the stubble on his face which seemed to have darkened even since they'd entered the building.

Scratching.

Staring at her.

Waiting.

Like she'd give up some big secret, if he could find the perfect way to irritate her. But he'd already done that nine ways to Sunday.

She slammed her hands against the metal table. "What are you waiting on? If you don't have any more questions, I need to go back to my shop."

A slow grin started in his eyes and made its way to lips that formed a halfhearted smile. "Oh, I have plenty of questions, sweetheart."

"Stop calling me that. I am not your sweetheart."

"She most certainly is not, and I would think you learned better technique in your law enforcement classes — careful Black, or you'll have a sexual harassment suit on your hands."

A rather large, older woman approached Callie's side of the table, set a brown leather Louis Vuitton briefcase down on the table, and held out her hand. "I'm attorney Adalyn Landt. Deborah asked me to represent you."

Callie nearly choked, still trying to process the sight of this woman who had barged in and now stood at her side, and the look on Gavin's face as he shrugged almost imperceptibly and exited the room. Then she turned and saw, for so brief an instant she might have imagined it, an expression of irritation pass across Black's face.

It was all the convincing she needed.

"Thank you, Miss Landt." She shook hands heartily. "I was just asking Officer Black if he had any further questions, but he doesn't seem to — "

"Wonderful, then I arrived in time to give you a ride home."

"Not so fast." Black grabbed the chair on the other side of the table, spun it around, and straddled it. "As I was explaining before you arrived, counselor, I have plenty of questions. I was merely giving Miss Harper time to recant her story from last night."

"And why would I do that?" Callie felt her temper rise again.

"I'm going to advise my client not to answer any further questions at this time, since she hasn't had the benefit of any counsel yet."

"That would be a bad idea." Black scowled and pulled a folder out of a scruffy looking bag which had been sitting on the floor. Slapping it on the table, he stared straight into Callie's eyes.

"This could be your best chance to come clean, Miss Harper. I suggest you take it. Your lawyer won't be much comfort to you when you're in the LaGrange County Jail."

"Psshhhh. Stop intimidating the poor girl. Show us what's in the folder and let's discuss this like the professionals we are, Shane."

He visibly flinched at the use of his given name. Callie realized he was losing his edge, finding it hard to bully her with a woman old enough to be his mother sitting at the table.

Then he sat back, and the cockiness returned.

Callie's stomach clenched into a small, tight fist—no bigger than the size of a rock she might as well have picked up and swallowed.

"You want to know what's in the folder? All right. I'll show you." He spun the folder once, twice, three times. Then stopped it with the flat of his hand, leaned forward, and stared into Callie's eyes. "What's in the folder is the testimony of four witnesses—four, Miss Harper. Do you know what they said?"

Callie shook her head, tried to look away but found she couldn't.

"They all say that last night, only hours before Stakehorn was found dead—" Black shook his head and sat back as if he was sad to deliver the last bit of news. "—you threatened Stakehorn, in public."

He opened the folder, made a show of running his finger down the printed lines. Callie could read them from where she sat, could read the names upside down.

His finger stopped at Baron Hearn and Gail Caldwell. She felt the sweat pool in the palms of her hands even before he began to read aloud. "Apparently you swore to—quote—get even." Continuing down the page he stopped at the names Kristen Smucker and George Simms. "You also said—again I'm quoting two witnesses—'You will regret making an enemy of me.'"

Chapter 14

BEFORE BLACK even finished speaking, Callie's left hand started trembling.

She grabbed it with her right hand and pulled it into her lap.

Her mind raced over the events of the night before. Somehow she'd been suppressing them the last twelve hours. That was the only explanation. She hadn't even told Deborah about the argument with Stakehorn — the episode at the deli, the peach mango tea, losing her temper . . . She hadn't thought to mention any of it.

"Something you'd like to say, Harper?"

"No, there is not anything she'd like to say." Adalyn pushed back her chair and picked up the Louis Vuitton bag. "Let's go, Callie."

Callie stood, surprised when her legs didn't betray her as her arm had.

Black stood as well, offering his lazy grin. "You both know it's best if she cooperates now."

"Do you have any indication that Stakehorn was killed?" Adalyn asked. "Could have been a heart attack or a stroke. The man likely had high cholesterol — be sure and run that test along with your toxicology reports."

"If I didn't have reason to suspect murder, do you think I'd even be conducting this investigation?"

"Do you have any evidence against my client?"

"We found Harper's phone at the scene, with calls to the deceased approximately one hour before his death."

"Which proves what?"

"It proves she was one of the last to speak with him, Adalyn. Even you have to acknowledge the significance of that. Perhaps she found a way to get even." Black's hands came up, his fingers adding quote marks to his last two words.

"A dozen people could have seen Stakehorn or talked to him in that hour." Adalyn shook her head, hooked her hand in Callie's arm, and practically dragged her toward the door. Opening it, she shoved Callie through, then turned and wagged her finger at Black. "You're going to need more than cell phone records and the testimony of a few gossips."

"Motive is half the battle. Means the other half. If she had both —" Black spread out both hands, indicating it was beyond him to control events after a certain point.

Callie watched them both, watched them as if she was sitting at her home in Houston, sitting in front of the big screen television, viewing an episode of some hour-long television series, some courtroom drama.

But it wasn't television.

It was her life.

She couldn't simply pick up the remote and change the channel on the big screen.

~

Deborah jumped when the door opened up again.

Adalyn had been in the back room less than ten minutes. When she marched back out, Callie in tow, Deborah wanted to shout for joy. Then she saw the pale look on Callie's face. She'd literally lost every ounce of color, and her eyes seemed unable to focus on any one thing.

Gathering her knitting and stuffing it into her bag, Deborah rushed over to join them. "What's wrong with her?"

"Not here," Adalyn said.

They walked out into the early afternoon sunshine, and Callie nearly dropped onto the steps of City Hall.

"Did he hurt her?"

"Course not. She's just had a bit of a shock." Adalyn placed her bag on the cement walk, stepped in front of Callie, and put both hands under her elbows. She waited until Callie's eyes settled on hers, then cocked her head in something bordering on amusement. "Where's the girl who was standing up to Black when I walked in the room? Hmm?"

Callie glanced down at the ground, as if lost. Then she looked up, over, and her eyes met Deborah's.

"You're okay, *ya?*"

"Yes. Maybe. I'm not sure." But she pulled in a deep breath, looked steadier.

"Would you like some *kaffi?*" Deborah tucked her hand into the crook of Callie's right arm, and Adalyn tucked hers into the bend of Callie's left.

"Coffee would be good," Callie murmured.

"And pie," Adalyn added, picking up her leather bag. "We could all use a piece of pie."

Ten minutes later they were seated at a back table inside The *Kaffi* Shop. The table had the double bonus of a side window which looked out over the parking lot (filled with both buggies and cars), while still affording them a bit of privacy. The waitress brought two steaming mugs of coffee and one hot tea, then returned with three pieces of pie—one cherry, one apple, and one chocolate.

"Officer Black acted as if he had evidence a murder had been committed," Callie said. "I've seen heart attacks before. Folks usually clutch their heart, pull at their clothes trying to catch their breath. Looking back, perhaps that's what frightened me. Stakehorn's body looked wrong—coffee spilled, hand stretched out as if he'd knocked it over, sitting at his desk like he was still working on the evening edition."

Adalyn pointed a forkful of cherry at Callie and said, "You don't have to tell me everything. Lawyers don't want to know everything in every case. But it's not like television either, where lawyers don't want to know anything. Shane Black is good at his job, and you can bet he's going to turn over every rock, or in this case every piece of newsprint." She swallowed the piece of pie and stabbed another. "Probably best to tell me all you can. I do my finest work with maximum information."

Callie nibbled around her apple pie and gave a replay of the last twelve hours. Deborah listened as she glanced around the café she'd been in many times. She often came here with Daisy; it was even a place Jonas liked to take her for a special treat.

While Callie spoke of the previous night's events, Deborah tried to piece together what it all meant for her new friend as well as the repercussions for Melinda and Esther and their quilting venture.

When Callie reached the part where she'd thrown the tea on Stakehorn, Deborah put down her forkful of chocolate pie and covered her mouth with her hand.

"You didn't, Callie."

"I did. I have a terrible temper, but I usually control it. When I'm finally pushed to the brink, I snap—but then it's over."

"Probably don't want to say those exact words if we do wind up in court." Adalyn pushed away her empty plate, smiling as she did. "Still, I wish I could have been there to see it. There are a lot of people in this town who would have applauded you for standing up to Stakehorn. Being new, you probably don't realize how much influence his little paper has."

"Had," Deborah said softly.

"Excellent point."

"I admit that I acted poorly in public," Callie said. "My mama would say that I forgot my southern manners, which is a sin where I come from, but not against the law in northern Indiana as far as I'm aware. I don't know what Black hoped to accomplish with his intimidation tactics, what he thought I'd confess—" Now her hands came out, gesturing and nearly knocking over her coffee. "Truth is I don't have anything else to tell."

Deborah hadn't heard Black's threats, but she could see how they had unnerved Callie. They had done something else as well; they had incensed her.

Now that she'd found her balance, she was becoming adamant about defending herself again, as she had been with Stakehorn. Her old spunk was returning. Deborah liked that side of Callie. It was what had drawn her to Daisy's niece in the first place, what had convinced her that Callie could help her with the quilts, and in the process help Melinda and Esther.

And suddenly, Deborah was reminded of Daisy.

The two women had the same determination and positive attitude—except in Callie it seemed to have been beaten down. At times she appeared lost, like the morning Deborah had first shown up at the shop, the morning Callie had still been in her bed clothes. She'd had the same bewildered look when she walked out of the police station. Other times though, her spunk returned, like now. It was as if Callie was trying to find her identity.

"Callie, do you have any family that I could contact if I need character witnesses? I don't think it's going to get that far, but I'd rather be ahead of this."

Callie shook her head, at first refusing to look up. When she finally did, there were tears in her eyes. "Daisy was the last of my family. My parents were both killed in a car accident when I was a freshman in college, which could be why I married young. At least that's what Rick—my husband—used to say."

"You're married?" Deborah asked. She had no idea.

"Was." Callie gulped the coffee, seemed to hesitate over revealing any more, then pushed on. "Rick wanted to wait to get married until I graduated, but I insisted I'd study better if we were married. He was older, ten years older, and claimed he'd grabbed me cradle and all." Callie smiled a bit.

"Where is he now, Callie?" Deborah ran her fingers down the strings of her prayer *kapp*. She wanted to reach out and touch her friend. This dear woman had so many things in her past that Deborah didn't know about.

"He died." Callie said it blandly, without emotion—but Deborah knew how the death of a beloved husband affected a person. "Cancer, over a year ago."

All three women leaned back in their chairs, studying one another. Finally Adalyn cleared her throat. "Do you have friends I can contact?"

"My job involved a lot of travel, so I wasn't close to anyone, not really." Callie turned the coffee cup once, twice, three times. "Why would Black suspect me? How could he suspect me? This is ridiculous and it is not fair." Callie sat up straighter and motioned the waitress for a refill on the coffee even as she continued to push the apple pie around on her plate.

"He must be floundering because he has no idea what happened," Deborah offered. "Or maybe he can't accept the man died of natural causes."

Adalyn had been watching Callie closely—not interrupting with questions or insights. Now she reached down for her bag and pulled out a wallet which matched the brown leather perfectly. "You could be right, but I suspect something else is at work here, and Shane simply isn't showing his hand yet. I've never known the man to bluff for the fun of it. Fishing? Possibly. But always with good cause."

"What would cause him to harass Callie?" Deborah asked, dread filling her stomach.

"He has reason to believe it was a murder. Remember the list of names he showed us? The man has already been busy interviewing witnesses. Who knows how many others he has brought in and questioned. He either believes Callie is guilty or knows something more that can lead him to the person who is."

"I'm not guilty though, and I don't know anything." Callie had been stirring cream into her coffee, but she dropped the spoon against the saucer in frustration. The clatter seemed to echo through the café.

"No doubt you think you don't, but you were on scene. Often people don't remember things for hours or days. My guess is he thought by scaring you, something would bounce out of your memory." Adalyn withdrew some money and laid it on the table.

"Well, it didn't work." Callie gulped the coffee, then glanced up at Adalyn. "Are you saying I don't have to worry about being arrested again?"

"No. I won't lie to you—I don't think you're paying me to give you false hopes."

"Which reminds me, we haven't discussed rates. I didn't exactly remember to put a line item in my budget for lawyer fees." Callie stared back into her coffee.

Deborah reached over and clasped her hand. "We'll help you if need be."

"Why would you do that?"

"Why wouldn't we?"

"You barely even know me."

Adalyn scooted her chair back from the table. "In a town like Shipshewana people either become friends or enemies real fast. Seems to me, you've made at least two friends, Callie, and they're both sitting here at the table."

Deborah was relieved when Callie nodded instead of arguing. She even looked a bit choked up.

"As far as what I said earlier—about paying me to give you false hopes—it was a phrase. I don't plan on charging you for this one." When Callie started to protest, she held up her hand to stop her. "I owe Deborah more than one favor. What you can do is let me know if you remember anything else. And call me if Shane Black contacts you again."

Adalyn handed Callie her business card as they walked out of the café.

Deborah drove her back to the shop in the buggy, and they discussed quilting, the auction, and how things were going at Deborah's farm. It helped to speak of normal things.

"As I mentioned the other day, we have no church service this Sunday. Instead we're meeting at one of the farms for dinner and to visit and play games."

Callie looked uncomfortable as she climbed out of the buggy and walked toward the shop. "I'll probably be busy."

"Say you'll try. It's at our home this week."

"I don't even know where you live."

"It isn't that hard, Callie. Shipshewana is small, and we're but a few miles on the outskirts of town. I'll draw you a map."

"Won't that be odd? Having an un-Amish person there?"

"Actually we call you Englishers, and it's not so unusual. We often have Amish, Mennonite, and Englishers. In spite of how outsiders paint us, we enjoy visiting with others. Come and see. There's always a volleyball game going. We can find out if you remember anything."

Callie gave her the look that said she knew she was being baited, but she didn't turn her down cold.

Deborah drew her a map before they left. When she and Melinda and Esther were on the road again, she couldn't help wondering how this turn of events would resolve itself.

The entire situation reminded her of a mystery quilt. She still remembered the first one she'd sewn as a teenage girl. It had seemed so exciting, and she kept pestering her *mamm*, asking her how it would turn out. "No one knows, until the day we sew the pieces together," her *mamm* had explained. "That's what makes it a mystery."

Callie's past was mysterious; she seemed to be keeping some things hidden. Amish were a closely knit people, so Deborah understood the desire for privacy, but it seemed to go deeper with Callie. Then there was their current situation.

Like the mystery quilt, each piece made sense when she considered it individually. For the life of her, she couldn't imagine the completed picture though.

In time she knew it would all make sense.

She just hoped when it did, she would like the final results.

Chapter 15

CALLIE WOKE to her alarm the next morning (her alarm being Max), surprised she had slept so soundly.

She expected to toss and turn.

She expected to dream of Stakehorn's still, lifeless form.

She expected to startle awake every time the summer breeze rattled the screen on her windows.

She didn't do any of those things. Perhaps it was exhaustion, or maybe the events of the previous two days had caught up with her. Whatever the reason, she slept the sleep of toddlers, oblivious to everything.

When Max crawled from the foot of her bed to place his cold nose in her hand, she stretched, scratched him between the ears once, and rolled out of bed refreshed.

Then she remembered Black and his round of questions — the way his eyes had stared into hers, accusing, never backing down — and her temper returned.

Snatching Max's leash up, she grabbed her robe and marched down the stairs. "Who does Shane Black think he is, anyway, Max? Man acts like a Texas Ranger. Well, he won't be pushing us around anymore."

Max whined and trotted off to do his business, leaving Callie to plot ways of getting even with Officer Black.

Once dressed and inside Daisy's Quilt Shop, her attention turned to different matters. She had a store to run, and she'd paid little attention to it the last two days. Inventory needed to be ordered, stock waited to be replenished, and customers had to be helped. She was grateful it wasn't a market day, so business was minimal.

She'd begun to catch up by late morning when the lunchtime customer surge hit and lasted until one-thirty. Relieved that no one was in the store, Callie decided to take advantage of the lull and take Max outside, then make herself a sandwich. She brought it to the counter and was placing an internet order of quilting notions when the bell over the front door rang.

Looking up, she nearly choked on her turkey and rye when Officer Gavin stepped inside.

"Miss Harper." He was in his uniform and stopped just inside the door, as if unsure whether he was welcome.

Callie took a drink of her unsweetened iced tea and waved him over. "You might as well come on in since you're here."

"Yes, ma'am." Gavin stepped up to the counter, his expression betraying none of his thoughts.

Callie was curious now. Obviously he wasn't here to arrest her again. That must be Black's department. So what could have brought the good officer by?

Instead of making it easier for him, she waited.

The man did carry himself as if he were still in the military. How many years and in what capacity had he served Uncle Sam?

She should have figured it out that first evening. She knew the military look, recognized the way an enlisted man carried himself. Her father had served in the Air Force, and she remembered how he stood in exactly the same stance—back ramrod straight, arms at his side, shoulders back, head still, but somehow the eyes were taking in everything. Years after her dad had retired from the service, he kept the military posture. The thought brought a smile to her face.

Gavin frowned all the more. "Wasn't sure you'd care to see me, after the other night at the *Gazette*, and then yesterday at the station."

Callie sighed and pushed the last half of her sandwich away. "Did Black send you over here?"

"No. Of course not." If it was possible, Gavin stood up straighter. His Commanding Officer would be proud, but as far as Callie could tell, no C.O. was in sight.

"Well?" she asked.

"Well, what?"

Callie's patience finally snapped. She slid off the stool, grabbed the basket of new magazines, and pushed past him to the magazine display near the front of the store. "Then why are you here? I'm sure you have plenty to do guarding the good folks of Shipshewana."

"That's just it. I realize I might have come off somewhat brusque at the scene of the deceased." Gavin paused as if waiting for her to contradict him. When Callie only shot him a look of disdain, he began speaking more rapidly, as if he needed to convince her before she ran him out. "Which is the point. It's why I came by. I don't want you thinking you can't call on local law enforcement—"

"Meaning you."

"Yes, me and the five other officers."

"Including Black?"

"Actually Officer Black is from the county office, but he does serve as back up when the need arises."

"And the need arose Tuesday night?" Callie finished with the magazines and moved past him toward the stock room. To her surprise, Gavin followed her back there as well. She bent down to pick up a box of Grab-N-Go Kits, but Gavin beat her to it.

"I can carry it," she said.

"I've got it." Blue eyes slammed into hers once again, just like two nights ago. This time instead of frightening her, they confused her. He had been a real jerk, but she'd been taught to respect a man who apologized.

"Where do you want it?" he asked.

"Front of the store, next to the carousel."

He turned and carried the box out of the storeroom, handling it as if it weighed nothing. Since his back was to her, he didn't see her roll her eyes. She realized it was immature, but it helped relieve her stress. The last thing she needed was a macho man, a macho officer, showing up to carry boxes for her.

Why was he here? To ease his conscience? To check up on her? To get more information? Whatever the reason, she'd rather he say what he'd come to say and get out of her store. The day had finally fallen into a nice rhythm. She'd managed to forget Stakehorn's lifeless form for a few minutes.

Until now.

Gavin set the box on the floor next to the carousel. "Might want to hire one of the Amish kids to help with your heavy lifting."

Callie put her hands on her hips. "I can handle it, Officer Gavin, but thank you for your concern."

His radio squawked, and though the garble that came through made no sense to Callie, Gavin pulled it off his belt, spoke into it once, and clipped it back to where it belonged.

"I have to go. Traffic problem."

"I'd say thanks for stopping by, but I still don't know why you bothered."

Gavin had reached the door. Now he turned and pierced her again with his stare. What he said next shocked her as much as anything that had happened since she'd arrived in Shipshewana. "Look, I don't have an opinion in these matters, okay? I just do my job, like I'm trained to do it."

Callie wanted to interrupt him, wanted to argue that being efficient didn't have to include being callous. Somehow she bit it back.

"But if I were to have an opinion," he continued, "I saw how scared you were Tuesday night. Killers might be frightened after they kill, might be afraid of being caught, but they're not terrified like you were."

"Then why were you so hard on me?" Callie felt her anger surge. She stepped forward, but Gavin held up his hand, stopped her with a shake of his head.

"I was doing my job, and I'll keep doing it. I'm just saying, if he was killed — and no I can't go into any details as to why it might have been a murder scene — but if he was killed, whoever did it is still out there. I don't want you being too mad, or too stubborn, to dial 911 if you need us."

Then Andrew Gavin turned and walked out of her shop.

Callie returned to the counter, considered her half-eaten lunch, but walked to the kitchen and tossed it in the trash.

"Whoever did it is still out there." Gavin's words circled in her mind.

Well of course he was. That was the point. She hadn't killed him. She didn't know who had. She was just the stranger in town who had stumbled on the body.

So which was it? Murder? Or old age? Callie's thoughts wavered between the two extremes like a child on a seesaw.

The man *was* old. He could have died of any number of diseases.

A stroke.

A heart attack.

An embolism.

Her mind went back over the limited medical training she'd had as a pharmaceutical drug representative, the part of her life she'd tried to forget. Nothing she'd seen from Stakehorn when

149

he'd first walked into the store on Saturday or at the deli on Tuesday matched up with any symptoms she was aware of, but then she wasn't a doctor.

"Whoever did it is still out there."

Gavin's words followed her around the store as she went back to work—disrupting the easy rhythm she'd found earlier.

~

Deborah finished the bulk of her chores by lunch. She had more to do—on a farm there was always more to do—but Wednesdays were when she went to see Esther. She hadn't missed a week since Seth had died, hadn't missed a week in over a year.

Jonas had the buggy hitched and ready when she gathered up baby Joshua.

"Would you like me to take the twins?" she asked.

"No need. They're helping me with the pigs today." Jonas placed the hamper she carried into the back seat of the buggy.

"You're a good *dat*. You know that, right?" Deborah reached up and ran her palm along his cheek. She liked the way his beard felt against her hand, loved the way he tipped his hat back and leaned forward to kiss her on the lips.

"Because I let the boys clean out the pig pens? It was my favorite job when I was their age."

Deborah laughed at his teasing. "Martha is inside sewing and keeping an eye on Mary."

"I'm sure they'll be fine. Enjoy your visit. If there's anything Esther needs, I can stop over Saturday afternoon."

Nodding, Deborah signaled to Cinnamon, and the horse set off at a quick pace. Jonas had always been generous with his time, but it was more than that with Esther. He understood the special connection that existed between her and Esther and Melinda. They'd been friends for such a long time. More than that, their love for and skill at quilting had drawn them together when they were only girls.

So many years ago, they could have never envisioned the twists and turns of life that would bind them together.

Deborah thought again of her mother-in-law's words. Ruth had said that sometimes pain had a place in their lives. Hadn't Esther had enough though? Wasn't it her turn for happiness? Deborah remembered how her friend used to participate in life, used to laugh and feel joy. Now when she was with her, sadness seemed to pour from her like moonlight had poured through her bedroom window last night.

Turning onto the lane that led to the Zook place, Deborah glanced over at Joshua, sleeping on the seat beside her. She couldn't imagine her pain if something happened to him or anyone in her family. And what if she had to live without Jonas?

There was the thing most people turned from when they looked at Esther. Easy enough to say she should move on, but few people stopped to think what their own life would be like if they were thrown into the same situation.

Deborah knew how barren her own life would be without her husband.

And the way Seth had died definitely made matters worse. A farming accident would have been difficult enough, but Deborah had been pushed to the brink by having to endure the police investigation, along with Shane Black's insistence that those responsible be brought to justice.

Now their lives were tangled with Shane's one more time.

God's doing or one more complication of living among the English?

Deborah murmured to Cinnamon and pulled under a shade tree outside of Esther's house. One thing she was sure of: she needed to be the best friend she could to Esther and Melinda, and at this point that seemed to mean befriending Callie Harper.

She was more than willing to do so.

The fact that friendship also involved her in another police investigation seemed a bit bizarre, but then life had always surprised her with its complexity.

Deborah gathered her sleeping son in her arms, picked up the basket, and walked up the steps of her best friend's porch.

Esther opened the front door of the single-story white house before Deborah had a chance to knock. Leah's head popped out from behind her *mamm's* dress, eyes wide, prayer *kapp* firmly pinned in place.

"Afternoon, Esther. Afternoon, Leah."

"Joshua sleeping?" Leah asked.

"He was on the ride over. I think he's awake now though." Deborah handed the basket to Esther as she walked through the door.

"When are you going to stop bringing me things, Deborah?"

"Can't a *freind* bring a *freind* fresh cookies?"

Joshua had begun to squirm, so Deborah set him down on the floor. He clung a bit to Deborah's dress, but stared at Leah and the basket.

"What kind of cookies, *Mamm*? I want to see." Leah's voice was soft, sweet, and unscarred.

"Take them to the kitchen." Deborah said. "Get Joshua a cup of milk and each of you a cookie."

Leah took the basket in her right hand, Joshua's hand in her left, and led him off to the kitchen.

Deborah and Esther could watch them from the sitting room, but talk more freely from a distance, without little ears picking up every word.

"You needn't do this, you know." Esther's eyes were on the children, and she had no real scolding in her voice.

"And you needn't fuss."

Deborah sank into the couch and gave Esther the once over. As usual, every blonde hair was in place, and her clothing was perfectly ironed. If anything though, she seemed to have lost more weight, and her face was devoid of color.

It occurred to Deborah for the first time that perhaps something more was wrong with Esther. What if she was sick? Maybe she should see one of the English doctors. Surely it was natural to mourn, but what if this was more than grief?

"It was nice of you to take the cookies you had to Callie. I thought I'd replace them is all. I know you only have time to bake once a week."

"And you have more time than I do? With your five *bopplin*?" Esther's right eyebrow arched with the question, but her hands remained folded in her lap. Esther had the patience of Job it seemed. Outwardly anyway. She would never ask probing questions, and she wouldn't volunteer any information. Deborah would have to jump right in.

"Have you heard anything new?"

"About what?"

"About ..." Deborah waved her hand, as if that would explain everything. "You know about what. Anything about Stakehorn? Anything new about Callie or Daisy's Quilt Shop? Anything else on Shane Black?"

Esther's face had been impassive until Deborah mentioned Black; then she flinched, just once.

"You're closer to town. You'd hear before I would."

"Hmm. Well, I haven't heard anything since Adalyn helped her out of Shane's interrogation room."

Esther nodded, but didn't respond.

"We finally catch a break," Deborah continued. "We finally get someone who can help us. Who is willing to help us, and now this."

"Now this?"

"Oh, Esther. You know what I mean."

"Stakehorn's death?"

"Yes. Could it have happened at a worse time?"

"A bit inconvenient," Esther agreed. Her blue eyes relaxed a bit, seemed to be amused though still she didn't smile.

"Now that's not what I meant. I wouldn't have wished it on him, and you know it."

Esther didn't contradict her, but she looked down at her apron, ran a finger over the hem.

"What? You might as well say it."

"*Mamm*? Can we have just one more? Joshua is still hungry."

Esther looked at Deborah. Deborah closed her eyes, then grinned. "Remember when we used to beg for more cookies?"

"You begged. I suggested we go to the orchard and pick apples." Esther leaned forward, caught her daughter's eye. "You may split one more, Leah. Then put the rest on the counter and cover them with the cloth so they will stay fresh for your *onkels*."

The sound of giggling trickled from the kitchen.

"Where were we?" Deborah slipped off her shoes and tucked her feet up underneath her. "You were about to say something."

"I was about to say nothing."

"About Stakehorn."

Esther looked out the front window, out over her fields that her brothers were even now working because her husband had died. Finally she turned, met Deborah's gaze. "I was going to say what we've all been thinking. It could have been the man was ill, or it could have been an accident."

"Or?"

"Or it could have been murder. We both know there are many here in town—both Amish and English—who did not like the man's ways."

"But enough to kill him?" Deborah felt a jolt of surprise at Esther's words, though they'd been tumbling around in her own mind.

"I wouldn't think so, but then what do I know of the motives for murder?"

The last three words were so soft that Deborah thought she might have imagined them. She wanted to remind her friend that

Seth's death was different. She wanted to assure her that her pain would eventually pass. There was so much she wanted to be able to do, but it all seemed out of her control.

And then the children were there on the rug between them. Leah was showing something to Joshua and they were both laughing, and that did bring a smile to Deborah's face. Before long, her hour was up. As they were leaving, Esther insisted they all walk out and look at her vegetable garden.

The garden was a thing of beauty. It seemed to be where Esther put all of her emotions, all of the things she couldn't say. Growing beside the onions were large pink roses. Next to the squash were tall yellow sun flowers. Even the giant ball of old fence wire, placed in a corner, bigger than the old wooden garden shed the women stood beside, looked impressive—like a giant ball of yarn artistically placed among three different kinds of flowering plants.

"This is beautiful, Esther. It really is. The entire thing looks like one of our quilts—as if you'd designed a new pattern."

"*Danki.*" Esther's cheeks pinked with color, and she smiled at the compliment. "I enjoy the time I spend out here. It's when I come closest to *gelassenheit.*"

"When Bishop Elam spoke of it again on Sunday, I prayed for you." Deborah looped her arm in Esther's. Together they watched Leah lead Joshua up and down the garden rows.

"It's an effort to maintain any composure at all," Esther admitted. "I pray for it each day when I rise, strive to seem calm and collected."

"For Leah's sake?"

"Yes, of course. But honestly, what good would wailing about do?"

Deborah squeezed her arm, stopped in front of the roses.

"It's been more than a year," Esther said. "I would think serenity would come, by now. That it wouldn't be something I have to reach for each day."

"Every week Bishop Elam reminds us of our need to find *gelassenheit* in all things. That alone proves it's hard for all of our people. You aren't the only one who struggles, Esther."

Esther pulled her hand away, broke off a few dead leaves from the rose bush. "My parents wish me to remarry."

Deborah started to ask if it was anyone she cared for, but she stopped herself when she saw the desolation in her friend's eyes.

When she and Joshua were in the buggy on their way back home, Deborah replayed the conversations of the last hour. And though her heart was on Esther's news about remarrying, her mind was on what she'd said about murder.

What were the motives for murder?

And who would have been angry enough to kill Stakehorn, because it most certainly was not Callie Harper. Who had reason to murder the editor, reason and opportunity? How long would it take Shane to find them so people like Gail Caldwell and Baron Hearn would turn their suspicions away from Callie?

~

Breaking into the *Gazette* was easy enough.

He ducked under the Crime Scene tape and moved back into the editor's office, snapping on rubber gloves as he turned on the small flashlight he'd brought.

He was almost certain the package wasn't here, but his boss had insisted that he look one more time. And his boss wasn't someone you said no to, not if you wanted to keep your job. Not if you wanted to wake up tomorrow. Stakehorn was proof of that.

So where had the editor stashed it?

All the factors seemed to indicate he'd sold it, but no deposits had been made to his accounts—which meant he'd hidden it.

The only question was where.

Chapter 16

CALLIE THOUGHT about trying out one of the churches in Shipshewana on Sunday, but in the end fatigue won and she spent the morning reading the paper, browsing the internet, and cleaning up her apartment. It didn't take much cleaning. She wasn't a messy person. Okay, she was a bit compulsive about picking up after herself.

Rick had always laughed and said they'd never need a maid.

Rick.

For some reason the day seemed thick with memories of him. She wasn't sure why. He'd never come to Indiana with her. In fact, he'd never met her family. Her parents had already died when her best friend, Nicole, had introduced them to one another.

Rick had claimed that her stolid independence was part of what drew him to her.

Today, she didn't feel so independent.

She felt vulnerable and restless and alone. She wasn't surprised when she picked up Daisy's journal, placed her finger in the middle, and opened it to October 15.

Be with Callie, Father. She needs you today. Be with her and Rick, wrap your arms around them; cover them in your love.

157

Her mind looped through the last week they'd spent together, the final days in the hospital as the brain cancer had ravaged his body. She'd stayed with him, showering in the bathroom that was supposed to be for patient use only. The fear that he would slip away as soon as she stepped outside the hospital gripped her, but in the end she'd been holding his hand when he'd pulled in his last breath.

Was that *Gotte's wille*? That they be allowed to share his final moment together?

Tears blurred her eyes, and she closed Daisy's journal, placed it back on the nightstand next to her bed.

When Max whined at the windows, she joined him at the seat looking down over Main Street.

"Shipshewana is closed on Sunday, pal. Nothing doing here. If we're twitchy it's either a trip to Middlebury or ..."

She looked over at the end table positioned next to the recliner she liked to read in at night. Deborah's directions sat there, tempting her. Why had she even brought them upstairs? She'd meant to throw them away, then decided she should keep them in case of an emergency.

Was loneliness an emergency?

Deborah had written "Come at noon and don't bring anything" across the bottom, and "P.S. Bring Max" along the edge. The map looked easy enough to follow.

A game of volleyball might be the cure she needed.

She wouldn't fit in though, and Callie hated not fitting in almost more than she hated this despondent, restless, itchy feeling. Then she looked back out the window and saw the Shipshewana Police Department vehicle slowly patrol down Main.

It was the final push.

She couldn't sit here thinking about Gavin or Black or Stakehorn. She needed to burn off some energy.

"Come on, Max." She paused long enough to check her reflection in the mirror. She wore jeans and a Southwest Texas University T-shirt—gray with a maroon logo. Checking Max's bandanas she found a maroon one that matched nicely, tied it on him, then snapped his leash onto his collar. After grabbing her car keys off the hook by the door, they trotted down the stairs.

The day's sunshine felt wonderful on her face, and the weather was nice enough to leave the windows down as she drove. Daisy must have taken Max riding in the car fairly often. He didn't attempt to hang his head completely out, only sat in the passenger seat with his muzzle resting on the door frame, snout pushed out in the wind.

When Callie had driven only a couple of miles, she passed a sign that said, "fresh produce." Pulling over she found they had a nice selection of strawberries, so she bought some for Deborah.

"Texans always take something," she murmured, pulling back out onto the two-lane road. Several buggies rolled along in front of her, but she'd grown used to the slow pace of driving behind them in town, and it didn't bother her like it had the first few times.

She set the radio to a country station, turned the tune down low, and enjoyed the view of the fields she was passing.

In no time at all, she saw the red barn and county road Deborah had drawn on the map. Turning down it, she had the feeling of stepping back in time. If she thought Shipshewana was old-fashioned, the back roads surrounding the little town were like something out of a Norman Rockwell poster.

It was easy enough to tell which farms were English and which were Amish, since some had cars and others had buggies. Also the English homes had electrical lines running to the house. If she looked closely she saw that the Amish farms had electricity only to the barns and some didn't have even that.

They sat side by side, and lay out before her like a patchwork quilt. Most had grain silos beside the barns, and all boasted barns bigger than the houses.

Callie was so intrigued by the farms, so busy comparing and contrasting them to the way farms and ranches were laid out in Texas that she almost missed the Yoder place altogether.

The reason she didn't was because the buggy in front of her slowed, then pulled into the lane. Quite a few buggies were pulled up at the tidy farm. To her surprise, even a few other cars were there. Glancing down at her map, she realized she was at her destination.

When she looked up, she'd nearly passed the entrance; she had to brake a bit harder than normal, and Max nearly fell into the floorboard. He whined once, then barked.

They both parked in front of the corral fence, in the line of buggies and cars.

She pulled slowly up beside the buggy that had been traveling in front of her, careful not to startle the mare. When she'd removed her key from the ignition, she finally noticed what was fastened to the back of the buggy — strapped tightly with bungee cords above the large black box where most Amish folk stored their packages.

Callie felt her hands go clammy and her heart rate increase. The wheelchair reminded her too much of Rick, of trying to wrestle the chair out of the trunk of her car, of their last few weeks together when he'd been too weak to walk. Though she knew she should step out of her little car, she felt frozen in place, as if she was caught in a spotlight and couldn't look away.

When it was Melinda Byer who stepped out of the buggy, Callie literally clutched her stomach, as if she'd sustained a double punch. Melinda wore a dress like the others Callie had seen her wear, this one a light gray with mid-length sleeves. Her light brown hair was pinned neatly beneath her white prayer *kapp*, and she was soon joined by a tall Amish man who handed her baby Hannah.

Melinda had two children? More than two children?

The boy who jumped out after Melinda was probably ten years

old. He wore the suspenders and wool cap that Callie had seen on most of the Amish boys around town.

Melinda's husband wore the traditional black hat.

Then Melinda's husband and the older boy moved to the back of the buggy and all thoughts of black hats and wool caps fled. They unfastened the wheelchair as if they'd done it a hundred times, which no doubt they had.

Callie had a sudden urge to flee, to back away and pretend she hadn't come.

But Melinda glanced over and spotted her at that exact moment. She said something to her husband, and walked toward her car, still holding baby Hannah in her arms.

"Callie, I didn't know you and Max were coming."

"I didn't know we were either." Callie stepped out of the rental, pulling Max's leash and fumbling with the strawberries. "Deborah invited us, and it seemed like a good day to be outside."

"*Ya*. The children were eager to get here. Would you mind holding Hannah for a moment?" Without waiting for an answer, Melinda thrust the infant in her arms and moved back toward her buggy.

Max contented himself with taking care of his business on the wooden fence, then sitting and staring at Melinda's horse. Callie juggled the baby, uncomfortable with the warm, sweet softness of her, afraid she might hold her wrong and injure the child somehow.

Then she saw why Melinda had left her with the baby.

She'd walked back to the buggy, had reached in for a box of food, and moved in front of the buggy door—holding it open with her body while her older son positioned the wheelchair next to it.

"Hurry, *Mamm*," the boy said. "They're starting the baseball game."

"There will be plenty of time for baseball, Matthew."

Her husband reached into the buggy and emerged with a boy

whose arms were wrapped around his father's neck. His hair and eyes were an exact replica of his mother's — a warm brown. He looked to be just about school-age, wore clothing identical to his brother's right down to the cap on his head, and even from where Callie stood she could tell he had trouble breathing.

"You promised I could play this time, Matthew," the boy said as his father placed him in the wheelchair.

"Sure, you can play. We'll put you in outfield." Matthew barely waited for the younger boy to shift his weight and find a comfortable position in the wheelchair before he flipped off the brakes and wheeled him away from his parents and in the direction of the barn, where a game of ball had already begun.

"Boys." Melinda's voice was quiet but firm.

Matthew stopped, turned the wheelchair in a half circle.

"Mamm?"

"You didn't say hello to Miss Callie." Both boys waved their right hand. "Callie, meet Matthew, our ten-year-old and Aaron who is six."

"Hello," Callie murmured.

"You may go now," Melinda said. They didn't hesitate; Matthew spinning the chair again and taking off at twice his previous pace. Melinda called after them. "Be careful."

Two hands waved back at her, though neither child bothered to turn around.

"Boys." Melinda smiled, gave the box to her husband, and turned back to take baby Hannah from Callie.

This time though, Callie wondered if she detected something hidden underneath the smile.

She'd been so busy with her own troubles, it had never occurred to her that other people might have a few of their own.

"I hope I didn't hurt her. I'm not sure exactly how to hold a baby."

"Hannah?" Melinda laughed and pushed up her glasses. "Can't hardly hurt a six-month-old, Callie."

"There was that time I laid her in the apple bin," Melinda's husband said. "You thought I'd hurt her, but she was fine." He had finished unloading two baskets from the box at the back of the buggy. Now he stood beside his wife, baskets in his left hand, box in his right, and a giant grin on his face. "Learned then that women tend to worry more than men."

Melinda shook her head and handed him the baby, taking the baskets of food from his hands. "Callie, this would be my husband, Noah."

"Nice to meet you."

"Same." He nodded toward Max. "I've missed seeing Daisy's dog."

"You know Max?" Callie's mind suddenly tripped back over an entry she'd read in Daisy's journal several nights ago — prayers for M. and her family and their special needs.

"Daisy used to join us every once in a while." Melinda pulled one last basket out of the back seat of her buggy, then peeked at Callie's bag of strawberries. "Those will be *wunderbaar* with the homemade ice cream Jonas makes."

"I haven't had homemade ice cream in ages." Callie put a hand to her stomach. "This is not going to be good for my waistline."

"Deborah mentioned you play volleyball," Melinda said. "You can run it off. Come on. I'll show you where to put the food."

As they walked toward the back of the house, under the shade of trees, Callie mentally slapped her forehead. She didn't know what she'd imagined an Amish home to look like, but it wasn't this.

This was a normal farm. In fact, other than the silo towering next to the barn, it could have been any country home in Texas. Of course there were community grain silos in far west Texas, but rarely right next to a house like she was looking at now.

A trampoline sat in the front yard under the shade of a giant tree. It was surrounded by a passel of children waiting for a turn, both boys and girls, while four at a time bounced.

The difference, of course, was in how the children were dressed.

It was Sunday though, and Callie could remember wearing dresses to church every Sunday, then coming home and waiting for her mom to set out fried chicken and mashed potatoes. These children didn't look that much different than the scene around her house would have looked twenty-five years ago. Other than the *kapps* on their heads.

She smiled at the thought.

"Want to share?" Melinda asked.

"I was thinking how normal it all looks."

"Oh, it's normal all right. You'll find that out when you get involved in the volleyball game."

The sight that greeted her as they turned the corner to the back of the house wasn't quite like anything she'd ever seen.

Tables were set up in two long rows, with enough chairs to feed forty to fifty people.

"I guess you need so many chairs because of all the children."

Deborah laughed as she came up and accepted the strawberries, giving them both a hug. "Most of the *bopplin* will eat in the barn or under the trees. The chairs are for the adults."

Within the next half hour, Callie realized adults were everywhere — women in the house still preparing cold dishes, men in the barn talking crops and horses. Things weren't completely segregated, though; a few couples walked under the trees. Callie noticed several younger women gathered around what looked like a brand-new colt, with a tall, beardless man proudly standing beside the mare.

"That's Jonas's brother, Stephen. He helps on all the family farms, since he isn't married yet."

"I could have guessed as much, the way he has so many young ladies around him." Callie smiled and followed Deborah toward the new tan colt.

"You can also tell because he has no beard. Our single men shave. Once married, they no longer cut their beards, though you'll notice they still have no mustache."

"Ah, a code."

Deborah laughed and accepted the flowers Mary brought her. "Would you like some flowers, Miss Callie?"

"I think I can just look at your mom's, but thank you, Mary."

Mary's smile fell away, and she stared down at the ground.

"What I meant to say was I'd love some flowers, if you wouldn't mind looking for some for me."

"Really?" The little girl brightened instantly.

"Really. I could put them on the counter in the shop."

Mary swung Deborah's hand and skipped along beside them. "Did you hear what she said, *Mamm*? She's going to put them on the counter."

"I heard. You better hurry. We're eating soon."

Mary's eyes grew wide and she dashed off, grabbing another little girl as she headed toward a field next to the barn.

"This little buckskin colt was born yesterday." Deborah proceeded to introduce Callie to Stephen and the women around him—who mostly seemed related in one way or another.

The image of the colt, wheat-colored with a black mane and one white sock, stayed with Callie through the afternoon. She thought of it as she ate. She pictured it as she tried to memorize names and faces though she knew she'd forget the vast majority of them. She even found herself looking up and trying to catch a glimpse of it as her attention returned again and again back to Melinda's little boy perched contentedly in his wheelchair.

Somehow images of the colt, Melinda's boy, and her husband Rick were determined to push their way into her day—awakening parts of her heart that she had coaxed to sleep over a year ago as she'd watched her husband take his last breath.

Chapter 17

CALLIE MANAGED to enjoy playing volleyball.

Everyone was surprisingly competitive.

Why did she expect the game to be a lay down? Because they were Amish? Turned out they wanted to win as much as she did.

She found herself jostling for the ball, diving for a save, even slamming one over the net—and she hadn't done any of those moves in years. The tension that had built up in her shoulders in the last week began draining away as a welcome exhaustion worked its way into her muscles.

When the third game ended, she looked over to see Mary sitting on the sidelines clutching the bouquet of flowers she'd picked for her in one hand, petting Max with the other.

"You won, Miss Callie."

"My team won."

"Same thing. Isn't it?" Mary squinched up her face, and tilted her head back, causing her *kapp* strings to touch the ground.

"I suppose it is, sweetie. How about you and I go find some of your mom's lemonade?"

"I'll get it. I know where it is." Thrusting the flowers into her hand, along with Max's leash, Mary was up and gone before Callie could argue.

"She's one with a lot of energy." The voice was a baritone, with no trace of German — most definitely not Amish.

Callie turned around in surprise and found herself face-to-face with a man six inches taller than herself, wearing jeans and a Notre Dame T-shirt.

"Bernie Richards." Crow's feet lined his hazel-colored eyes, and his properly trimmed hair held a light smattering of gray.

"You're—"

"English? Yes, I suppose I am."

"I'm sorry. I don't mean to stare. It's just that I feel as if I'd spent the afternoon at the bottom of Alice's proverbial rabbit hole. Now that I think about it, I did see other cars parked when I drove in, but for some reason I'd been thinking I was the only person here who wasn't Amish."

Mischievous eyes panned left, then right. "I believe we might be it, other than a few Mennonites."

"Yes, Deborah said Mennonites might be here. I don't see any."

Bernie Richards' smile spread into a full grin. "You are new. Mennonites wear English clothing, though they usually dress modestly. The men don't always sport the long beard, and the women cover their hair differently. See the woman there by the table? She has a handkerchief covering her head, instead of the traditional prayer *kapp*."

Mary interrupted their conversation, proudly clutching the promised glass of lemonade, though she'd spilled a bit of it down the side in her trek across the yard.

"Thank you, Mary."

"*Gern gschehne*, Miss Callie." The young girl looked up at Bernie and cocked her head, then rubbed her nose with the back of her hand. "Sorry, Doc Richards. I didn't brung you any."

"It's no problem, dear. But I believe your *grossdaddi* is trying to get your attention."

Mary pivoted in a circle and finally caught sight of an older man with a long white beard waving at her. "I have to go now." She ran three steps, then turned and threw herself at Callie's legs, wrapping chubby arms around her thighs and giving her a tight hug.

The girl's sticky hands sent a warm, sweet feeling into Callie's heart. She thought of saying something, but before she could translate her emotions into words, Mary had knelt in the grass and hugged Max around his neck.

"In case I don't see you before you go," she whispered to the Labrador. Then like the imp she was, she flew away, across the lawn.

"Her grandfather?" Callie asked, nodding toward the older man who welcomed Mary into his arms.

"Yes, Deborah's father."

"And you're a doctor?"

"I am. You are Miss Callie, I take it."

Nearly choking on her drink, Callie lowered the glass and offered her right hand. "I've completely forgotten my manners. Callie Harper, from Houston, Texas. More recently the shop owner of Daisy's Quilt Shop."

"So you are Daisy Powell's niece. I'm sorry for your loss. Daisy was a sweet woman and an important part of our town."

"She was a dear, and I'm learning how much she meant to Shipshewana." Callie walked slowly to an oak rocker sitting in the shade of the front porch. She was a little surprised when the doctor followed her, but found she didn't mind the company.

Some of the families with younger children were starting to leave. Others were settling down on blankets or in the small groupings of chairs—resting from the afternoon's games.

"You're the doctor here in town?"

"Not exactly," Bernie said.

Just then the boys returned from a second round of baseball, Matthew still pushing Aaron in his wheelchair.

"I've been coming here for years." Bernie said. "To see about Aaron. I feel like one of the family now. They've all become very special to me, and Aaron—well Aaron is an extraordinary child."

"So you're not a regular doctor?"

"No. I'm what some people call a disease chaser."

Callie took a sip of her lemonade, then set it down on the floor of the porch. "I don't understand. Why would you chase a disease?"

⁓

Deborah had kept an eye on Callie all afternoon. She wasn't surprised that she got on so well with everyone. Callie struck her as a people person—at times uncomfortable with shows of emotion like hugs or a hand laid across her arm, but still a people person. She couldn't help wondering if in her other life, in her Texas life, she'd built a kind of box around herself to protect her heart from the hurt of her losses. For some reason Callie reminded her of the box turtle the twins had found down by the pond.

The turtle had huddled inside his shell for nearly a week, only coming out to eat when no one was around. Eventually though he'd learned to trust the boys, when he was sure it was safe, when he was sure his environment was a place that wouldn't harm him.

Was it the same for Callie?

Now that she was in Shipshe, would she stay out of her box? She certainly seemed completely different than the woman she'd met that first morning.

And at first she looked at ease sitting on the porch with Dr. Bernie. Deborah noted the moment Callie set down her glass of lemonade, hugged her arms around herself, and stared off into the distance. She'd seen that posture before—when she'd first met her outside Daisy's Quilt Shop and again when they'd left the police station.

So what had upset Miss Callie this time?

Deborah glanced over to make sure baby Joshua was doing fine, which he was. Currently he was being passed from one *onkel* to another, being spoiled rotten by each of them. An article had come out in one of the English magazines just last week about how the Amish didn't treasure their children, perhaps because they didn't indulge their every wish. Deborah only knew about it because one of the women who shopped in the bakery where her sister worked had brought it in, upset that they were being raked through the English press once again.

Deborah wished those writers could spend one afternoon watching her youngest son being passed from loving arms to loving arms. She'd yet to hold him herself, and her mother's heart ached a bit at that thought. Soon he would be like the twins, off chasing frogs and playing baseball.

Soon he wouldn't tolerate her kisses.

Shaking away the motherly thoughts, she picked up a platter of cookies and headed to the front porch.

"I've actually been doing this for quite some time," the doctor was saying. "I find it more rewarding than working in a large city setting."

"What is it that you do — exactly?" Callie looked up as Deborah walked up the porch steps.

"A disease chaser looks for folks with rare diseases in the hopes of being able to find them, help them, and thereby help other people."

"And Aaron is one of those people?"

Doc Bernie began to stand from his rocker, but Deborah motioned for him to stay seated. She offered them the cookies, then sat next to the steps, resting her back against the porch column.

"Yes, Aaron is," Bernie admitted.

"I don't understand why you had to search for him." Callie tucked her hair behind her ears, and looked from the doctor to Deborah.

Bernie pulled a pipe out of his front pocket and began gesturing with it. Deborah had yet to see the man actually light it, but he seemed to find comfort in holding it. "While the Amish community does use medical facilities, they're less eager to do so. More often they'll wait and see if a condition improves on its own, and since they don't participate in insurance programs, the entire process is different."

Deborah watched as Callie processed all she was hearing. Somewhere in the back of her mind, she had known that Callie would see Aaron if she came to the luncheon today; there was no keeping a child like Aaron secret. And why should they? Aaron was a precious gift from God.

Still, by the look on Callie's face, she wondered if today had been too soon. After all, she'd only known Melinda for less than two weeks.

"Did Melinda and Noah wait to seek medical help?" Callie leaned forward in the rocker.

Doc Bernie glanced at Deborah. She took that as a signal he would rather she answer this question.

"They didn't, not really." Deborah set the plate of cookies on the porch beside her, folded her hands in her lap. "Aaron was a small baby, but fairly normal. Then when he was about a month old his *grossmammi* noticed that his body would shiver uncontrollably."

"Not unusual in a baby with nemaline myopathy," Doc Bernie added, then stuck the pipe in his mouth.

"The Amish call it chicken breast disease. I had never seen it before, but Melinda's grandparents moved here from Pennsylvania. The disease is somewhat more prevalent there."

Callie's frown deepened. "It sounds ... terrible. Chicken breast disease?"

"The common name, because the variant found among the Amish causes the sternum to rise straight up from the chest symmetrically, making the breastbone more prominent."

"But he was playing baseball." Callie's eyes sought out the two boys, found them sharing watermelon in a group of children near the tables of food.

"Matthew wheels him out there, hands him a glove. The children are good about involving Aaron as much as possible." Deborah didn't look away when Callie's eyes bore into hers.

"Is he all right?"

Doc Bernie smiled. "Aaron is a very stubborn young man."

"And God is *gut*," Deborah added quietly.

"But what exactly is my-opia ..."

"Myopathy. It's an inherited muscular disorder. Aaron's *grossmammi* saved his life by recognizing it so early—"

"And then the bishop found out about Dr. Bernie and his work here in Indiana."

"So he doesn't need to be in a hospital?"

"They couldn't do for him in a large urban medical facility much more than what we are doing right here. Melinda and Noah feel—and I agree—that Aaron belongs with his family. Aaron lacks a structural protein. We treat that by giving him a drug called albuterol. It seems to be working."

"But he's in a wheelchair." Callie again hugged her arms around her middle.

Doc Bernie removed the pipe, stuck it back into his shirt pocket. "Most children with this type of nemaline myopathy don't live past the age of two. Aaron's quite the exception, and we have every reason to believe he'll continue to grow and improve."

The conversation eventually turned to other things as they were joined first by Esther, then her parents who were carrying Leah.

Within the hour, Callie stood and began saying her good byes.

Deborah and Mary walked her to her car.

"I'm so glad you came."

"I am too." Callie hesitated before opening her car door. "Why didn't you tell me about Aaron?"

Deborah looked into her new friend's eyes, then glanced out over the small groups of people that remained around her home, Melinda and Esther among them.

"I don't know, Callie. It seems everyone has their hurts. I didn't mean to keep anything from you, but I didn't want to overwhelm you either. Do you want me to write out a report of all the ailments in our community and bring it by in the morning?" She aimed for casual, but knew her words fell short.

"We're in business together, Deborah — the four of us, you, myself, Melinda, and Esther. I would have liked to know."

"Would it have made a difference? Would you have auctioned the quilts for more or changed the terms of the contract?"

"No, of course not. It's just — "

"Just what?" Deborah moved now so that she was standing directly in front of her.

"I would have liked to know. I feel so badly ..."

"Callie, she doesn't want pity."

"I didn't mean that."

"And yet pity is everyone's first reaction, and it does her no good. She doesn't want it and neither does Aaron. Would you?"

"Would I?"

"Would you want people feeling sorry for you?"

Callie drew back, busied herself with putting Max in the car. "No, of course not. That's not what I meant though."

"She's the same person she was before. We have the same agreement we had before, and I'm sure you'll do as good a job as you would have done." Deborah smiled at her as Callie shut the door, buckled the seat belt, and rolled down the window.

"Why are you smiling?" Callie asked.

"Here less than a month and you're starting to care about everyone. You are very much like your aunt."

Callie glanced into her rearview mirror and her worried expression changed to a slight smile, then a full-blown grin.

173

It did Deborah's heart good to see that Callie was settling in so well.

Callie pulled her sunglasses down a tad against the setting sun, and said, "I do care, Deborah. Especially about those sweet twins of yours."

"My twins?"

"Beautiful boys. In fact, I think I just saw them running back behind the barn chasing several of Jonas's pigs. At least it looked like them. Hard to tell with all the mud covering them from head to toe."

Chapter 18

DEBORAH WAS STANDING at the kitchen sink, cleaning the last of the dishes. Jonas slipped up behind her, wrapped his arms around her waist, and snuggled her neck.

"Are all the children in bed?" she asked.

"Every last one."

"Even Joseph and Jacob?"

"Especially Joseph and Jacob."

Sighing, she slipped the last cup into the soapy dish water, twirled her dishcloth through it, then dipped it in her rinse water. "I never thought the mud would come out of their hair."

"I never thought the pigs would go back in their pen." Jonas reached past her, pulled the plug on the water, then took the dishrag from her hand and placed it over the middle of the sink.

"Looks like you're finished here. Why don't you come and sit in the swing with me?"

"Jonas Yoder. Are you serious? After washing all these dishes, and I still have darning in that basket—"

"Come." He turned her around in his arms, pulled her close, and traced her jaw line with his thumb. "The darning will wait, but the stars won't. They're beautiful tonight."

"Do not tell me you're going to use the star line."

"I will if it works."

"It always works."

"That's why I always use it." Loosening the pins from her hair, he pulled off her *kapp* and set it on the table. "Come sit outside with me."

She stood on her tiptoes, placed her still damp hands on both sides of his face, and planted a kiss on his lips. "You win. The darning will wait for another night."

As she ducked under his arms, Jonas dimmed the gas lantern to its lowest setting, then left it there on the hook over the kitchen sink.

The moment Deborah walked outside, the cool night air hit her like a welcome caress. Jonas again put his hand on her neck, under her hair, and they walked leisurely across the yard to the swing.

"It was a good day, *ya?*"

"It was. It's one of the things I like most about our life." Jonas eased himself into the swing and pulled her down close beside him. "I remember it from my own childhood. The resting on Sunday—the sermons and gathering too, but mostly that it was a day where we took a break and came together with each other. It's what I want for our children, and why I was so happy when we bought this place and were able to stay in LaGrange County."

"It's *gut* land, Jonas, and it's *gut* to be able to keep the old ways, to teach our *bopplin* the important things."

"Like how to catch pigs." Jonas's laughter moved out into the night, merging comfortably with the evening breeze.

They sat there for a few minutes, rocking, listening to the sounds of the evening birds and the crickets.

He brought it up before she did. "Miss Callie seemed to enjoy herself."

"She did." Deborah thought of the conversation on the porch with Doc Bernie, thought of Aaron, but decided not to pursue it. It was Stakehorn's murder though, that she needed to talk about.

"So what are you fretting about?"

"I'm trying to puzzle out who might have killed Stakehorn," Deborah admitted.

"You don't know it was murder, and it's not your place to figure it out even if it was."

"*Ya*, but ..." Deborah moved to shift away from him, but Jonas pulled her back.

"I'm only saying what you already know. Don't be shying away from the truth. You try to solve every puzzle, even those not in your own yard."

"But this one keeps popping up around my *freinden*. You heard about the break-in at the *Gazette*?"

"I did. Reuben was talking about it to my *daed*." Jonas pushed the swing once to keep it rocking.

"I heard it from Esther. By tomorrow everyone will know — it would be in the paper if the paper were running. Doesn't it strike you as odd that Stakehorn is found dead and then three days later someone breaks into the paper?"

Jonas took his time answering, something that bothered Deborah immensely when they were first married. Over the years, she'd learned it meant he was considering the different angles of a topic before he answered. "Could be related, I suppose. Then again, maybe it's nothing."

"How in the world would you figure that?" Deborah studied him in the darkness.

"I suppose everyone knows about Stakehorn now."

"Oh, everyone's heard. Shipshewana may be growing, but it's still a small town. Even without a funeral everyone knows."

"And that's a shame."

"The police haven't released his body yet."

"Well, they should," Jonas said. "Family should be able to bury their own."

"His family isn't even here."

177

"Heard his son is coming."

"*Ya.* I heard the same. He's never been here before though, so I'm thinking he can't be much of a son."

"Bit judgmental my *lieb.*"

Deborah sighed, realizing he was right. "I've forgotten what your point was. You distracted me."

"I was trying to say that everyone knows the *Gazette*'s office is empty. It's an easy place to vandalize."

"Mrs. Caldwell is there — but who would dare mess with her? She's tough. Trust me."

"Anyway, the break-in occurred at night — if you can believe Reuben's version, which came from Tobias."

"He's still working late nights at the feed store?"

Jonas laughed and pulled her back to his side. "I think it's a way of avoiding some of the chores and all of the younger children at home."

"But he's living at his *grossdaddi's.*"

"Still expected to show up at home and help."

"The boy needs to fall *in lieb*, marry, and get a place of his own, then he wouldn't have to avoid his parents' house."

"Know anyone you want to set him up with?"

"I do not, and you're changing the subject again."

"Which was?" Jonas began to run his fingers through her hair, massaging her scalp, neck, and shoulders as he did.

He held her hair up, allowing the breeze to cool her skin, sending a light shiver down her back. Then he started planting kisses on her neck, which Deborah did her best to ignore. "Someone broke in, then took nothing?"

"*Ya.* Have I told you how beautiful you are?"

"It's dark, Jonas."

"There's starlight. I can see your beauty in the glow of the stars."

She knew her husband well enough to guess there was a grin on his face as he teased her.

"The bishop spoke on humility just last week," she reminded him.

"You are humble—that's part of your beauty."

Deborah tried to catch the idea lurking in the corner of her mind, but Jonas's distractions were too strong. Before long he had her full attention, first in the swing, then upstairs under the quilt she'd made as a young girl, hoping to find the man of her dreams.

She did dream later—of a quilt she was piecing together, only she couldn't see the pattern. Each time she looked down at the blocks of fabric, everything in her hands was obscured as if by a cloud, but a cloud couldn't exist in her sitting room. She'd laugh and attempt to push it away, but her hand would go through the fluffiness, like batting between layers of a quilt.

In the dream, it suddenly became important that she know the pattern, that she put this one quilt together correctly. Again and again she would look up from where she sat, sewing more intensely. Once she saw Aaron outside her window, wheeling himself across her yard. She wanted to call out to him, but she couldn't. She had to stay with the quilt, had to figure out the pattern. When she looked down though, all she could see was the white of summer clouds.

Except the clouds were no longer white; they became gray, then black like the color of the sky darkening before a storm.

She woke to the sound of rain upon her roof, Jonas already gone from her bed, and with worries for Callie still dogging her thoughts.

～

Callie was learning to enjoy the routine of her weeks.

She'd taken Deborah's advice and decided to keep the shop closed on Mondays, but she enjoyed the increase in activity in the downtown area that followed Sunday's silence. Most of the shop owners around her were in their stores, stocking inventory, setting up new displays, and taking care of yard work.

Since she had on blue jeans and a brown T-shirt, she let Max choose his own bandana.

"We might be taking this coordinated thing too far," she admitted as she tied the blue one with small silver stars around his neck. She had to admit it looked nice though. Who had said dogs were color-blind? Max was proof that was an urban myth.

A few tourists strolled up and down the streets.

Mr. Simms stopped by to apologize about answering Black's questions. "I hope what I said didn't cause you trouble."

"Don't worry about it, Mr. Simms. Shane Black is turning over every rock he can find, but I've nothing to hide. I lost my temper—that's true. I didn't hurt anyone though."

"Of course you didn't, and I told Officer Black as much. He doesn't listen though. He's stubborn like an old mule. Though if it makes you feel any better, I heard he also pulled in three other people who had argued with Stakehorn in the last month. The editor had more than one enemy." The older gentleman picked up a few of the quilt flyers to place in his deli on his way out.

Several of the adjacent store owners stopped to talk to her as she added new plants to her window boxes and tacked WEEKLY SPECIAL flyers on her outdoor announcement board.

She was surprised when Deborah drove up in her buggy.

"How about we grab some lunch together?" Deborah asked after admiring the new flowers. "I wanted to run some ideas by you."

"Sure. I needed to return a few things to the General Store. Let me go inside and grab the bag."

"I can put Max in the side yard for you if you like."

Within five minutes they were standing outside the store door, ready to leave.

"I'm not complaining, but how do you manage to get away from the farm so often? I mean you do have five children."

"Are you kidding me? They have one *grossmammi* and two

grossdaddis who clamber to take care of them, not to mention all those *aentis* and *onkels*."

Callie squinted and shook her head as she locked the shop behind her. "My car or yours?"

"How about we walk?" Deborah asked.

"Um, sure." She pocketed her keys and resumed their conversation. "I've had friends with children before. They always had trouble finding sitters, and you have five children. It can't be easy."

"But with Amish families, we all live close to one another. Think about it, Callie. I come from a family of eight children, seven of us are married."

"Okay."

"Jonas comes from a family of ten."

"Yeah."

"All married except Stephen."

"So, if you don't count the in-laws ..."

"Which we do."

"I'm not great at math."

"Want a calculator?"

"Eight plus ten, minus you two equals sixteen."

"Right." Deborah smiled and stopped between the deli and The *Kaffi* Shop. "Which do you prefer for lunch?"

"Umm, either is fine, but I could probably use a bit more caffeine."

"*Kaffi* it is."

Callie continued with the math as they pushed into the shop and Deborah studied the menu board above the counter. "So sixteen, but you said two weren't married."

"One's not old enough. One's a bit stubborn."

"Okay. So fourteen times two equals twenty-eight." She'd grabbed a napkin from the counter and was jotting down the math now. "Plus the two hold-outs who aren't married equals thirty aunts and uncles?"

"Ya, and they all live close and all have cousins who want play dates."

Callie turned and stared at her in amazement. "What is Christmas like with your family?"

"Very special, very holy, and a time we spend with our families. You'd have to see to understand."

"I suppose you do need two days for the holiday with so many people. How many gifts do you have to buy?"

"We usually give handmade things, and then only one or two items even for our closest family. No, holidays are simply different for the Amish."

Callie shook her head, as they turned their attention to ordering.

"Gudemariye," Deborah said.

"Actually it's afternoon." Margie, the woman who owned The *Kaffi* Shop, had bright red hair cut in a spiky fashion. "Good to see you Deborah, Callie."

Deborah turned and looked curiously at Callie. "You come here often?"

"Oh, Callie's become quite the regular." Margie smiled. "I believe she needs the caffeine."

Callie focused on ordering her lunch. "Could be that I was a bit used to a certain coffee chain."

"No Starbucks in Shipshewana," Margie explained.

"Starbucks?"

"Strong coffee."

"Don't forget they have wireless," Callie muttered.

"We have wireless." Margie grinned.

"Which is why I come so often."

"She's here so often, we allow her to bring Max inside."

"How do you manage to come at all?" Deborah shook her head in disbelief. "I don't see how you have a free minute what with all the time you put in at the shop."

"A girl has to eat. I come in the evenings after the shop closes, force myself to get away from work for an hour or so. I learned at my last job ..." Callie hesitated, then pushed on. "I learned that it doesn't pay to be married to your work. An hour off here and there is healthy. I didn't do that before, and I paid a steep price."

"Sounds as if your last employment wasn't a good situation."

"No. No, it wasn't." Callie looked around her, half expecting to see copies of the *Houston Chronicle* and the *Wall Street Journal*. When she glanced out the window though there was only a few tourists, two buggies, and a Honda Accord Hybrid. There wasn't even a pickup truck in sight. "This shop is the one thing that feels familiar. Everything else seems so alien—not at all what I'm accustomed to. I still feel as if I've settled on a different planet."

"We all feel that way sometimes, sweetie." Margie smiled, took her order, then handed her a receipt and change. "Don't worry. It gets easier with time."

"I've told her the same, Margie."

They chose a booth near the window, looking out over the old train station. Callie pushed her large plastic shopping bag with SHOP SHIPSHEWANA emblazoned on the front across the seat.

"What's in the bag?" Deborah asked.

"I had purchased some things for Max, then I found Daisy had most everything. It was all in a cupboard in her apartment."

"You're a very good niece—caring for her dog, taking over the shop ..."

"The shop is still for sale," Callie reminded her.

"I know. I'm just saying, I think Daisy would be proud of you."

Callie didn't speak for a moment, focusing instead on stirring the whip cream topping into her coffee while Deborah sipped her iced tea. Then she looked up, a grin splitting her face. *"Danki,"* she said.

"And your mastery of the Amish language is truly amazing."

"Next week I'll teach you Texan."

"Texas has a different language?" Deborah's eyes widened, and Callie realized she could have a lot of fun with this.

"Absolutely." She cocked her head sideways, then pointed to the music speakers which were currently sporting a wonderfully familiar George Strait tune. "Do those words make sense to you?"

"Not at all."

"Texan. That's what I'm talking about. Now, back to your kids. You've convinced me it's not a problem for you to get away when you want."

"No. It's not. But then you might stop by and find me with ten *bopplin* instead of my usual five."

Callie held up her hands, palms out. "Stop. I don't even want to envision it. At this point, Max is the most I can handle." She took a deep drink of the coffee and smiled in satisfaction. The coffee shop was becoming a place of refuge for her, country music and all.

"How would you like to help me out part-time in the shop?"

Deborah placed her napkin in her lap, seemed to choose her words carefully. "I'd love to, but I wouldn't be dependable enough. While it's true I can get away from the house often, other times I'll have *bopplin* cutting teeth or one with a cold. Then I need to be home for a week at a time."

Callie dug back into her salad. "I figured you might say that, but I also have realized I'm going to need some help."

"You should hire one of the Amish girls in town. They're very dependable."

"Have anyone particular in mind?"

Deborah pulled a napkin toward her and began writing down names and phone numbers. "Remember those cousins I told you about?"

"Wait. How do they have phones?"

"Many are in their *rumspringa* and have cell phones, but we're not supposed to know about it."

"We?"

"Adults, *aentis*, *onkels*, parents." Deborah pressed on. "These are *gut* girls though. They will be good employees for you."

Callie stuffed the list into her purse.

"So what did you want to talk to me about?" Callie asked.

"Did you hear about the break-in at the *Gazette*?"

"I did. Several people mentioned it yesterday, and the owner of Yesterday's Pansies came over and talked to me about it this morning."

"What did you think about it?"

"I didn't, really."

"Just seems a bit odd."

"Probably someone heard the building was empty. Didn't Stakehorn used to live out back of the place? Which is a little creepy since I live over Daisy's Quilt Shop."

"I wouldn't worry, honey." Margie set their sandwiches down in front of them. "I heard it was kids."

"*Ya*, that's what Jonas thought too." Deborah stared down at her sandwich.

"Should stop now that the new editor is in town."

Chapter 19

DEBORAH'S GAZE locked with Callie's.

"New editor?" they asked at the same time.

"So I heard this morning." Margie said. "My daughter saw it on someone's Facebook page. Of course, I don't use those things. I only use the internet to check my email and catch the news occasionally, but apparently someone knows someone who knows the brother of this person who's coming. He was due to arrive this morning."

Margie looked pleased with her bullet-proof information. Deborah waited until Margie had moved away before she leaned forward. "What are you thinking?"

Callie popped a mini muffin into her mouth. "We go see the new editor. We might be able to get that retraction."

They sat smiling at each other as the noon-day rush began to pick up in The *Kaffi* Shop.

"Oh!" Deborah said. "More good news: Bishop Elam has allowed us to leave the three quilts on eBay. I don't know if he'll approve additional ones though. He's still thinking on it."

"First auction ends today."

Deborah relaxed for the first time in weeks. The quilt sale could continue, Callie was staying—at least for now—and the newspaper would soon be back in business. Maybe everything would return to normal. After they finished eating their meal, Callie dug around in her purse, apparently pulling out change for a tip. She didn't see Shane Black pull up outside the little shop and get out of his Buick, but Deborah did, and she didn't like the look on his face.

It was an expression she'd seen before.

The door to The *Kaffi* Shop opened. Black glanced around the booths, zeroed in on theirs, and began walking toward them.

"Callie—"

Callie zipped the change holder on her wallet shut. "What is it?"

"Mrs. Yoder. Miss Harper."

Callie's face froze the moment she heard Black's voice, before she even looked up. Placing her wallet carefully in her purse, she pulled the strap over her shoulder, then turned toward him. "Officer Black."

"I'm going to need you to come with me, Miss Harper."

"Oh, no you don't. We're not doing this again."

"I'm afraid we are, sweetheart. And it would be better if you don't make a scene."

"I'll make a scene all right, because I'm not going with you. How did you even find me here? Are you following us now?"

"Don't flatter yourself. I asked around and folks saw you walking down Main."

"I'm not going with you," Callie repeated.

Deborah watched the exchange in horror, dread rising in her like a fever. She knew firsthand that arguing with Shane Black was pointless. One could win against him slowly, with other means, like water dripping against a rock ... but when he showed up like this, bent on something, there was no changing his mind.

"Maybe you should go with him, Callie. I'll get Adalyn."

"No. I won't do it." Callie shook her head and scooted to the far side of the bench, reminding Deborah of her oldest child Martha when she was younger and didn't want to take her bath. "You can't make me."

Shane didn't look away, didn't appear embarrassed or perturbed, but he did lean forward slightly and lower his voice. "I can make you, Miss Harper, and I will if you insist. Do you want me to handcuff you and drag you out of here?"

"You wouldn't dare," she hissed, her face turning a bright red.

"I'd actually enjoy it."

He had to jump back, she came out of the booth so quickly. "Well, don't put yourself out, Officer Black. I wouldn't want you to have to exert yourself." Callie paused only long enough to toss her store keys to Deborah. Instead of going quietly, she stormed out of the shop, waiting by the back door of his Buick, looking as if she might kick the tires or begin slamming her purse against the windows.

Deborah noticed that several people walking by spoke to her, but Callie appeared not to hear. While Black was unlocking the door and waiting for her to get inside, Mr. Simms, the owner of The Deli, walked outside. Deborah heard him ask if everything was all right.

Shane told him to go back into his store. Then the officer drove away, toward the station.

Deborah grabbed her own bag and headed for the door.

"Why did he do that?" Margie demanded. "What was Shane Black thinking?"

"I don't know. I need to run to Adalyn Landt's office. She can help Callie. She'll want to be at the station as soon as she can."

"All right." The woman began stacking dishes from their table haphazardly while still watching out the window.

Deborah was pushing her way out the door, when Margie called out to her. "Oh, wait. Callie forgot her shopping bag." She dropped the dishes back onto the table with a clatter, picked up the large shopping bag, and rushed toward the front door of the shop.

"Can you keep it for her? One of us will return to pick it up later."

"Yes, sure. I'll put it behind the counter. You come back when you can. And call me if you need anything—use the station phone."

Deborah was on the street, eyeing the crowd that was still staring at Shane's Buick, when she realized what Margie had just said. She turned and hurried back into the shop. "On second thought, could you call Adalyn for me? Her number's in the book."

"Absolutely."

"*Danki.*" Deborah reached up, making sure her *kapp* was firmly in place. She had the sense that things were moving quickly now, that she might miss something if she weren't careful. "I need to go back to The Quilt Shop and check on Max, then get my buggy. If you could call Adalyn and tell her what happened, tell her Shane took Callie to the station. She'll know what to do."

"Of course I will. You go on, dear."

Deborah walked back outside and straight into Mr. Simms, the owner of the deli. She had to pause and assure him that Callie would be fine.

"Why is Officer Black bothering her? He should be looking for the man who killed Stakehorn, and whoever broke into the newspaper on Friday night."

"They're saying it was just children who broke in, Mr. Simms."

Mr. Simms swept the walk a little harder than was necessary. "Children would not know how to break into a business without busting the lock, now would they?"

"I suppose you're right."

"You go and help Miss Callie. The police should not be harassing the shop owners of Shipshewana."

"Yes, Mr. Simms."

Deborah hurried down the street, thinking that it seemed Callie had made quite a few friends in the short time she'd been in town.

The gawkers dispersed as she walked through the heat, hurried up the walk, and unlocked the door to Daisy's Quilt Shop. She felt as if eyes were on her, but surely that was her imagination. Curiosity was natural; after all, it wasn't every day that a person was picked up by Shane Black on the streets of Shipshewana.

At least the new editor would have plenty to write about.

~

He stood across the street milling among the group of people watching the short brunette get into the unmarked car with the cop.

"What a shame," one of the dames with a bonnet on her head muttered.

"You know Callie Harper had nothing to do with killing Stakehorn." This from a man with a long beard and a black hat like he had seen in an old movie once. These people all looked liked they stepped out of a Hollywood set. Why his boss had picked Shipshewana, Indiana, for the site was beyond him, but then it wasn't his place to question the boss or his plan.

His place was to clean up the mess, and that was exactly what he meant to do.

"I was in Daisy's Quilt Shop last Saturday. She's fixed the place up as cute as ever." This from a young woman who was at least dressed halfway normal, though she wore a doily on her head.

"Well, it might be cute, but it's *different.*" The last word was pronounced by an old biddy as if it tasted poisonous.

The thought brought a smile to his lips.

He pretended to study his map of downtown merchants as the little crowd watched the vintage Buick drive slowly down Main Street.

"Different isn't always bad, Thelma."

"Say what you want, but in my opinion she had no right putting those quilts on the in-ter-net." Thelma said *in-ter-net* as if it were three different words. Though she wasn't dressed in old-fashioned clothes, obviously she'd never used Twitter or tweeted.

The BlackBerry in his pocket vibrated, but he ignored the text. It was more important that he listened to the local gossip.

"Wasn't a crime to sell the quilts that way," the man in the hat piped in. "Whether you agree with it or not."

"No, I suppose it wasn't." Thelma sniffed and pulled her pocketbook closer to her side, as if she suspected someone of stealing it. No one had even glanced at him, but then he was standing under the shade of the tree, studying his map, supposedly ignoring them. "Folks who have strange ways, there's no telling what they're capable of."

One or two seemed to agree with her. A few shook their heads as if they were tolerating her odd ideas, but they were exactly that—odd.

He wondered what they'd say if they knew who was standing in their midst, exactly what he was capable of and the things he had done.

They wouldn't know though.

He'd clean things up, reclaim the boss's package, and head out of town. They'd never be one bit wiser.

If the brunette took the fall, so be it.

The crowd began to disperse, so he walked on down the sidewalk, pretending to be interested in the wares offered in the various windows.

He'd heard and seen enough.

Time to call the boss.

Harper had taken a bag identical to the one he was supposed to pick up—large, plastic, with the words SHOP SHIPSHE-WANA—into The *Kaffi* Shop.

A bag just like the one Stakehorn had found. If the man had handed it over, he wouldn't have died, but apparently he'd decided to pass it off to someone else.

This Harper dame?

And now she'd given it to the owner of The *Kaffi* Shop. Maybe these people weren't as backward as they looked. They recognized quality goods when they saw them. Knew a once in a lifetime opportunity when it showed up in their little town.

No doubt there were hundreds of bags exactly like it around Shipshewana, but he didn't believe in coincidences. He'd seen Harper with Stakehorn.

Stakehorn had taken what belonged to the boss.

It was time for him to take it back.

He hadn't found it in the *Gazette* on Friday night.

Tonight he'd try again.

Chapter 20

CALLIE SEETHED ALL THE WAY TO THE POLICE STATION.

Each time Black looked into the rearview mirror she glowered at him. This was nothing like the first time. Oh, she was shaking the same — but it was from anger instead of fear.

How dare he take her in again?

In front of everyone *again*! At this point she'd soon have her own locker at the police station.

When Black opened the door and motioned for her to go first, she couldn't stop the smart remark. "I think I remember the way."

The dark eyebrows arched up, but still he said nothing. It infuriated her, made her want to stomp her feet on the steps of Shipshewana Police Department, but she resisted. She would not give him the satisfaction of a tantrum. No doubt he expected one.

She passed Andrew Gavin heading out as she walked in. Whatever was going on, he knew about it. He met her eyes, but said nothing. His gaze lingered, locked with hers, and Callie realized there was something there she didn't want to see. Disappointment?

But why? She hadn't done anything.

Black picked up a case folder from the girl working the desk as he ushered her into the same interrogation room—same freshly painted white walls, same drab metal table, same three chairs.

The only thing that gave her any comfort was knowing Adalyn would soon occupy one.

As if Black read her thoughts, he dropped the file folder on the table and perched on the edge of a chair. "Before your lawyer gets here, how about you tell me where you got the poison?"

"What?"

"Come on, Harper. You know how this works. Smart city gal like you, bet you watch all the crime shows—*CSI, Law and Order*, and old reruns of *Murder, She Wrote*." He paused to offer a smile, but it wasn't genuine. It was sad, and seemed almost filled with regret. "Things work differently in small towns though. We're more like Max hunting a bird. We don't let go until we catch our man—or woman."

"Is this supposed to intimidate me, Officer Black?" Callie leaned well across the halfway point of the table though she had to scootch to the end of her chair to do it. "I don't know what you're talking about."

"Sure you want to play it that way?" The black in his eyes turned to steel, and it occurred to Callie that here was an adversary she didn't want to cross if she didn't have to.

So why did she have to?

He opened the file.

A picture of Stakehorn, laid out on a morgue slab, was stapled to the left. On the right was one of those two prong fasteners she hadn't seen since she used to go into her father's engineering office and help his receptionist with the filing during the summer. The top sheet was a toxicology report.

"How long did you think it would take us to learn that you were a pharmaceutical rep?"

"What?"

"That you have a degree in bio-medical science?"

"But—"

"In fact, you graduated cum laude."

"I didn't think—"

"Clearly."

"What difference does it make?"

"Maybe because Stakehorn was killed with poison."

Callie felt the salad in her stomach tumble and turn sour.

"Maybe because the poison used was something any pharmaceutical rep would have access to." Black stood, walked around the table, and moved behind her chair, leaning in until his voice was just inches from her ear—a voice that was no longer loud, but had instead become a whisper. "Maybe because now you have more than motive—you have access to the substance used to commit murder."

The scene flashed back in her memory as her fingers gripped the edge of the metal table. Stakehorn at his desk, his face pale, lifeless. His hand reaching out over the stack of papers. Brown liquid on the floor...

Callie's hand came up, covered her mouth, even as her pulse thudded through her veins. "It was in his coffee."

"Okay. We're getting somewhere. When did you put it in his coffee?" Black walked back around the table, sat down opposite her, and waited.

"No. I didn't do it. You know I didn't even get there until he was already dead."

"How would I know that?" Black sat back, crossed his arms, and waited.

"Most poisons would have broken down in a hot liquid. It would have had to been administered fairly quickly ..."

"Say by the person who made his cup of coffee?"

Callie had recovered her equilibrium. Now her mind was back at the university, back in the classroom and the textbooks. She barely heard Black or the accusatory note in his voice.

"Depending on what the substance was, the person could have stirred it in his coffee and handed it to him, but only a few pharmaceuticals wouldn't have a bitter taste." Callie sat back, mirroring Black's posture. "And as I said, the chemicals would have broken down in the hot, acidic liquid quickly. Unless he drank at least half the cup, he would have become sick, likely very sick, but he wouldn't have died from it."

"From what?"

"Any number of things. Atropine is deadly. Anyone could have access to it. The common plant is called nightshade."

Callie noticed he didn't take notes.

"Many ordinary seeds are toxic — cherries, potatoes, peaches, and apple seeds. This information is available on the net, Shane." She liked using his first name, liked the way it made her feel he didn't have the superior hand here.

"Or in a bio-med class."

Narrowing her eyes, Callie forced her voice to remain steady. "Surely even you know that the castor bean is the deadliest plant poison on earth."

His relaxed pose was infuriating her.

"One tiny castor bean is enough to kill an adult within a few minutes. Instead of questioning me, maybe you should be checking people's gardens." When he still didn't answer, she snatched at the folder. "What does your report say? What killed him?"

"Inconclusive, sweetheart." Black slapped the folder shut. "Thanks for the toxicology lesson though. Now if you'll sign a confession stating exactly how you did it, we can move on to the next phase of this investigation."

Callie's temper spiked at the same time her hand came down on top of his, on top of the folder, surprising them both. "I didn't do it. You know I didn't do it."

"Because you say you didn't?"

"Check your autopsy report again." Callie pulled the folder

out from under his hand and threw it across the table at him. "Does it or doesn't it show toxic levels of poison?"

An impenetrable mask covered Black's features. "I'm the one asking questions here, Miss Harper."

"Maybe Stakehorn ingested some, but I seriously doubt he swallowed enough to kill him. He might have taken enough to induce a coronary." Callie shook her head. "I don't know. Check with his doctor. See who knew enough about him and who had access to the drugs."

"Pharmaceutical reps have access to samples. Samples of the wrong drug would have been enough. Samples of the wrong drug—possibly something meant to make it look like a natural herb ..." Black's voice was a low growl, though his expression remained impassive.

"Shane, think about it. I barely knew this man. I had no reason to want him dead."

"You had every reason. According to witnesses, you did. Shall we go back over their testimony again?"

Callie waved away the sheets he was flipping through.

"How long had he been dead when I arrived?" she asked.

"Why did you move to Shipshewana?"

"What?" Why was he changing the topic when they were clearly on to something?

"You hadn't seen your aunt in over fifteen years, then you suddenly come back because she died. You suddenly quit your job and moved here. Why?"

"What's that have to do with anything?"

"Was Daisy Powell really your aunt? Would you be willing to submit to a lie detector test? Offer a DNA sample?"

"You're completely insane. Is this even about Stakehorn's murder?"

"Of course it is. Why did you put poison in his coffee?"

Callie took a deep breath, tried to push away the absurd

questions he'd just thrown at her. "What substance was in it? Maybe I can help you. Maybe I can help your investigation and together we can find who did this."

"I don't need your help, sweetheart. I need your confession." Black stood, both hands braced against the table, leaning toward her, the wolf-smile playing on his lips.

"And I'm telling you I have nothing to confess." Callie stood as well, though the top of her head didn't reach his chin. She wasn't about to take his accusations sitting down.

She didn't care about the one-way mirror, or the gun he was wearing, or the scowl on his face.

This was absurd.

She had not killed a man she barely knew.

Shane Black bullying her wouldn't change that fact.

Adalyn walked in and found them that way.

"My. Looks like I'm missing out on all the fun." Adalyn didn't bother with preliminaries, simply took her seat beside Callie and began pulling out a pad of paper, pen, and tape recorder from her bag.

This time the Louis Vuitton was a summer white. The sight of it temporarily snapped Callie out of her battle with Black.

Where did Adalyn purchase her handbags? They weren't briefcases exactly. They were incredibly stylish. How did she afford them? Everything else about the woman screamed fiscal responsibility. The bags—they were a thing of beauty.

She locked eyes with Adalyn, and the lawyer smiled, nearly winked.

"Ladies? Hello? Did I lose you? Some sort of secret ESP going on? Because I have a murder investigation I'd like to wrap up if you two are finished grinning at one another." For the first time since she'd known him, real irritation and bewilderment filled Black's voice.

Adalyn clicked the ON button so that the micro-recorder

began whirling, and she gestured with her right hand. "By all means, Shane. Go right ahead and investigate."

"Tell me about your concealed handgun license, Miss Harper."

"Why, was he shot?"

Adalyn laughed and wrote on her pad, "Good, girl."

"So you admit you have one," Shane continued.

"Of course I have one."

"Why?"

"Why not?"

Shane switched tactics. "How long have you had it?"

"Since I was twenty-two."

"What type of weapon do you own?"

"None of your business."

Adalyn placed a check by her earlier comment.

"Don't you find it unusual for a woman to have a concealed permit?"

"Not where I come from, Officer Black. Does it intimidate you for a woman to be able to defend herself?"

"Did you bring your weapon with you to Indiana?"

"I did not."

"You can prove that?"

"I flew. You can check with the airlines. They tend to be itchy about such things."

He continued in the same vein for another thirty minutes, ending with a warning that she remain in the Shipshewana area.

"I own a shop here. Where would I go?"

"Just wouldn't want you to have any ideas about running home to Texas. I'd hate to have to come looking for you."

"Are you threatening me?"

Adalyn reached out and put her hand on Callie's arm. "Next time you need to speak with my client, call her or myself. Pick her up again, with no more than this, and I'll file a harassment charge."

Black made an annoying sound, but Adalyn paused long enough to let him know she was serious.

"It might not stick, Shane, but it will bury you in paperwork."

This time when they stepped out into the afternoon, storm clouds were building in the north.

"I'll give you a ride home. Wouldn't want you to get caught in a downpour."

"Thanks. Couldn't ask for much more than a lawyer who's free and provides taxi service."

Callie filled Adalyn in on the first part of the interrogation until they'd rounded the corner on Main Street.

"He's still fishing, Callie, and he's trying to intimidate you. I've known Shane Black since he was the star pitcher in LaGrange County. He could throw a fast ball better than anyone before or since, but the real secret in Shane's game was the way he could stare a batter down." She patted her on the arm as she pulled in front of Daisy's Quilt Shop. "Look, Max is glad to see you."

"Thank you, Adalyn."

"You're welcome, dear. If you come up with any ideas on the poison angle, email or call me. Otherwise let's meet on Thursday for lunch and see if there have been any other developments."

～

Deborah watched Callie exit Adalyn's car. She'd been gone less than an hour, but it seemed much longer.

Deborah rushed out into the side yard, reached Callie at the same moment Max did. "How are you?"

"I'm fine."

"He didn't—"

"What?"

Deborah laughed. "I don't know. I suppose I was afraid he might keep you there or something."

Callie sank onto the bench. "He has no evidence, just a lot of hunches—which are wrong."

Deborah rested a hand on her shoulder. "You stay here with Max. Catch your breath. I'll go back and finish stocking for tomorrow."

"No, you need to get home. I'm sure baby Joshua is ready for his *mamm*."

Smiling, Deborah gave Max a firm pat on the head. "Joshua is fine. My *schweschder* stopped in earlier and said she'd left him with her oldest girl. He'd had his lunch and was napping. Take your time here. Rest."

Thirty minutes later, Callie was inside, explaining about the poison, about her job in Houston, and about how Black had connected the two.

"Because you had the knowledge doesn't mean you did it."

"Tell that to Black."

"He has to investigate every possibility. It's his job."

Callie stopped refilling the thread display. "How exactly do you know so much about him?"

Deborah didn't answer, and Callie pushed harder. "It was a criminal matter, wasn't it? But I thought the Amish don't pursue matters in court."

"I can't speak to you of this, Callie." Deborah's brown eyes looked directly into Callie's dark ones as she spoke.

She wanted to be honest, but she couldn't give Callie the details about Esther she wanted. Just remembering those days brought tears to her eyes. She looked up at the ceiling, prayed for wisdom, then refocused on Callie.

"It's not my place to share what happened, and I won't. But I can tell you he operates within the English law. He is quite persistent. He follows a thing through to the end, and won't let it go until he's sure he knows the answer. Whether that is a good thing or a bad thing is hard to know."

"So you're warning me about him?" Callie sat back on her haunches.

"I don't know if warning is the correct word. I will pray that God leads Shane onto a different path, onto the path of the killer, because I know you didn't do this."

"In my past, praying hasn't been very effective," Callie said softly. "It feels as if everything is falling to pieces. As if my life is one of those old quilts I found in Daisy's closets — one I have no idea how to restore."

Deborah didn't argue. She merely leaned forward, hugged her, and whispered, "We will pray diligently."

"Perhaps while we're praying we should start looking for the real killer ourselves."

Deborah began gathering up her things. "I can't say that I know what a killer would look like," she teased. "But I can certainly ask around about any suspicious-looking persons."

"And I'll keep my ears open here in the store. I also think I'll pay a visit to the new editor."

Deborah stopped with her hand on the door. "You're not still worried about him printing a retraction, are you?"

"Honestly, not so much." Callie stepped closer as an English woman and child paused outside the store to study the window display. "But Deborah, if Stakehorn was murdered, and then someone broke into the shop, it could be that the new editor is in danger. We should at least warn him."

"I'm sure the police warned him."

"They probably warned him about *me*. I didn't do it. He needs to know someone else is out there, and that they might be after him next."

"*Ya.* You might be right."

"Or maybe the new editor could find a clue in the print shop as to what actually happened."

"Callie, the police went all over the print shop looking for evidence."

"I know they did, but police can miss things that someone with an eye for the news will find." She shrugged and pushed her friend out the door. "Go home to your *bopplin*."

"You promise to be careful?"

"Yes, of course. Kiss the baby for me."

It wasn't until she was in her buggy and traveling out of town, that Deborah remembered about the bag Callie had left in The *Kaffi* Shop.

Chapter 21

DEBORAH DIDN'T go straight home.

It wasn't yet three, and her *schweschder* Miriam had said she didn't need to pick up the children until five. If she hurried, she had enough time to stop and see Tobias and Reuben.

If Jonas's information was accurate, Tobias helped with the fields at their *grossdaddi's* place during the day, caught a brief nap in the afternoon, then pulled the late night shift at the feed store most weeknights. She should be able to catch him before he left for town.

Pulling up at the old farm house, she put her hand to her mouth to stifle a laugh. It looked as if the two men weren't bothering to put much work into the old place. In fact, as she walked up the steps of the old farmhouse that were in sore need of repair, she began to wonder if she'd misunderstood Jonas. Peeking in the front window, she saw a few pieces of furniture, but they had old bed sheets covering them.

Tobias and Reuben stayed here?

Spinning in a circle she studied the fields.

They looked well tended enough.

Then her eyes landed on the barn.

The windows near the door were clean. A clothesline peeped

out from behind the back corner of the building, and she could just make out pants and a shirt flapping in the breeze.

She glanced at the northern sky where the clouds were building. The clothes would get wet from the storm darkening the skies if they weren't brought in soon.

She made sure Cinnamon was settled, then hurried around the corner of the barn and began removing the clothing. Her arms were full and she was unfastening the last shirt when Tobias appeared from the back door of the barn.

"Deborah? What? What are you doing out here?"

Tobias was tall, easily six and a half feet, and skinny as a pole. He hurried to help her, one hand holding his straw hat on his head, the other taking the bulk of the clothes from her arms.

He motioned her toward the door of the barn. When she stepped inside, she looked around in amazement.

"You're living here?"

Reuben stepped through a doorway that was cut into a partition, separating the barn neatly into two halves. The complete opposite of his cousin, he was closer to Jonas's height — maybe five foot eight — and solidly built.

"*Ya. Gut* idea, right? We figured why keep both places clean, when we spend most of our times out here anyway."

Deborah closed her eyes, considered arguing with them, then realized their sisters had probably already given it a good try. Why bother? "Closer to your woodwork too."

"Exactly. Step through the door and I can work on an order or check on an animal." Reuben and Tobias smiled at one another.

"Want some *kaffi* or tea? We just finished eating an early dinner." Tobias led her through the entry room into a bigger room, which apparently served as their sleeping area and sitting area both. Beds were pushed up to the north wall, and a stove, sink, and cupboard took up the southeast corner. A square wooden table separated the two.

"*Danki*, but no. I need to head home before the rain starts."

"*Ya*, looks like it will be a *gut* storm." Reuben looked at Tobias. He was the older of the two, the one who stayed on the farm full time. He'd also recently started a small woodworking business that was doing well.

It was obvious that neither were used to having callers, so Deborah plunged right in. First she set her bag on the table and pulled out a chair. The men followed her lead.

"I came by because I wanted to talk to you about the *Gazette*."

Both men nodded. Reuben pulled on his suspenders. Tobias drummed on the table. Neither offered any information.

"About Mr. Stakehorn?" Deborah prodded.

"*Ya*, that was a terrible thing." Reuben looked to Tobias, and the younger man nodded in agreement.

"I know it was a terrible thing. What I'd like to know is what you saw, specifically."

"Well, I didn't see anything." Frowning into his *kaffi* grounds, Reuben shook his head slowly. "Nope. Haven't been into town at all this month. Been through town, when we had church meeting, but I haven't stopped in town at all."

"Reuben isn't one to go into town much. Mostly I'm the one who picks up supplies," Tobias explained.

Deborah sighed, closed her eyes again, and prayed for patience. These two had lived alone so long, they'd forgotten the art of conversation. Either that or they were being purposely slow.

Her eyes popped open.

She studied them a moment, like she would two quilt pieces that didn't want to fit together. Reuben shifted uncomfortably under her gaze. Tobias shot a glance at his cousin, but Reuben refused to meet the look. Did he put his hand up to stave off any question or comment the younger man might make? Or maybe he was reaching for his napkin. She could be imagining things at this point.

"My mistake. I thought you two might know something about the paper. My friend is having a bit of a problem, and I was hoping you could clear up some misunderstanding."

"Would be happy to help if we could," Reuben muttered.

"Sure we would," Tobias agreed.

"But we can't," Reuben added, a bit quickly.

"Well, I suppose I should be going then." Deborah stood as if she was about to leave, then paused as she looked out at her horse. "Say, Reuben, I noticed that Cinnamon seemed to be limping a bit on her right front hoof. I wonder if you'd mind checking it before I start home."

She didn't squirm at all over the lie, since it was only a half-truth. Jonas had promised to check the hoof after dinner. It would be a neighborly thing for Reuben to do it for him.

"I'd be happy to, Deborah." He visibly relaxed that the questioning was over. Grabbing his hat off the hook on the wall, he hurried out of the room, like a boy let out for recess.

Tobias squirmed in his seat. "Sure I can't get you something to drink?"

"Maybe *kaffi* would be good. If you have some left."

"Sure do." He jumped up, began fiddling with the pot on the stove, pulling a cup out of the cabinet and finding sugar.

"So, Tobias, how do you like your job at the feed store?"

"I like it all right. Gets me off the farm a little. Don't take me wrong. I like working in the fields, but a guy likes to spend time in town as well."

"Sure. I know what you mean. I go in town fairly often myself."

"You?" Tobias looked up in surprise as he poured the boiling *kaffi* into a chipped cup. "I thought you loved being on the farm with Jonas."

"Oh, I do. But I quilt you know."

"I remember now. *Mamm* and my *schweschders* brag about your quilting."

Deborah smiled at the compliment. "It's why I go into town so often. Callie Harper, she's the friend I spoke of earlier. She's also the new owner of Daisy's Quilt Shop."

Tobias brought the cup over to her along with the sugar and some cream. He didn't refill his own cup, but sat down and began to twirl the spoon he had been using. "I suppose she's had a hard time, what with Stakehorn and all."

"*Ya*. It was quite a shock for her to find him."

Staring at the table, Tobias muttered, "Would be for anyone."

"You were there that night?"

"Reuben said it would be better not to talk about it to anyone, Deborah."

"Did he say anyone, or the English?"

Tobias ran his hand over the back of his neck. "Suppose he meant the English, or more specifically, Black."

"Black was here?"

"*Ya*. Here and the feed store."

"He talked to you?"

"Not just me." Tobias looked up quickly. "He talked to all the guys."

"Sure. But you didn't have much to tell him, right? I mean it's not like you were staring out the window when it happened."

"That's what I told him. I had stepped outside to crush some boxes, so I was the one who saw her running down the alley. Stopped to watch and make sure she was okay. Of course I wasn't the only one to hear the lady's car alarm go off. Then I saw her fussing with the keys, jump in, and sit there a while."

Deborah thought about his explanation.

It matched up with what Callie had said.

"I didn't lie to him, Deborah. You know I wouldn't do that."

"Of course you wouldn't."

"Black seemed to think we were all holding back. It made him angry, but he had no evidence to pull any of us in. Everyone had what the English call an alibi. Remember, we were all at work. But as far as involving ourselves in their investigation, we'd rather stay separate. Reuben is right. It's not our place. You know how it is between the Amish and the police. We'll help them if there's a need, but no one at the feed store saw any need. Stakehorn's dead, and nothing we can say will change that fact. It goes against our ways to become involved."

Deborah nodded, took a sip of the bitter *kaffi*, and tried not to wince at the taste. "It's only that I'm trying to help Callie out, and we're not exactly sure what happened before she arrived."

Tobias didn't say anything, but he did rub his hand along the back of his neck again, as if he had an ache that no amount of massaging would ease.

"This woman, Callie Harper, she means a lot to you?"

"She does. I believe the Lord brought her to Shipshewana for a reason. But now—with all that has happened—I'm worried she's going to be scared away. Or worse yet, that Shane Black is going to harass her until she runs away."

"She's English though."

"*Ya*, but being English isn't a sin, Tobias. I believe your *mamm* taught you better than that. We're to help those we can."

Deborah looked out the window, saw the dark storm clouds closing in, and knew she needed to head home. Although their farms were close to one another, she didn't want to risk driving the buggy through a heavy rain.

Reuben was walking back toward the barn. She only had another minute or so. Somehow she needed to think of the right question to ask Tobias, because he wasn't going to offer up the information she needed.

But the thought had no sooner crossed her mind, when he cleared his throat and did just that.

"Here's the thing. We didn't lie to Black. None of us did. I know I didn't, but perhaps I didn't tell him everything either."

"What didn't you tell him?"

"He asked me about Tuesday night and what I saw then. Since I'm the one usually carrying the boxes outside during the late shift, maybe I'm the only one who heard. He probably would have pursued the line of questioning more, but he received a phone call and we were interrupted. I thought to go back and tell him, but I can't see how it would make any difference. Dead is dead." Tobias rubbed his neck again, then pushed on. "Stakehorn had people there arguing with him nearly every night the entire week before. I don't know what was going on with the man—he'd never been easy to get along with—but the week before he died, well, it was worse than ever."

Reuben was nearly at the door, but Deborah had enough time to pull out a scrap of paper from her bag and jot down the short list of names Tobias gave her.

It wasn't proof, but it was a place to start. She'd begin first thing in the morning.

~

Callie made it to the *Gazette* ten minutes before closing as the first raindrops began to hit the pavement on Main Street.

Mrs. Caldwell once again sat behind the front desk, like a guard at a front gate. She looked as stoic as ever—like a tough battleship; no smile adorned her face, every gray hair remained in place, and her glasses hung from a chain around her neck. Still, it seemed to Callie that the last few days had taken its toll on the woman.

Callie waited for Stakehorn's receptionist to finish a phone call. Then she noticed the two no-nonsense shoes peeking out from the bottom of the desk—one blue, one black.

Hanging up the phone, Caldwell turned to her without changing her deadpan expression. "We close in eight minutes, Miss Harper. I doubt we can do anything for you; and as *you* are aware, Mr. Stakehorn isn't here."

Did she emphasize the word *you?*

What was that supposed to mean?

"I was wondering if I could speak with the new editor?"

"Mr. McCallister? Were you wanting to threaten him as well?"

"No, of course not."

"He's busy."

"I can wait."

"We're closing."

"How long is he going to be busy?"

"That's irrelevant. Come back tomorrow if you want to see him."

"But this can't wait until tomorrow."

Caldwell put on her glasses and peered over them at Callie. "I doubt that seriously, unless you are here to threaten him. In which case I want to warn you that I won't tolerate a repeat of last week's performance." A muscle began to twitch on the right side of the older woman's mouth, and Callie watched in fascination as tears began to pool in her eyes.

"I'm not here to threaten anyone."

Caldwell stood and pointed to the front door. "Go."

"But—"

"Just go."

Callie looked from the receptionist to the door and back again. Caldwell opened a desk drawer, and Callie had the absurd thought that there was a gun in there and she was going to be shot, when the door to the back office burst open.

"I demand that you give me my father's things."

Mrs. Caldwell groaned.

"You have your father's things, Mr. Stakehorn—" said a man's voice.

"All of his things!" The response was a shriek and Callie automatically stepped closer to the desk.

A stockier, younger version of the former editor exploded out of the back office. Already balding, he was built like a bull with no visible neck at all — and his face was bright red.

Standing beside him was a slender man with shoulder length sandy hair. He wore wire-framed glasses and looked to be in his early thirties. "You have all of his things, but you can't have the things which belong to the paper. Now if you want Mrs. Caldwell to call the police to come and escort you out, she'd be happy to do so."

The new editor, Mr. MacCallister, looked at Caldwell. She put one hand on the phone. The younger Stakehorn glared at them both.

"This isn't over," he vowed. "I'll be back, and I will get my father's things. All of his things."

Brushing past Callie, he stormed out into the street.

McCallister shrugged in a what-can-you-do kind of way and walked toward the two women. "Would you like me to call the police, Mr. McCallister?"

"That won't be necessary. Stakehorn's just blowing off steam, and who can blame him." The editor was speaking to Caldwell, but his eyes were on Callie.

She stepped forward and stuck out her hand. "Mr. McCallister, the new editor I assume?"

"You assume correctly. And you are?" McCallister reached out and shook hands, his hazel eyes twinkling as he smiled down at her.

"This here is Miss Harper," Mrs. Caldwell cut in, "and I already told her we're closed." Caldwell pulled her bag out of the bottom drawer and slammed it shut.

"No need to hurry the lady out. It's not as if we have a line at the door."

"Suit yourself, but the last editor she spoke with ended up dead." Caldwell strode out of the office, never bothering to look back.

"She one of your biggest fans?" McCallister asked.

"Let's hope not. If she is, I better stop my city council bid right now."

"You're running for city council?" McCallister leaned back against the receptionist's desk, crossing his long legs at the ankles and studying her.

"No. Not at all. I tend to become sarcastic when I'm in awkward situations."

"This situation is awkward?" McCallister leaned forward, looked right down the empty hall, then left out the front windows on to the deserted street, and finally pointed to his chest. "Surely you don't mean because of me?"

"You didn't see the neckless man storm out of your office and threaten you?"

"Oh, him. Well, I tend to cut a guy some slack when he hasn't seen his dad in ten years and then learns he died on the night shift."

"So you're not buying the murdered angle?"

McCallister pushed up his wire glasses. "Who did you say you were?"

"Callie Harper, owner of Daisy's Quilt Shop."

"Right, and you were first on the scene when old man Stakehorn croaked."

"Please, couldn't you use a more—" Callie waved with her hands, then turned to study a plastic tree in the corner that didn't have a speck of dust on it. How often did Caldwell dust the plants? Who bothered to dust plastic plants?

"A more what? Politically correct term?"

"Yes. Maybe." Callie crossed her arms and turned to stare at McCallister. She usually made first impressions rather quickly, but she didn't know what to think of him. He seemed confident, but also a bit out of place here.

She could certainly relate to that feeling.

"Mr. McCallister—"

"Trent." Now she had no doubt his eyes were laughing at her.

"Fine, Trent. The reason I came by today was because I wanted to warn you."

"Warn me?"

"Yes."

"About what? Small towns? Tough receptionists? Angry sons?"

"None of those things." Callie stepped closer, knew how the next words would sound, but forced herself to say them anyway. "I wanted to warn you that whoever killed Stakehorn might be after you next."

Chapter 22

TRENT MOVED OVER to the two chairs that made up the waiting area and sprawled in one. "I thought I'd had the oddest first day of a news editor's career. Then you stepped through my door and confirmed it."

"This isn't a laughing matter." Callie moved to the chair beside him and perched on the edge of it. "Do you think I would have bothered coming by here if I were joking?"

"Oh, I believe you're serious." Trent removed his glasses and began rubbing the bridge of his nose.

"Someone killed Stakehorn here in this office."

"You're telling me nothing new. His death is why I was assigned to this town."

"Officer Black thinks it was poison, but I'm not so sure . . ."

Trent had been staring at the floor, but now he peered up between the locks of hair that had fallen forward, gave her a serious once-over—which she noticed lingered a bit long on certain portions of her anatomy—and finally let his gaze meet hers. "Go on."

"It's a hunch. I'll admit that, but things aren't adding up like they should."

"And how does this spell danger for me?"

"I'm not sure."

Trent looked exasperated. He stood up. "Look, lady, I appreciate your concern, but I have a paper to put together, and I'm already behind schedule. Not to mention I have one of the oldest presses in the state which is determined not to cooperate with me."

"Are you forgetting about the break-in on Friday?" Callie scooted herself farther back in the chair, as if she could grasp the arm rests and refuse to leave until he heard her out.

"I'm not even sure it was a break-in."

"What are you talking about?"

Trent pushed his glasses back on and walked over to the front door, turned the sign hanging there to CLOSED. "Look, yeah someone was here Friday night, but there was no sign of forced entry. More than likely, Caldwell forgot to lock up when she left."

"You think Caldwell forgot something? Are we talking about the same Sergeant Caldwell?"

Smiling, Trent motioned to the front door. "I believe she's a little upset about her former boss. Did you notice her mismatched shoes? Not exactly the sign of a woman with it all together. Could be she's a little past the retirement age. Kind of makes you wonder why she was hanging on so long, but it's not my place to come in and start changing things the first day on the job."

"You can't be serious." Callie jumped up and began pacing the area between them. "Caldwell would have never forgotten to lock the door."

"Nothing was missing, and no damage was done."

"But—"

"Look, I'm touched at your concern, especially considering you met me ten minutes ago. Now if you don't mind, I have a paper to put out before morning."

"So you're not going to do anything about it?"

"Anything about what?" Trent opened the door, put a hand on her back, and practically shoved her out onto the walk.

"The danger you're in."

"If it makes you feel any better, I'm well armed with my wit and charm. And while your theories are interesting, they're not interesting enough for copy."

Callie turned around to tell him sarcasm wouldn't save him against a criminal who'd already killed once, but she found herself facing a closed door and beyond that Trent McCallister's back retreating toward the press room.

She considered knocking on the glass, but suddenly the sky opened up and the rain began to fall in sheets.

Turning, she ran for her car.

As she did, she noticed the windows of the feed store across the street. Direct line of sight to the newspaper. Perfect place to watch, or plan, a murder.

The streets of town had emptied out as the storm moved in. Callie drove slowly back to the shop, playing the conversation with Trent McCallister over in her mind. She had to find a way to convince the man to listen to her. She was so caught up in her imaginary conversation that she nearly missed her own parking lot and had to slam on her brakes.

As the back end of her car hydroplaned slightly, she heard the screech of brakes, glanced up into the rearview mirror, and saw a car practically collide with her bumper.

Who had been following so closely?

Callie couldn't identify the make or model of the car as it accelerated and sped past her shop, spewing more water and further obscuring her view.

Probably didn't matter. No doubt the person would stop by tomorrow and chastise her for braking late and nearly causing a collision. Callie parked, searched in the floorboard for an umbrella but found none, so she stepped out into the pouring rain.

∽

He thought about turning around and going back to the quilt shop.

He knew now that the woman lived alone and would be an easy mark. What he didn't know was if she had the package. He had no real reason to think she would have it, but he was curious to know what she'd been doing back at the newspaper office.

Then there was the police department's interest in her.

That piece of luck caused him to smile as lightning brightened the evening. Not everything had gone wrong during this operation — almost, but not everything. Having a newcomer in town that would distract the police was the best thing to happen to him in the last month.

Now he just needed to find the package.

~

For perhaps the first time since she'd come to Shipshewana, Callie was completely relaxed. She was wrapped in a blanket, curled onto the sofa chair, her feet propped up on the ottoman. A warm mug of tea rested on the plate warmer on the table beside her — a marvelous invention she never would have considered purchasing, but one her aunt had obviously enjoyed.

Her attention was completely absorbed in the Agatha Christie book she was reading, and only when Max whined and inched closer in her lap did she raise her eyes to the storm raging outside her window.

"This weather is nothing, boy. You should experience a Houston storm."

But Max wasn't impressed. He buried his nose into the tiny crevice between the hand-stitched pillow and her side, as if he could hide from the clap of the thunder or the lightning that pierced the darkness. When his entire body began to tremble, Callie braced the book with her right hand and commenced to rubbing him between the ears with her left.

They both jumped when the police sirens split the night.

Callie tossed back the lap blanket and walked to the front windows. The light from the police cruiser vanished down the far end of Main Street, but she could still make out its peal.

Looking across the road at the streetlight, she noted that the rain had nearly stopped. The thunder and lightning were now following the storm to the south, but the police sirens continued to beckon from down the street.

From near the *Gazette*.

Callie snapped a light rain jacket on over her T-shirt and jeans, clipped on Max's leash, and hurried down the stairs.

She took off at a fast walk down Main. Halfway down it occurred to her it would have been faster to drive. Amazing how used to walking she'd become, something she hadn't done much of in Houston. When in Rome . . .

She came to the corner of Main and First and stopped so quickly Max skidded in his tracks.

She'd automatically headed straight, toward the *Gazette*, but the front of the newspaper remained cloaked in darkness — as it always was in the evening.

Plainly she could still hear the sound of the police sirens though. If anything, they blared louder.

Pivoting on her toes, she turned and felt her heart plummet.

The Shipshewana Police squad car was pulled at an awkward angle in front of The *Kaffi* Shop. And next to it, red lights pulsing out an emergency beacon, was an ambulance from The LaGrange County Hospital.

She rushed up to the small knot of people who had formed across the street.

Callie was too short to see over the dozen or so men and women pressed close to the police tape that had been hastily wrapped around a few trees and a street light.

She tried to push forward, but no one parted for her. She was hemmed in by police cruisers on the left, shop walls on the right, and a crowd of a dozen in front of her.

"Need some help, Harper?"

She turned and bumped into Trent McCallister, wearing jeans, a Harley Davidson T-shirt, and a Nikon camera around his neck.

"Where did all these people come from? I thought Max and I were the only ones in this part of town at night."

"Max?"

Callie reached down to calm her dog at the same time he pressed his wet nose into Trent's hand.

"Got it. Well, looks like there's more people than you or I knew about." Trent began snapping pictures of the crowd, including one of her and one of Max who happened to still be wearing his blue bandana.

"What were you doing down here this late?"

"Putting out a paper, remember? I started late due to some Paul Revere dame who wouldn't go away."

She gave him her best irritated look, but his grin only widened.

"I need to see what's happening in there." She stood on her tiptoes, but it didn't help a bit. The Amish residents wore their black hats and prayer *kapps*. She couldn't see over them. And the English residents were all taller than she was.

"Want me to put you on my shoulders?" Trent asked, closer this time.

"No, I do not. Can you see anything?"

"Sure, but I don't know what I'm looking at other than a squad car and an ambulance. Can't hardly make a story out of that."

Callie tried hopping, but that didn't help either.

"Hang on, gorgeous. I think I have a better idea."

Trent grabbed her hand and began to pull her away from the scene.

"I can't leave. I know the owner of that shop—Margie. I stop by nearly every day, and she always has a treat for Max. I was there earlier this afternoon."

He didn't bother answering her, didn't even seem to be listening, just kept pulling her back and around the old train station building. When they reached the other side, she understood why.

They had a perfect view of all that was going on.

Callie's legs suddenly felt like jello. She reached for Max, touched Trent's hand instead, and dropped straight to the ground.

This couldn't be happening. Just when she found her balance, it was as if she was dropped into a nightmare. She needed to stand up, barge over there, and demand some answers.

"You all right?"

Callie didn't answer, couldn't answer.

Her mind kept jumping between images of Stakehorn at his desk and the ambulance stretcher in front of The *Kaffi* Shop. She had held out hope that perhaps the paramedics were working on someone next door, that maybe there had been a car accident at the corner of the intersection.

"Talk to me, Harper."

Sweat broke out along her neck and trickled down her back, even as the cool night air caused her to shiver.

Max whined and licked her cheek once.

"You need me to call somebody?" Trent was kneeling in front of her now, his face mere inches from hers.

Callie shook her head, continued to stare at the ground in the darkness.

"Are you going to look at me? You going to tell me what's going on?"

When she finally did find the courage to look up though, it wasn't at the new editor; it was at the shattered glass from the front door of The *Kaffi* Shop, littering the sidewalk.

Andrew Gavin was speaking to the ambulance driver, while a paramedic was working on a person lying on the gurney—a woman with bright red hair.

"That's Margie," she whispered, and then she felt the night begin to spin.

Chapter 23

THE NEXT AFTERNOON Deborah, Esther, and Melinda all waited expectantly for Callie as she turned the lock on the door, flipped the sign below the words Daisy's Quilt Shop to CLOSED, and walked back over to the counter.

"Now tell us everything," Melinda said, bouncing her baby in her arms.

"Yes, we've been waiting for over an hour." Esther continued to straighten things on the counter, but the worry lines between her eyes remained.

"Girls, give her a chance to catch her breath. This was only Callie's second week of market days. She looks a bit in shock."

"Remember, one of those days last week I was in jail and missed most of the crowds." Callie sank on to a stool, slipped off her shoes, and began to rub her feet.

"Maybe you shouldn't have worked today," Melinda suggested. "After last night."

"I'm fine." Callie shook her head and her cheeks reddened in embarrassment. "Last night was just—bizarre."

"Trent McCallister actually carried you across the street?" Deborah asked.

"I fainted—nothing more. Which I have never done before

and never plan to do again. Smelling salts and a bottle of water fixed me right up.

"And Marjorie is still in the hospital?" Melinda pulled a teething ring out of her bag and gave it to Hannah to play with. "Is she going to be all right?"

"I think so."

Callie looked ready to cry, and Deborah wondered if they should talk of something else. She realized again, for perhaps the hundredth time since Jonas had told her about the assault on The *Kaffi* Shop owner, that her new friend had been through a lot since arriving in Shipshewana.

"Maybe we should talk of something else. Callie has good news about the auction of the Medallion quilt."

Both Melinda and Esther stopped what they were doing and looked up expectantly.

"You tell her, Deborah."

"No, you are the one who did all of the computer work. You tell."

"Someone tell!" Melinda said. "I'm so *naerfich* my stomach is tumbling like children's toys left out in a storm."

Deborah said nothing, but she did stand and begin worrying the strings on her prayer *kapp*.

"It's good news, so stop looking anxious." Callie smiled over at Deborah. "The Medallion quilt went for double our minimum bid."

Melinda squealed and buried her face in Hannah's neck to plant a kiss. Esther smiled broadly, the first genuine smile Deborah had seen from her in some time.

"There's more," Deborah said. "The second quilt went up for auction yesterday, as soon as the first closed. It started out quite high."

"We've decided to lessen the buying period on the second. I think this will increase interest, which is already building. We'll close bids in forty-eight hours."

"Tomorrow?" Esther asked, as she walked over to the kitchen area.

"Tomorrow." Callie paused and looked around the room. "I researched previous auctions, and I believe this will earn you the highest return."

"We're so glad for your business sense, Callie." Deborah sank back onto her chair. "I hoped it might work, but still it's hard to believe that customers who have never seen our work would be willing to buy it."

"Oh, they've seen it," Callie reminded her. "They just haven't seen it in person."

"Do you think this is why your store was so crowded today?" Melinda asked.

"Could be. I don't know exactly what's normal for a market day."

"Market days are busy, but what I saw in the last hour was a bit *narrisch*," Esther said as she walked back into the room with a tray of four cups, all filled with hot water, and a basket of assorted teas and cookies.

"Crazy?" Callie asked.

"*Ya*," Melinda smiled. "Definitely crazy."

"Things have been *narrisch*. If you could have been there last night ..." Callie dunked her tea bag in her cup of hot water and sighed. "I just couldn't believe that Margie's store was broken into. What are the odds?"

"Are you worried staying here alone? Not that I think anyone will bother you with Max here." Melinda reached across and took one of the cookies off the tray.

"It's not so much that I'm worried about my own safety. I took a personal defense course in Texas, and I do have my concealed handgun license." At the look on her friends' faces she smiled and shook her head. "No worries, I didn't bring my gun with me. It's in storage in Texas, and I would need to reapply for a permit to carry here in Indiana. I'm just saying I know how to protect myself."

"It's odd," Deborah said, not ready to deal with the fact that her friend was used to carrying a weapon. Of course policemen carried weapons, but members of the Amish community believed passionately in nonviolence. "What's going on in Shipshewana?"

"I don't know. At first I thought it might have to do with the quilts and our fight with Stakehorn, but murder? And now Margie in the hospital?" Callie shook her head, took a tentative sip of the tea. "It doesn't make any sense."

"She's going to be all right though?" Melinda rubbed Hannah's back in small circles.

"Yes. Andrew Gavin stopped by this morning. Said they were keeping her a few days for observation. Turns out blunt force trauma to the back of the head is nothing to mess with."

"She couldn't tell them anything about what happened?" Deborah asked.

"I don't think so. Gavin wouldn't tell me much, but Trent also stopped by—"

"To check on you?"

"Maybe. It's hard to tell with Trent whether it's real concern or if he's trying to pump you for tomorrow's front page story."

Deborah noticed she turned a pretty pink even as she complained about Trent. She also rushed on with her story before anyone could ask questions.

"He had been to the hospital in the hopes of interviewing Margie for the *Gazette*. The nurses allowed him less than ten minutes, but apparently he found out whoever broke into the shop expected the place to be empty. Margie thought she'd forgotten to turn off the espresso machine, so she came back to check it. When she saw the shattered glass, she went straight in before calling the police. She doesn't remember anything after walking in the front door and being smacked on the head."

"Anything missing this time?" Esther asked.

"Nothing." Callie put down the mug, hugged her arms around herself. "When I looked up and saw Margie's red hair, Margie's still form lying on the stretcher ... I don't know. I just lost my equilibrium for a moment."

"And Trent McCallister actually carried you over to the ambulance?" Melinda asked, a smile lighting up her face.

"Please don't remind me," Callie groaned. "I still can't believe I fainted."

"You've been through a lot since coming to Shipshewana, Callie." Esther reached out and patted her arm.

"I think it's sweet that he helped you," Deborah added.

"I am mortally embarrassed. He insisted on seeing me home, and I thought he'd never leave. If it weren't for Max, he'd still be here, watching over me."

"Callie, maybe you shouldn't be here—downtown—alone." Esther spoke quietly as they all began picking up their things, preparing to go home.

"I won't be alone much, but thanks for worrying. I've hired two teens to work part-time. A boy, Zeke, will come before I open in the morning and help move a lot of the stock for me."

"Who else?" Deborah asked.

Callie smiled, sure she already knew. "Lydia, your cousin, Deborah. She's seventeen, right?"

"*Ya.* Lydia is a sweetheart."

"She'll work in the afternoon, running the register and staying if I need her to stock after close. They both start tomorrow."

"But being here at night alone," Deborah said. "It might not be a good idea until this person is caught. We have room at our house. You could stay there for a few nights."

Callie was already shaking her head. "I don't think that's necessary, but thank you for the offer."

"We worry because not many shopkeepers live down here anymore. It's not like in the old days." Melinda stuffed Hannah's toys into her bag.

"Turns out Trent is going to be staying in the little room behind the shop until he can find a place to rent. And Andrew has promised whoever is on patrol will keep an eye on the place. Not to mention Shane Black continues to watch me like a hawk. The man still acts as if I'm guilty, or I know something that I'm not telling him."

Deborah noticed Esther flinch when Callie mentioned Shane's name.

"I'll be fine, ladies." Callie herded them all out the door as she walked to the side fence to let Max back inside from his afternoon yard time. "I appreciate your worrying about me though."

"All right. We'll see you later in the week." Melinda waved baby Hannah's hand as she climbed into her buggy.

Deborah jostled Joshua to her shoulder, gave Callie a hug, then moved off toward Cinnamon and her own buggy.

Callie noticed though that Esther hung back as Leah knelt beside Max, petting him softly. In fact, Esther still hadn't moved toward her own buggy by the time Deborah had moved out on to Main Street.

～

Callie looked at Esther curiously. "Did you forget something?"

"Actually, I'd like to stay for a moment." Esther looked around uncomfortably.

"Okay, well, we could go back inside."

"No." Esther's reaction was too quick, her moves too sharp. She pulled herself up into an even more erect posture, if that was possible, then gestured to the side yard. "I feel more comfortable in the garden, if that's all right with you."

"Certainly, Esther. Though the word *garden* is a bit of a euphemism."

They walked into the yard which was still quite wet from the recent storm. Though Callie had made huge strides in the shop and apartment, she hadn't done much here except hire a neighboring Amish boy to mow the grass when it had reached knee-high after Jonas had mowed it the first time they'd had their initial cleanup.

Leah spotted a ball and began to toss it to Max.

In the corner of the yard was a garden area which must have once been quite beautiful. A brick path ran through it, but the flowers had long since run wild. What birdbaths and pottery her aunt had placed there were hidden beneath the raucous growth.

Esther walked to the edge, reached out, and touched a branch of miniature white roses which looked as if it were trying to make an escape.

"I've been meaning to come out here and attempt to tackle the weeds, but all I've done so far is bring a few pots of herbs. I had so much to do inside."

"Daisy loved the garden, though she had trouble keeping up with it as well."

"Deborah told me this is where she found my aunt. Perhaps that's why I've been avoiding it. I'm not sure how I feel about being in the same place where she died."

"She died doing what she loved, in a peaceful place." Esther hesitated, then pushed on. "I would consider that a blessing. Here, more than any other place, you can be close to who she was and what mattered to her."

"You sound as if you knew my aunt fairly well."

"Not as well as Deborah, but I counted her my *freind*. She helped me through a hard time in my life."

"When your husband died." Callie flinched at the words as soon as she said them, images of Rick blossoming in her mind. She realized, not for the first time, that she and Esther had that pain in common.

Esther nodded, but continued studying the garden, reached out and took hold of the branch of white roses. "Plain people believe that all things happen for a reason, that it is *Gotte's wille.*"

Callie didn't interrupt. It was obvious enough what she meant.

"I was willing to accept that, at least outwardly, and grieve inwardly. But Shane would not allow Seth's death to rest."

"Shane Black?"

Esther turned to her now, though she continued to hold on to the branch of white roses. "Yes, Callie. Shane Black. This is why I stayed to speak with you. I want you to understand about him, to understand that he is a formidable man."

"I'm not sure I'm following what you're trying to tell me." Callie reached into the pocket of the gardener's apron she now wore as she worked around the store. She snipped off the end of the branch of roses and handed it to Esther. "Let's go and sit. You can explain to me what you mean."

They sat in the Adirondack chairs, under the shade tree, Callie's brand new shiny pots of herbs between them. Leah continued to play with Max, running back and forth. Finally, Callie voiced the question which hung heavy between them.

"Why would Shane be involved in Seth's death?"

"Because he thought it was a matter for the authorities, but we did not. It was an accident. It was *Gotte's wille.* Shane though, he wanted to prosecute the boys."

Esther's voice remained calm, but she clenched the rose branch so tightly her fingers turned as white as the petals on the flowers.

"What type of accident was it, Esther?"

"They were in our old barn. We didn't know it. We didn't use the old barn except to store things. The boys, they were in those years we call their *rumspringa.*" She paused, glanced at Callie. "You're familiar with the term?"

"Their running-around years?"

"*Ya.* So these boys had a car hidden in there, but we didn't know it. The barn is a little ways from our house, and as I said, we didn't have cause to go there often—mainly when one of us needed to fetch something we'd stored in it."

She stared across the yard, though it was plain to Callie that she was seeing something else entirely.

"It was late that evening. Leah was still quite young, and I had gone to bed early." She stopped, drew in a deep breath. "Seth tiptoed into our room. I remember appreciating how he didn't want to wake me, but I turned over to ask him what was wrong. He told me he'd heard some of the cattle near the old barn and thought perhaps they'd gotten into one of the old pens."

Esther smiled then, but there was no joy in it, only sadness and a bit of solace in the telling—like a worry stone she'd turned over so many times that perhaps it had become a bit of consolation to her to touch the smoothness of the memory one more time.

"We always meant to one day fix those old pens. Cattle are somewhat stupid animals, and ours kept going to the old barn, nosing around. They'd wander into the old areas, then not be able to find their way out. It seemed no matter how Seth wired them shut, some bull or cow would find a way back in."

Once again her story stuttered to a stop, and Callie wondered if she'd become lost in her remembering. She reached out, touched her lightly on the arm. "What happened, Esther? What happened when Seth went out to the barn?"

Esther shook her head, turned away from the past, and looked directly at Callie. "I didn't know at first. I fell back asleep. That haunts me still. The doctor said it wouldn't have made any difference, that Seth was most likely dead immediately, but I still wonder."

Standing, she turned and looked out at Main Street. "When I woke and realized that he wasn't back, I went looking for him. He lay dead, outside the door of the barn. There were tire tracks. I couldn't understand that. How could there be tire tracks in the dirt? We owned no car."

Looking at Callie, her eyes widened as if she were taking it in all over again, but she had no tears. Perhaps in the time since her husband's death, she had cried herself out.

"Later, I pieced together the stories—as the boys came back and asked for my forgiveness. They had hidden the car there. When they sneaked inside to get it, that was the noise Seth heard; and when they started it, they didn't realize he was standing outside the big barn doors."

Her voice took on a hollow sound. "One boy opened the door, the other floored the gas pedal, and then the first boy jumped in. They had to do it this way because it was an older model car and prone to dying after they started it. Seth was unfortunate to be standing in their path when the door flew open. He never saw what ran over him—an old Dodge truck."

Callie waited, letting the words sink into the afternoon around them. She wanted to say she was sorry, but surely a hundred people had said that to Esther before. She wanted to fold the woman into her arms, but Esther remained ramrod straight. So she waited.

Finally, Esther continued.

"Shane used words like vehicular homicide, involuntary manslaughter, and negligent homicide."

"Did they ever catch the boys?"

Esther stared down at the white rose she still clutched. "I knew the names of both boys almost immediately."

A feeling of dread crawled through Callie's stomach. "But you didn't tell Shane."

"No, of course not. It is not our way."

"Even for murder?"

"Was it murder? Or was it two boys who had a terrible accident?"

"But ..." Callie felt her arguments fall away before she even uttered them.

"They were sixteen. Their going to prison or having a record in the English courts wouldn't bring back Seth. It was an accident."

"But you live in America, under our laws."

"This is true, but we reserve the right not to bring suit."

"Even in criminal matters?"

"Was this criminal?" Esther turned to her, and Callie finally saw the battle that she must have fought for over a year, fought and finally won. "Those boys will have to live with what happened all of their lives. One is Seth's cousin. The other the son of a very *gut* friend. Within a month, each had come to the bishop to confess and to me to ask forgiveness."

"Easy enough to ask forgiveness—"

"And not so easy to live with having taken a life. I know. They still see me when they are in town, still send money to help with Leah. One lives here even now. The other has moved to live with his cousins in Ohio." Esther shook her head, watched her child playing with Max, then stood and motioned Leah toward the gate. "I am telling you this for a reason, Callie."

"Shane."

"Yes. He would not let it go. He was determined to know the names of the boys, but it is not the Plain way to prosecute our own. We have ways within our church to deal with such matters."

"And you're satisfied with that?"

"Yes, I am. It was a difficult time, nonetheless; and it was made more so by Shane Black."

"He was only doing his job though."

"I understand, but you need to understand *how* he does his job. He will not let a thing go. Even when he's told to by his superiors."

"What do you mean?"

"Our bishop went to Officer Taylor, the head of the Shipshewana Police Force. He in turn asked Black to back off. Still he wouldn't. He was determined to know the names of the boys and to arrest them."

Esther called again to Leah, who gave Max one final hug and

ran to catch up with her mother. Callie walked them through the gate and to her buggy.

"I am not saying he's a bad man. I'm saying that he is tireless. It's the same with the way he is chasing Stakehorn's murderer, and if it means relentlessly pursuing you for answers that you may not have, then he will. He'll do whatever it takes to catch his man."

"What made him finally stop with the boys?"

Esther helped Leah into the buggy, then turned back to Callie. When she did, she was smiling. It was a genuine smile, and Callie realized for the first time what a beautiful woman she was.

"Amish do not normally involve themselves in politics, at the local or state level, but that doesn't mean that we don't have *freinden* or aren't owed favors. Our bishop called in such a favor by a man at the state level; that man spoke with Black and insisted that he call off the investigation. If it hadn't been for this connection though, for this favor that was owed to our bishop, I believe he would have learned the names of the boys and ruined their lives forever."

Chapter 24

DEBORAH DID NOT START checking on her list of names the next morning.

Though she'd done laundry on Monday, with twin boys, laundry had ways of creeping into other days of the week. Wednesday she threw an extra load into the gas washer, and strung it up on the line when the skies finally cleared and allowed the sun to peek out.

While the laundry dried in the morning breeze, she did some baking, then realized she hadn't worked in her vegetable garden all week.

"Mamm, have you decided if you want to have another *bop-pli?"* Martha sat at the end of the row Deborah was hoeing, caring for baby Joshua, while Mary went behind her picking up the weeds and putting them in the basket they'd then empty into the compost pile.

"It's not totally up to what I decide, Martha. You know where *bopplin* come from."

"Bopplin come under cabbages," Mary declared, stooping to check under the lettuce plant her mother had just weeded around.

Martha and Deborah shared a smile, but didn't bother correcting Mary.

"Of course I know," Martha said in a lower voice when Mary had stepped away to chase a rabbit. "I was asking because Anna's mother is expecting another already, and her baby is less than a year old. So I don't really understand how this works."

Deborah paused to wipe the sweat away from her forehead and gazed out over the fields. She could barely make out Jonas at the north end of the hay patch. He'd stopped under a grove of trees and pulled the jug of tea off the back of the tractor. Joseph and Jacob were climbing the tree rather than resting under it.

"It's a bit confusing, I'll admit." She moved to the next row of vegetables and continued weeding. "Probably the midwife or your *grossmammi* could explain it better, but I can tell you it's different for every woman. We waited four years between you and Mary, but then only one year between Mary and the boys."

"So it's a little like when we come out to harvest the vegetables." Martha stood with Joshua, held on to his fingers as he took tentative steps down the row. "Sometimes we pull squash, and more comes out right away. Other times we have to wait."

Deborah's laughter bubbled out of her, causing Joshua to plop on the ground and begin laughing as well. "Yes, I suppose it is a little like the vegetables. We never know when God is going to give us more very soon or ask us to wait a bit."

As she worked on the garden, Deborah thought of Tobias's list of names. She had a plan in her mind, much as she designed her quilts before she began sewing.

She wanted to visit with Mrs. Caldwell first, but she thought it would be best to do it outside the *Gazette* office. As long as she'd known her, the receptionist always took her lunch at the deli on Main, and she always took it at half past noon.

"Add more tomatoes to that basket, Martha."

"It's near full now. I'm afraid it will spill over."

"Then add the cherry ones, and put my checkered cloth over the top."

"We're taking them to town?"

"*Ya*, and it would help me if you'd clean up Joshua and put his suspenders on him."

Martha didn't question her, only smiled.

It wasn't every day that she dressed the baby in the traditional Amish clothes, but she would for church and for Mrs. Caldwell. The woman had a soft spot for her children. Deborah planned to use every tool at her disposal.

She would have taken the twins, as they tended to look charming and most Englishers couldn't help but smile when they saw the two boys together. Then again, most Englishers didn't have to clean up after the two of them. However when they arrived in from the field, ready for lunch, they were darker than the work horses Jonas used to pull the plough.

"How does that happen?" Deborah asked. "It looks as if you had them roll in the dirt."

The boys shrugged and offered no reason, but Jonas seemed to think he should explain. "I believe the first of it began when Joseph was pulling Patch by the bridle and slipped into the mud—"

"I didn't slip exactly, *Dat*. Patch pushed me with his nose."

"*Ya*, Patch is stubborn when he doesn't want to move," Jacob agreed, reaching out to play with baby Joshua.

"Don't touch your brother. He's clean." Deborah pushed his hand out of the way without coming in contact with too much of the mud, then she took the reins to Cinnamon in her hand and looked at her girls. They were clean as a new dawn in fresh *kapps* and aprons. "We'll be back well before dinner."

"Sounds *gut*. We're working in the barn this afternoon."

"Keep the boys out of the pigs, please."

Joseph and Jacob cast a glance at each other, but both muttered, "Yes, *Mamm*."

∽

She pulled up in front of the deli a few minutes before one, which seemed like perfect timing. Mrs. Caldwell should be done with her lunch, but not yet ready to leave.

"Carry the basket for me, Mary?"

"Sure." Mary scrambled out of the buggy, and carefully placed the basket over her arm.

Martha took baby Joshua, and Deborah led them all into the store. Since it was a Wednesday and a market day, the sidewalks were a bit more crowded than usual. Deborah noticed a few Englishers stopping to stare at both her and her children.

Tourists, more than likely. She knew they meant no harm by their long looks and pointing. Most knew enough not to take pictures, or if they did they stayed at a distance to snap with their little instant cameras.

Smiling politely, she hustled the children inside and looked for Mrs. Caldwell.

She breathed a sigh of relief when she spied her sitting at a table near the back, reading a magazine.

"Hello, Mrs. Caldwell. Do you mind if we join you?"

Caldwell peered over the top of her magazine, a frown automatically in place. Then she spied Martha, baby Joshua, and Mary carrying the basket of vegetables. Deborah realized how picture-perfect her children looked, and almost felt guilty for using them to soften the woman's heart. But she told herself it was for the greater good, and pushed aside her remorse.

"Deborah, of course you can sit down. Your children look so nice today. I always did say that you have such nice-mannered, well-kept children. That tells a lot about a person."

The children smiled, but didn't speak.

"Danki," Deborah said.

"Sit, sit. There are plenty of chairs."

"I hope we're not interrupting."

"Of course you're not. I had already finished eating. What brings you to town?"

"We were working in the garden this morning, and I found that we had more vegetables than I could use without canning them." Deborah paused—again what she said was half-true. She could have given them to any of a number of people, but it seemed most expedient to offer them to Caldwell.

"And you thought of me?"

"I did," Deborah said with relief; at least that part was completely true.

Mary hopped off her chair and walked around the table, as if on cue. "Here you go. We looked under the lettuce and there were no *bopplin.*"

Caldwell raised an eyebrow and glanced at Deborah, then accepted the basket. "Well, thank you for checking for me, and thank you for the vegetables."

"Gern gschehne." Mary slipped back around to her seat.

"Such polite children. Not always the case you know. Not at all. In fact it seems more and more people are moving into Shipshewana who are outright rude." Caldwell looked as if she was about to say more, then pressed her lips together. Finally she added. "It was kind of you to think of me."

Martha and Mary turned and watched as a mother and father with two English children walked through the deli with ice-cream cones. Deborah was proud that her children didn't ask for any money or any treats, but she noticed how their gaze followed the family all the way out the door.

"Martha, would you like to take your sister and buy some ice cream for you both?"

Martha's face brightened immediately. "Yes."

"I'll take the baby." She handed her daughter her change purse, thought to tell her to buy only a single dip each, but then bit back the words. Martha was frugal. She would spend the money wisely.

Taking Mary by the hand, Martha led her over to the ice-cream counter.

"It must have been a hard week for you," Deborah said. "I wanted to do something to make it easier."

"Thank you." Caldwell sighed, took a sip of her iced tea. "I have always wanted to start my own garden like yours, but it just isn't possible with the hours I put in at the paper."

Again Caldwell seemed to want to say more, but didn't.

"*Ya.* I know the new editor will be glad to have you, to help show him the way of doing things."

"What man actually listens to a woman, tell me that—Amish or English I imagine it's much the same. It was the same with my late husband." Caldwell reached for the baby, bounced him on her lap. "New editor or old editor, I don't think it will be any different. No, I don't expect Mr. McCallister will listen to me any better than Mr. Stakehorn did. If he had—"

Again she stopped, looked around as though she were checking to see if anyone else could hear their conversation.

"If he had listened to me, perhaps we wouldn't need a new editor."

Deborah's eyes widened. "You tried to warn him? You knew—"

"I suspected." Caldwell leaned forward. Deborah tried not to focus on the bright red of her lipstick. "He had been angering people for many years over his column. I warned him time and again that he was going to push too far."

She sat back, looking relieved that she had finally had her say. When Joshua picked up a fork and began playing with it, she gave him a spoon instead.

"You told the police this, *ya?*"

"Black? Of course I told him, but do you think he listened? No. He's like every other man—thick headed. He wanted to know who had been in the office that afternoon, who had called that day, as if the person who murdered Dennis would have made an appointment first."

"Gail, I hope you're not in danger."

Caldwell's eyes jerked up at the sound of her given name. She studied Deborah for a moment, then shook her head. "No, of course not. I'm a receptionist. Whatever grudge the murderer held was obviously against Dennis, against the paper, not against the way the phone was answered."

Deborah stood as the older woman pushed her chair back from the table, accepted her baby so that Caldwell could pick up the basket of vegetables, and walked with her to the front of the store where her girls waited. "So you think that's what it was then, a grudge?"

Caldwell stepped closer as they walked outside into the afternoon sunshine. It was warmer there after the artificial coolness of the air conditioning. But though the warmth of the sun felt comforting on Deborah's skin, it did nothing to stop the chill sliding down her spine at Caldwell's next words.

"I can think of a dozen people who held a grudge against Dennis. Can't say I blame them, either. The man even angered me."

Deborah thought Caldwell would stop there, but she added, "It's wrong to make promises, don't you agree? Promises that you have no intention of keeping."

"*Ya.* It is."

Caldwell glanced over at Martha and Mary and a look passed over her face that differed from anger or bitterness. It was closer to regret.

Had Gail Caldwell been in love with Dennis Stakehorn?

Then the look passed, and Caldwell planted her smile firmly back in place. "Not that I would have killed him. I would have been smart enough to hire someone else to do it."

∽

The children stayed in the buggy while Deborah checked out one more person on her list that afternoon — Mr. Beiler, the owner of the feed store where Tobias worked. He was Amish and in his late forties. Amish folk took a vow of non-violence when they joined the church. But he was on her list, on the list she'd made when speaking to Tobias, so she spoke with him anyway.

"*Ya*, I argued with him quite often," Mr. Beiler admitted, as he shuffled through a stack of papers that covered nearly every square surface of his desk. "And don't you be judging me for it, Deborah. The man was not a *gut* neighbor — not by English or Amish standards."

"Of course I wouldn't be judging you, Mr. Beiler. I'm simply trying to figure out what happened here. The police don't seem to be making much headway, and my friend, Miss Harper, is very distressed by the situation. Do you have any idea what might have happened to Mr. Stakehorn?"

"I don't." Mr. Beiler said, standing and shooing her out of his office. "But I'll tell you this — he won't be missed."

The meeting was unsettling to say the least. She'd seen crotchety old men among her district before, but she'd rarely seen one with so little compassion.

Ten minutes later, Deborah was showing her list of four names to Callie, explaining what she'd learned so far and Mr. Beiler's odd reaction to her questions.

"Doesn't make him guilty of murder though," Callie said.

"*Ya*. I was thinking the same thing." Deborah remained in her buggy in the parking lot of Daisy's Quilt Shop. Callie had stepped outside to help a customer carry a large order to their car. "So you called and spoke with Margie?"

"No. They wouldn't put me through, but the nurse who's caring for her said her condition is the same."

"That's a shame. Try not to worry. I'm sure she'll improve soon."

Callie nodded, reached forward and tussled the baby's hair, waved at the girls. "Say, I just remembered. I was going to take that sack of things for Max back, but I can't find it. You know the one I had at The *Kaffi* Shop before Black picked me up—*again*. Any idea where it is?"

"Oh. I asked Margie to keep it for you, until you could come back for it. I believe she set it behind the counter."

"I don't suppose the shop is open today. I'd like to return what was in the bag and purchase more supplies for Max." Callie tucked her hair behind her ears, looked over at her dog who was sitting behind the fence staring at her as if she'd single-handedly invented dog chow. "He's needing more dog biscuits already. He eats like a bear instead of a dog."

"*Ya*, much like my boys. I believe The *Kaffi* Shop is open. I drove by there on my way back from the feed store. They'd placed plywood over the broken glass, but a big sign out front said OPEN. I suppose they don't want Margie losing money as well as being laid up sick."

"Maybe Max and I will walk over there when I close then."

"Okay, and come out to our place if you decide you don't want to stay alone."

"We'll be fine." Callie smiled and waved as Deborah pulled her buggy out on to Main Street.

"As if anyone would mess with you, Max."

Chapter 25

Callie didn't leave at six when her shop closed.

The Fed-Ex man showed up with the load of supplies she'd ordered. Fortunately, Zeke had stopped back to pick up the cell phone he'd left charging in the supply room, a cell phone he'd mentioned his parents knew nothing about.

He kindly offered to stay and help her move the boxes into the storeroom.

"We can unpack them in the morning," she said once the last box had been stacked against the shelves.

"You're sure? I don't mind staying." He cast an eye toward the front window as he spoke, and Callie had heard his phone beep several times in the last half hour, indicating either a call or a text message. He'd been respectful enough not to check it while they were working, at least not while she was in the room.

"I'm positive. It can wait. Now go and meet your friends."

The grin that spread across his face nearly eased the fatigue that was beginning to wash over her. Was there ever a time when a ride in a buggy made her evening?

Come to think of it, probably not. But there was that old mustang her parents had helped her purchase her senior year in high school.

"Go. Max and I have plans too."

Zeke didn't wait for further coaxing. He pulled his wool cap a bit lower on his head, then headed out the door. His friends were waiting at the curb by the time he made it to the street. Funny how he still wore the wool cap but kept the cell phone tucked in his back pocket. He had one foot in both worlds, but then what teen didn't?

Callie grabbed her own cell phone, the replacement for the replacement since Shane had insisted on keeping hers, and the Agatha Christie book she was reading, and locked up the shop.

Max started prancing as soon as he saw the leash. He was a good walker, and never pulled or strained on the leash, but the amount of energy he had at the beginnings of their walks some-times made her wonder what his "full-speed-ahead" would look like.

They made it to The *Kaffi* Shop in record time.

The sight of the boarded up window in the front door tugged at Callie's heart, but she took a deep breath and marched inside nonetheless.

As usual, country-western music played over the speakers. Booths were fairly crowded with customers. And Haiden, Margie's assistant, worked behind the counter. She wore blue jeans and a bright pink sun-top layered over a yellow T-shirt, but no Margie hovered near her—helping with orders, making sure she operated the espresso machine correctly, smiling at customers, exchanging comments about the latest bizarre item to pop up at the market.

"How are you doing, Haiden?"

"Hi, Miss Harper. Hey, Max." Red-rimmed eyes contradicted her cheery tone, but she raised her chin, waved at the display of baked goods and sandwiches, and pulled a pen out of her pocket. "I'm okay."

"It's good to see you're open."

"Regular hours—same as if Mrs. Margie were here. Margie's husband said it would be okay, and Kristen and I thought it would be a good way to, you know, show our support."

Kristen was the other part-time help, a sweet teenaged Amish girl.

Callie peeked behind her. "Is Kristen here?"

"No. She opened and was pretty worn out, so I told her I'd close."

"Are you going to be here alone?"

"No, ma'am. Kristen was going to come back after she'd gone home for a few hours."

"Well, you girls are doing a fine thing."

"Thank you. Can I get you some dinner?"

"Sure. I'll take my regular sandwich and a coffee with a shot of espresso."

"Kind of late for that; isn't it?" Gavin's voice sounded as serious as ever, but when Callie turned she found him out of uniform—wearing blue jeans and a Hike Montana shirt.

Hike Montana? She had envisioned him in a Go Army shirt, but not Hike Montana.

He was standing directly behind her, looking as stiff and formal as ever, but she thought she saw a glimmer of humor in his eyes.

"It's never too late for espresso, Officer Gavin."

"Doesn't it keep you awake?"

"No. It used to, when I was younger. Now it just recharges me enough to keep me awake until dark."

"Anything else?" Haiden asked.

"No. That will do it." Callie paid with a twenty, and Haiden was handing her the change when Callie remembered why she'd stopped by in the first place.

When she asked about the bag, Haiden remembered it immediately. "I helped her store it right here under the cabinet, but it's not here. Let me check in the back."

"Great. I need to return it to the General Store and buy Max more treats."

Max yelped lightly and several customers turned to look at him.

"Harper, I'm sure you're not supposed to bring animals in here."

"Could you do me a favor?" Callie turned, smiled sweetly at the officer who could not have been older than her. "Lighten up."

Before Gavin could answer, Haiden returned. "No bag. I looked where we put it and on the Lost and Found shelf."

"It was kind of large. Had SHOP SHIPSHEWANA on the outside, and it was filled with dog stuff."

"Yeah, I remember."

Max lay down on the floor and put his head on his paws.

"Does that dog actually understand what you're saying?" Gavin asked.

"Are you sure it's not behind there?" Callie asked Haiden, ignoring both Gavin and Max.

"You can look for yourself, but it would be hard to miss."

Callie thrust Max's leash into Gavin's hand and walked around the counter. "That's strange. I left it here Monday when Black showed up and arrested me again."

"Technically you weren't arrested." Gavin still hadn't moved. He stood there, still not smiling, holding Max's leash, studying the two women. "What? I'm just saying."

"Thank you for that observation, Officer." Callie rolled her eyes.

"I remember," Haiden said. "I was working Monday. You left, Deborah rushed out with the bag, then rushed back in, and asked Margie to hold it for you. Margie placed it right here under the shelf. It was here when we closed Monday night. I know it was, because I asked Margie if she wanted me to take it by your place."

"Monday night was when the burglar—" Callie turned

slowly and stared across the counter at Gavin. "Was anything else reported missing?"

"I can't reveal the details of an ongoing—"

Callie sprinted back around the counter. Gavin backed up two paces, but Callie closed the gap. "Was anything else missing?"

When he didn't answer, she turned back to Haiden.

The girl shook her head. "Nothing."

"Don't tell me someone broke into this store and assaulted Margie so they could steal Max's dog toys. That doesn't make any sense. Why would they do that?"

"Maybe you should calm down," Gavin said.

"I don't want to be calm. I want answers. Tell me it didn't happen that way, because it doesn't make any sense. There has to be more to it. There has to be another answer." Callie suddenly knew that she had to have fresh air, she had to be out of the little shop that was becoming smaller by the second.

She pushed past Gavin, heard him say to Haiden, "Hold her order. We'll be back for it in a minute."

Some part of her knew that he was following her, bringing Max, but she kept walking, across the street to the bench. The same place she had sat with Trent less than forty-eight hours ago when they'd first seen the ambulance pulled up outside The *Kaffi* Shop.

Gavin stood in front of her, still holding Max's leash. "I don't know what you're thinking, but I'll wager it's wrong."

Callie didn't bother answering him. She was trying to deal with all the images and ideas going through her head—quilts, eBay, Stakehorn, murder, Shane Black, Margie, Max.

What did they have in common? Or did they have anything in common?

Was she trying to force a connection where none existed?

"Talk to me, Harper."

He crouched in front of her, and when she continued to stare at the ground he reached out, placed his hand under her chin, and gently raised her head until her eyes met his.

"Talk to me."

"Nothing was missing from the store."

His silence confirmed what she already knew.

"The same way nothing was missing from the *Gazette* office."

"You're not a detective, Callie."

"I know that." She felt her temper snap, and for the first time he smiled. Why did her anger make him smile? "I wish I were a detective. I'm just a shop clerk, out of my league. But somehow I'm caught in this, and it's not making any sense."

Andrew stood, handed her Max's leash, then sat beside her on the bench.

"So sometimes it helps to talk things out, rather than chasing them around in your head."

"I talk them out," she mumbled. When Gavin leaned forward and gave her the look, she added. "I tell Max almost everything."

Then the tears started tracking down her cheeks, and it made her even angrier. She did not want to cry in front of this man. She didn't want to feel vulnerable and weak. The last thing she wanted to be was helpless—again—helpless. She'd traveled twelve hundred miles, yeah she'd looked up the distance on Google maps and wasn't that absolutely pitiful. Twelve hundred miles from Houston to Shipshewana.

But what difference had it made?

She was as lost here as she'd been there.

And it seemed she was no more in control of her life now than she had been then.

Gavin reached over and tapped the book she didn't realize she was still clutching. "I guess you know your aunt was fond of Agatha Christie."

"Yeah." Callie swiped at the tears with the heels of her hand. "There's an entire shelf in her apartment."

"Did you know Max's name came from Agatha Christie?"

What escaped was half laugh, half sob. "You're making that up."

"I'm not. She told me so one day when I stopped by to help her with a flat tire on her old truck."

"You know more about my aunt than I do." More tears threatened to fall, but Callie blinked them back. "I found a journal of hers. I've started reading it, and it's like I'm getting to know her, but I didn't realized she had a truck."

"Everyone seems to know everyone in a small town — I'm sure you've figured that out in the short time you've been here. Daisy had that old truck the entire time I knew her, a couple of years at least. She finally got rid of it last summer when she realized she liked walking and it was cheaper to hire a driver like the Amish."

"So Max was a character in a mystery novel?"

"No. He was Agatha Christie's second husband. They were married forty-six years. I remember it struck me as amazing how she knew the exact number of years. She said Max was faithful to her, same as the author's husband had been faithful."

Callie reached down, rubbed her dog as he leaned against her leg. He felt warm and safe and comfortable. He provided a connection to her past and her family — to people who loved her.

"Thanks, Gavin. Guess I needed to hear that right now."

"Call me Andrew."

"Andrew, huh?"

"Yeah."

So she did, and she told him her fears about being connected to Stakehorn's murder and Margie's assault.

Andrew wasn't buying it though. "I've seen a lot of coincidences. Sometimes when you're afraid, you connect things that don't belong together at all."

"But what about the bag of Max's things? Why would that be the one thing missing?"

"You don't know it was. Until Margie can tell us what she did with it, you're making an assumption."

Callie pulled in a deep breath. One part of her knew he was right. Another part, a small nagging part that felt more like a twitch, wondered.

"I'm not saying I blame you," he continued. "Shipshe is a small, safe community. For two random acts of violence to happen in less than a week is disconcerting, but you don't have anything to be afraid of."

"I suppose you're right." Suddenly Callie remembered Deborah's list and the two names she hadn't spoken to yet. "Can I ask you one more thing?"

"Of course."

"You argued with Stakehorn — the night he was murdered."

She didn't think he would answer, though she felt him stiffen beside her. "Is there a question in there somewhere?"

"I was wondering what it was about."

"I didn't always agree with what Dennis wrote in his columns. The newspaper was his business, though. He was the editor."

"Do I hear a *but* in there somewhere?"

"But sometimes he stepped over the line. Actually most of the time he did. Hurt people, and hurt them unnecessarily." Andrew stood, refused to meet her eyes.

Callie moved in front of him, even put her hand on his arm until he looked down into her eyes. This intimacy didn't feel odd to her like it might have just a few weeks earlier. The shell she'd so carefully kept around her life was beginning to crack, and it wasn't as painful as she'd expected. Callie looked down at her hand still on his arm, then back up into his eyes. "Are you saying you confronted Dennis Stakehorn over what he wrote about me?"

"Yeah, Callie. I did."

"Why would you interfere? You didn't even know me then. We hadn't even met."

Andrew shrugged and the slow smile that spread across his face was charming enough to melt even Callie's heart, a heart she'd kept well guarded since the day her husband had died, maybe longer.

"I knew you well enough to understand you were doing a good thing helping the ladies out with those quilts, taking over your aunt's shop, even coming here." He waved out and over the town which lay in front of them. "Many people would have sent a packing company to ship her things. You came and looked after family. That says something about you."

"It always comes back to family, doesn't it?"

"For the good guys I think it does. We're mostly doing the best we can and chasing the American dream — two-point-five kids, a little garden, and a roof over our head."

Callie nodded, emotionally drained, but certain that they could wipe Andrew Gavin's name off Deborah's list. He might have the technical ability to kill someone, but he didn't have the heart, that much she was sure of.

"Let's go pick up your dinner. I'll walk you back home."

"I'm fine now."

"It's no problem." Suddenly Andrew's phone blipped, not once but three times in quick succession. He pulled it out of his back pocket and checked the screen. "There's been a wreck out at the highway intersection. I need to go. If you'd like to wait here and eat your dinner, I could swing back by when I'm done and — "

"Don't worry about us. I'm going to grab it to go and head home. We'll be fine."

"You're sure?"

"Positive."

"All right. Put my private cell number in your phone though."

"Officer, is that really necessary?" Now Callie was smiling full throttle, and Andrew was smiling back.

"It might not be necessary, but it's not going to hurt either."

"I bet you use that line on every girl."

"No, ma'am. Only the ones with great dogs."

~

Gordon watched through his scope, saw when Andrew received the text about the accident.

He spoke to the brunette a moment longer, then left in his truck.

Good. All of Shipshewana's police department—the entire force of half a dozen—seemed to be accounted for. He'd have the half hour he needed to search Daisy's Quilt Shop.

There was a marketing scheme that made no sense to him. An entire shop just for quilts?

Regardless, this job had turned into a fiasco. Time to get back on top of things. He'd been hired because he guaranteed results.

He watched the lady walk back into The *Kaffi* Shop as dusk began to settle on the sleepy little town.

With any luck she'd spend half an hour eating dinner and reading whatever novel she had stuck under her arm. And wasn't he fortunate she'd taken the mutt with her?

It was about time his luck changed.

He disassembled the rifle, placed it back in his bag, and hustled down the stairs of the vacant building.

Find the package, and he could put this town in his rearview mirror by the time darkness had fully settled.

Which was a good thing since their famous market days were over for the week. Once the Wednesday crowd left, he stuck out like a sore thumb—he was not looking forward to another five days of lying low in a town of six hundred.

He'd pulled bad assignments before, but this was one for the books. Not that it was a real problem, since he'd recently been promised a bonus for completing the job. He could imagine the money in his off-shore account.

It wasn't solely about the money he realized as he made his way down the back alleys.

A man had to have pride in his work.

Chapter 26

THAT SAME EVENING, Deborah was a bit late traveling the final stretch of road home. She'd stopped by her *grossmammi's* house to check on her. While she was there, she had decided to stay and work in the garden for a bit. She'd also picked up another quilt top Irma had been helping her with. Though she was in her eighties, she still found time and energy to quilt. By the time she'd loaded the children back in the buggy the sun had set, though darkness hadn't yet settled over the fields.

Murmuring to Cinnamon, she allowed her to settle into a good trot as they headed toward home.

She was nearly to the turnoff for their lane, thinking of dinner and quilting and the boys and Jonas, which might be why she didn't at first notice the English car speeding up behind her.

Cinnamon began to toss her head, and Martha jerked around to look out the back window of the buggy. "He's not slowing, *Mamm.*"

"Whoa, girl." Deborah calmed the mare as best she could, spied the double lane just ahead, and aimed for it. By the time they reached the passing lane, all of her children were staring out the back window, and Cinnamon was the most agitated she'd ever seen her.

Instead of passing, the little sports car pulled in front of the buggy, slammed on its breaks, and parked at an angle, causing, Cinnamon to rear and neigh.

"Easy girl. Settle down." Deborah calmed her, then attempted to back her up a few paces. Before she could put much distance between her and the Englisher's automobile he was out of it and storming toward them.

"*Mamm*, why is he walking back here?"

"I don't know. Hand the baby back to your *schweschder.*"

Martha did as she was told, and Mary had taken Joshua into her lap just before Roger Stakehorn charged their buggy. There was really no other word for it. With his red face, blocky build, and angry face, he reminded Deborah every bit of an old bull she'd seen in her *dat's* field when she was a girl.

Deborah had wondered how she'd reach the other name on her list, the other name Tobias had given her of people arguing with Dennis Stakehorn, and now it seemed that problem had been solved. Tobias had plainly heard the editor outside, on his cellular phone, arguing with his son. He'd shouted the words "Roger" and "son" several times into the phone, before slapping it shut, marching back into the newspaper, and slamming the door.

It would seem Deborah would have her chance to speak to the younger Stakehorn now.

"You," he sneered. "You are the reason I'm stuck in this God-forsaken town. Doesn't even have a good tavern. Drove all the way to the next town and all I could find was a convenience store that sold *this*." He waved a brown paper bag containing a bottle. "Man shouldn't have to drink alone," he added as an afterthought.

The foul odor of his breath left no doubt as to what Stakehorn had been drinking. Deborah wondered if she had enough room to signal to Cinnamon, but he blocked her on the left, and a pasture fence blocked her on the right.

"Mr. Stakehorn," she aimed for calm and polite though her heart was thudding in her chest. "What's the problem?"

"What's the problem?" Though it didn't seem possible, his face turned an even deeper shade of red. "The problem is that I just came from the reading of my old man's will. Yeah, that's right. We have wills, though I guess you Amish people don't bother with such things."

Deborah felt Martha move closer to her on the seat. She put a protective arm across the front of her daughter, hoping it would somehow shield this man from seeing her. Instead his blood-shot eyes took in Martha, Mary, and Joshua.

"And what did he leave me? Nothing. All those years working in this stinking town, and what was left? Nothing! Well I don't believe it—he had money, and I'll find it. I'll find it, and I'll have it. So what if I didn't see him the last ten years? Why would I come to this poor excuse for a town? He still owed me. Man owes his only son. Miser never spent a dime. The money's here somewhere, and I will find it. I'll find it, and I'll have it, because it's rightfully mine."

Deborah said nothing, only waited, prayed he would turn and go away. Prayed someone would pass by and stop to help her.

"Isn't it mine?" he shouted.

She jumped in spite of her resolve not to show fear. "Certainly it is."

Stakehorn's eyes darted from her to the horse and past them to the fields. "Old man wouldn't share with me while he was alive." He uncapped the bottle in the paper bag and took a swig. Leaning in, he lowered his voice. "I told him he'd regret not helping me, and do you know what he said?" Instead of waiting for an answer, he pushed on. "He said I wasn't the first one to threaten him. Said lots of people threatened him every week, and he knew how to get even. Said he was always getting even in that paper of his. Said you and that short quilt-shop woman had already been by and threatened him once."

Deborah's face must have registered the surprise she felt.

Stakehorn leaned in closer. "That's right. Surprised to hear he mentioned you by name? Well, he did. And I was able to track you down. Wasn't I? Even if you don't have a phone. I might not be a *reporter*, but I can find an address in a town of six hundred." His stare traveled over her to the quilt folded on the seat. "You're her, all right — Deborah Yoder."

Deborah tightened her grip on Cinnamon's reins.

"So how do I know you didn't kill him, kill him and take all his money, kill him and take what was mine?"

Stakehorn was practically inside the buggy now. "Black might suspect me; they always suspect the next of kin, but it could just as easily have been you and that quilt-shop woman."

Deborah inched away from him, though she still gripped Cinnamon's reins tightly.

Joshua picked that moment to let out a healthy holler.

Instead of irritating Stakehorn, it seemed to pull him out of his trance. He snarled something out, something incomprehensible, and staggered back toward his car.

"He shouldn't be driving," Martha whispered, over the crying of Joshua.

"No, you're right. He shouldn't."

They turned and watched as he fell into the car and maneuvered it into a U-turn in the middle of the road. He'd driven less than another thirty feet, when he swerved off the road into a pasture fence, where the car came to a rest, apparently unharmed.

Though Stakehorn revved the engine and spun the tires, the car was stuck in the ditch and the mass of fence wire.

"Should we stop and help him?"

"No. He wasn't going fast enough to hurt himself. There's a phone shack a mile up ahead. We'll call the police, and they will send someone to pick him up."

Deborah clucked to Cinnamon, and they hurried down the lane and toward home.

~

Callie carried her to-go dinner in one hand, and held Max's leash in the other as she walked back toward her shop. The streets were quiet now. It was amazing how quickly town cleared out at the end of a market day. She supposed folks were too tired to hang around, though far down the road she could still make out quite a few cars parked at the Blue Gate Restaurant.

When her shop came into sight, when Daisy's shop came into view, she nearly stopped there on the sidewalk. She'd seen her aunt's name on the sign many times, had even climbed up on a ladder and cleaned off the letters a few days ago. But it struck her tonight, for the first time, that if someone else bought the shop they'd probably change the name. It would become Belinda's Quilt Shop or Jane's Quilt Shop or worse yet, something catchy like Sunshine Stitches. The small legacy her aunt had left in Shipshewana would be erased.

Why did she feel a pain in her chest at the thought? She switched the to-go sack of food to her left hand, to the hand that held Max's leash, and reached up and rubbed at her chest. Felt like she had a stitch there, like she used to get in her side when she jogged.

Absurd. Probably she was just tired.

She needed to go upstairs, eat her dinner, and rest.

She'd nearly made it to her parking lot when a man on a Harley-Davidson Sportster pulled up beside her.

"Need a ride?" he asked.

Max barked once, but didn't seem too perturbed. Callie took that as a good sign, that and the grin on Trent McCallister's face.

"I thought you drove a truck."

"I do."

"And a motorcycle? I didn't realize editors make so much."

"Have you seen my truck? I'd have to pay someone to haul it off."

"The bike on the other hand ..."

"The bike is primo." Trent motioned toward the back with his thumb. "Hop on. I'll take you around the block."

"Actually I'd love to, but—" She held up the dinner sack and Max's leash. "Kind of bogged down here."

Trent cut the engine and walked the bike into her parking lot, parking it in the first slot he came to.

"Yeah, I only have one extra helmet, and it probably wouldn't fit the dog."

"So have you ridden for a while?"

"Since I graduated high school. My dream was to ride to Sturgis, but I've never made it. Always been too busy. This is the year though."

"Ahh. I'm not really up on my motorcycle lore, but isn't that in South Dakota?"

"Yes ma'am. The motorcycle convention has been going on since 1938."

"Long way from here."

"Eleven hundred miles." Trent's grin said it all, so Callie just smiled.

"I hope you make it then."

"Oh, I'll make it—ten days vacation was the one condition of my taking this assignment. Six weeks from now, I'll be headed northwest."

"Goals. That's good to see in a man."

"You're not kidding. Some guys my age have nothing to aim for."

He carried her sack as they walked toward the back door, and she held on to Max's leash. When they were a few feet from the door, Max let out a growl and ripped the leash from her hand, bounding through the back door.

"You didn't lock it?"

"Yes, I locked it. I always lock it."

"Stay here." Trent thrust the sack in her hands and took off through the open back door, after the Labrador who could be heard barking and snarling like a rabid hound.

Callie started through the door, had made it halfway down the hall when she heard the gunshot.

She dropped the sack of food and started running.

She heard the sound of broken glass, heavy footsteps, and her front door slamming.

Her pulse was pounding in her ears, and she could only focus on reaching Max's side, on finding Trent. When she came around the corner of the main room and saw him kneeling over her dog it occurred to her that Max had stopped barking. Then she saw the blood on the floor, and Trent with his shirt off and pressed to the dog's side.

Max's dark eyes were on her, trusting her.

Some part of her mind registered that whoever had been there, whoever had shot her dog had run out, had escaped, but she didn't care.

She dropped to her knees beside her new best friend and ran her hand over his silky ear. He licked her hand once, and then he lay completely still.

～

Deborah hopped out of Trent's truck and ran up the steps of the veterinary hospital.

She found Callie sitting in one of the orange plastic chairs. Andrew Gavin flanked her on one side. Officer Stan Taylor, still in uniform, sat on the other. Though it had been only a month or so since Deborah had seen him, he looked older in the fluorescent lights. His bushy white eyebrows over his drawn face accented how tired he must be, and Deborah could well imagine how the weight of the past week's incidents had affected him.

Callie looked up, saw her, and flew into her arms.

"Trent told me," Deborah said. "Any word?"

"No. We're still waiting." Callie rubbed her sleeve across her nose, laughed then sobbed when Deborah pulled a handkerchief out of her bag. "Thank you."

"Gifts between *freinden*," Deborah said softly.

Taylor moved over a seat so that Deborah could sit beside her. Trent remained standing, his arms crossed, a look of anger on his face. "Have you heard from Black yet?"

"Nothing new since you left," Gavin said.

"I can't believe there's no fingerprints at all. Whoever is doing this can't be that good."

"He left a slug, son." Taylor looked at him calmly. "We'll get something from that. Give him enough time and he'll leave something else behind."

"Give him enough time and he'll shoot something besides a dog." Trent began pacing.

"What about the items moved around in my shop?" Deborah's head snapped up.

"It's true," Callie told her. "Seems our cat burglar likes to return to the scene of the crime—and play."

"We're working on it," Taylor insisted.

Deborah felt Callie begin to tremble beside her. She put her arm around her, rubbed her shoulder. "Have you had any dinner at all?"

"No, I was walking home when, when …" she tried to finish and failed.

"Trent, would you mind finding Callie a soft drink and perhaps a package of crackers? I believe we passed some vending machines when we came in."

"It only takes change," Gavin muttered.

"You've been here before?" Callie looked up in surprise.

"Last week. My cat decided to fight with a raccoon and needed stitches."

Deborah tried to hide the smile which insisted on forcing its way out. "You have a cat, Officer Gavin?"

"He looks more like a dog person, doesn't he?" Callie leaned forward and studied Gavin who was now turning a nice shade of pink.

"I don't have a cat. This stray showed up at my place, so I started feeding it, and now ..."

"Never feed a stray," Taylor muttered.

"*Ya*, I tell my children the same thing," Deborah said.

"I only have fifty cents," Trent said.

The men all stood and began going through the change in their pockets, then moved off toward the vending machines.

"Thank you."

"For?"

"Getting rid of them for a few minutes. They've been very kind, but they're also teeming with energy and busting to do something. It's exhausting."

"I have four males in my house. I know exactly what you mean."

They sat there, quietly, and Deborah thought Callie had just begun to relax a bit when two things happened at once.

The men returned—laden down with sodas and junk food—and Dr. England walked in through the double doors, holding a clipboard and looking exhausted.

He sat down directly across from Callie.

Gavin, MacCallister, and Taylor took three chairs to the left of her.

Callie sent Deborah a grateful look when she reached over and clasped her hand, entwining their fingers together.

"First, I want to say you have one very brave dog."

Deborah squeezed Callie's hand.

"The bullet passed through, as you know. It did quite a bit of muscular damage. I was able to repair everything. Max lost a lot of blood, and I want to give him antibiotics for at least forty-eight hours to fight infection, but I think he's going to be fine. Again, he will have to stay here several days."

Callie leaned forward, dropped her head into her hands, and began to cry.

"This is *gut*. He's going to be fine." Deborah rubbed her back in soft circles.

"Thank you, Doc." Taylor asked.

"No problem. Terrible thing, to be happening in Shipshewana."

"Well, I believe we're close to catching him." Taylor walked with the doctor back toward the double doors.

Gavin knelt in front of Callie. "I don't want you going back to the shop tonight."

She sat up, scrubbed at her face with the handkerchief. "He's not running me off from my house. I don't know who's doing this, but I'm going home."

"Callie—"

"You can't stop me."

"You're not thinking straight."

"Yes, I am. You want to patrol the streets, fine. But I won't be run off. Whoever did this only came by because he thought I wasn't home. He's a coward and a thief." She stood now, giving her anger full rein.

"I can stay downstairs if you insist on going back," Trent offered. When everyone turned and stared at him, he added, "Think of the front page story when I snap a picture of the guy and manage to single-handedly catch him."

"No, you won't stay downstairs." Callie turned on him like a whirlwind undecided as to which path it would take.

Deborah caught her by the shoulders, turned her around. "Callie, look at me. They're only trying to help. They're concerned."

"*Ya*, I know that."

They smiled at the same time at her use of the Amish word.

"But don't you see?" Callie continued. "Whoever this is keeps hitting places he thinks are empty. He's not going to come back while I'm there. I haven't figured it all out, but that much I'm sure of."

"What about Stakehorn?" Trent asked. "He's dead. We don't want you to end up like him. So don't be angry at us for caring."

Callie took a deep breath, looking back toward the double doors where Taylor still stood speaking with the doctor. "I appreciate it. I do, but I need to go home, okay? I need to not be afraid anymore."

Taylor turned and walked toward them, and Deborah knew no one would change Callie's mind.

But she also had a sense that they were running out of time, as if the windup clock like the one she kept by her bed was ticking down ... but to what she didn't know.

Chapter 27

CALLIE WALKED OUT to her car after closing up the shop Friday afternoon. Her arms were loaded with things she was taking to Deborah's—the new fabric Deborah had ordered, the novel Callie was currently reading, cuttings from her herb garden, and charts showing the auction results.

The first quilt had brought a respectable price. They'd barely paid attention to the closing price of the second quilt, since it occurred on the night Max was shot—but as she'd hoped, the shorter auction period resulted in a higher price. The third quilt—the signature quilt—was closing at midnight tonight. So far, the bids were higher than either of the previous two.

Setting everything in the front passenger seat, her heart ached that Max wouldn't be sitting there, but the doc had assured her he'd be ready to come home soon—maybe even tomorrow.

She had slammed the door shut and walked around to the driver's side, when she saw Shane Black pull into the parking lot in his vintage Buick.

Funny how seeing him didn't anger her anymore.

He could still be here to arrest her, but somehow she didn't think so. Since Max had been shot, she figured the focus of the investigation was officially off her, though Adalyn had said yesterday at their meeting that according to her inside sources, she wasn't completely off the radar yet.

Black unfolded himself from the car. It was painted a mustard yellow with a black hood and black stripes down the sides, and it looked like something an Amish teen would drive on his *rumspringa*, or an English teen would drive to college—in his dreams. He covered the distance between the two cars in a few easy strides.

"Officer."

"Harper."

"What brings you out tonight?"

He didn't answer right away; he took a few minutes to study her intently, as if he were assessing her condition. What did he have to do that for? She was fine as long as they were bantering back and forth. If he was going to get serious on her, she might tear up.

A month ago she'd never have thought she could care so much about a dog, but then Max was more than a dog. Acknowledging that was hard. It was as if her heart had begun to thaw and she was feeling things so much more acutely now.

It hurt, like a fresh sunburn.

But it felt better than the numbness she had lived with for over a year.

"I wanted to check on you."

"I'm okay," she said honestly.

"Good." He joined her, leaning against the blue rental. She really needed to do something about finding a permanent car if she was staying.

Was she staying?

"How's Max?"

"Doing well. He might come home tomorrow, or the next day."

"Glad to hear it. Place isn't the same without him."

Callie nudged him with her shoulder. "You act as if you stop by every day."

"I might, if you were a bit more friendly."

"Tell me you have something new to report, because your people skills are terrible."

"No. Not really. I was just driving by and saw you loading stuff in this little car. Why do you drive such a small car?"

"I was just wondering the same thing myself."

"Own a shop, have a big dog, probably will get married and have a passel of kids—"

"That's a bit personal, don't you think?"

"I'm just saying. You might want to think about a bigger car when you get rid of this rental."

"I appreciate the advice, *Officer* Black."

"Sure. It's free."

"Suspected it was." Callie opened her door, buckled up, and thought to turn down the radio before she started the ignition.

Black made as if he was going to step away, but then pushed the door open wider, stuck his head back in, and said casually, "Poison doesn't always kill a person."

Callie nearly popped the car out of park by mistake. "Say again?"

Looking out at her yard, Black ran his hand over his face, which already sported a dark shadow, though no doubt he had shaved it that morning. The man had to have Italian genes. "Turns out poison doesn't always kill a person, like you said. Interesting, don't you think?"

"I don't . . . what . . . why would you say such a thing?"

He shrugged, stood up straighter. "Just found it interesting."

Slapping the top of the car, he waved. "I won't keep you. Have a good evening." Then he shut her car door and walked away.

The man was infuriating. Why had he told her that? Was she off the hook? Had he learned that something else killed Stakehorn? Or maybe he was tired and had let it slip? Only Shane Black didn't strike her as the kind of detective who just let things slip. So there was a reason he'd told her that poison hadn't killed Stakehorn. In fact, it was probably the reason he'd stopped by.

The question was, why?

~

Callie and Deborah sat on the front porch, looking out over the fields that were now full of grain. Crops looked different here than they did in Texas, at least they did to Callie. Even from where they sat she could see Jonas on his rig, planting a second summer crop, the twins on the seat next to him.

It was an image she couldn't recall from home—fathers and sons working in the field together.

Home.

Was Shipshewana home? Or was Texas?

She couldn't imagine going back there, though she'd only been here a short time—four weeks to be exact.

It felt right here. It felt as if she were connected to the last of her family.

Finding the journal from Daisy had soothed something in her soul, had healed an ache that she hadn't realized was long in need of repair. What else would she discover if she stayed? What other secrets remained hidden among her aunt's things, within the folds of her aunt's life?

"Is lemonade okay?" Deborah set a tray with a pitcher and two glasses on the weathered table between them, then sank with a sigh into the opposite oak rocker.

"Perfect." Callie drank gratefully from the ice-cold glass. When she visited Deborah now, she no longer wondered at the lack of electricity, how the gas refrigerator worked, or that they were able to have running water both hot and cold—though it didn't spew out of the faucet like it did at her place. Everything here seemed as it should be, even the heat, and the lemonade which soothed it. "Where's the baby?"

"Martha took him to the barn to show him the new kittens." Deborah frowned and followed Callie's gaze out toward the fields. "Remember when kittens and a nicely planted row solved everything?"

"Yes. Well, no, truthfully I don't, since I grew up in the city, but I catch your meaning." Callie sipped again from the tart drink, pressed the cool glass against her forehead, and gazed over at Deborah.

Callie shared with her the price the second quilt had brought.

"It's *gut*. It will help Melinda and Esther a lot."

"How is Aaron?"

"His *bruder* tried to sneak him out to the pond for some late-night fishing, got his wheelchair stuck in the mud. If you could have seen the mess they'd created on the wheels of that chair..." Deborah paused and took a sip of her drink. "There are things he'll need, especially as he grows older. The money will go a long way to helping."

"And Esther?"

"Her parents want her to marry again, and she's not ready. Perhaps the money will help to ease their worries a while longer."

They sat there in the late afternoon heat, thinking of their friends, and of all they'd been through together since the auctions had begun.

"We need to end this, Deb. Before someone else gets hurt."

"*Ya*. I was thinking the same thing. First Margie and now Max. How is he?"

"Fine. Doctor England said he might be ready to come home tomorrow. He wanted to keep him another night for observation."

"It's *gut* he wasn't hurt any worse, and he was there to protect you. It was God's provision, Callie."

Callie looked out at Jonas and the boys. One of the twins had dropped his hat behind the plough, and Jonas stopped the rig so he could jump down, fetch his hat, then climb back on board. It was a simple act, one probably replayed many times in a summer, but it struck Callie as being intimate and precious. She didn't want this family to be hurt as Margie had been, as Max had been.

"I understand what you're saying about God's provision." Callie tucked her hair behind her ears, comfortable with the silence between them as she searched for the words she needed to share. "If Max hadn't been there, I could have been the one shot. But I feel as if I somehow started this sequence of events, as if I brought evil into this place by first putting the quilts on the internet."

"Do you realize how *narrisch* that sounds?"

"Crazy."

"Yes, crazy. It sounds crazy. First of all, other people in Shipshe had been on eBay before you put my quilts there."

Callie smiled at her correct pronunciation of the word, but it didn't stop her.

"Secondly, we don't know whether the person doing this is from the outside. He could very well be a part of our community."

"One more thing we've been unsuccessful in finding out."

"Agreed, but if he's from within, he was here before you arrived. If he's from without, he didn't arrive because of your efforts." Deborah smiled sadly, pushed a stray hair into her *kapp*. "What I mean is you've done a fine job with the shop, but the number of people who come to market each week has remained steady at around thirty thousand for several years now."

"*Danki* for the compliment, if there was one in there." Callie reached over and tapped her lemonade glass against Deborah's. "Thirty thousand people. That is part of our problem. If it were only the people of Shipshewana we had to work through, I think we could figure out who the murderer is, but with all those people traipsing through our town every week ..."

Deborah set her glass on the table and drummed her fingers against the arm of the rocker. "God promises us in his Word that he has plans for us, *gut* plans that include hope and a future, plans to prosper us and not to harm us."

"You're sure solving murders is covered in the Bible?"

Instead of answering, Deborah cut her eyes toward her and smiled, then stood and went inside to check on dinner. Callie heard her in there, opening the oven door, pulling out the casserole which was slow-cooking, adding water from the tap.

She would offer to help, but knew it was useless. Her cooking abilities were limited and usually resulted in more work for all involved.

Instead she focused on Stakehorn's murder, the recent burglaries, and how they were tied together.

~

Deborah walked back out on the front porch to find Callie on her hands and knees in front of her little rental car. Kneeling beside her were Martha, Mary, and baby Joshua. All she could see were the rumps of all four of them, because their heads were practically under the car.

"I can almost reach him," Callie was murmuring.

Martha sat back on her heels and shook her head. "Your arms are too short. They're not any longer than mine. I think you're going to have to stay the night if he doesn't come out."

Callie sat back and brushed at the hair that had flopped in her eyes.

Joshua climbed over into her lap, and Mary scooched closer, placing her hand inside of Callie's. "Stay here tonight, Miss Callie."

Joshua reached up with one hand and twirled Callie's hair; with the other hand he popped his thumb into his mouth.

Callie looked down at the boy, drew one arm around his waist, then kissed him on top of his head.

"Maybe he'll come out if we get a bowl of milk," Callie suggested.

"He doesn't drink from a bowl yet," Martha explained. "Only from her *mamm*."

They all continued to stare at the car, as if it might produce whatever had vanished.

"Lose something?" Deborah asked.

Everyone turned and looked up at her at once.

"The smallest of the kittens, *Mamm*." Mary jumped up and grabbed hold of her hand, tugged her toward the car. "We brought him to show Miss Callie. We thought she might be lonely, since Max is still in the hospital. But the kitten scratched her by accident and she dropped him."

"I didn't drop him, I set him down," Callie corrected her.

"And then he run under there." Mary pointed under the car.

"We were trying to lure him out, but he stays just out of our reach." Martha studied the car, as if it would produce an answer to their puzzle.

Deborah looked at the car, then at the children, and finally at Callie. She felt the hairs on the back of her neck bristle, the same way they did when Jonas ran his hand lightly under her hair. Why hadn't she thought of it before? The solution was so simple.

With absolute certainty, Deborah knew how they could catch Stakehorn's killer — the same way they could catch Martha's kitten.

"Run inside, Martha. Fetch a length of my brightest yarn."

Martha cocked her head to the side, thought about it only a few seconds, then rose and dashed into the house.

They ended up having to tie a small twig onto the end of the yarn to give it some weight. As soon as they did, luring the kitten out was as easy as fishing for perch in the pond. The calico kitten was powerless to resist the temptation. He chased the twig and yellow yarn closer and closer, until Mary was able to pounce on him.

"Gotcha!" she exclaimed, pulling the kitten into her arms.

"Take the kitten back to her *mamm*, children. She'll be worried."

Mary carried the kitten, and Martha held on to Joshua's hand. They hurried toward the barn, giggling and whispering—all once again right in their world.

"Emergency averted." Callie laughed as they walked back to the porch.

"More than that, I think I have a solution to our problem."

"What did you do, spy something under my car?" Callie picked up her glass, took a long drink.

"*Ya*. I spied what we've been missing. Someone poisoned Stakehorn, right?"

"Possibly, though I had a strange visit from Shane Black just before I came out here." She repeated what Shane had said.

Deborah listened, then waved her hand in front of them, as if she were waving away a pesky fly. "Maybe it doesn't matter."

"Doesn't matter?"

"Right. Forget for a minute how Stakehorn died. What's important is that the murderer wanted you to take the fall. We can assume he was happy about that."

"No doubt."

"But just three days later—someone broke into the newspaper." Deborah stood now, walked to the edge of the porch. "Which everyone thought was a burglar or kids who heard the place was empty." "What if it was the same person, looking for something?"

Callie rubbed her finger over her bottom lip. Finally she said, "I tried that angle. I tried it when my bag was missing."

"Stay with me a minute."

"All right. Go on."

"When the paper reopened, Trent McCallister noticed a few strange things." Deborah sat back down in the rocker. "He told us at the vet that several times things have been in the wrong place, the paper hasn't been locked up—at first, things that he attributed to Mrs. Caldwell being old and past retirement age." Callie began tapping her finger against the arm of the rocker.

"But after Max was shot, he changed his tune. What if all of this is caused by the same person?"

A bird called out, then took flight across the field in front of them.

"Margie's shop, your shop, even Max being shot ... it's all the same person, looking for the same thing." Deborah sat back, picked up the lemonade, and rubbed at the condensation running down the sides of the glass.

"You thought of all this while looking under my car?"

"It's just like pieces of a quilt, Callie. It took time for them to come together into a pattern. What I saw under the car was that we need to lure the person out, just like we enticed the kitten. We need to finally give this guy what he's been looking for."

"But we don't know what he's looking for."

"He doesn't have to know that."

Callie continued to worry her bottom lip, studied Jonas and the twins as they made their way in from the field, then said what Deborah had known all along she'd say. "I'm in."

Chapter 28

CALLIE DROVE STRAIGHT to the *Gazette*. Trent answered her knock on the front door of the newspaper, though it was nearing eight in the evening.

"Hello, Callie. Rather late to be placing an ad."

He had a bit of newsprint smeared on his right cheek. Callie struggled with whether to tell him or ignore it. In the end, she stood on her tiptoes and smudged it off with her thumb.

"Oh, uh. Thanks. I've been working on tomorrow's edition and the press broke down again."

"Did you get it working?"

"Yeah. Surprisingly I did, and I only hurt one foot kicking it in the process."

They stood there in the fading sunlight, and suddenly Callie felt a bit awkward. She wondered if her skirt was soiled from kneeling in the dirt with the children, then she wondered why she cared. Her palms started to sweat and she wanted to wipe them on her blouse, but she felt self-conscious doing it.

Why was she so nervous?

Did she actually think he would refuse them?

Their plan couldn't work without his cooperation, without the *Gazette*. It had all begun with the newspaper, and now it could all end with it. But she'd need his help.

"How's Max?" Trent asked.

"He's going to be all right. He should be home tomorrow." Unless Trent agreed to their plan, then she'd ask Doc England to keep him an extra night.

"That's good news. I ran his picture on page one—the one I took the night Margie was attacked."

When Callie only shook her head, he ducked back into the office, came out with a copy of page one. Max had a nice four by five photo in the top left column. He was wearing his blue bandana with silver stars.

"He looks like a real hero," Trent said.

"Yeah, he does." Callie stared down at the picture, determined she wouldn't let her tears fall. "I still owe you for that shirt—the one you put over his wound, but um ... actually I was here to ask another favor."

Trent looked at her quizzically, pushed his glasses up, then stuffed his hands in his pockets. "So you weren't here to place an ad."

"No, I, uh, needed to talk to you about something."

"I was headed out to grab a bite to eat. Are you hungry?"

"Actually I ate with Deb and her family."

"Oh." He nodded as if he had expected her to say no.

"I'd love to join you though, if you don't mind."

The smile that covered his face was slow, genuine, and left her a bit confused. Trent McCallister was all about the story. She could easily imagine him as an editor in Fort Wayne or even Indianapolis. The man had drive. In many ways he reminded Callie of who she had been in Houston. Then there was the personal side of him. When he turned on the charm, she couldn't help melting a bit.

"Want to take my truck or the bike?"

"Let's go with the truck."

"All right, but you're living dangerously if you're betting the truck will make it there and back. I can grab a to-go sandwich at the deli; then we can sit outside and talk."

"Sure. Sounds perfect."

When they arrived at the deli, she declined to go inside with him, opting to wait outside. She needed the night air, needed to hear the sounds of the evening birds and feel the breeze.

It seemed like karma that she was back where the incident had started.

Or had it started here?

What had happened before she'd become upset with Stakehorn?

That was what they really needed to know.

Callie leaned against the side of the truck, studying Trent as he walked back out of the deli — short-sleeved button-up shirt pulled out of his khakis, sand-colored hair badly in need of a cut and extending far past his collar. He looked like such a bad boy, someone who should be climbing on his Harley and riding out of town at sunset, not grabbing a bite to eat then heading back to work on tomorrow's paper.

Depending on Trent McCallister might be one of the most reckless things she'd ever done, but then she remembered the way he'd knelt beside Max with his shirt pulled off. The way he had hurried back to the paper for his truck while she'd called ahead to the clinic. How he'd carried her dog to his truck. The hours he'd spent sitting with her in the vet's waiting room.

He smiled his crooked smile, lowered the tailgate on the truck, and perched on the edge. Callie walked slowly around to the back, her skirt brushing against her legs, her legs brushing against the warm metal of the truck.

Callie had been careful to maintain her independence after Rick's death. Trusting Deborah had been a giant leap of faith. Now she needed to trust Trent. More than that she wanted to trust him. She wanted to give him a chance to prove that he was the good guy here.

He gave her a hand up, and she joined him on the tailgate, with her legs swinging. She felt like a child again, and all things were possible. From where they sat, they were able to watch the last of the travelers down Main Street. Since it was a Friday, there weren't many people.

Again, she wondered if that had figured into what had happened. Was it one of Deborah's quilt pieces? Part of the pattern she always spoke of, part of the answer that would lead them to understanding the identity of Stakehorn's murderer? And it had been a murder, no one doubted that anymore, although Shane hadn't put up any WANTED posters. The way he'd conducted his investigation made it plain enough.

"Deborah and I think the person who killed Stakehorn is still in Shipshewana. We think he or she has been trying to find something."

Trent finished chewing the large bite he had taken of the sandwich.

"How do you figure?"

"One murder, an attack on Margie, break-ins at the paper, The *Kaffi* Shop, my shop, Max shot ..."

"Slow down." A frown formed between Trent's eyes, and she knew he was putting this together like a reporter, which was good. They needed some objective thinking applied to the situation.

The more they talked, the more accurate Deborah's theory felt.

"If we're right, this person is going to keep coming back to the same places until he finds what he's looking for. You're going to keep finding things misplaced, doors unlocked—"

Holding his hand up to stop her, Trent took a drink of the soda he'd bought with the sandwich. "You think the person who killed Stakehorn, and did all that other stuff, is still nosing around in my newspaper office?"

"Yes."

"Why?"

"We don't know why. Maybe we don't need to know why. We want to know who. I met with Adalyn yesterday, and according to her I'm still on Black's short list regarding the murder. I give you my word I didn't do it. I didn't kill Stakehorn, and I didn't break into the paper. I sure didn't shoot my own dog. So who did? We want to know. We want to stop what's happening in Shipshewana."

"And you're telling me because—"

"We need your help."

"Whoa there, hoss. I report the news. I don't star in it."

"Tell me it's not in your best interest to find out."

"I'm not sure it matters to me, if they're not taking anything."

"Of course it does. They've killed once, and they won't hesitate to kill again." Callie crossed her arms, feeling frustrated at his immediate resistance. "Think about what a headline it would make on the front of your paper when we catch this person."

"If I were to agree, what kind of help are you talking about?" The frown was quite pronounced now. "And I'm not saying I would because my MO is to stay uninvolved."

Callie pulled in a deep breath. She'd been a good salesperson when she was a pharmaceutical rep, partly because she knew her product, but also because she was able to gauge what a client needed.

Looking at Trent, she put herself in his shoes. He didn't need the murderer's identity, not like she did.

But there was one thing he did need.

"We need you to run a story."

"Uh-huh."

"And if it works, we'll catch our man."

"Or woman."

"Just say you'll help." Callie waited while Trent considered what she'd said.

"What if it doesn't work?" Trent balled up all the trash, placed it in the bag, and sat back against the side panel of the truck—studying her, assessing her, looking for the weakness in her plan.

"It will. All you have to do is run the story. Say that according to undisclosed sources you've learned Stakehorn had amassed a large sum of money—money that is now missing from his safe."

Trent began shaking his head, but Callie pushed on.

"The police have not formally charged anyone yet, but it's possible charges will be filed in twenty-four to forty-eight hours—against the same person they have considered their prime suspect for murder."

"Which everyone knows is you." Trent crossed his arms, cocked his head, and looked at her as if she were insane or two-years-old, or possibly both.

"Exactly. An indictment for murder and burglary is expected to be handed down at the same time. Think what a scoop that will be for your paper."

"Except it's completely bogus."

"I'm not done yet." Callie leaned forward and lowered her voice as Mr. Simms walked out of the deli and began changing the sign on the front marquee. "On the second page, you run a story that states Daisy's Quilt Shop has been temporarily closed and that I am unavailable for comment."

"You are?"

"Yes."

"And why are you not available?"

"As a good reporter, it's your job to find out."

"Of course it is." Trent now looked as if he was actually enjoying this. He offered her a drink of the soda, which she waved away.

"So you contact the store."

"But there's no answer."

"Then you contact the Chamber of Commerce."

"But they haven't heard from you."

"Finally you call—"

They both stopped talking as Mr. Simms walked by. "Night, Mr. McCallister, Miss Callie."

"Mr. Simms." They said his name simultaneously.

He turned, looked at them as if he expected they might say something more. "Did you need anything?"

"No, sir. That is, not at this moment." Callie smiled mischievously.

"You go ahead and knock if you do. We're closed now, but for you, Miss Callie, I will open up again." He shuffled off into the store, waving a hand spotted with age as he did.

"Where was I?" she asked.

"I had just called Mr. Simms to find out why you're unavailable for comment, and why Daisy's Quilt Shop is closed."

"He saw me get in the back of Shane Black's car."

"Tell me it's not true." Trent's hazel eyes practically danced in the darkening night. "Why, pray tell, would the good officer arrest you yet again?"

"Simms doesn't know, but he did overhear something."

"Of course he did."

"He overheard me ask to make a last minute stop by my place."

"You practically begged."

"I did."

"Request denied though."

"How did you know?"

"Simms told me."

Callie sat back, satisfied at last.

"That's the craziest story I've ever heard, Callie. Maybe you should give up being a shop owner and become a writer."

"*Danki.*"

"Huh?"

"That's Amish. It means thank you."

"Okay. Thanks for the lesson in Dutch. Now suppose I bought

into this, which I haven't. What's the point? Why are you planting these two stories?"

Callie grinned at him, more sure than ever that he would agree and that their plan would work. "Because Deborah and I are going to be hiding upstairs, waiting for the murderer—who has to be Stakehorn's son. He's the only person on Deborah's list who makes sense."

Callie was certain the real killer would never know he was being set up.

It took her another twenty minutes to convince Trent. Finally he shrugged, pushed his hair out of his eyes, and aimed for nonchalant. "I have a hard time believing Stakehorn did this."

"Greed is the most frequent motive for murder. Haven't you read any Agatha Christie?"

"No, but I've read a lot of newsprint. Greed, I accept. Killing your own father . . ."

"They were estranged."

"Takes an abnormally cold person, and someone who might be dangerous. Why don't you go and talk to Black?"

"We don't have any proof. That's what we need! Do you really think Roger Stakehorn is dangerous? He's more like the bumbling crook in some comedy flick."

"If what you say is true, he's dangerous enough to have killed."

"With poison, probably from long distance." Callie combed her fingers through the back of her hair as they walked toward the deli. "I don't even think he was in town. I think he mailed the poison to his father. Hid it in some coffee creamer and waited for it to do its work. He's a coward, Trent, and I for one am not afraid of him. All we need is for you to run the stories."

"I'm not completely convinced. Remember I'm only on temporary assignment here. If this crazy idea of yours works, maybe I'll secure my job here. If it doesn't, I'll claim I had a terrible source I'll never use again."

"Me?" Callie gave him her best smile, thought he might kiss her by the way he smiled that half smile and shook his head slightly.

"You," he said, leaning forward, then past her to open the door to the closed deli.

Mr. Simms was easier to convince. They didn't need to tell him all of the details, only that they had a plan to end what was going on in Shipshewana, catch the guilty party, and disperse the cloud of suspicion hanging over Callie.

He reached an age-spotted hand across the table and patted hers. "I've liked you since you walked into my deli and threw tea on Stakehorn."

"Mr. Simms, I'm not exactly proud of that moment."

"Proud or not, he had been less than kind to many of my customers. You were not afraid to stand up to him. Though you are small, you are incredibly brave."

"Or incredibly stupid," Trent muttered, then grabbed his ankle when Callie kicked him under the table.

"Do you understand what you're to say if anyone comes by and speaks with you, Mr. Simms?" Callie's biggest fear was that another innocent person would be hurt before the murderer was brought to justice.

"Sure, sure. I tell them I saw you put into Black's car. This is true. I was walking down the street the day he arrested you. It was a terrible thing."

"Too bad that was actually a week ago." Trent stood, signaling to Callie that it was time for them to go.

"Dates and times—sometimes these things blur for me. I have a deli to run and can't always be looking at a calendar or a clock." He chuckled and walked them to the door. "Be careful, young lady."

"Don't forget—I insisted on going back to the shop first."

"I've got it. You don't need to write it down."

For a moment the jesting demeanor was gone, replaced by a wiser man who had perhaps seen his share of evil. "Whoever this person is, he isn't playing a game, and he won't hesitate to hurt anyone who steps in his way."

Callie stepped closer, kissed his weathered cheek. "I will be careful."

Callie stepped out into the night, but as she did, she heard Simms pull Trent back and mutter, "Take care of her, or you'll need more than a newspaper to hide behind."

Chapter 29

Saturday evening, Deborah parked her buggy at Mr. Simms's deli, promised him one last time they would be fine, and hurried in the waning light down Main Street.

When Daisy's Quilt Shop came into sight, she skirted near the overhang of the buildings, hoping no one saw her. If they did, she had her excuse ready—a cup of plant fertilizer in her basket for Callie's window plants.

Come murder or burglary she was not about to see the shop fall into disrepair like it had before. Now that she thought about it, maybe they'd have time to fertilize the ferns and spider ivy before they hid upstairs in the apartment.

Letting herself in with the key Callie had given her, she locked the door behind her, then turned around and let out a shriek when she bumped into Callie.

"Having second thoughts?" Callie asked, a grin splayed across her face.

"Of course not, though my stomach has been *naerfich* all day." Deborah smiled back at her, and thrust the basket into Callie's hands. "It's as if we've stepped into one of those Agatha Christie novels you are so fond of reading."

"Yes, turns out my Aunt Daisy had good taste in authors.

284

Remember though, this isn't a book. We follow the plan—lock Stakehorn in the storage room, leave the shop, call the police."

"That's exactly what I told Jonas—lock, leave, and call. The way the man drinks, he'll probably fall asleep in the storage room before the police arrive."

Callie pulled up the cloth napkin and peered into the basket. Squirreling up her nose she took a step backward, holding the basket at arm's length. "This is not food."

"No, it isn't for human consumption. How would it look for me to be bringing food here when the entire town is talking about your probable arrest?" Deborah smirked, then walked into the shop, which was growing dark. Enough light was still coming in the front windows for her to see that the plants looked healthy.

"So they're buying the story?" Callie followed, trying to push the basket back into Deborah's hands.

"*Ya*. It's the gossip of the town. Most folks are so mad at Black they won't speak to him. Gavin is walking around looking as if he's been sideswiped by a two-by-four. And Trent had to pretend he'd gone over to Middlebury for supplies so people would stop pestering him for more details."

"*Most* folks are mad?" Callie plucked on Deborah's arm as she walked into the kitchen to fill a pitcher with water. "Most? You mean some people actually think I deserved to be arrested? They think I'm guilty?"

"Some people are always willing to believe the worst. You know that. It's true whether you're in Shipshe or in Texas."

"I suppose." Callie sighed, set the basket on the counter, then looked at the pitcher of water. "What are you planning on doing with that, throwing it at the killer?"

"Of course not." She reached into the basket and pulled out a pot, then untied the string that was holding a cloth over the top. "I'm going to feed the plants while I'm here. It's why I brought the fertilizer—a special mixture of manure and herbs Jonas makes up for me to use on my own garden plants."

Callie followed her out toward the front window.

"Throw that at whoever comes through the door. He'll run for his life. Smells like something Max did after I fed him one of my failed attempts at cooking."

Deborah heard the downturn in her voice at Max's name. "No doubt it was hard for you to leave Max at Doc England's, but you know it was for the better. If he'd been here, he would have tried to take another bite out of the intruder."

At the word intruder, they both heard noise at the back door.

Her heart thumping in her chest, Deborah snatched Callie by the arm, pulling her behind the aisle of cotton fabric. Looking into her eyes, she saw surprise, a healthy dose of fear, and steely resolve—the very emotions she was feeling.

"It's not even completely dark yet," Callie muttered.

Deborah shushed her and reached on a nearby table for a weapon. All she came up with was a pair of quilting scissors. Callie stared at her as if she were truly *narrisch*, and perhaps she was. But when Deborah handed them to her she took them and gripped them like a stake she planned to ram into the ground.

Deborah slowly pulled out one of the bolts of fabric from the shelf they crouched near and held it like a softball bat. She hadn't played since she was a girl, but she still remembered the way it felt to swing the bat and connect with the ball. Would it feel the same to swat a man with a heavy bolt of cotton cloth?

They squatted there, waiting for the intruder to make his way into the back room where the safe was located.

Instead they heard footsteps slowly trudging toward the front room. So much for hiding. If the murderer was coming toward them, maybe they could knock him over, run out the door, and get help.

Motioning for Callie to creep toward the right end of the aisle,

Deborah headed toward the left. Then holding up her fingers she counted one, two, and finally three.

They jumped out at the same time, shouting "Don't move," and "We have you surrounded."

Trent stumbled backward and knocked over the lamp on the check-out counter. "Easy, ladies. I'm not your man."

Deborah and Callie exchanged glances, as if they weren't quite sure they could trust him.

"What are you doing here?" Deborah asked, still not relinquishing her bolt of calico print cotton.

"I came to help, maybe snap a few pictures. Now would you mind dropping the flowery material?" Trent righted the lamp and pushed his glasses back into place. "Callie, put down those scissors, before you hurt someone."

"We hadn't planned on needing to defend ourselves. Stakehorn won't be walking up and down the fabric aisles. He'll be headed straight for the safe. Now would *you* mind getting out of here? We're trying to be inconspicuous, which we can't do if you're on a photo opp." She pointed her scissors at the camera around his neck. "We also can't have people just dropping by."

"I wasn't exactly here for a social visit, gorgeous."

Deborah noticed Callie's eyes widen slightly at the nickname, but decided it was something she'd have to ask about later. "Why are you here, Trent?"

"Like I said, it'll make good cover copy in the paper. Besides I couldn't leave you two here to greet a killer by yourself."

"How did you get in?" Callie stepped forward.

"I thought about jimmying the lock, but there was a key hidden under the frog."

"You didn't bring that in?" Deborah asked Callie.

"I thought you did."

"Ladies? Could we hide before he gets here?"

Callie switched the scissors to her other hand, wiped her

sweaty palm on her skirt. "You know we don't need a man. We can do this by ourselves."

"Actually it might be a good idea," Deborah interrupted. "Jonas wanted to come, but I needed him to stay home with the *boppli*."

"I'm glad someone here is willing to listen to reason." Trent smiled, apparently happy that he'd won a round.

"Well, you didn't say anything last night about wanting to be here."

"Maybe that's because I didn't have time to think it through when you sprung this crazy idea on me."

"If it's so crazy, why did you agree to it?"

They were now only inches apart, and Deborah wondered if arguing was some strange English courting ritual. "Umm, guys. I think we probably should move upstairs."

Trent and Callie turned to glare at her.

Deborah pointed out the front window. "Pretty dark out there. I wouldn't put it past our guy to show up any minute."

But in fact he didn't show up then, and they could have stayed downstairs arguing for quite some time.

~

Upstairs, they sat in the darkness of Callie's apartment on the floor in front of the bay windows and watched the streets of Shipshewana grow less crowded and then deserted.

One by one the lights went out in each store.

Twice Andrew Gavin drove by, even stopping once to shine his flashlight in the front door of Daisy's Quilt Shop.

"I feel a little guilty about not telling him," Callie confessed.

The light of a quarter moon slipped through the front window of the apartment, dispelling enough of the darkness for them to see each other's expression.

"Now you grow a conscience." Trent rolled his eyes, but Deborah also heard the concern in his voice.

"You can come clean tomorrow," Deborah reminded her. "After we catch the murderer."

"If we catch him." Callie traced the pattern in the wood grain on the floor. "What if he doesn't show? What if I remain Black's best suspect?"

"Adalyn said he doesn't have enough evidence to prosecute, Callie. Try not to worry about tomorrow's problems." Deborah reached out and squeezed her hand, which was when they heard the tinkle of glass breaking downstairs.

Then the back door of Daisy's Quilt Shop opened once again.

Callie felt every hair on her neck prickle up.

She stared at Trent and Deborah and knew they were as shocked as she was. They had planned everything so carefully, but now that it was actually happening, they could hardly believe it.

Downstairs, someone was moving toward the safe in her back room — and that someone was most certainly the person who had killed Stakehorn, the person who had hurt Margie, and the person who had shot her dog.

Anger surged through Callie's veins.

She leapt off the floor and would have hurdled herself down the stairs if Trent hadn't caught her by the waist. "Slow, Callie Grace. Slow and quiet."

He'd never used her middle name before. She had no idea how he even knew it, unless he'd been doing some investigating into her background. Would he have done that? Before she could fully consider the question, he'd encircled her waist with both arms and pulled her back across the room, his lips lingering near her ear. His words were like cold water in her face. The effect of those two words was like her mother's sensible voice in her memory. It slowed her down, calmed the fury just enough to allow caution a bit of room.

She pulled in a deep breath, nodded once, and picked up the scissors off the end table.

They took the stairs in that order.

Callie first, carrying her wickedly sharp fabric scissors. Trent following, fists clenched at his side, his camera apparently left behind. Deborah bringing up the rear, still clutching her bolt of fabric.

As they crept down the stairs, then around the corner into the back hall, they lost the light of the moon.

Callie met a wall of blackness, but was finally able to make out a pin-prick of light, which slowly broadened to a glow the size of her fist.

It had to be coming from a flashlight.

As they tip-toed closer, she made out a figure, hunched over the tiny desk which was stored against the east wall. The person was shuffling through papers and pulling out drawers. Deborah had suggested they write the safe's combination on an index card and tape it inside the middle desk drawer, under the pencil keeper—something a burglar might expect an old lady to do.

Callie knew the moment he found it. She could have sworn she heard him cackle.

Then he spun away from them and toward the safe in the wall at the back of the room.

She could almost make out who it was. There was something familiar about the shape of his head, the way he hunched his shoulders as he worked in the near darkness. She couldn't see well enough to be sure, but she had the distinct impression she'd seen him before.

When he turned away, she lost the light from his flashlight. He was turning the combination on the lock, had just opened the safe's door, and pulled out the envelope stuffed with one dollar bills, when Callie, Trent, and Deborah reached the door to the little back room.

As planned, they didn't confront him, didn't holler out, didn't try to stop him from taking the money or the package they'd planted in the safe.

Instead Callie slammed the door shut, Trent braced it closed with his shoulder, and Deborah grabbed the chair they'd placed in the next room. They moved it under the knob in one smooth motion.

"Find something else," Trent said. "In case this doesn't hold."

Callie and Deborah hurried into the next room.

Callie ran into an old oak trunk Daisy had used to keep extra supplies in, smashing her knee into the brass fixture on the side.

"William Barret Travis," she groaned. "I think I broke my knee."

Deborah was too focused on the task at hand to comment on the obscure reference — or even the injury. "Hurry, Callie! Let's drag this back to Trent."

Ignoring the throbbing in her knee, she grabbed the trunk by one handle and began to pull it out of the room and down the hall. She couldn't see Deborah, but she could feel her on the other end, pushing with as much effort as she was pulling.

They fumbled down the dark hall, where Trent was leaning with all of his weight against the door.

"Why didn't you turn the lights on?" he asked.

"Didn't think of it." Callie wondered if she could lift the trunk up enough to drop it on his foot. Leave it to a man to have a better idea in the midst of a crisis. Maybe if he felt the full weight of the trunk he'd cut her some slack.

"I thought of it," Deborah pushed her end in place. "Electricity isn't working."

Why didn't the electricity work? Had the man cut the power before he'd broken into the shop? Why would he do that?

The person on the other side of the door had realized his predicament by this point. He'd begun banging on the door and hollering — demanding to be let out. Swearing he'd get even once he found a way through the solid wood door.

"Have to admire the construction in these older buildings." Trent's voice sounded tight and uncharacteristically nervous.

Callie thought she heard him sit down on top of the chest.

"This should hold him for a while, but I'd feel better if you ladies stayed in the next room."

"Whatever for?" Deborah asked.

Next to her, Callie felt Deborah pick up the bolt of cloth she had dropped and hug it to herself. She stood so close that their shoulders were touching, and Callie could feel the slight tremor passing through her arms.

The rattling at the door continued, its shaking a noise as nerve-wracking as fingers on a chalkboard.

"Trent's worried he has a gun," Callie explained, as she pulled out her phone and dialed nine-one-one. "I really don't think he does, though."

"Why not?" Trent asked.

"I know who it is," Callie said. "I'd know that sniveling voice anywhere. And I'm betting all he has in his pocket is a bottle of whiskey."

In what she hoped was a calm voice she told the dispatch operator that she'd like an officer sent over to Daisy's Quilt Shop, yes *that* quilting store. Snapping the phone shut, she pulled Deborah back into the doorway of the main room.

If they glanced left, they could stare into the darkness where Trent sat on the trunk and the sounds of the door rattling, of the murderer trying to break free, continued.

If they glanced to the right, they could barely make out a bit of ambient light from the street.

"What about Trent? Shouldn't he be with us? What if the guy does have a gun?" Deborah stuck her head out into the hall, and Callie pulled her back.

"He probably should be with us, but he's a man. English men need to be the protector. Plus if the guy did have a gun, he'd already have used it."

"I hope we don't have to wait long. I'm ready for this to be over." Deborah's voice was calm, but she reached over and clasped Callie's hand.

Though it was still pitch dark, Callie looked down, tried to see their fingers entwined together. She suddenly realized how close they'd become in such a short time.

Maybe extreme circumstances did that to people — forged relationships that otherwise might have taken years to build. Or maybe it was the Amish way. How could she know?

She didn't have long to think about it though. The darkness of the night was split by the light and blip-bleep of a Shipshewana Police Department vehicle.

Andrew Gavin's voice was one of the sweetest sounds Callie had ever heard.

"Shipshewana Police. Whoever is in there needs to come out with your hands in the air."

"Gavin, it's us. Don't shoot!" Callie and Deborah hurried to the back door, their shoes crunching on broken glass as they practically ran out into the night, out into the light of Andrew Gavin's flashlight.

"Callie? Deborah? What's going on?" Gavin reached into his squad car and silenced the siren.

"We caught him. We caught the murderer!" Callie couldn't stop herself from hopping up and down. She pointed into the still dark shop.

"He's locked in the storage room." Deborah pointed back to the hallway, only slightly more calm. "Trent McCallister is guarding the door."

"You two are sure you're all right?"

"We're fine, but you better hurry. He's trying to bust his way out. We braced the door with a chair and a trunk." Callie shuffled from one foot to the other.

She should feel calmer now that the guy they'd been searching for was about to be arrested, but suddenly everything felt wrong. She had an abrupt overwhelming urge to be back inside.

"Trent's worried he might be armed," Deborah explained.

Gavin pulled out his radio. "This is Officer Gavin. I'm at Daisy's Quilt Shop on Main Street. We have a burglary in progress. I'm requesting back-up, over."

Callie took a step toward the door. "We can't wait, Andrew. We need—"

They'd been standing between the shop and the police cruiser, but everyone turned when they heard Trent yell out for help.

"Guys, I think you should get in here, and you better hurry."

Chapter 30

DEBORAH FOLLOWED Callie and Officer Gavin back inside. She'd never feared the darkness or the night, but something told her this evening held danger—danger of a kind she hadn't faced before.

She said a prayer for safety and a prayer for wisdom, then reached for her bolt of cloth while Gavin directed Trent and Callie to remove the trunk and the chair.

And why did she find such comfort from holding the fabric?

She'd always been soothed by the sight, smell, and texture of cotton—whether she was quilting, sewing, or doing a simple task such as laundry. It seemed that in many ways fabric was a gift from God which held her family together physically, much as his love and grace held them together spiritually.

The light from Gavin's flashlight flooded the hall. He handed it to Callie; then he held up his weapon and nodded at Trent to open the door.

Deborah tried to focus on what was happening; but her mind kept returning to the fabric, to the quilt squares she sewed into patterns.

This pattern was coming together all wrong. Something was missing, but she couldn't put her finger on exactly what.

Trent opened the door—now cracked and splintered from the

battering it had received from the inside, and Roger Stakehorn nearly fell out into the hall.

Sweaty, flushed, and wild-eyed, he looked ready to charge at the first thing that moved.

"Hands in the air," Gavin barked.

Stakehorn froze, blinking in the bright light. "What? I don't understand. What's going on here?"

"Why don't you tell us, Mr. Stakehorn? Looks like a pretty clear case of breaking and entering." Gavin motioned with his gun. "Turn around, walk to the back of the storage room, and put your hands on the wall. You can drop the envelope of money on the desk."

Stakehorn looked at the envelope he was holding as if he were seeing it for the first time. "This is my money to begin with. I'm not stealing it. I'm taking it back."

"Tell it to the judge. Now turn around."

Finally noticing Callie, Stakehorn's face turned red as the plums at the local market. "You! This is your fault. You're the one who killed my father and now you're getting away with his things. Well, I won't allow it."

He moved toward Callie. Trent moved in between them at the same moment Gavin raised his gun higher, sending Trent back to Callie's side with a single look.

"I will shoot, Mr. Stakehorn. This is your last warning. Turn around and walk toward the back walk."

"This isn't over, Harper." Stakehorn practically spit the words, but he turned slowly, walked to the back of the storage room, and stopped when his fingers touched the wall.

Deborah noticed he did not drop the envelope of money.

～

To Callie it seemed that everything happened at once.

She had the absurd notion she was inside a dream, one where

she had no ability to control events and was powerless to stop what would occur next.

Stakehorn threatened her, Trent moved in between them, and Gavin raised his gun.

Stakehorn sneered, said something else, finally turned and walked toward the back wall.

It all happened as if from a distance.

She noticed the beam of light from Gavin's flashlight wavering and realized her hand must be shaking.

Then she felt, more than saw, Deborah leave the room.

Where was she going?

Before she could turn to ask, before she could fully formulate any reasons to explain what might be happening, Gavin stepped forward so that he too was in the beam of light.

Callie wanted to call out, wanted to stop him, but again she was frozen—exactly like in a dream.

He lowered his gun so that he could put handcuffs on Stakehorn. Trent moved forward a step, maybe two.

And that was the moment when her dream fell away, the slow motion of sleep time dropped like a cloak, and reality snapped into events that moved too quickly, events that became a full-fledged nightmare.

The cold hard metal against her neck could only be a gun, and the voice in her ear sent shivers all the way down to her toes.

"Real quiet, and don't drop the flashlight or I'll shoot the officer first."

More loudly he called out. "Drop the gun, Officer Gavin. I don't want to cap the girl, but I will if you insist."

Everyone in front of them froze, like in some graphic cartoon. For the space of a few seconds no one spoke. It seemed to Callie that no one dared to breathe.

Finally Gavin raised his right hand, with his weapon clearly palmed there, but his fingers well away from the trigger.

"Good. Bend down, place it on the floor, turn around, and kick it back toward me. Real slow like."

When Gavin turned, he only glanced at her for a second. It was long enough for Callie to see a myriad of emotions in his eyes. She saw feelings she hadn't expected to see in another man's glance ever again—despair, concern, and something more than friendship. She felt her heart catch in her throat, but before she could understand the emotions behind his deep blue eyes, his gaze turned to the man behind her, hard as steel.

"Whatever you want, we can work it out," Gavin said. "Everyone just needs to stay cool."

"Exactly my sentiments. Now your back-up weapon. Very slowly. I have an itchy finger as long as someone else is armed."

Gavin's moves were deliberate and non-threatening. Had he been taught this in some training seminar?

"Same thing with the radio."

Gavin did as he was told, never taking his eyes off the man who was holding a gun to Callie—though she realized too late he was staring into darkness. She was the one holding the light, and it was all pointed toward them.

"Let her go. She's not a part of this."

"Oh, but she is. It would seem she's been a part of this from the beginning."

He was going to kill them all.

The thought shot into Callie's mind with the force of a lightning strike. Trent would never take that motorcycle ride to Sturgis. Gavin wouldn't get a chance to settle down and have those two-point-five kids. And Deborah—

Where was Deborah?

She had left.

Had she heard him coming? Had she escaped?

Callie's hands started shaking and the light wavered.

"Easy, honey." The voice was gravelly, reminding her of a pharmaceutical client she'd had who was a heavy smoker. "Remember our deal? The light stays steady, and you'll be okay."

She didn't believe him for a minute, but she nodded and gripped her right arm with her left, forced the tremor to stop.

She needed to do something, needed to warn Deborah away. Deborah had children. She couldn't die in the back hall of Daisy's Quilt Shop.

"God has plans for us, Callie." Deborah's words came back to her so strongly that for a brief second it seemed she was standing there, uttering them again.

Was this God's plan?

Callie didn't know, but for the first time in over a year, she began to pray.

Deborah couldn't have said why she'd ducked out of the room after Trent had opened the door. The urge had been too strong to deny.

She'd slipped into the main room of the shop at the exact moment the dark, hulking figure had entered the back door, gun raised. She'd just made out his shadow by the light of the moon, but it was all she'd needed to see.

The man locked in the storage room wasn't the murderer. Deborah hadn't stayed long enough to figure out who he was, but he wasn't the person they needed to fear. The one holding the larger gun, creeping down the hall — the one now threatening her friends — was the person they had to stop.

Suddenly she understood why the pieces hadn't fit earlier, why this entire plan of theirs had felt like a quilt she was sewing together incorrectly, tugging at the different squares, forcing them into positions where they didn't belong. And in that moment, she realized that she couldn't fix this — it was bigger than her. She was only a woman, who liked to quilt, who cared for her friends. She wasn't someone who could stand up to a real killer.

It was easy to remind Esther and Melinda and even Callie about *Gotte's wille*, but could she trust him now? Images of her *kinner* flashed through her mind even as her heart rate continued to accelerate. Panic flooded her bloodstream.

Then Jonas's words came to her, soft and low, or was it *Gotte's*? "Small steps ..."

She couldn't escape out the front door; the bell would ring and alert him.

She couldn't flee out the back. He'd hear her step on the broken glass.

This man was a professional at what he did. She could tell that by the way he'd slid along the wall, holding the gun with the same confidence Jonas held his farming tools. The gun to him was second nature.

No, he would hear the smallest sound.

She couldn't escape either of those ways, and she had to escape.

Finding help for her friends would be their only hope.

Slipping her flip-flops off her feet, she turned the corner into the hall and crept up the stairs. Once in Callie's apartment, she opened the side window, praying the old wooden pane would raise silently. If she remembered correctly, there was a lattice work trellis on this side of the building.

She put her shoes back on, and started down in the darkness. Daisy's white roses had made healthy progress up the trellis, reaching well past the first floor. Deborah didn't worry about them biting into her fingers, though she was careful not to let them tangle her dress. She had to hurry.

She didn't have long now.

She landed softly in the grass below, saw a car on the far end of Main, and began to run.

Not caring how she looked or what the Englisher driving the car thought, but knowing that they were down to a few minutes, she ran down the middle of the road. Arms waving, her *kapp* knocked askew, Deborah ran with all her might.

She didn't realize it was Shane Black until he screeched to a halt in front of her and jumped out of the unmarked car.

"Deborah, you're bleeding. What happened? Tell me what's wrong." He grabbed her hands, tried to wipe away the blood from the thorns.

"Callie and Trent and Gavin. You have to hurry." Deborah sucked in a breath. "He's going to shoot them."

Shane looked in her eyes, and then he did the one thing she knew she could count on Shane Black to do. He acted first, and left the questions for later.

"Get in the car."

"No, he'll hear us. We need to run." Deborah turned and took off back down the street. Shane ran beside her.

They left the car, sitting there, idling in the middle of Main Street.

∼

Gordon Stone had rarely been so glad to have a job finally finished. At last he could leave this hick town behind him, hit the toll road going eighty, and never look back.

He should have been finished weeks ago.

He would have been too, if his boss had picked a normal place for the drop. But no, he had to pick the flea market in Shipshewana. The place was like stepping back in time. Everything about it gave Gordon the willies — from the clip clop of the horses to the absurd way people had of dressing.

"Walk forward." He tapped the brunette lightly with the gun. If he had time he would have talked her into going with him. This was one broad who did not belong in a do-nothing town. Unfortunately he needed to grab the boss's package quick and split.

"Hand the flashlight to your boyfriend."

When she started to look at him, he pushed the gun a little bit harder into the flesh on her neck. "Don't turn around, hon. Hand it to McCallister, like I told you."

She moved forward, did as instructed.

That was another thing he liked about this one; she followed directions well. Maybe he would take her with him.

"Don't worry, Callie. We'll be all right," McCallister said as he accepted the flashlight.

Gordon raised his gun and cuffed the editor on the side of the head.

"If I want to hear from you, I'll ask you a question."

While he didn't say anything else, Gordon noticed the guy did give Harper a weak smile. The last thing he needed was a hero in this group. At least the officer knew how to keep his trap shut, though he suspected the cop was simply biding his time, waiting for a chance to make his move. No problem there; he'd dealt with the law before this assignment. He'd be long gone by the time Gavin figured a way out.

"Okay, Harper, first I want you to take out Officer Gavin's handcuffs and cuff his right hand to those utility shelves. They look like someone had the sense to weld them to the floor."

"I'm sorry," she whispered to the officer as she took the cuffs off his belt and did as Gordon directed her.

"Now take the other half of the cuffs and secure our burglar to the same shelf."

Stakehorn growled but didn't argue. Apparently he'd learned from McCallister's example.

"You want this, I guess." She took the package of one dollar bills from Stakehorn's other hand, though he looked like he might fight her for it.

"Nah. It was yours to begin with. You keep it. I'm guessing there isn't that much in there anyway. Now tell her where the keys to the cuffs are, Gavin."

"Front shirt pocket, Callie."

Harper retrieved them. As she unbuttoned his pocket and pulled the keys out, Gordon noticed her hands were shaking. He thought that was kind of sweet.

"All right. Toss them over here to me."

Catching them, he pocketed them in the front pocket of his jeans. "Here's the easy part, and listen carefully or I'm going to have to kill everyone in this room. I need to know what you did with the package that old man Stakehorn found. If you give me the bag, then I'll take it and leave. That's all my boss wants."

Harper looked at the blond guy. He shook his head slightly and cut his eyes to the younger Stakehorn. Gavin was trying to catch Harper's attention.

Gordon figured he'd seen enough sleezeballs in his life to know one, and Roger Stakehorn qualified. As soon as everyone looked at him, he started singing prettier than the canary Gordon's mama had once kept in the house.

"Don't start staring at me. You know I don't have any package." He tried to stand, tripping when he forgot that he was handcuffed to the shelf. "She probably stole it, just like she stole my old man's money. She killed him too."

If Gordon had the time, he'd teach the little leech some manners. Instead he opted for pulling back the slide on his SIG Sauer P226. The feel and sound of the pistol brought him a measure of pleasure, as did the looks of fear on the four faces in front of him.

"Shut up," he said. "I told you I'm in a hurry, and I don't have time to listen to this sort of thing."

"But she—"

"She did nothing. You think she killed your old man? How'd she do that? He was already dead when she got there. You know how I know? Because I killed him, and I wouldn't have had to do it if he'd just given me the package." His voice rose and his pulse began throbbing in his temple as his patience ebbed away. "Now I'm going to count to three, then I'm shooting somebody if I don't see that bag."

"One."

"We don't have it," Harper said.

"Two."

McCallister moved and grabbed Harper, shoving her down on the floor behind him.

"Three."

"I wouldn't do that if I were you."

The unmistakable feel of a pistol pressed into the nape of his neck was enough to send Gordon into a rage. Then again, he didn't want the guy standing behind him to do anything they'd both regret.

"Easy, pal."

"Don't speak. Don't move." The voice was calm and cool. Too calm. Whoever it was, he'd handled this sort of situation before, and that most certainly was not a good thing.

The man leaned forward and relieved him of his semi-automatic, never easing up on the pistol's pressure that was biting into his neck.

Gordon didn't like the way Harper was staring over his shoulder, like she'd spotted a knight in shining armor ride up on a white horse.

He didn't like the smugness in the guy's voice.

And he sure didn't like knowing what his boss was going to say when he used his one phone call.

Chapter 31

Shipshewana, Indiana
June 28

"I STILL DON'T UNDERSTAND," Callie said, staring down into her coffee, squished between Deborah and the wall of the booth. "If the poison didn't kill Stakehorn, what did?"

"And why was poison in his *kaffi*?" Deborah asked.

Adalyn took a bite of the apple strudel in front of her and grinned. "You want to explain it, Trent? Or do you want me to?"

"Be my guest." He leaned back in the booth at The *Kaffi* Shop, tapping a rolled up sheet with his notes for Tuesday's paper against the table.

"This is all off the record, mind you." She looked across at Trent and wagged her finger.

"No problem. I have my own sources—some who are on the record and some who aren't." He grinned across at Callie and she felt her heart rate trip, then accelerate.

She still hadn't digested all her feelings from the last forty-eight hours. Max groaned and rolled over on her feet underneath the table, his bright red bandana resting nicely against his golden coat. Since the news had spread around Shipshewana, and the *Gazette* had come out featuring Max as a hero, he was allowed into any store or restaurant.

Callie was grateful for that. She felt better with the Labrador at her side, though she knew she was perfectly safe with Stone behind bars.

"From what we've been able to put together," Trent said, "through Stone's confession, a more complete revelation of Shane's investigation, and of course most importantly finding the package is the following."

Callie pushed away her coffee and leaned forward, fidgeting with the plastic placemat that had cracked on the corner.

Adalyn chimed in: "Gordon Stone was here to pick up twelve windsocks—all stuffed in a single shopping bag—a bag with SHOP SHIPSHEWANA on it." She popped the final bit of strudel into her mouth and motioned to Trent to finish.

"That's why he broke into Margie's place? He thought my bag was his bag?" Callie turned her cup round and round.

"Correct." Trent leaned back. "Margie took your bag home the day you were arrested. She meant to bring it by to you the next day. Apparently Stone thought he'd break in and pick it up."

"Why? What did he want the windsocks for?" Deborah sounded truly puzzled.

"Each windsock was stuffed with a kilo of cocaine."

"I don't understand." Deborah scooted farther into the booth as Jonas approached the table with baby Joshua.

"I thought I might find you here." Jonas smiled at his wife as if he hadn't just dropped her off at Callie's shop an hour ago.

What did that feel like, Callie wondered? She had experienced love and devotion once before, but it seemed like a lifetime ago.

"Adalyn and Trent were explaining Gordon Stone's motive to us." Deborah told her husband.

"Greed, I would imagine. Isn't that usually the motive?"

"In this case, you might be right—since the street value for that amount of cocaine is more than a quarter of a million dollars." Trent's grin broadened. "Guess they figured our little police department wouldn't catch an organization like theirs."

"I'm not sure Stone's motive was greed." Adalyn put her elbows on the table, steepled her fingers and stared at them, as if she might find answers there. "I don't personally believe any of that money was going to Mr. Stone. He does seem rather confident that he'll be taken care of—both legally and financially before, during, and after his probable incarceration."

"Then what would be his motivation?" Callie's palms went clammy at the mention of Stone's name, as they did whenever she allowed her mind to travel back over what had happened two days ago—Stone's voice, his hand on her arm, or the way he had held the gun to her head. She hadn't yet dealt with the terror she'd felt then, and she wasn't sure when she would.

"I think possibly loyalty. Whoever he works for has been a good employer, has taken care of him in the past, and he seems confident that boss will take care of him now."

Shane Black appeared at their table, and Callie wondered if they'd be forced to take their little party outside since there was not enough room for one more person.

"I was headed over to the livery," Jonas said, standing. "This little guy wanted his *mamm*."

"Meet you at the quilt shop?" Deborah asked, accepting the baby.

"Sure, but no hurry. I still need another half hour."

Jonas stood, tapping the top of his straw hat to be sure it was firmly in place. Facing Shane, he hesitated, then held out his hand. "I haven't had a chance to thank you for what you did, for protecting my wife. *Danki*."

"You're welcome, Jonas. I'm not sure we'd have caught Stone if she hadn't thought to climb out that window." He left unsaid that Callie, Trent, Gavin, and Roger Stakehorn might all be dead.

"*Ya*. She's a good one for thinking fast on her feet." Jonas left and Shane took his place at the table.

"What's the meeting about?"

"Just catching everyone up," Adalyn said.

"Off the record," Trent added.

"Well, if we're off the record I might be able to add a few things. If anyone deserves to know, you all do." He was speaking to them all, but he sat a bit sideways and leaned forward so he could look directly at Callie as he spoke. "I knew a week ago that Stakehorn didn't die of poison."

"What?" Callie nearly came out of the booth, but there was nowhere for her to go; she was pinned between Deborah and the wall.

"The autopsy reports came back and showed conclusively that he died of a heart attack."

"But you said—"

"What exactly did I say, Callie?" Shane pierced her with his dark eyes.

She thought of the time she'd spent across from him in the interrogation room, thought of the visit he'd made to her parking lot, thought of the moment he came in and saved her from Gordon Stone.

"I *asked* you about the poison. I *asked* you to make a confession."

"What was the point then?"

"I wasn't sure. I was chasing it down. I suspected though, that the poison in the coffee was a diversionary tactic. I didn't know by whom, and I didn't know what side you were on. You claimed to be Daisy's niece, but no one here remembered meeting you before. I had a bit of background investigation to do before I could be sure, to tell you the truth."

Now Callie's temper overrode the debt she owed him. Deborah must have sensed it, because she ran her hand down Callie's arm, whispered "Peace" in her ear.

"This morning, with his Chicago lawyer present, Stone admitted to part of what happened." Everyone at the table sat up a little straighter.

"The evening Stakehorn died, Stone was there. He confronted

308

him about a missing package—a package he claims had sentimental value but to his knowledge did not contain any illegal
substances. Stone confronted him in the office, the night you
found him, Callie." Shane accepted the cup of coffee the waitress
offered, then continued. "Stakehorn denied ever having posses-
sion of it, but Stone claims he saw the editor pick it up at the flea
market and walk away with it."

"You don't believe that do you? The part about Stone not
knowing there were drugs in it?"

"Doesn't matter what I believe. All that matters in a court of
law are the facts and the evidence. Some of those facts have been
corroborated by video recordings, now that we know what to look
for. Stone claimed he followed Stakehorn from the market, followed him down the alley behind your shop, Callie. We pulled
video surveillance tapes from local business on the night in question. Some had been erased, but Pots and Pans had installed a new
security system. It shows Stakehorn stopping outside the back of
their shop and peering into a shopping bag. He apparently didn't
know what he had, but if he'd turned it in at that point, he might
still be alive today."

The group at the table grew quiet, trying to soak in all of the
information.

"There's more." Shane pushed away the coffee cup, cleared
his throat as if he was uncomfortable with what he was about to
say. "We can't be sure, and our techs are still working on it, but
it looks as if your aunt saw both Stakehorn and Stone creeping
down the alley. She appears in a corner of the frame. It's hard to
see, and she's across the alley, just peeking out from the foliage in
her garden. It was the night she died, Callie."

Deborah reached over and clasped her hand, as Callie processed Shane's words. Aunt Daisy had died in the garden, after
seeing Stakehorn running from Stone?

"It must have been quite a shock for her," Deborah murmured.

"So how did Stakehorn die, Shane?" Adalyn cocked her head, curious now by the look on her face.

"Heart attack—we knew that, and Stone confirmed it. He pressured him to give up the location of the package. When Stakehorn didn't, Stone became more persuasive, and Stakehorn's ticker gave out."

"Pressured him how?" Trent asked.

"I can't go into details."

"So where is the package?" Trent had resumed tapping his notes against the table.

"Not at liberty to say." Shane grinned now. "I can say that our K–9 unit is ninety-nine percent successful. The dogs did their job well and are already on their way back home."

"And Stakehorn's money?" Deborah asked. "The money his son was sure he was hiding?"

Adalyn set her fork across her plate. "People who don't trust lawyers or banks tend to hide things."

"Right," Shane confirmed. "He hid his stocks in the same place he hid the package he'd stumbled upon. Those stocks—and they totaled a large sum of money—automatically go to his only heir."

"So Roger Stakehorn just walks with a stash of money?" Trent asked. "He broke into Callie's store and he terrorized Deborah on the road, and he walks away with the prize?" Trent asked.

"I'm not pressing charges. I want him out of town." Callie couldn't let one thing go though. Shane Black had harassed her for weeks. "Why did you continue questioning me?"

Shane again turned in the booth, though there was barely enough room. He looked her directly in the eyes, one arm across the back of the booth, one on the table. "Someone put poison in his coffee. Given your background, you were a suspect—at first. I also had to verify that you were, in fact, Daisy's niece."

"How could I not be her niece?"

"People impersonate other people all the time, Callie. They read the obits and show up with false identification."

"That's awful," Deborah murmured.

"The *Chicago Trib* did a story on that very thing last year. Reporter won a big award." Trent sounded wistful.

"So sorry I couldn't help you out with that," Callie snapped. She turned back to Shane. "You really thought I was impersonating ... myself! How ridiculous."

"It's not ridiculous," Adalyn admitted. "Actually that's part of what makes Shane a good detective. He leaves no suspect unscrutinized."

"Once I'd confirmed your identity, I sent an investigator from Fort Wayne to interview some of your Texas friends."

"You what?"

"Relax, sweetheart. They all gave you glowing recommendations. Even your ex-employer. Apparently they were still recovering from losing their best sales rep. By the way, you still have a job waiting for you in Houston if you want it."

All eyes turned to Callie, but she only shook her head, still shocked at the latest revelations. She had friends in Texas? Why had she felt so alone then?

"Though I was convinced of your innocence when Max was shot. That's why I stopped by and saw you at the shop."

"And told me poison doesn't always kill—"

"It was the most I could say at the time. Meanwhile I continued interviewing other suspects here, which we had plenty of. As you know, Stakehorn had his share of enemies."

"What was the purpose of the poison?" Deborah asked.

"My best guess is that Gordon did it so that we'd spend our time looking for the murderer while he spent his time looking for the package."

"Still doesn't make sense to me. Dennis Stakehorn was an old man. A heart attack would have been natural at his age."

"He'd had a physical two weeks before, been given a clean bill of health, with one caveat—a weak heart. The doctor advised no drama, no big scares, no huge stories. The doctor even suggested he retire."

"How could this man, Gordon, know that?" Callie worried the hair which now reached well past the collar of her shirt.

"We found evidence on Gordon's phone that he'd broken into Stakehorn's home first. While he was there he read the doctor's report, looked for the stash of drugs, but didn't find it, then moved on to the office."

"This was in his texts?" Callie asked.

"Exactly."

"My head is beginning to ache," Deborah murmured.

"The autopsy would have revealed the heart attack eventually, but in the meantime we spent our resources looking at the poison. It's a pretty common tactic among the Chicago mob, divert the investigation with another investigation. Can't hurt and it might buy them enough time to find what they need and get out of town."

"Why did they pick our town, Shane?" Deborah had been quietly absorbing all the news, snuggling Joshua in her lap. Now she caressed the top of his head. "Why Shipshewana instead of a big place like Chicago or Indianapolis?"

"Pressure is on due to the crack-down on drug operations. They're looking for smaller towns to ship through. Shipshewana was the perfect location. We have a small police force to handle such things, but swell to a large crowd during market days. This operation was a test to see how it would work."

"They won't try again, will they?" Callie forgot her anger, forgot everything except the families she'd grown close to—Deborah and Melinda and Esther. It was one thing to accept that drug usage and distribution was a common occurrence in a city like Houston, but it wasn't supposed to happen in Shipshewana.

"I doubt it. They know we'll be watching now." Shane stood, straightened his light summer jacket, and adjusted his belt, which she now knew held his pistol. Well, of course it did. He was an officer. And wasn't she glad about that?

He had saved her life.

The words echoed through her mind a dozen times a day.

"Ladies, Trent." Shane turned and walked out of the diner.

"Guess he'll stop bothering you now, Callie." Adalyn picked her red leather bag up off the seat between her and Trent. "Bill's on me this time."

"Thank you, ma'am. I'm not fired, but I didn't receive a raise either." Trent rolled up his notes and grinned. "No promotion — yet."

"So you think Roger Stakehorn is innocent in all this?" Callie asked as they walked outside.

"He didn't kill his father. That's what I'll print in tomorrow's paper." Trent looked off toward the *Gazette*, then pulled her aside and lowered his voice. "Want to go out to dinner sometime?"

When Callie only looked at him in surprise, he added, "I owe you. I'm going to get at least a week's worth of copy from this story, and they're picking some of it up for the big papers in Indianapolis and Fort Wayne. Dinner's the least I could do."

Callie thought to resist, considered pulling back like she would have in Houston. Her mind jumped to an image of Gavin and then — inexplicably to Shane Black, though she couldn't imagine why. She realized in that split second that she still missed Rick, but she knew he would want her to move on with her life. Was that what Deborah meant by accepting *Gottes wille*?

Truth was she couldn't think of a reason not to go out to dinner with Trent. Truth was she rather enjoyed time spent with him, and he had saved Max. She wouldn't be forgetting that anytime soon. "Sure, Trent. Give me a call and we'll work something out."

～

Trent waved and walked off down Main Street.

It was only then that Callie noticed he hadn't driven the bike or the truck. Maybe the Amish ways were rubbing off on him as well.

"Gals, stay in touch." Adalyn said. "I'm going to miss our little meetings."

"We can get together, even if it doesn't involve a murder," Deborah pointed out.

"True." Adalyn rubbed Joshua's back, then reached down and gave Max a pat. "My experience is I usually don't see a client unless they have problems though."

Deborah shook her head, causing the strings of her *kapp* to bounce in the summer sunshine. "We're not clients, Adalyn. We're *freinden*."

Adalyn didn't respond. She did squeeze both of their hands, then climb into her little Prius, and drove off in the direction of her office.

"Would you like me to go and get my car?" Callie asked.

"Can Max walk that far?"

"Doc England said a short walk every day was good for him. What about you? We didn't know you'd be carrying a sleeping baby when we walked down here."

"I'm used to carrying him. It's not a problem. When you work on a farm, your arms grow used to bearing quite a bit of weight."

Callie thought on that as they walked side by side down Main. Was Deborah talking about carrying physical things or was she trying to convey a spiritual lesson again?

She was learning that with Deborah one could never be sure.

A few of the shop owners called out a greeting as they walked toward Daisy's Quilt Shop.

She realized suddenly that she had friends here — casual friends, like the shop owners and real friends, like Deborah and Adalyn. She was closer to those two women than she was to anyone in Houston, over a thousand of miles to the south.

314

It was good to hear that she'd left things in Houston in a better state than she remembered—it helped to ease some of the bitterness. She had changed since coming to Shipshe, and now she couldn't imagine herself moving back. She couldn't claim to fully understand the Amish lifestyle, hadn't completely acclimated to small-town life, but she knew a trade-up when she experienced one—and Shipshewana, Indiana, was without a doubt a trade-up for her.

"I'm relieved Margie is home," Callie said.

"The Lord was looking after her," Deborah agreed. "How's it working out having Lydia watch the store when you're out?"

"Wonderful. I would never have thought a seventeen-year-old girl could be so responsible, but she's not your ordinary teenager."

"I don't know, Callie. Amish teens are responsible. They're eager to work, and Lydia has always loved quilting, but she is a normal teen in other ways. Have you seen her giggle and blush when Phillip walks by or caught her daydreaming when the sun is about to set?"

Callie laughed. "I might have noticed those things once or twice."

"She's a *gut* girl. I'm just saying, don't expect her to be perfect because she's Amish."

Callie nodded and tucked her hair behind her ears as they approached the parking lot.

"I expected Gavin to appear at our meeting earlier." Deborah smiled, looked out from her *kapp* in a suggestive way that Callie couldn't resist laughing over. "Tell me he hasn't taken a personal interest in protecting you."

"Actually he called earlier this morning. He's on traffic duty today and couldn't make it, but he made me promise I'd tell him everything this evening."

"This evening?"

"We're going to dinner, but it's dutch."

"Dutch?"

"*Ya.*"

"German?"

"No, Deborah. Dutch means we each pay our own way."

"Why would you want to do that? If Gavin wants to take you to dinner and asks you out, why not let him pay your way?"

"I'm not quite ready to call it that kind of a date," Callie admitted.

~

Deborah's heart jumped at the sight of Jonas waiting by their buggy, whittling a piece of wood into some shape she couldn't recognize. It was funny how after twelve years of marriage and five children, she still felt flushed when he smiled at her.

He took the sleeping Joshua from her arms and laid him across the back seat of the buggy.

"We've no church this Sunday, so we'll meet at Melinda's for supper and games. Will you join us again? Doc Bernie will be there." Deborah snagged Callie's hand and waited for a reply. "He told me he wants to thank you for something. Will you join us?"

"I will," Callie promised.

"Want to tell me what Doc Bernie was talking about?"

"Not really."

"It wouldn't have anything to do with an anonymous donation he received; would it? One that was specifically marked for Aaron?" When Callie only shrugged, she hugged her and whispered, "They're picking up his new wheelchair today. Melinda is thrilled. It will be very helpful for when he returns to school."

"*Wunderbaar,*" Callie said with a smile.

Deborah held her at arm's length, then admitted what was on her mind. "My life was a bit simpler when your Aunt Daisy ran this shop, Callie Harper. I always knew what to expect when I walked in the door. With you, I'm not so sure."

Callie laughed and glanced down at the ground.

"I have something for you." Deborah stuck her head back in the buggy and pulled out the quilt she'd tucked in there before leaving home.

"Another quilt?" Callie took it from her with near reverence. "Deborah this is beautiful. I didn't realize you had finished another."

"We finished it."

"You and Melinda and Esther."

"Correct."

"So do you want me to auction it, like the others?"

"The bishop is still deciding about whether we should auction more quilts on eBay or not, but we don't want you to sell this quilt, Callie. We're giving you this quilt—it's a friendship quilt. See our names stitched in—all four of our names? This is our gift to you, our way of thanking you for all you have done for us."

When Callie looked up tears had pooled in her eyes, and Deborah thought for a moment that she would refuse the gift. Instead she hugged it to her, and patted Max's head.

Callie always went to Max now, when she needed reassurance.

Then she grabbed Deborah and hugged her tight.

"Thank you," she whispered.

"*Gern gschehne,*" Deborah said.

Callie stepped back and Deborah joined Jonas in the buggy. As they pulled out of the parking lot, she hung out the window and waved. Callie was still standing there, holding the quilt with one hand, patting Max with the other.

Perhaps her mother-in-law had been right. There was no stopping the pain that ran through their life like dishwater down a drain, no avoiding the lessons that God allowed. But given time, joy returned bit by bit.

The last few years had been difficult for her *freinden;* however, Deborah had the distinct feeling that better times were ahead.

Looking back at Daisy's Quilt Shop—neat, trimmed, and minus one FOR SALE sign—gave her a feeling of satisfaction.

Callie Harper had brought an interesting change to the pattern of her life. As a quilter, she was fascinated by the new design and couldn't help wondering where it would lead them all next.

Acknowledgments

THIS BOOK IS DEDICATED to my mom, Wanda Van Riper. She is a talented seamstress, a patient woman, and believes I have the ability to do anything. Above all, she is a loving mom and grandmother. I'm blessed to have her in my life.

I also would like to acknowledge the help of my agent, Mary Sue Seymour, my editor, Sue Brower, and all of the wonderful team at Zondervan — they are a writer's dream to work for.

Many other authors were instrumental in guiding my way through the process of writing this book, including Barbara Cameron, Amy Clipston, Mary Ellis, and Beth Wiseman. Each of these ladies has been a help and encouragement to me.

I can't thank the members of ACFW and FHL enough.

I would like to acknowledge Dr. Richard Kelley and his work among the Amish community. He served as inspiration for Dr. Bernie, though any errors made in medical details are my own.

As always, I could not write a book without the support and help of my pre-readers: Donna and Kristy, you have been with me from the very beginning. Martha, thank you so much for help with quilting details. Cindy and Toot, I appreciate you both being available to help with all of my equestrian questions.

To all the friends I've made in Shipshewana, I count it a

pleasure to know you. Thank you for enduring my questions. You were very kind to a country girl from the heart of Texas. I hope to be back to see you often.

And last, but never least, my family makes it all possible. I couldn't write if my husband didn't feed me and make sure my car was filled with gas before I take off on my many crazy trips — Bobby, you are the greatest.

Kids — I know you are grown, but I still think you're tops. You mean more to me than a thousand books — Cody, Kylie, Yale, and Jordyn.

Mom, Pam, and Loyall — thank you for being my first fans.

I thank the Lord for giving me the chance to follow my dreams, for putting stories in my heart, and for giving us all lives filled with grace.

Questions for Group Discussion

1. There's a stark contrast between Deborah and Callie in chapter 1. Deborah is in her home, dressed, working on something she loves to do, and she is surrounded by friends and family. Callie is hiding beneath her covers as the clock approaches noon; she has no food in the pantry, and she has no plans for how to address her problems. Have there been times in your life when you were able to relate to either character?

2. In chapter 9, Ruth makes the observation that "there's a place in this life for pain." Deborah doesn't like this answer any more than I do, but her heart acknowledges the truth of what her mother-in-law is saying. Do you agree that God sometimes uses the pain in our lives? Why or why not?

3. In chapter 15, we see Esther's garden. This is where she has buried all of her grief, and also where God seems to be working with her, slowly mending her heart. Where do you go and what do you do when you're hurting the most?

4. Chicken breast disease, or *nemaline myopathy*, is a real disease, and there are real doctors like Doc Bernie who travel

among the Amish and treat their children. Doctor Bernie explains to Callie that Melinda and Noah have made the choice to treat their child Aaron at home. In chapter 17, Doc Bernie agrees with this choice. How did you feel about it?

5. In chapter 23, Esther explains to Callie exactly how her husband died. Her decision not to prosecute the boys responsible for Seth's death is in keeping with Amish beliefs. Although this situation is fictional, it seemed to me that this was an extreme, real-world example of someone extending God's grace and forgiveness. What was your reaction to this scene?

6. I mention white roses twice in the story. The first time is in chapter 23, when Esther is speaking to Callie, describing her husband's death. The second time is in chapter 30, when Deborah is climbing out the window, running away — though she doesn't yet know why. What do you think the white roses represent in these scenes?

7. At the end of the story, Callie notes that she now has casual friends and real friends. Do you think we need both?

8. If you've read Amish books before, was the portrayal of Amish people different in this book than in others? If you haven't read any Amish books before, was the portrayal of the Amish here what you expected?

9. When the novel opens, Callie is very disconnected from those around her. She first opens up slowly — through Max, and then more so through Daisy's journal, Daisy's books, and the friends and community that her aunt was a part of. Could this transformation also have taken place in a large metropolitan area like Houston? Why or why not?

10. From the beginning scene to the closing one, quilting is the lens through which Deborah understands her world. It is her frame of reference, and when she's confused, she tries to envision the "problem" as she would a quilt that isn't cooperating. What helps you solve your problems?

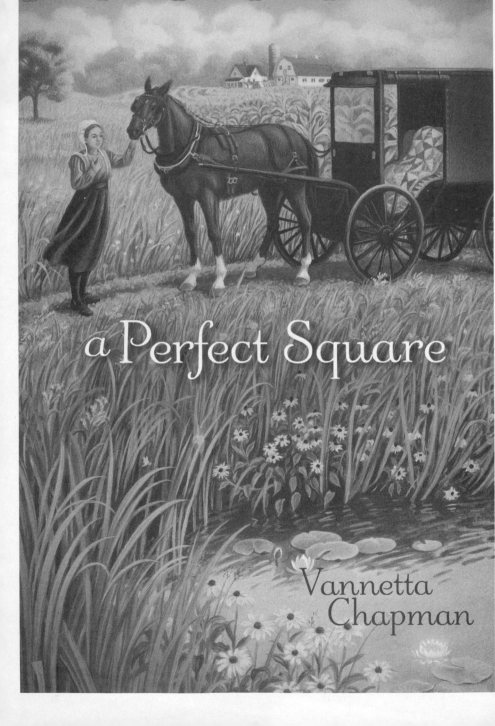

a Perfect Square

Vannetta Chapman

Read an excerpt from book 2: *A Perfect Square*.
Coming soon!

Chapter 1

Shipshewana, Indiana
Late October

"LESS THAN TWO WEEKS UNTIL THE WEDDING." Deborah Yoder glanced once at Esther, then focused again on the dirt lane, her horse Cinnamon, and guiding the buggy down the rutted path.

On both sides of them, fields of fall corn rose, golden and plump, ready for harvest. They shaded the lane so that the midmorning sun broke through in a slatted fashion, as if it were winking at them.

Joshua and Leah spoke in hushed tones from the back seat, caught up in some game that children played. It never failed to amaze Deborah how they managed to find amusement in the smallest things. Yesterday it had been twisting stalks of corn shucks into absurd figures.

When Esther didn't comment, Deborah looked at her again. Her hands clutched the casserole bowl firmly, but she managed a radiant smile.

"*Ya*. Less than two weeks. One part of me wishes it were tomorrow. That I could wake up and we would be living our life together, as man and wife."

"And the other part?"

"The other part agrees with Tobias. There's still much to do before he moves into my home. We're not ready, and as much as I'd like to wish the days away, I know it's all a part of the season and something I won't want to forget. Less than two weeks. I should be grateful for each day, as Tobias reminds me."

Deborah smiled as she began circling the small pond at the far end of Tobias's and Reuben's place—actually it was their *gross-daddi's* place, but they'd been farming it for the last several years. "Tobias has become quite industrious since he asked you to marry him. He's always been a hard worker, but in the last few months it's as if he's a man on a mission. He wants everything to be perfect."

"I know. He's working even more hours at the feed store, and he still needs to help with the harvest." Esther's hands worried over the top of the casserole dish. "It's why I wanted to bring them dinner. I'm not sure they eat well with Reuben's cooking."

Deborah laughed out loud, causing both children to pop up and hang over the front seat. "I've no doubt they'll be glad you made the chicken and potatoes. They don't strike me as *wunderbaar* cooks. Reuben burned the *kaffi* the last few times I stopped by. I wouldn't fuss over them too much though. I think their *schweschders* bring them dinners fairly often."

"I spoke with Tobias's mother Saturday when I saw her in town. No one was coming by tonight so—" Esther reached out and clutched Deborah's arm. "Could you stop the buggy? Just for a moment?"

Following her friend's gaze, Deborah immediately spied the tall bunches of wildflowers growing on the pond's southwestern side.

Black-eyed Susans swayed among autumn goldenrods, dipping and rising beside the blue water of the small pond in the October morning. Nearly buried in switch grass that was close to three feet tall, Deborah was surprised they'd seen the cluster of wildflowers at all. If they hadn't been riding in the buggy, they would have missed the beautiful sight, which looked to Deborah like colors from a patchwork quilt.

Esther's fingers tightened their grasp on her arm. "Can we stop?"

"We don't have to be at Daisy's Quilt Shop for another hour. Let's pick a few."

"Callie will love them," Esther agreed.

"And when they're dried, you can keep the seeds for your garden." Deborah pulled the buggy to the side, noticed that Cinnamon acted a bit nervous, tossing her head and dancing to the right of the road. "Whoa, girl."

"Will she be okay?" Esther asked, even as she pulled her small quilting scissors out of her sewing bag.

"I'm sure. I'll stay here. You go and gather the flowers."

"Later I'll regret using sewing scissors for gardening."

"Callie will have cleaning solution, and you'll only snip a few. You use those for thread, not cloth. It will be fine."

"I want to go, *mamm*." Leah's sweet little face peeped forward from the back seat. She had recently turned three, and had come out of her shell quite a bit over the last few months — perhaps because her mother was no longer so sad. Perhaps because her mother was *in lieb*.

Joshua wasn't far behind her.

"Me, too," he said. "I wanna go with Leah."

Deborah studied her son. He would turn two next month, and she worried some days that he'd be the last baby she'd ever hold in her arms. "You? I thought you'd stay with me and Cinnamon."

"Leah needs me." He pulled his wool cap down around his ears and climbed out of the buggy after his best friend. "Kay, Ceemon?"

The horse shook her head again, rattling the harness.

"I'll look after Cinnamon." Deborah followed them out of the buggy and stood with her hand on the mare. "You two go with Esther, but stay close to her, and come back as soon as she says. We're going to see Miss Callie this morning."

Esther allowed each child to clasp one of her hands as they walked toward the flowers by the water's edge.

Deborah kept one eye on them as they wound their way through the tall grass, but another part of her mind was focusing on the mare. She ran one hand down her neck, whispering and stroking, attempting to calm her. Still Cinnamon shook her harness and tried to pull away. Deborah ran a hand down the length of the mare's leg, wondering if perhaps she had something in one of her hooves.

She'd seemed fine trotting down the lane.

"Easy, girl. What's wrong?" Again running her hand down the mare's neck, she found the horse was actually trembling. Sweat slicked her coat though the morning was cool.

Deborah's own heart rate kicked up a notch as she responded to the mare's anxiety.

She must have missed something.

Perhaps there was a snake nearby or an animal carcass in the weeds. She was scanning the surrounding area when she noticed where the dry grass was stamped down to the north. It looked as if someone had traveled the opposite direction as Esther and the children, though still close to the water, sometime earlier. The path that had been beaten down was wider than footsteps — smaller than a buggy.

More like something had been dragged.

The path extended well past the area where she'd stopped with the buggy ...

She glanced back to where Esther still stooped among the flowers, where the children continued to play.

Yes, the paths led to almost opposite ends of the pond. She was surprised she hadn't noticed it earlier, but she'd been so focused on the flowers. It was hard to imagine Tobias and Reuben taking the time to come out here, unless they'd been fishing. But Tobias had been so busy working double shifts at the feed store and on the farm, which had left Reuben pulling extra weight in the fields.

She focused again on the scene, tried to find the piece she was missing.

Esther and the children stood beside the water, snipping flower stems.

A slight breeze stirred the water.

Geese crossed the blue autumn sky, heading north, their cry piercing the morning, then fading, leaving it quiet but not peaceful.

Cinnamon tossed her head one more time, nearly pulling the harness out of Deborah's hand when the morning's silence was broken by Esther's scream.

~

Callie Harper clomped down the stairs from her apartment to her quilt shop, tugging at the long, plain dark green dress with one hand and readjusting the tie to her apron with the other. Oh how Rick would laugh to see her now. There were a lot of things her husband would be amused to know about her new life. There wasn't a day since he'd died that she didn't miss him, didn't wish he could share things with her. This though, oh he would laugh about the dress.

She wanted to reach up and scratch under the *kapp* on her head, but it had taken so long to corral her shoulder-length dark hair underneath the white bonnet, she didn't want to displace any of it.

When she turned the corner into the shop's main room, her yellow Labrador, Max, let out a whine and placed his head on his paws.

Lydia, the seventeen-year-old girl who worked for her full time now, dissolved into a torrent of giggles.

"Why are you laughing?" Callie spun in a circle. "Don't I look exactly like you?"

"No." Lydia collapsed onto the stool behind the counter. "You do not look like me at all."

"But I pinned the dress right."

"*Ya.*"

"And I put the apron on correctly, though I don't know how you manage to tie it in the back just so. I had the hardest time with that."

"The tie is fine."

"It's the *kapp*, isn't it? My hair isn't long like yours, but still it didn't want to stay in." She moved to a mirror that ran along the top of a fabric display. As she suspected, her dark hair had begun to escape from various corners of the white *kapp*. She looked nothing like the neat Amish women who were her friends.

She looked like what she was — an imposter.

"I don't think the *kapp* or the clothing is the problem." Lydia propped her chin on her hand and studied her employer. "It's not our clothes that make us Amish. It's obvious you're only pretending — an Englisher in Plain clothing."

"Fix me." Callie's hands flapped at her side. "I have to sneak into Mrs. Knepp's store. To do that, I need to look Plain."

"Why?"

"Because."

"I like how you normally dress. Why can't you look English?"

"She's suspicious of all English."

"Mrs. Knepp is suspicious of everyone — Amish or English." Lydia hopped off the stool and joined Callie in front of the narrow mirror.

"You look a bit like her. Mrs. Knepp is exactly your size, only much older."

"She's old and her eyesight is poor. If I wear this, maybe she won't recognize me." Callie narrowed her eyes at the mirror. "No doubt she does a better job taming her hair."

Carefully pulling the hairpins away one by one, Lydia removed the *kapp*, freeing her boss's dark curls.

"Now I look like a prairie girl," Callie said.

"*Ya*. You should change before our mid-morning rush of customers begins. Wouldn't want Trent McCallister to happen in and snap a picture of you in this dress, then splash it across the front page of the *Shipshewana Gazette*."

Both girls turned to look at the framed photo of Callie, Deborah, and Max. The words "Burglar apprehended" were printed in large letters under their name. Max padded over and pushed his head between their legs, as if he understood what they were staring at.

"Those were the days, right boy?" Callie reached down and rubbed the Labrador between his ears, pausing to adjust his orange colored bandana. She might as well change back into her clothes. She preferred to match Max's wardrobe to hers, though she knew it was silly—and his orange bandana definitely clashed with this green dress. Together they looked like something out of a fall window display. "I'm not worried about Trent. I'm worried about Mrs. Knepp. She hates me, and I don't know why."

"You can't please everyone. That's what my *grossmammi* says."

"We're losing customers because of her." Callie walked to the counter and straightened the stack of flyers announcing her weekly sales. "I don't mind competition, but this is growing nasty. We could work with each other instead of against each other. Her store is different than mine. We could be referring customers to each other if she weren't so stubborn."

"You said last month's profit was better than ever. The best since you re-opened the store four months ago."

"True, but—"

The store to the shop burst open and Trent McCallister nearly fell through it. Wearing jeans and a long-sleeved Harley T-shirt, with a souped-up Nikon digital camera slung around his neck, he looked as if he belonged on the cover of a magazine rather than in Shipshewana, Indiana. Shoulder-length brown hair was pulled back in a pony tail, and wire-rimmed glasses completed the West Coast look.

His eyes widened at Callie's outfit, but he didn't comment on it. "I'm headed out to Tobias's place. A call came in ten minutes ago over the police scanner."

"Tobias?" Callie moved forward. When she did, Max moved with her, on alert as if he'd been called to hunt.

"Is Tobias all right?" Lydia asked.

"I don't know, but ..."

"Is there anything we can do?" Callie began fumbling with the tie on the back of her apron.

"Callie." Trent stepped closer, put his hand on her arm, waited until she was still and looking directly at him. "Deborah and Esther are there."

"They're at Tobias's?" Callie reached for something to sit on, nearly stumbled. "But they're all right."

"I don't know."

"They have to be. Tell me there's nothing wrong with Deborah or the children." Her hand covered her mouth, as if to stop the words that were tumbling out. "Esther and Leah, they're fine—"

"I'm not sure. Callie ..." Again his hazel eyes sought hers. "All I know is that someone called in a homicide."

Experience
- people
- food
- culture

Amish Visit-in-Person Tours

Traditional Amish Farm Feast

Heritage Amish homestead tours

www.AmishExperience.com
www.PlainAndFancyFarm.com

the Amish Experience

the amish experience at plain&fancyfarm
- ten pristine acres on an AAA scenic byway -

discover luxury with a view at www.AmishViewInn.com

Share Your Thoughts

With the Author: Your comments will be forwarded to the author when you send them to *zauthor@zondervan.com*.

With Zondervan: Submit your review of this book by writing to *zreview@zondervan.com*.

Free Online Resources at
www.zondervan.com

Zondervan AuthorTracker: Be notified whenever your favorite authors publish new books, go on tour, or post an update about what's happening in their lives at www.zondervan.com/authortracker.

Daily Bible Verses and Devotions: Enrich your life with daily Bible verses or devotions that help you start every morning focused on God. Visit www.zondervan.com/newsletters.

Free Email Publications: Sign up for newsletters on Christian living, academic resources, church ministry, fiction, children's resources, and more. Visit www.zondervan.com/newsletters.

Zondervan Bible Search: Find and compare Bible passages in a variety of translations at www.zondervanbiblesearch.com.

Other Benefits: Register to receive online benefits like coupons and special offers, or to participate in research.

ZONDERVAN®

ZONDERVAN.com/
AUTHORTRACKER
follow your favorite authors